Patricia Campbell's life has never felt ⬠ **P9-DWI-522** workaholic, her teenage kids have their own lives, her senile mother-in-law needs constant care, and she's always a step behind on her endless to-do list. The only thing keeping her sane is her book club, a close-knit group of Charleston women united by their love of true crime. Then James Harris walks into her life during the summer of 1993. He makes her feel things she hasn't felt in years, but when children on the other side of town go missing, Patricia wonders if he's connected. Is he a Brad Pitt, a Bundy, or something much worse?

NEW YORK TIMES BOOK REVIEW
2020 SUMMER READING SELECTION

NEW YORK PUBLIC LIBRARY
TOP 10 BOOKS FOR ADULTS IN 2020

GOODREADS TOP HORROR NOVELS OF 2020

GOODREADS CHOICE AWARD FINALIST (HORROR)

AMAZON BEST BOOKS OF 2020

BARNES & NOBLE BEST FICTION OF 2020

SOUTHERN BOOK PRIZE NOMINEE FOR FICTION

#1 APRIL 2020 LIBRARYREADS PICK

APRIL 2020 INDIE NEXT PICK

LIBRARY JOURNAL EDITORS PICK FOR APRIL 2020

THE A.V. CLUB BEST BOOK OF APRIL 2020

POPSUGAR BEST OF APRIL 2020

THE SOUTHERN
BOOK CLUB'S
GUIDE TO SLAYING
VAMPIRES

ALSO BY GRADY HENDRIX

Horrorstör

My Best Friend's Exorcism

Paperbacks from Hell

We Sold Our Souls

THE SOUTHERN BOOK CLUB'S GUIDE TO SLAYING VAMPIRES

GRADY HENDRIX

QUIRK BOOKS

PHILADELPHIA

First paperback edition, Quirk Books 2021
Originally published by Quirk Books in 2020

Library of Congress Cataloging in Publication Data
Hendrix, Grady, author.
The southern book club's guide to slaying vampires / Grady Hendrix.
Summary: "A supernatural thriller set in South Carolina in the
'90s about a women's book club that must protect its suburban
community from a mysterious stranger who turns out to be a real
monster"—Provided by publisher.
2019037437
GSAFD: Horror fiction. | Suspense fiction.
PS3608.E543 S68 2020 | 813/.6—dc23
ISBN: 978-1-68369-251-5

Printed in the United States of America

Typeset in Scotch Roman MT and Bembo
Cover designed by Andie Reid
Cover illustration by Liz Wheaton
Interior designed by Molly Rose Murphy
Interior illustration by Dan Funderburgh
Production management by John J. McGurk

Quirk Books
215 Church Street
Philadelphia, PA 19106
quirkbooks.com

10 9 8 7 6 5

For Amanda,
Wherever all the pieces of you are . . .

AUTHOR'S NOTE

A few years ago I wrote a book called *My Best Friend's Exorcism* about two teenage girls in Charleston, South Carolina, in 1988, at the height of the Satanic Panic. They become convinced that one of them is possessed by Satan and, consequently, things go poorly.

That novel was written from a teenage point of view, and so the parents seemed awful because that's how parents seem when you're a teenager. But there's another version of that story, told from the parents' point of view, about how helpless you feel when your kid is in danger. I wanted to write a story about those parents, and so *The Southern Book Club's Guide to Slaying Vampires* was born. It's not a sequel to *My Best Friend's Exorcism*, but it takes place in the same neighborhood, a few years later, where I grew up.

When I was a kid I didn't take my mom seriously. She was a housewife who was in a book club, and she and her friends were always running errands, and driving car pool, and forcing us to follow rules that didn't make sense. They just seemed like a bunch of light-weights. Today I realize how many things they were dealing with that I was totally unaware of. They took the hits so we could skate by obliviously, because that's the deal: as a parent, you endure pain so your children don't have to.

This is also a book about vampires. They're that iconic American archetype of the rambling man, wearing denim, wandering from town to town with no past and no ties. Think Jack Kerouac, think Shane, think Woody Guthrie. Think Ted Bundy.

Because vampires are the original serial killers, stripped of everything that makes us human—they have no friends, no family, no roots, no children. All they have is hunger. They eat and eat but they're never full. With this book, I wanted to pit a man freed from all responsibilities but his appetites against women whose lives are shaped by their endless responsibilities. I wanted to pit Dracula against my mom.

As you'll see, it's not a fair fight.

PROLOGUE

This story ends in blood.

Every story begins in blood: a squalling baby yanked from the womb, bathed in mucus and half a quart of their mother's blood. But not many stories end in blood these days. Usually it's a return to the hospital and a dry, quiet death surrounded by machines after a heart attack in the driveway, a stroke on the back porch, or a slow fade from lung cancer.

This story begins with five little girls, each born in a splash of her mother's blood, cleaned up, patted dry, then turned into proper young ladies, instructed in the wifely arts to become perfect partners and responsible parents, mothers who help with homework and do the laundry, who belong to church flower societies and bunco clubs, who send their children to cotillion and private schools.

You've seen these women. They meet for lunch and laugh loudly enough for everyone in the restaurant to hear. They get silly after a single glass of wine. Their idea of living on the edge is to buy a pair of Christmas earrings that light up. They agonize far too long over whether or not to order dessert.

As respectable individuals, their names will appear in the paper only three times: when they're born, when they get married, and when they die. They are gracious hostesses. They are generous to those less fortunate. They honor their husbands and nurture their children. They understand the importance of everyday china, the responsibility of inheriting Great-Grandmother's silver, the value of good linen.

And by the time this story is over, they will be covered in blood.

Some of it will be theirs. Some of it will belong to others. But they will drip with it. They will swim in it. They will drown in it.

Housewife (n)—a light, worthless woman or girl
—*Oxford English Dictionary*, compact edition, 1971

CRY, THE BELOVED COUNTRY

November 1988

CHAPTER 1

In 1988, George H. W. Bush had just won the presidential election by inviting everyone to read his lips while Michael Dukakis lost it by riding in a tank. Dr. Huxtable was America's dad, *Kate & Allie* were America's moms, *The Golden Girls* were America's grandmoms, McDonald's announced it was opening its first restaurant in the Soviet Union, everyone bought Stephen Hawking's *A Brief History of Time* and didn't read it, *Phantom of the Opera* opened on Broadway, and Patricia Campbell got ready to die.

She sprayed her hair, put on her earrings, and blotted her lipstick, but when she looked at herself in the mirror she didn't see a housewife of thirty-nine with two children and a bright future, she saw a dead person. Unless war broke out, the oceans rose, or the earth fell into the sun, tonight was the monthly meeting of the Literary Guild of Mt. Pleasant, and she hadn't read this month's book. And she was the discussant. Which meant that in less than ninety minutes she would stand up in front of a room full of women and lead them in a conversation about a book she hadn't read.

She had meant to read *Cry, the Beloved Country*—honestly—but every time she picked up her copy and read *There is a lovely road that runs from Ixopo into the hills*, Korey rode her bike off the end of the dock because she thought that if she pedaled fast enough she could skim across the water, or she set her brother's hair on fire trying to see how close she could get a match before it caught, or she spent an entire weekend telling everyone who called that her mother couldn't come to the phone because she was dead, which

Patricia only learned about when people started showing up at the front door with condolence casseroles.

Before Patricia could discover why the road that runs from Ixopo was so lovely, she'd see Blue run past the sun porch windows buck naked, or she'd realize the house was so quiet because she'd left him at the downtown library and had to jump in the Volvo and fly back over the bridge, praying that he hadn't been kidnapped by Moonies, or because he'd decided to see how many raisins he could fit up his nose (twenty-four). She never even learned where Ixopo was exactly because her mother-in-law, Miss Mary, moved in with them for a six-week visit and the garage room had to have clean towels, and the sheets on the guest bed had to be changed every day, and Miss Mary had trouble getting out of the tub so they had one of those bars installed and she had to find somebody to do that, and the children had laundry that needed to be done, and Carter had to have his shirts ironed, and Korey wanted new soccer cleats because everyone else had them but they really couldn't afford them right now, and Blue was only eating white food so she had to make rice every night for supper, and the road to Ixopo ran on to the hills without her.

Joining the Literary Guild of Mt. Pleasant had seemed like a good idea at the time. Patricia realized she needed to get out of the house and meet new people the moment she leaned over at supper with Carter's boss and tried to cut up his steak for him. A book club made sense because she liked reading, especially mysteries. Carter had suggested it was because she went through life as if the entire world were a mystery to her, and she didn't disagree: *Patricia Campbell and the Secret of Cooking Three Meals a Day, Seven Days a Week, without Losing Your Mind. Patricia Campbell and the Case of the Five-Year-Old Child Who Keeps Biting Other People. Patricia Campbell and the Mystery of Finding Enough Time to Read the Newspaper When You Have Two Children and a Mother-in-Law Living with You and Everyone Needs Their Clothes Washed, and to Be Fed, and the House Needs to*

Be Cleaned and Someone Has to Give the Dog His Heartworm Pills and You Should Probably Wash Your Own Hair Every Few Days or Your Daughter Is Going to Ask Why You Look Like a Street Person. A few discreet inquiries, and she'd been invited to the inaugural meeting of the Literary Guild of Mt. Pleasant at Marjorie Fretwell's house.

The Literary Guild of Mt. Pleasant picked their books for that year in a very democratic process: Marjorie Fretwell invited them to select eleven books from a list of thirteen she found appropriate. She asked if there were other books anyone wanted to recommend, but everyone understood that wasn't a real question, except for Slick Paley, who seemed chronically unable to read social cues.

"I'd like to nominate *Like Lambs to the Slaughter: Your Child and the Occult*," Slick said. "With that crystal store on Coleman Boulevard and Shirley MacLaine on the cover of *Time* magazine talking about her past lives, we need a wake-up call."

"I've never heard of it," Marjorie Fretwell said. "So I imagine it falls outside our mandate of reading the great books of the Western world. Anyone else?"

"But—" Slick protested.

"Anyone else?" Marjorie repeated.

They selected the books Marjorie wrote down for them, assigned each book to the month Marjorie thought best, and picked the discussants Marjorie thought were most appropriate. The discussant would open the meeting by delivering a twenty-minute presentation on the book, its background, and the life of its author, then lead the group discussion. A discussant could not cancel or trade books with anyone else without paying a stiff fine because the Literary Guild of Mt. Pleasant was not fooling around.

When it became clear she wasn't going to be able to finish *Cry, the Beloved Country*, Patricia called Marjorie.

"Marjorie," she said over the phone while putting a lid on the rice and turning it down from a boil. "It's Patricia Campbell. I need to talk to you about *Cry, the Beloved Country*."

"Such a powerful work," Marjorie said.

"Of course," Patricia said.

"I know you'll do it justice," Marjorie said.

"I'll do my best," Patricia said, realizing that this was the exact opposite of what she needed to say.

"And it's so timely with the situation in South Africa right now," Marjorie said.

A cold bolt of fear shot through Patricia: what was the situation in South Africa right now?

After she hung up, Patricia cursed herself for being a coward and a fool, and vowed to go to the library and look up *Cry, the Beloved Country* in the *Directory of World Literature*, but she had to do snacks for Korey's soccer team, and the babysitter had mono, and Carter had a sudden trip to Columbia and she had to help him pack, and then a snake came out of the toilet in the garage room and she had to beat it to death with a rake, and Blue drank a bottle of Wite-Out and she had to take him to the doctor to see if he would die (he wouldn't). She tried to look up Alan Paton, the author, in their *World Book Encyclopedia* but they were missing the *P* volume. She made a mental note that they needed new encyclopedias.

The doorbell rang.

"Mooooom," Korey called from the downstairs hall. "Pizza's here!"

She couldn't put it off any longer. It was time to face Marjorie.

Marjorie had handouts.

"These are just a few articles about current events in South Africa, including the recent unpleasantness in Vanderbijlpark," she said. "But I think Patricia will sum things up nicely for us in her discussion of Mr. Alan Paton's *Cry, the Beloved Country*."

Everyone turned to stare at Patricia sitting on Marjorie's enormous pink-and-white sofa. Not being familiar with the design of

Marjorie's home, she had put on a floral dress and felt like all anyone saw were her head and hands floating in midair. She wished she could pull them into her dress and disappear completely. She felt her soul exit her body and hover up by the ceiling.

"But before she begins," Marjorie said, and every head turned back her way, "let's have a moment of silence for Mr. Alan Paton. His passing earlier this year has shaken the literary world as much as it's shaken me."

Patricia's brain chased itself in circles: the author was dead? Recently? She hadn't seen anything in the paper. What could she say? How had he died? Was he murdered? Torn apart by wild dogs? Heart attack?

"Amen," Marjorie said. "Patricia?"

Patricia's soul decided that it was no fool and ascended into the afterlife, leaving her at the mercy of the women surrounding her. There was Grace Cavanaugh, who lived two doors down from Patricia but whom she'd only met once when Grace rang her doorbell and said, "I'm sorry to bother you, but you've lived here for six months and I need to know: is this the way you *intend* for your yard to look?"

Slick Paley blinked rapidly, her sharp foxy face and tiny eyes glued to Patricia, her pen poised above her notebook. Louise Gibbes cleared her throat. Cuffy Williams blew her nose slowly into a Kleenex. Sadie Funche leaned forward, nibbling on a cheese straw, eyes boring into Patricia. The only person not looking at Patricia was Kitty Scruggs, who eyed the bottle of wine in the center of the coffee table that no one had dared open.

"Well . . . ," Patricia began. "Didn't we all love *Cry, the Beloved Country*?"

Sadie, Slick, and Cuffy nodded. Patricia glanced at her watch and saw that seven seconds had passed. She could run out the clock. She let the silence linger hoping someone would jump in and say something, but the long pause only prompted Marjorie to say, "Patricia?"

"It's so sad that Alan Paton was cut down in the prime of his life before writing more novels like *Cry, the Beloved Country*," Patricia said, feeling her way forward, word by word, guided by the nods of the other women. "Because this book has so many timely and relevant things to say to us now, especially after the terrible events in Vander . . . Vanderbill . . . South Africa."

The nodding got stronger. Patricia felt her soul descending back into her body. She forged ahead.

"I wanted to tell you all about Alan Paton's life," she said. "And why he wrote this book, but all those facts don't express how powerful this story is, how much it moved me, the great cry of outrage I felt when I read it. This is a book you read with your heart, not with your mind. Did anyone else feel that way?"

The nods were general, all over the living room.

"Exactly." Slick Paley nodded. "Yes."

"I feel so strongly about South Africa," Patricia said, and then remembered that Mary Brasington's husband was in banking and Joanie Wieter's husband did something with the stock market and they might have investments there. "But I know there are many sides to the issue, and I wonder if anyone wanted to present another point of view. In the spirit of Mr. Paton's book, this should be a conversation, not a speech."

Everyone was nodding. Her soul settled back into her body. She had done it. She had survived. Marjorie cleared her throat.

"Patricia," Marjorie asked. "What did you think about what the book had to say about Nelson Mandela?"

"So inspirational," Patricia said. "He simply towers over everything, even though he's really just mentioned."

"I don't believe he is," Marjorie said, and Slick Paley stopped nodding. "Where did you see him mentioned? On which page?"

Patricia's soul began ascending into the light again. *Good-bye*, it said. *Good-bye, Patricia. You're on your own now . . .*

"His spirit of freedom?" Patricia said. "It pervades every page?"

"When this book was written," Marjorie said. "Nelson Mandela was still a law student and a minor member of the ANC. I'm not sure how his spirit could be anywhere in this book, let alone pervading every page."

Marjorie drilled into Patricia's face with her ice-pick eyes.

"Well," Patricia croaked, because she was dead now and apparently death felt very, very dry. "What he was going to do. You could feel it building. In here. In this book. That we read."

"Patricia," Marjorie said. "You didn't read the book, did you?"

Time stopped. No one moved. Patricia wanted to lie, but a lifetime of breeding had made her a lady.

"Some of it," Patricia said.

Marjorie let out a soul-deep sigh that seemed to go on forever.

"Where did you stop?" she asked.

"The first page?" Patricia said, then began to babble. "I'm sorry, I know I've let you down, but the babysitter had mono, and Carter's mother is staying with us, and a snake came out of the commode, and everything's just been so hard this month. I really don't know what to say except I'm so, so sorry."

Black crept in around the edges of her vision. A high-pitched tone shrilled in her right ear.

"Well," Marjorie said. "You're the one who's lost out, by robbing yourself of what is possibly one of the finest works of world literature. And you've robbed all of us of your unique point of view. But what's done is done. Who else would be willing to lead the discussion?"

Sadie Funche retracted into her Laura Ashley dress like a turtle, Nancy Fox started shaking her head before Marjorie even reached the end of her sentence, and Cuffy Williams froze like a prey animal confronted by a predator.

"Did anyone actually read this month's book?" Marjorie asked.

Silence.

"I cannot believe this," Marjorie said. "We all agreed, eleven months ago, to read the great books of the Western world and now, less than one year later, we've come to this. I am deeply disappointed in all of you. I thought we wanted to better ourselves, expose our-selves to thoughts and ideas from outside Mt. Pleasant. The men all say, 'It's not too clever for a girl to be clever,' and they laugh at us and think we only care about our hair. The only books they give us are cookbooks because in their minds we are silly, lightweight know-nothings. And you've just proven them right."

She stopped to catch her breath. Patricia noticed sweat glistening in her eyebrows. Marjorie continued:

"I strongly suggest y'all go home and think about whether you want to join us next month to read *Jude the Obscure* and—"

Grace Cavanaugh stood, hitching her purse over one shoulder.

"Grace?" Marjorie asked. "Are you not staying?"

"I just remembered an appointment," Grace said. "It entirely slipped my mind."

"Well," Marjorie said, her momentum undermined. "Don't let me keep you."

"I wouldn't dream of it," Grace said.

And with that, the tall, elegant, prematurely gray Grace floated out of the room.

Robbed of its velocity, the meeting dissolved. Marjorie retreated to the kitchen, followed by a concerned Sadie Funche. A dispirited clump of women lingered around the dessert table making chitchat. Patricia lurked in her chair until no one seemed to be watching, then darted out of the house.

As she cut across Marjorie's front yard, she heard a noise that sounded like *Hey*. She stopped and looked for the source.

"Hey," Kitty Scruggs repeated.

Kitty lurked behind the line of parked cars in Marjorie's driveway, a cloud of blue smoke hovering over her head, a long thin cigarette between her fingers. Next to her stood Maryellen something-or-other, also smoking. Kitty waved Patricia over with one hand.

Patricia knew that Maryellen was a Yankee from Massachusetts who told everyone that she was a feminist. And Kitty was one of those big women who wore the kind of clothes people charitably referred to as "fun"—baggy sweaters with multicolored handprints on them, chunky plastic jewelry. Patricia suspected that getting entangled with women like this was the first step on a slippery slope that ended with her wearing felt reindeer antlers at Christmas, or standing outside Citadel Mall asking people to sign a petition, so she approached them with caution.

"I liked what you did in there," Kitty said.

"I should have found time to read the book," Patricia told her.

"Why?" Kitty asked. "It was boring. I couldn't make it past the first chapter."

"I need to write Marjorie a note," Patricia said. "To apologize."

Maryellen squinted against the smoke and sucked on her cigarette.

"Marjorie got what she deserved," she said, exhaling.

"Listen." Kitty placed her body between the two of them and Marjorie's front door, just in case Marjorie was watching and could read lips. "I'm having some people read a book and come over to my house next month to talk about it. Maryellen'll be there."

"I couldn't possibly find the time to belong to two book clubs," Patricia said.

"Trust me," Kitty said. "After today, Marjorie's book club is done."

"What book are you reading?" Patricia asked, groping for reasons to say no.

Kitty reached into her denim shoulder bag and pulled out the kind of cheap paperback they sold at the drugstore.

"*Evidence of Love: A True Story of Passion and Death in the Suburbs*," she said.

It took Patricia aback. This was one of those trashy true crime books. But clearly Kitty was reading it and you couldn't call someone else's taste in books trashy, even if it was.

"I'm not sure that's my kind of book," Patricia said.

"These two women were best friends and they chopped each other up with axes," Kitty said. "Don't pretend you don't want to know what happened."

"Jude is obscure for a reason," Maryellen growled.

"Is it just the two of you?" Patricia asked.

A voice piped up behind her.

"Hey, everyone," Slick Paley said. "What're y'all talking about over here?"

CHAPTER 2

The last bell of the day rang somewhere deep inside the bowels of Albemarle Academy and the double doors opened and disgorged a mob of small children strapped beneath bulging, spine-bending book bags. They hobbled to the car pool area like elderly gnomes, bent double beneath three-ring binders and social studies books. Patricia saw Korey and pecked at the horn. Korey looked up and broke into a loping run that made Patricia's heart hurt. Her daughter slid into the passenger seat, hauling her book bag onto her lap.

"Seat belts," Patricia said, and Korey clicked hers in.

"Why're you picking me up?" Korey asked.

"I thought we could stop by the Foot Locker and look at cleats," Patricia said. "Didn't you say you needed new ones? Then I was in the mood for TCBY."

She felt her daughter begin to glow, and as they drove over the West Ashley Bridge, Korey explained to her mom about all the different kind of cleats the other girls had and why she needed bladed cleats and they had to be hard ground cleats and not soft ground cleats even though they played on grass because hard ground cleats were faster. When she stopped for breath, Patricia said, "I heard about what happened at recess."

All the light went out inside Korey, and Patricia immediately regretted saying anything, but she had to say something because isn't that what mothers did?

"I don't know why Chelsea pulled your pants down in front of the class," Patricia said. "But it was an ugly, mean thing to do. As soon as we get home, I'm calling her mother."

"No!" Korey said. "Please, please, please, nothing happened. It wasn't a big deal. Please, Mom."

Patricia's own mother had never taken her side in anything, and Patricia wanted Korey to understand that this wasn't a punishment, this was a good thing, but Korey refused to go into Foot Locker, and mumbled that she didn't want any frozen yogurt, and Patricia felt like it was deeply unfair when all she'd tried to do was be a good mother and somehow that made her the Wicked Witch of the West. By the time she pulled into their driveway, steering wheel clenched in a death grip, she was not in the mood to see a white Cadillac the size of a small boat blocking her drive and Kitty Scruggs standing on her front steps.

"Hellooooo," Kitty called in a way that immediately set Patricia's teeth on edge.

"Korey, this is Mrs. Scruggs," Patricia said, smiling too hard.

"Pleased to meet you," Korey mumbled.

"You're Korey?" Kitty asked. "Listen, I heard what Donna Phelps's little girl did to you today at school."

Korey looked at the ground, hair hanging over her face. Patricia wanted to tell Kitty she was only making it worse.

"The next time Chelsea Phelps does something like that," Kitty said, barreling ahead, "you tell everyone at the top of your lungs, 'Chelsea Phelps spent the night at Merit Scruggs's house last month and she wet her sleeping bag and blamed it on the dog.'"

Patricia couldn't believe it. Parents didn't say things like that about other people's children. She turned to tell Korey not to listen but saw her daughter staring at Kitty in awe, eyes round, mouth open.

"Really?" Korey asked.

"She tooted at the table, too," Kitty said. "And tried to blame *that* on my four-year-old."

For a long, frozen moment, Patricia didn't know what to say, and then Korey burst into giggles. She laughed so hard she sat down on the front steps, fell over sideways, and gasped until she started to hiccup.

"Go inside and say hello to your grandmother," Patricia said, feeling suddenly grateful to Kitty.

"Aren't they such little pills at that age?" Kitty said, watching Korey go.

"They are peculiar," Patricia said.

"They're pills," Kitty said. "Bitter little pills who ought to be tied up in a sack and let out when they're eighteen. Here, I brought you this."

She handed Patricia a glossy new paperback copy of *Evidence of Love*.

"I know you think it's trash," Kitty said. "But it has passion, love, hate, romance, violence, excitement. It's just like Thomas Hardy, only in paperback and with eight pages of photos in the middle."

"I don't know," Patricia said. "I don't have a lot of time . . ."

But Kitty was already retreating to her car. Patricia decided that this mystery should be called *Patricia Campbell and the Inability to Say No*.

To her surprise, she tore through the book in three days.

Patricia almost didn't make the meeting. Right before she left, Korey washed her face in lemon juice to get rid of her freckles and wound up getting it in both eyes, sending her shrieking into the hall, where she ran face-first into a doorknob. Patricia flushed her eyes with water, put a bag of frozen peas on her goose egg, told Korey she'd had just as many, if not more, freckles when she was her age, and got her settled on the sofa with Miss Mary to watch *The Cosby Show*. She made it to the meeting ten minutes late.

Kitty lived on Seewee Farms, a two-hundred-acre chunk of Boone Hall Plantation that had been parceled off a long time ago as a wedding present to some Lord Proprietor or other. Through misadventure and poor decision making it had come to Kitty's grandmother-in-law, and when that eminent old lady had declined elegantly into her grave, she'd passed it on to her favorite grandson, Kitty's husband, Horse.

Way out in the middle of nowhere, surrounded by flooded rice fields and tangled pine forest, dotted with broken-backed outbuildings inhabited solely by snakes, it was anchored by a hideously ugly main house painted chocolate brown and wrapped in sagging porches and rotting columns with raccoons in the attic and opossums in the walls. It was exactly the kind of grand home, suspended in a state of gracious decay, Patricia thought all the best Charlestonians owned.

Now she stood before the massive double doors on the sprawling front porch and pressed the bell and nothing happened. She tried again.

"Patricia!" Kitty called.

Patricia looked around, then up. Kitty leaned out the second-floor window.

"Go around to the side," Kitty hollered. "We haven't been able to find the key to that door in forever."

She met Kitty by her kitchen door.

"Come on in," Kitty said. "Don't mind the cat."

Patricia didn't see a cat anywhere, but she did see something that thrilled her: Kitty's kitchen was a disaster. Empty pizza boxes, schoolbooks, junk mail, and wet bathing suits crowded every flat surface. Back issues of *Southern Living* slid off chairs. A disassembled engine covered the kitchen table. By comparison, Patricia's house looked magazine perfect.

"This is what five kids looks like," Kitty said over her shoulder. "Stay smart, Patricia. Stop at two."

The front hall looked like something out of *Gone with the Wind* except its swooping staircase and oak floor were buried beneath a mudslide of violin cases, balled-up gym socks, taxidermied squirrels, glow-in-the-dark Frisbees, sheaves of parking tickets, collapsible music stands, soccer balls, lacrosse sticks, an umbrella stand full of baseball bats, and a dead, five-foot-tall rubber tree stuck inside a planter made of an amputated elephant's foot.

Kitty picked her way through the carnage, leading Patricia to a front room where Slick Paley and Maryellen Whatever-Her-Name-Was perched on the lip of a sofa covered with approximately five hundred throw pillows. Across from them, Grace Cavanaugh sat ramrod straight on a piano bench. Patricia didn't see a piano.

"All right," Kitty said, pouring wine from a jug. "Let's talk about axe murder!"

"Don't we need a name first?" Slick asked. "And to select books for the year?"

"This isn't a book club," Grace said.

"What do you mean, this isn't a book club?" Maryellen asked.

"We're just getting together to talk about a paperback book we all happened to read," Grace said. "It's not like it's a real book."

"Whatever you say, Grace," Kitty said, thrusting mugs of wine into everyone's hands. "Five children live in this house and it's eight years before the oldest one moves out. If I don't get some adult conversation tonight I'm going to blow my brains out."

"Hear, hear," Maryellen said. "Three girls: seven, five, and four."

"Four is such a lovely age," Slick cooed.

"Is it?" Maryellen asked, eyes narrowing.

"So are we a book club?" Patricia asked. She liked to know where things stood.

"We're a book club, we're not a book club, who cares?" Kitty said. "What I want to know is why Betty Gore came at her good friend, Candy Montgomery, with an axe and how the heck she got chopped up instead?"

Patricia looked around to see what the other women thought. Maryellen in her dry-cleaned blue jeans and her hair scrunchie and her harsh Yankee voice; tiny Slick looking like a particularly eager mouse with her pointy teeth and beady eyes; Kitty in her denim blouse with musical notes splayed across the front in gold sequins, slurping down a mug of wine, hair a mess, like a bear just woken up from hibernation; and finally Grace with a ruffled bow at her throat, sitting straight, hands folded perfectly in her lap, eyes blinking slowly from behind her large-framed glasses, studying them all like an owl.

These women were too different from her. Patricia didn't belong here.

"I think," Grace said, and they sat up straighter, "that it shows a remarkable lack of planning on Betty's part. If you're going to murder your best friend with an axe, you should make sure you know what you're doing."

That started the conversation, and without thinking, Patricia found herself joining in, and they were still talking about the book two hours later when they walked to their cars.

The following month they read *The Michigan Murders: The True Story of the Ypsilanti Ripper's Reign of Terror*, and then *A Death in Canaan: A Classic Case of Good and Evil in a Small New England Town*, followed by *Bitter Blood: A True Story of Southern Family Pride, Madness, and Multiple Murder*—all of them Kitty's recommendations.

They selected next year's books together, and when all the blurry black-and-white photos of crime scenes and minute-by-minute timelines of the night when it all happened began to blur, Grace came up with the idea of alternating each true crime book with a novel, so they would read *The Silence of the Lambs* one month, and *Buried Dreams: Inside the Mind of John Wayne Gacy* the next. They read *The Hillside Stranglers* by Darcy O'Brien, followed by Shakespeare's *Titus Andronicus*, with its children baked into a pie and fed to their mother. ("The problem with that," Grace pointed out, "is you would need extremely large pies to fit two children, even minced.")

Patricia loved it. She asked Carter if he wanted to read along with her, but he told her he dealt with crazy patients all day, so the last thing he wanted to do was come home and read about crazy people. Patricia didn't mind. The not-quite-a-book-club, with all its slow poisoners and murderers-for-hire and angels of death, gave her a new outlook on life.

She and Carter had moved to the Old Village last year because they'd wanted to live somewhere with plenty of space, somewhere quiet, and somewhere, most importantly, safe. They wanted more than just a neighborhood, they wanted a community, where your home said you espoused a certain set of values. Somewhere protected from the chaos and the ceaseless change of the outside world. Somewhere the kids could play outside all day, unsupervised, until you called them in for supper.

The Old Village lay just across the Cooper River from downtown Charleston in the suburb of Mt. Pleasant, but while Charleston was formal and sophisticated, and Mt. Pleasant was its country cousin, the Old Village was a way of life. Or at least that was what the people who lived there believed. And Carter had worked long and hard so that they could finally afford not just a house but a way of life.

This way of life was a slice of live oaks and gracious homes lying between Coleman Boulevard and Charleston Harbor, where everyone still waved at cars when they went by and no one drove over twenty-five miles per hour.

It was where Carter taught Korey and Blue to crab off the dock, lowering raw chicken necks tied to long strings into the murky harbor water, and pulling up mean-eyed crabs they scooped up in nets. He took them shrimping at night, lit by the hissing white glare of their Coleman lantern. They went to oyster roasts and Sunday school, wedding receptions at Alhambra Hall and funerals at Stuhr's. They went to the Pierates Cruze block party every Christmas, and danced the shag at Wild Dunes on New Year's Eve. Korey and Blue went to Albemarle Academy on the other side of the harbor for school, and made friends, and had sleepovers, and Patricia drove car pool, and no one locked their doors, and everyone knew where you left your spare key when you went out of town, and you could go out all day and leave your windows open and the worst thing that might happen is you'd come home and find someone else's cat sleeping on your kitchen counter. It was a good place to raise children. It was a wonderful place to be a family. It was quiet, and soft, and peaceful, and safe.

But sometimes Patricia wanted to be challenged. Sometimes she yearned to see what she was made of. Sometimes she remembered being a nurse before she married Carter and wondered if she could still reach into a wound and hold an artery closed with her fingers, or if she still had the courage to pull a fishhook out of a child's eyelid. Sometimes she craved a little danger. And that was why she had book club.

In the fall of '91, Kitty's beloved Minnesota Twins made it to the World Series and she got Horse to chain-saw the two pine trees in their front yard and lay out a scaled-down baseball diamond in white lime. She invited all the members of their not-quite-a-book-club over to play a game with their husbands.

"Y'all," Slick said, at their last meeting before the game. "I need to unburden my conscience."

"Jesus Christ," Maryellen said, rolling her eyes. "Here it comes."

"Don't talk about who you don't know," Slick shot back. "Now, y'all, I don't like asking people to sin—"

"If baseball's a sin, I'm going to Hell," Kitty said.

"My husband, he . . . well," Slick said, ignoring Kitty. "Leland wouldn't understand why we read such morbid books in our book club—"

"It's not a book club," Grace said.

"—and I didn't want to worry him," Slick forged on, "so I told him we were a Bible study group."

No one said anything for a full fifteen seconds. Finally, Maryellen spoke. "You told your husband we've been reading the Bible?"

"It rewards a lifetime of study," Slick said.

The silence stretched on as they looked at each other, incredulous, and then they all burst out laughing.

"I'm serious, y'all," Slick said. "He won't let me come anymore if he knows."

They realized she was serious.

"Slick," Kitty said, solemnly. "I promise, on Saturday, all of us will profess a sincere and deep enthusiasm for the word of God."

And on Saturday, they all did.

The husbands bumbled together in Kitty's front yard, shaking hands and making jokes, with their weekend stubble and their Clemson logos and their Polo shirts tucked into their stonewashed jean shorts. Kitty divided them into teams, splitting up the couples, but Patricia insisted Korey be allowed to play.

"All the other children are swimming off the dock," Kitty said.

"She'd rather play baseball," Patricia said.

"I'm not going to pitch underhanded just because she's a child," Kitty told her.

"She'll be fine," Patricia said.

Kitty had a strong swing and on the pitcher's mound, she threw lethal fastballs. Korey watched her strike out Slick and Ed. Then she was up at bat.

"Mom," she said. "What if I miss?"

"Then you tried your best," Patricia told her.

"What if I break one of her windows?" Korey asked.

"Then I'll buy you a frozen yogurt on the way home," Patricia said.

But as Korey walked to home plate, a bolt of worry shot through Patricia. Korey held the bat uncomfortably and its tip wobbled in the air. Her legs looked too thin, her arms looked too weak. She was just a baby. Patricia got ready to comfort her and tell her she tried her best. Kitty gave Patricia an apologetic shrug, then drew her right arm back and sent a fastball screaming at Korey in a straight line.

There was a crack and the ball suddenly reversed direction, sailing in a high arc toward Kitty's house, and then at the last moment it lifted, soaring over the roof, over the house, coming down somewhere deep in the woods. Everyone, even Korey, watched, frozen.

"Go, Korey!" Patricia screamed, breaking the silence. "Run!"

Korey circled the bases and her team took the game, 6–4. Korey was at bat for every single one of those points.

Six months later, it became clear Miss Mary could no longer live on her own. Carter and his two older brothers agreed to take turns having their mother stay with them four months at a time, and Carter, being the youngest, took her first.

Then Sandy called the day before he was supposed to drive down and pick her up, saying, "My kids are too young to be around Mama when she's confused like this. We want them to remember her the way she used to be."

Carter called his oldest brother, but Bobby said, "Mom wouldn't be comfortable in Virginia, it's too cold up here."

Harsh words were exchanged, and then Carter, sitting on the end of their bed, jammed his thumb down hard on the portable phone's hang-up button and held it there for a very long time before he said:

"Mom's staying."

"For how long?" Patricia asked.

"Forever," he said.

"But, Carter . . . ," she began.

"What do you want me to do, Patty?" he asked. "Throw her out on the street? I can't put her in a home."

Patricia immediately softened. Carter's father had died when he was young and his mother had raised him alone. His next-oldest brother was eight years his senior and so it had been Carter and his mother on their own. Miss Mary's sacrifices for Carter were family legend.

"You're right," she said. "We have the garage room. We'll make it work."

"Thank you," he said after a long pause, and he sounded so genuinely grateful, Patricia knew they'd made the right decision.

But Korey was starting middle school, and Blue couldn't focus on his math and he needed a tutor and he was only in fourth grade, and Carter's mother couldn't always say what she was thinking, and she was getting worse every day.

Frustration poisoned Miss Mary's personality. Once she had doted on her grandchildren. Now, when Blue accidentally knocked over her buttermilk she pinched his arm so hard it left a black-and-blue mark. She kicked Patricia in the shin after finding out there was no liver for her supper. She demanded to be taken to the bus station constantly. After a series of incidents, Patricia learned she couldn't be left home alone.

Grace stopped by early one afternoon on a day when Miss Mary had already thrown her bowl of cereal on the floor, then clogged her toilet in the garage room with an entire roll of paper.

"I wanted to invite you to be my guest for the closing night of Spoleto," Grace told Patricia. "I have tickets for you, Kitty, Maryellen, and Slick. I thought it would be nice if we did something cultural."

Patricia ached to go. Closing night of Spoleto took place outdoors at Middleton Place. You had a picnic on a blanket on the hill facing the lake while the Charleston Symphony Orchestra played classical music and it ended with fireworks. Then she heard Ragtag yelp from the den and Miss Mary say something ugly.

"I'm sorry, but I can't," Patricia said.

"Can I help?" Grace asked.

And it all came out, how scared Patricia felt about Miss Mary living with them, how hard it was for her to sit at the table for dinner with the children, how much of a strain it was on her and Carter.

"But I don't want to complain," Patricia said. "She did so much for Carter."

Grace said she was sorry Patricia wouldn't make Spoleto, then left, and Patricia cursed herself for talking too much.

The next day, a pickup truck pulled into Patricia's driveway with Kitty's boys in the back along with a portable toilet, a walker, bedpans, washing basins, large-handled plastic cutlery, and boxes of unbreakable plates. Kitty heaved herself out of the driver's seat.

"When Horse's mother lived with us we wound up with all this junk," she said. "We'll bring the hospital bed over tomorrow. I just need to round up some more fellas to lift it."

Patricia realized that Grace must have called Kitty and told her the situation. Before she could call Grace to say thank you, her doorbell rang again. A short black woman, plump but sharp-eyed, her hair set in a stiff old-fashioned helmet, wearing white slacks and a white nurse's tunic under a purple cardigan, stood on her front porch.

"Mrs. Cavanaugh said you might be able to use my help," the woman said. "My name is Ursula Greene and I take care of old folks."

"It's very nice of you," Patricia began. "But—"

"I'll also look after the children occasionally at no extra charge," Mrs. Greene said. "I'm not a babysitter, but Mrs. Cavanaugh said you might step out from time to time. I charge eleven dollars an hour and thirteen dollars an hour at night. I don't mind cooking for the little ones, but I don't want it to become a habit."

It was cheaper than Patricia thought, but she still couldn't imagine anyone being willing to deal with Miss Mary.

"Before you make a decision," she said, "let me introduce you to my mother-in-law."

They walked onto the sun porch, where Miss Mary sat watching television. Miss Mary scowled at the interruption.

"Who's this?" she snipped.

"This is Mrs. Greene," Patricia said. "Mrs. Greene, I'd like you to meet—"

"What's she doing here?" Miss Mary said.

"I've come to brush your hair and do your nails," Mrs. Greene said. "And make you something to eat later."

"Why can't that one do it?" Miss Mary asked, jabbing a gnarled finger at Patricia.

"Because you're working that one's last nerve," Mrs. Greene said. "And if that one doesn't get a break she's liable to throw you off the roof."

Miss Mary thought about it for a minute, then said, "No one's pushing me off any roof."

"Keep acting like that and I might help her," Mrs. Greene said.

Three weeks later, Patricia sat on a green plaid blanket at Middleton Place, listening to the Charleston Symphony Orchestra play Handel's "Music for the Royal Fireworks." Overhead, the first firework unfolded until it filled the sky like a burning green dandelion. Fireworks always moved Patricia. It took so much time and effort to get them right and they were over so quickly and could only be enjoyed by such a small number of people.

By the light of the fireworks she looked at the women sitting around her: Grace in a lawn chair, eyes closed, listening to the music; Kitty, asleep on her back, plastic wineglass tipping dangerously in one hand; Maryellen in her overalls, legs stretched out in front of her, taking in Charleston's finest; and Slick, legs tucked beneath her, head cocked, listening to the music like it was homework.

Patricia realized that for four years, these were the women she'd seen every month. She'd talked to them about her marriage, and her children, and gotten frustrated with them, and argued with them, and seen all of them cry at some point, and somewhere along the line, among all the slaughtered coeds, and shocking small-town secrets, and missing children, and true accounts of the cases that changed America forever, she'd learned two things: they were all in this together, and if their husbands ever took out a life insurance policy on them they were in trouble.

HELTER SKELTER

May 1993

CHAPTER 3

"But if I can't get Blue to come to the table for supper when Carter's mother eats with us," Patricia said to her book club, "then Korey will stop coming, too. She's already picky about food. I'm worried it's a teenager thing."

"Already?" Kitty asked.

"She's fourteen," Patricia said.

"Being a teenager isn't a number," Maryellen said. "It's the age when you stop liking them."

"You don't like the girls?" Patricia asked.

"No one likes their children," Maryellen said. "We love them to death, but we don't like them."

"My children are a constant blessing," Slick said.

"Get a life, Slick," Kitty said, biting into a cheese straw, showering crumbs into her lap, brushing them off onto Grace's carpet.

Patricia saw Grace flinch.

"No one thinks you don't adore your children, Slick," Grace said. "I love Ben Jr. but it will be a happy day when he leaves for college and we can finally have some peace in this house."

"I think they don't eat because of what they see in magazines," Slick said. "They call it 'heroin chic,' can you imagine? I cut out the ads before I'll let Greer have a magazine."

"Are you kidding me?" Maryellen asked.

"How do you find the time?" Kitty asked, snapping a cheese straw in half and sending more crumbs to Grace's carpet.

Grace couldn't contain herself. She got Kitty a plate.

"Oh, no thank you," Kitty said, waving it away. "I'm fine."

The nameless not-quite-a-book-club had settled into Grace's sitting room with its deep carpets and soothing lamplight. A framed Audubon print hung over the fireplace, reflecting the room's pale colonial colors—Raleigh peach and Bruton white—and the piano in the corner gleamed darkly to itself. Everything in Grace's house looked perfect. Every early American Windsor chair, every chestnut end table, every Chinese porcelain lamp, it all looked to Patricia as if it had always been here and the house had grown up around it.

"Teenagers are boring," Kitty said. "And it only gets worse. Breakfast, laundry, clean the house, dinner, homework, the same thing, every day, day after day. If anything changes even the slightest bit, they have a cow. Honestly, Patricia, relax. Pick your battles. No one's going to die if they don't eat every meal at the table or if they don't have clean underwear one day."

"And what if that's the day they get hit by a car?" Grace asked.

"If Ben Jr. got hit by a car I think you'd have bigger problems than the condition of his underpants," Maryellen said.

"Not necessarily," Grace said.

"I freeze sandwiches," Slick blurted out.

"You what?" Kitty asked.

"To save time," Slick said in a rush. "I make all the sandwiches for the children's lunches, three per day, five days a week. That's sixty sandwiches. I make them all on the first Monday of the month, freeze them, and every morning I pull one out of the freezer and pop it in their bag. By lunchtime it's thawed."

"I'll have to try that," Patricia started to say because it sounded like a fantastic idea, but her comment got lost beneath Kitty and Maryellen's laughter.

"It saves time," Slick said, defensively.

"You can't freeze sandwiches," Kitty said. "What happens to the condiments?"

"They don't complain," Slick said.

"Because they don't eat them," Maryellen told her. "They either throw them in the trash or trade them to the dummies. I bet you money they've never eaten a single one of your freezer-burn specials."

"My children love my lunches," Slick said. "They wouldn't lie to me."

"Are those new earrings, Patricia?" Grace asked, changing the subject.

"They are," Patricia said, turning her head to catch the light.

"How much did they cost?" Slick asked, and Patricia saw everyone recoil slightly. The only thing tackier than bragging about God was asking about money.

"Carter gave them to me for my birthday," Patricia said.

"They look expensive," Slick said, doubling down. "I'd love to know where he got them."

Carter usually gave Patricia something he bought at the drugstore for her birthday, but this year he'd given her these pearl studs. Patricia had worn them tonight because she was proud he'd gotten her a real gift. Now she worried she was being a show-off, so she changed the subject.

"Are you having a problem with marsh rats?" she asked Grace. "I had two on my back patio this week."

"Bennett keeps his pellet gun with him when he sits outside and I don't get involved," Grace said. "We need to start talking about the book if we're going to get out of here at a decent hour. Slick, I believe you wanted to start?"

Slick sat up straighter, shuffled her notes, and cleared her throat.

"*Helter Skelter* by Vincent Bugliosi was this month's book," she said. "And I think it's a perfect indictment of the so-called Summer of Love as being the decade when America lost its way."

This year, the not-quite-a-book-club was reading the classics: *Helter Skelter, In Cold Blood, Zodiac,* Ann Rule's *The Stranger Beside Me,* and a new edition of *Fatal Vision* with yet another epilogue updating the reader on the feud between the author and his subject.

Only Kitty had read much true crime before 1988, so they'd missed a lot of the essentials, and this year they were determined to fill those gaps.

"Bugliosi tried the case all wrong," Maryellen said. Because Ed worked for the North Charleston police she always had an opinion about how a case should have been handled. "If they hadn't been so sloppy with the evidence they could have built a case based on physical evidence and not gotten stuck with Bugliosi's Helter Skelter strategy. They're lucky the judge found in his favor."

"How else would they have brought charges against Manson?" Slick asked. "He wasn't at any of the crime scenes when people were killed. He didn't personally stab anyone."

"Except Gary Hinman and the LaBiancas," Maryellen said.

"He never would have gotten a life sentence for those," Slick said. "The conspiracy strategy worked. Manson is the one I want off the streets. Beware false prophets."

"The Bible is hardly the best source for legal strategy," Maryellen said.

Kitty leaned forward, grabbed another cheese straw, fumbled it, then picked it up off the carpet and crunched into it. Grace looked away.

"That first chapter, y'all," Kitty said, chewing. "They stabbed Rosemary LaBianca forty-one times. What do you think that feels like? I mean, I think you feel every single one of them, don't you?"

"You all need to get alarms," Maryellen said. "Ours connects directly to the police, and the Mt. Pleasant police department has a three-minute response time."

"I think you could still get stabbed forty-one times in three minutes," Kitty said.

"I won't have those ugly stickers all over my windows," Grace said.

"You'd rather get stabbed forty-one times than ruin the curb appeal of your home?" Maryellen asked.

"Yes," Grace said.

"I thought it was fascinating to see into so many different lifestyles," Patricia said, expertly changing the subject yet again. "I was in nursing school so I always felt like I missed out on the hippie movement."

"It was a bunch of baloney," Kitty said. "I was in college in '69 and, trust me, the Summer of Love skipped South Carolina completely. All that free love was out in California."

"My summer of love was working in the live specimens lab at Princeton," Maryellen said. "Some of us had to pay our way through school, thank you very much."

"What I remember from the sixties is people being so nasty to Doug Mitchell when he came home from the war," Slick said. "He tried to go to Princeton on the GI Bill but everyone just spat on him and asked him how many babies he killed, so he wound up back in Due West working at his father's hardware store. He'd wanted to be an engineer, but the hippies wouldn't let him."

"I always thought the hippies were so glamorous," Patricia said. "In the nurses' lounge I'd see pictures of those girls in *Life* magazine with their long dresses and feel, well, life passing me by. But in *Helter Skelter* it all seemed so squalid. They lived on that ranch with all the flies, and they didn't wear clothes half the time and were dirty *all* the time."

"What good is free love if nobody showers?" Maryellen asked.

"Can you believe how old we are?" Kitty said. "Everyone thinks of the hippies as being a million years ago, but we all could've been hippies."

"Not all of us," Grace said.

"They're still around," Slick said. "Did you see in the newspaper today? In Waco? They followed that cult leader in Texas the same way all those girls followed Manson. These false prophets come wandering into town, take hold of your mind, and lead you down the primrose path. Without faith, people fall for honeyed words."

"Wouldn't happen to me," Maryellen said. "Anyone new moves into our neighborhood and I do what Grace taught me: I bake them a pie and take it over and by the time I leave I know where they're from, what their husband does for a living, and how many people live in their house."

"I did not teach you that," Grace said.

"I learned by example," Maryellen said.

"I just want people to feel welcome," Grace said. "And I ask them about themselves because I'm interested."

"You spy on them," Maryellen said.

"You have to," Kitty said. "So many new people are moving here. It used to be you'd only see bumper stickers for the Game-cocks, or Clemson, or the Citadel. Now you've got people driving around with Alabama and UVA stickers. Any one of them could be a serial killer for all we know."

"What I do," Grace said, "is if I see an unfamiliar car in the neighborhood, I write down their license plate number."

"Why?" Patricia asked.

"If something happens later," Grace said, "I have their license plate number and the date and make of the car so it can be used as evidence."

"So who does that big van belong to in front of Mrs. Savage's?" Kitty asked. "It's been there for three months."

Old Mrs. Savage lived half a mile away down Middle Street, and even though she was a deeply unpleasant woman, Patricia loved her house. The wooden clapboard sides were painted Easter egg yellow with bright white trim, and a glider hung on her front porch. Whenever she drove past, no matter how horrible Miss Mary was being, or how detached she felt from Korey as she got older, Patricia always looked at that perfectly proportioned little house and imagined herself curled up on a chair inside, reading her way through a stack of mysteries. But she hadn't noticed any van.

"What van?" she asked.

"It's a white van with tinted windows," Maryellen said. "It looks like something a child snatcher would drive."

"I noticed it because of Ragtag," Grace said. "He adores it."

"What?" Patricia asked, overcome by a sinking feeling that one of her shortcomings was about to be exposed.

"He was doing his business on Mrs. Savage's front yard when I drove by tonight," Kitty said, and started laughing.

"He's gotten in her garbage cans," Grace said. "More than once."

"I saw him raising his leg on that van's tires once, too," Maryellen added. "When he's not sleeping under it."

Everyone started to laugh and Patricia felt a hot flush creeping up her neck.

"Y'all, that's not funny," she said.

"You need to put Ragtag on a leash," Slick said.

"But we never used to have to," Patricia said. "No one in the Old Village ever put their dogs on a leash."

"It's the nineties," Maryellen said. "The new people sue you if your dog so much as barks at them. The Van Dorstens had to put Lady to sleep because she barked at that judge."

"The Old Village is changing, Patricia," Grace said. "I know of at least three animals Ann Savage called the dogcatcher on."

"Putting Ragtag on a leash seems"—Patricia looked for the right word—"cruel. He's used to running free."

"The van belongs to her nephew," Grace said. "Apparently Ann is too sick to get out of bed and the family sent him down to look after her."

"Of course," Maryellen said. "What'd you take over? Pecan pie? Key lime?"

Grace didn't dignify that with an answer.

"Should I go down there and say something about Ragtag?" Patricia asked.

Kitty picked up another cheese straw and snapped it in half.

"Don't sweat it," she said. "If Ann Savage has a problem, she'll come to you."

CHAPTER 4

Two hours later they bubbled out of Grace's house, still talking about hidden messages in Beatles albums, and whether Joel Pugh's suicide in London was an unsolved Manson murder, and blood spatter patterns at the Tate crime scene. As the other women walked across the front yard to their cars, Patricia stopped on Grace's moss-covered brick steps and inhaled the scent of her camellia bushes, lying in perfect rows on either side of the front door.

"It's so hard to go home and pack tomorrow's lunches after all that excitement," Patricia said.

Grace stepped outside, pulling her front door partially closed behind her in a halfhearted attempt to keep the air conditioning in. Which reminded Patricia. She made a mental note to call the air-conditioning man.

"All that chaos and mess," Grace said, shaking her head sadly. "I can't wait to return to my housekeeping."

"But don't you wish that something exciting would happen around here?" Patricia asked. "Just once?"

Grace raised her eyebrows at Patricia.

"You wish that a gang of unwashed hippies would break into your house and murder your family and write *death to pigs* in human blood on your walls because you don't want to pack bag lunches anymore?"

"Well, not when you put it like that," Patricia said. "Your camellias look wonderful."

"I spent this week planting my annuals," Grace said. "Those vincas, and the marigolds, and I have some azalea bushes around the side that are already blooming. When it's light I'll show you the noisettes I planted in back. They'll smell heavenly this summer."

They said good night and Patricia walked onto Pierates Cruze and Grace's door clunked softly shut behind her. The Cruze was a dirt horseshoe hanging off Middle Street in the Old Village, and the fourteen families who lived there would rather die than have it paved. The rocks on the road crunched beneath Patricia's feet, and she felt them through the thin soles of her shoes. The steamy evening air closed around her like a fist. The only sounds were her feet grinding rocks into the dirt and the angry rasp of crickets and katydids crowding around her in the dark.

The book club buzz evaporated from her veins as she left Grace's perfect yard behind and approached her house, huddled behind overgrown groves of wild bamboo and gnarled trees choked by ivy. She got closer and saw that the garbage cans weren't at the end of the driveway. Taking out the trash was one of Blue's chores, but after the sun went down the side of the house where the rolling cans lived got pitch-black and he would do everything in his power to avoid it. She'd suggested that he bring the rolling cans around to the front steps before it got dark. She'd given him a flashlight. She'd offered to stand on the front porch while he went to get them. Instead, he waited until the last possible moment to collect the trash, put all the cans and bags by the front door, and informed her that he was going to take them out in five minutes, just as soon as he finished doing this *Wordly Wise* crossword puzzle, or this long division worksheet. And then he disappeared.

If she could catch him before he made it to bed, she'd make him get the cans and take them out to the street, but not tonight. Tonight she stood in the doorway to his dark room, the hall light slashing across him where he lay under the covers, eyes squeezed shut, a copy of *National Geographic World* rising and falling on his stomach.

Pulling his bedroom door halfway closed, she paused outside Korey's door and listened to the rise and fall of her daughter's voice on the telephone. Patricia felt a prick of envy. She hadn't been popular in high school, but Korey captained or co-captained all her teams, and younger girls showed up at games to cheer her on. Inexplicably, girls being sporty had become popular. When Patricia was in high school, the only girls who talked to the sporty girls were other sporty girls, but Korey's list of friends seemed endless, and they'd finally gotten a second phone line so Carter could make phone calls without call waiting going off every five seconds.

Patricia plodded downstairs to check on Miss Mary. She walked down the three steps from the den to the converted garage room and let her eyes adjust to the orange glow of the night-light. She saw the old woman, thin and deflated under the sheets of her hospital bed, eyes glittering in the dim light, staring at the ceiling.

"Miss Mary?" Patricia said softly to her mother-in-law. "Do you want anything?"

"There's an owl," Miss Mary croaked.

"I don't see any owls," Patricia said. "You should get some rest."

Miss Mary stared at the ceiling, her eyes leaking tears that ran down her temples and into her sparse hair.

"Whether you like it or not," Miss Mary said, "you've got owls."

She acted worse at night, but Patricia had even noticed that during the day she often couldn't follow the give-and-take of a conversation anymore and covered her confusion with long stories about people from her past that no one knew. Even Carter couldn't identify two-thirds of them, but to his credit he always listened and never interrupted.

Patricia checked that Miss Mary had water in the sippy cup by her bed, then went to take out the trash. She took the flashlight with her because Blue wasn't wrong—it was scary around the side of the house.

The humid night air buzzed with insects as Patricia walked across the harsh black slash where the light from the front porch ended. She walked into the thick darkness around the side of the house at a brisk pace, forcing herself to wait three steps before clicking on the flashlight, just to prove she was brave. The first thing she saw was one of Miss Mary's blue incontinence pads in the dirt. A short length of fence projected from the side of the house, hiding the rolling cans from the street, but even from here Patricia could tell both cans had been tipped over. The nervousness she felt vanished in a flash of irritation. Blue really should be the one cleaning this up.

Behind the fence two mounds of fat white garbage bags spilled from both cans. The oven-hot air smelled thick with the dank, earthy scent of coffee grounds and Miss Mary's adult diapers. Mosquitoes buzzed in her ears.

Patricia scanned the damage with her flashlight: napkins, coffee filters, apple cores, Toaster Strudel boxes, wadded Kleenex, folded blue incontinence pads. Either raccoons or really big marsh rats had gotten into the trash and torn everything to shreds.

The biggest white bag had been dragged into the narrow alley between the blank brick wall of their house and the stand of bamboo marking the boundary of the Clarks' house behind them. She heard the slurping sound of someone eating jelly as she flicked her flashlight up to the bag.

It was cloth, actually, and not white but pale pink, and covered in rosebuds. It had dirty bare feet and when the flashlight beam struck it, it turned its face into the light.

"Oh!" Patricia said.

The harsh white beam picked out every detail with unforgiving clarity. The old woman squatted in a pink nightgown, cheeks smeared with red jam, lips bristling with stiff black hairs, chin quivering with clear slime. She crouched over something dark in her lap. Patricia saw a raccoon's nearly severed head hanging upside down over the old woman's knees, tongue sticking out between its bared fangs. The old woman reached one gory hand into its open belly and scooped up a fistful of translucent guts. She raised that hand, shiny with animal grease, to her mouth and gnawed on the pale lavender tube of intestines while squinting into the flashlight beam.

"May I help you?" Patricia asked, because she didn't know what else to say.

The old woman slowed her gnawing and sniffed the air like an animal. The heavy smell of fresh feces, the suffocating stench of spilled garbage, the iron reek of the raccoon's blood forced their way up Patricia's nose. She gagged, stepping backward, and her heel hit something soft. She sat down suddenly in the pile of greasy white bags, struggling to get up, trying to keep the flashlight beam centered on the old woman because she was safe as long as she could see the old woman, but the old woman was halfway to her already, crawling on her hands and knees, coming too fast, plowing through the spilled garbage, dragging the raccoon's forgotten corpse along by its head.

"Oh, no, no, no, no, no," Patricia chanted.

A hand gripped her shin, hot through her pants leg. The other hand released the raccoon and gripped Patricia's hip. The old woman put all her body weight on Patricia, pressing her down onto something that dug into her right kidney. Patricia tried to thrash backward, or up, or away, but she couldn't get any leverage and sank deeper into the pile of bags.

The old woman hauled herself up Patricia's body, mouth open, slaver swinging from it in glistening ribbons, eyes wide and mindless like a bird's. One of her filthy hands, tacky and rough with raccoon gore, burrowed past Patricia's collar and clutched the side of her neck, and then she dragged her body, warm and soft like a slug's, completely over Patricia's front.

Something about her long white hair pulled back in a ponytail, frail neck, and clunky digital watch worn around one wrist snapped into place.

"Mrs. Savage?" Patricia said. "Mrs. Savage!"

This face hanging over hers, slobbering with mindless hunger, belonged to the woman who, for years, had been the bane of the neighborhood. This yawning mouth whose white teeth had raccoon fur stuck between them belonged to the woman who grew beautiful hydrangeas in her front yard and patrolled the Old Village in the midday heat wearing a floppy canvas hat, carrying a stick with a nail in one end to spear candy wrappers.

Now all Mrs. Savage cared about was getting her open mouth onto Patricia's face. She was on top, and gravity worked in her favor, and Patricia's world filled with white teeth smeared with blood and bristling with raccoon fur. Patricia felt things tickling her face and realized they were fleas leaping from the raccoon's corpse.

Full of panic, Patricia grabbed Mrs. Savage's wrists and rolled to one side, scraping her back painfully, and Mrs. Savage lost her balance and fell heavily against the wooden fence, her face hitting it with a hollow *donk*. Patricia squirmed backward through the garbage bags and pushed herself to her feet. The flashlight lay on the ground, shining directly on the disemboweled raccoon.

Patricia didn't know what to do as Mrs. Savage writhed in the bags, and then the old lady was on her feet, lurching toward Patricia, and Patricia ran through the absolute blackness of the side yard, toward the front yard. She could see it, lit by the porch lights, as serene and peaceful as ever. She burst into the light, wet grass under one foot, realizing she'd lost one shoe, and she opened her mouth to scream.

It was one of those things she'd always thought she could do if she were ever really in trouble, but now, at ten p.m. on a Thursday night surrounded by people who were either already asleep or getting ready for bed, Patricia couldn't make a sound.

Instead, she ran for the front door. She'd get inside, lock up, and call 911. That was when Mrs. Savage grabbed her waist and the old lady tried to mount her from behind, taking Patricia down to her knees, which thudded into the grass painfully. The old woman crawled up her body, forcing Patricia onto her hands, and Mrs. Savage's mouth slobbered hot and wet and intimate into Patricia's ear.

I drive car pool, Patricia's mind gibbered. *I'm in a book club. Well, it's not really a book club, but essentially it's a book club. Why am I fighting an old woman in my front yard?*

Nothing fit together. None of it added up. She tried to drag herself out from under Mrs. Savage, but a screaming pain ripped through the side of her head and she thought to herself, *She's biting my ear. Mrs. Savage, whose yard won the Alhambra Pride Award two years ago, is biting my ear.*

The old lady's small, sharp teeth clamped down harder and Patricia's vision went white—and then a blinding light smashed into her face as a car turned into the driveway slowly, slowly, so slowly and pinned them both with its headlights. A door clunked open.

"Patty?" Carter said over the sound of the idling engine.

Patricia whined.

Carter ran to her, pulling Mrs. Savage off her back, but something went wrong as he lifted Mrs. Savage and Patricia's head snapped backward with a flash of searing pain, and she realized that Mrs. Savage wasn't letting go. She heard a crunch deep inside her skull and then a pop and then the entire side of her head was pressed to a red-hot stove.

That was when Patricia screamed.

It took eleven stitches to close the wound and she had to have a tetanus shot, but they couldn't reattach her earlobe because Mrs. Savage had swallowed it. Fortunately, neither Mrs. Savage nor the raccoon seemed to be rabid, but they'd need more tests to make sure so Patricia had that to look forward to.

On the drive home, she felt heavy from the painkillers, and she dreaded saying anything to Carter, but finally, she had to speak.

"Carter?" she asked.

"Don't talk, Patty," he said, merging onto the Cooper River bridge. "You're pretty out of it."

"They need to monitor her bowel movements," Patricia said, head rolling from side to side against the headrest.

"Whose?" Carter asked, accelerating up the second rise of the bridge.

"Ann Savage's," Patricia said, overwhelmed with sadness. "She swallowed my earlobe and, and the earring you gave me . . . it's going to come out, and I suppose they can wash it . . ."

She started to cry.

"Relax, Patty," Carter said. "You're not wearing those again."

"But you bought them for me," Patricia wailed. "And I lost them."

"One of my patients sells costume jewelry," Carter said. "He gave them to me for free. Just put the other one in the trash and I'll pick you up something from the Pitt Street Pharmacy."

It was probably the painkillers, but that made her cry even harder.

CHAPTER 5

Patricia woke up the next morning with the entire side of her face swollen and hot. She stood in front of her bathroom mirror and looked at the enormous white bandage that covered the left side of her head, wrapped beneath her chin, and around her forehead. Sadness flooded her chest. She'd had a left earlobe all her life, and suddenly it was gone. She felt like a friend had died.

But then that familiar fishhook wormed its way into her brain and got her moving:

"You have to make sure the children are all right," it said. "You can't let them feel frightened."

So she brushed her hair over the bandage as best she could, went downstairs to the den, and made Toaster Strudel. And when Blue came down, followed by Korey, and they sat on their stools on the other side of the counter, she smiled as best she could, even though her face felt tight, and asked, "Do you want to see it?"

"Can I?" Korey asked.

She found the beginning of the gauze at the back of her head, untaped it, and began the long process of unwrapping it around her forehead, beneath her chin, over her skull, until she got down to the final cotton pad and gingerly began to pull it away. "Do you want to look, too?" she asked Blue.

He nodded, and she lifted the square bandage and felt cool air wash over her sweaty, tender tissue.

Korey sucked in her breath.

"Gnarly," she said. "Did it hurt?"

"It didn't feel nice," Patricia said.

Korey came around the counter and stood so close her hair brushed Patricia's shoulder. Patricia inhaled her Herbal Essences shampoo and realized that it had been a long time since they'd been this close. They used to squeeze in together on the La-Z-Boy and watch movies on the sun porch together, but Korey was almost as tall as Patricia now.

"I can see teeth marks, Blue, look," Korey said, and her little brother dragged over a kitchen stool and stood on it, balanced with one hand on his sister's shoulder, both of them inspecting their mother's ear.

"Another person knows what you taste like now," Blue said.

Patricia hadn't thought about it that way before, but she found the idea disturbing. After Korey ran to get her ride to school, and Blue's car pool honked, Patricia followed him to the door.

"Blue," she said. "You know Granny Mary wouldn't do something like this."

By the way he stopped and looked at her, Patricia realized it was exactly what he'd been thinking.

"Why?" he asked.

"Because this woman has a disease that's affected her mind," Patricia said.

"Like Granny Mary," Blue said, and Patricia realized that was how she'd described Miss Mary's senility to him when she'd moved in.

"It's a different disease," she said. "But I want you to know that I would not let Granny Mary stay with us if it weren't safe for you and your sister. I would never do anything that put the two of you in danger."

Blue turned this over in his head, and then his car pool honked again and he ran out the door. Patricia hoped she'd reached him. It was so important that the children have good memories of at least one of their grandparents.

"Patty," Carter called from the top of the stairs, a paisley tie in one hand, a red striped tie in the other. "Which do I wear? This one says I'm fun and think outside the box, but the red says power."

"What's the occasion?" Patricia asked.

"I'm taking Haley to lunch."

"Paisley," she said. "Why are you taking Dr. Haley to lunch?"

He started putting on the red tie as he came down the stairs.

"I'm throwing my hat in the ring," Carter said, wrapping his tie around his neck and looping the knot into existence. "I'm tired of waiting in line."

He stood in front of the hall mirror.

"I thought you said you didn't want to be chief of psychiatry," Patricia said.

He tightened his tie in the mirror.

"We need to make more money," he said.

"You wanted to spend time with Blue this summer," Patricia said as Carter turned around.

"I'll have to figure out a way to do both," Carter said. "I'll need to be at all the morning consults, I'll have to spend more time on rounds, I'll need to start bringing in more grants—this job belongs to me, Patricia. I only want what's mine."

"Well," she said. "If it's what you want . . ."

"It'll only be for a few months," he said, then stopped and cocked his head at her left ear. "You took off your bandage?"

"Just to show Korey and Blue," she said.

"I don't think it looks so bad," he said, and examined her ear, his thumb on her chin, cocking her head to the side. "Leave the bandage off. It's going to heal fine."

He kissed her good-bye, and it felt like a real kiss.

Well, she thought, *if that's the effect trying to become chief of psychiatry has on him, I'm all for it.*

Patricia looked at herself in the hall mirror. The black stitches looked like insect legs against her soft skin, but they made her feel less conspicuous than the bandage. She decided to leave it off. Ragtag clicked into the front hall and stood by the door, wanting to go out. For a moment Patricia thought about putting him on a leash, then remembered that Ann Savage was in the hospital.

"Go on, boy," she said, opening the door. "Go tear up that mean old lady's trash."

Ragtag charged off down the driveway and Patricia locked the door behind him. She'd never done that before, but she'd never been attacked by a neighbor in her own yard before either.

She walked down the three brick steps to the garage room, where she unlatched the side of the hospital bed.

"Did you sleep well, Miss Mary?" she asked.

"An owl bit me," Miss Mary said.

"Oh, dear," Patricia said, pulling Miss Mary into a sitting position and swinging her legs out of bed.

Patricia began the long, slow process of getting Miss Mary into her housecoat and then into her easy chair, finally getting her a glass of orange juice with Metamucil stirred into it just as Mrs. Greene arrived to make her breakfast.

Like most elementary schoolteachers, Miss Mary had drunk from the fountain of eternal late middle age; Patricia never remembered her as young, exactly, but she remembered when she had been strong enough to live on her own about a hundred and fifty miles upstate near Kershaw. She remembered the half-acre vegetable garden Miss Mary worked behind her house. She remembered the stories of Miss Mary working in the bomb factory during the war and how the chemicals turned her hair red, and how people came to tell her their dreams and she would tell them lucky numbers to play.

Miss Mary could predict the weather by reading coffee grounds, and the local cotton farmers found her so accurate they always bought her a cup of coffee when she came by Husker Early's store to pick up her mail. She refused to let anyone eat from the peach tree in her backyard no matter how good the fruit looked because she said it had been planted in sadness and the fruit tasted bitter. Patricia had tried one once and it tasted soft and sweet to her, but Carter got mad when she told him about it, so she'd never done it again.

Miss Mary had been able to draw a map of the United States from memory, known the entire periodic table by heart, taught school in a one-room schoolhouse, brewed healing teas, and sold what she called fitness powders her entire life. Dime by dime, dollar by dollar, she'd put her sons through college, then put Carter through medical school. Now she wore diapers and couldn't follow a story about gardening in the *Post and Courier*.

Patricia's pulse throbbed in her bandaged ear, sending her upstairs for Tylenol. She had just swallowed three when the phone rang, exactly on time: 9:02 a.m. No one would dream of calling the house before nine, but you also didn't want to appear too anxious.

"Patricia?" Grace said. "Grace Cavanaugh. How are you feeling?"

For some reason, Grace always introduced herself at the beginning of each phone call.

"Sad," Patricia said. "She bit off my earlobe and swallowed it."

"Of course," Grace said. "Sadness is one of the stages of grief."

"She swallowed my earring, too," Patricia said. "The new ones I had on last night."

"That is a pity," Grace said.

"It turns out Carter got them for free from a patient," Patricia said. "He didn't even buy them."

"Then you didn't want them anyway," Grace said. "I spoke with Ben this morning. He said Ann Savage has been admitted to MUSC and is in intensive care. I'll call if I find out anything further."

The phone rang all morning. The incident hadn't appeared in the morning paper, but it didn't matter. CNN, NPR, CBS—no newsgathering organization could compete with the women of the Old Village.

"There's already a run on alarms," Kitty said. "Horse said the people he called about getting one told him it would be three weeks before they could even make it out here to look at the house. I don't know how I'm going to survive for three weeks. Horse says we're safe with his guns, but trust me, I've been dove hunting with that man. He can barely hit the sky."

Slick called next.

"I've been praying for you all morning," she said.

"Thank you, Slick," Patricia said.

"I heard that Mrs. Savage's nephew moved down here from someplace up north," Slick said. She didn't need to be more specific than that. Everyone knew that any place up north was roughly the same: lawless, relatively savage, and while they might have nice museums and the Statue of Liberty, people cared so little for each other they'd let you die in the street. "Leland told me some real estate agents stopped by and tried to get him to put her house on the market, but he won't sell. None of them saw Mrs. Savage when they were there. He told them she couldn't get out of bed, she was so poorly. How's your ear?"

"She swallowed part of it," Patricia said.

"I'm so sorry," Slick said. "Those really were nice earrings."

Grace called again later that afternoon with breaking news.

"Patricia," she said. "Grace Cavanaugh. I just heard from Ben: Mrs. Savage passed an hour ago."

Patricia suddenly felt gray. The den looked dark and dingy. The yellow linoleum seemed worn, and she saw every grubby hand mark on the wall around the light switch.

"How?" she asked.

"It wasn't rabies, if that's what you're worried about," Grace said. "She had some kind of blood poisoning. She was suffering from malnutrition, she was dehydrated, and she was covered with infected cuts and sores. Ben said the doctors were surprised she lasted this long. He even said"—and here Grace lowered her voice—"that she had track marks on her inner thigh. She'd probably been injecting something for the pain. I'm sure the family doesn't want anyone to know about that."

"I feel just miserable about this," Patricia said.

"Is this about those earrings again?" Grace asked. "Even if you got back the one she swallowed, could you ever really bring yourself to wear them? Knowing where they'd been?"

"I feel like I should take something by," Patricia said.

"Take something by to the nephew?" Grace asked, and her voice climbed the register so that *nephew* was a high, clear note of disbelief.

"His aunt passed," Patricia said. "I should do something."

"Why?" Grace asked.

"Should I take him flowers, or something to eat?" Patricia asked.

There was a long pause on Grace's end, and then she spoke firmly.

"I am not sure what the appropriate gesture is to make toward the family of the woman who bit off your ear, but if you felt absolutely compelled, I certainly wouldn't take food."

Maryellen called on Saturday and that was what decided things for Patricia.

"I thought you should know," she said over the phone, "we did the cremation for Ann Savage yesterday." After her youngest daughter had entered first grade, Maryellen had gotten a job as the bookkeeper at Stuhr's Funeral Homes. She knew the details of every death in Mt. Pleasant.

"Do you know anything about a memorial service or donations?" Patricia asked. "I want to send something."

"The nephew did a direct cremation," Maryellen said. "No flowers, no memorial service, no notice in the paper. I don't even think he's putting her in an urn, unless he got one from someplace else. He'll probably just toss her ashes in a hole for all the care he showed."

It ate at Patricia, and not merely because she suspected that not putting Ragtag on a leash had somehow caused Ann Savage's death. One day, she would be the same age as Ann Savage and Miss

Mary. Would Korey and Blue act like Carter's brothers and ship her around like an unwanted fruitcake? Would they argue over who got stuck with her? If Carter died, would they sell the house, her books, her furniture, and split up the proceeds between themselves and she'd have nothing left of her own?

Every time she looked up and saw Miss Mary standing in a doorway, dressed to go out, purse over one arm, staring at her silently, not seeming to know what came next, she felt like it was only a few short steps from there to squatting in the side yard stuffing raw raccoon meat into her mouth.

A woman had died. She needed to take something by the house. Grace was right: it made no sense, but sometimes you did a thing because that was just what you did, not because it was sensible.

CHAPTER 6

Friends and relatives had dropped by the house all Friday and brought Patricia six bunches of flowers, two copies of *Southern Living* and one copy of *Redbook*, three casseroles (corn, taco, spinach), a pound of coffee, a bottle of wine, and two pies (Boston cream, peach). She decided that regifting a casserole was appropriate, given the situation, so she took out the taco one to thaw.

Carter had gone to the hospital early even though it was the weekend. Patricia found Mrs. Greene and Miss Mary sitting on the back patio. The morning felt soft and warm, and Mrs. Greene leafed through *Family Circle* magazine while Miss Mary stared at the bird feeder, which was, as usual, crawling with squirrels.

"Are you enjoying the sunshine, Miss Mary?" Patricia asked.

Miss Mary turned her watery eyes toward Patricia and scowled.

"Hoyt Pickens came by last night," she said.

"Ear's looking better," Mrs. Greene said.

"Thank you," Patricia said.

Ragtag, lying at Miss Mary's feet, perked up as a fat black marsh rat streaked out of the bushes and dashed across the grass, making Patricia jump and sending three squirrels fleeing in terror. It dashed around the edge of the fence separating their property from the Langs next door and was gone as fast as it had appeared. Ragtag put his head down again.

"You ought to put out poison," Mrs. Greene said.

Patricia made a mental note to call the bug man and see if they had rat poison.

"I'm just going down the street to drop off a casserole," Patricia said.

"We're about to have some lunch," Mrs. Greene said. "What are you thinking about for lunch, Miss Mary?"

"Hoyt," Miss Mary said. "What was his name, that Hoyt?"

Patricia wrote a quick note (*So sorry for your loss, The Campbells*) and taped it to the tin foil over the taco casserole, then walked down the warming streets to Ann Savage's cottage, the freezing cold casserole held in front of her.

It was turning into a hot day so she had a little bit of a shine on her by the time she stepped off the road onto Mrs. Savage's dirt yard. The nephew must be home because his white van sat on the grass, underneath the shade. It looked out of place in the Old Village because, as Maryellen had pointed out, it seemed like the kind of thing a child snatcher would drive.

Patricia walked up the wooden steps to the front porch and rattled her knuckles against the screen door. After a minute she knocked again and heard nothing but the hollow echo of her knock inside the house and cicadas screaming from the drainage pond that separated Mrs. Savage's yard from the Johnsons next door.

Patricia knocked again and waited, looking across the street at where developers had torn down the Shortridges' house, which used to have the most beautiful slate roof. In its place, someone from out of town was building an ostentatious miniature mansion. More and more of these eyesores were popping up all over the Old Village, big heavy things that sprawled from property line to property line and didn't leave any room for a yard.

Patricia wanted to leave the casserole, but she hadn't come all this way not to speak to the nephew. She decided to try the front door. She'd just leave it on the kitchen counter with a note, she told herself. She opened the screen door and turned the doorknob. It stuck for a moment, then swung open.

"Yoo-hoo?" Patricia called into the dim interior.

No one answered. Patricia stepped inside. All the blinds were drawn. The air felt hot and dusty.

"Hello?" Patricia said. "It's Patricia Campbell from Pierates Cruze?"

No answer. She'd never been inside Ann Savage's house before. Heavy old furniture crowded the front room. Liquor store boxes and paper bags of junk mail covered the floor. Circulars, catalogs, and old rolled-up copies of the *Moultrie News* spilled from the seats of every chair. Four dusty old Samsonite suitcases were lined up against the wall. Built-in shelves around the front door were crowded with waterlogged romance novels. It smelled like the Goodwill store.

A doorway on her left led into a dark kitchen, and a doorway on her right led to the back of the house. A ceiling fan spun lethargically overhead. Patricia looked down the hallway. There was a half-open door at the far end leading to what she assumed was the bedroom. From it, she heard the groaning of a window-unit air conditioner. Surely the nephew wouldn't have gone out and left his air conditioner on.

Holding her breath, Patricia walked carefully down the hall and pushed the bedroom door all the way open.

"Knock knock?" she said.

The man lying on the bed was dead.

He lay on top of the quilt, still in his work boots. He wore blue jeans and a white button-up shirt. His hands were at his sides. He was huge, well over six feet, and his feet hung off the end. But despite his size, he looked starved. The flesh clung tight to his bones. The sallow skin of his face looked drawn and finely wrinkled, his blond hair looked brittle and thin.

"Excuse me?" Patricia asked, her voice a shaky rasp.

She forced herself to step all the way into the room, put the casserole dish on the end of the bed, and took his wrist. His skin felt cool. He had no pulse.

Patricia examined his face closely. He had thin lips, a wide mouth, and high cheekbones. His looks lay somewhere between handsome and pretty. She shook his shoulder, just in case.

"Sir?" she croaked. "Sir?"

His body barely moved beneath her hand. She held the back of her forefinger under his nostrils: nothing. Her nursing instincts took over.

She used one hand to pull his chin down, and the other to pull his upper lip back. She felt inside his mouth with one finger. His tongue felt dry. Nothing obstructed his airway. Patricia leaned over his face and realized, with a tickling in the veins on the inside of her elbows, this was the closest she'd been to a man who wasn't her husband in nineteen years. Then her dry lips pressed against his chapped ones and formed a seal. She pinched his nose shut and blew three strong breaths into his windpipe. Then she performed three strong chest compressions.

Nothing. She leaned down for a second attempt, made the seal with their lips, and blew into his mouth, once, twice, then her trachea vibrated backward as air blasted down her throat. She reared back coughing, the man bolted upright, his forehead smacking into the side of Patricia's skull with a hollow knock, and Patricia staggered backward into the wall, knocking all the breath out of her lungs. Her legs went out from under her, and she slid to the floor, landing hard on her butt, as the man leapt to his feet, wild-eyed, sending the casserole dish clattering to the floor.

"What the fuck!" he shouted.

He looked wildly around the room and found Patricia on the floor at his feet. Chest heaving, mouth hanging open, he squinted at her in the dimness.

"How'd you get in?" he shouted. "Who are you?"

Patricia managed to get her breathing under control enough to squeak, "Patricia Campbell from Pierates Cruze."

"What?" he barked.

"I thought you were dead," she said.

"What?" he barked again.

"I performed CPR," she said. "You weren't breathing."

"What?" he barked one more time.

"I'm your neighbor?" Patricia cowered. "From Pierates Cruze?"

He looked out the hall door. He looked back at his bed. He looked down at her.

"Fuck," he said again, and his shoulders slumped.

"I brought you a casserole," Patricia said, pointing at the upside-down casserole dish.

The man's chest heaved slower.

"You came here to bring me a casserole?" he asked.

"I'm so sorry for your loss," Patricia said. "I'm . . . your great-aunt was found in my yard? And things got a little bit physical? Maybe you've seen my dog? He's a cocker spaniel mix, he, well . . . maybe it's better you haven't? And . . . ? Well, I so hope that nothing happened at our house to make your aunt worse."

"You brought me a casserole because my aunt died," he said, as if explaining it to himself.

"You didn't come to the door," she said. "But I saw your car outside so I stuck my head in."

"And down the hall," he said. "And into my bedroom."

She felt like a fool.

"No one here thinks twice about that," she explained. "It's the Old Village. You weren't breathing."

He opened his eyes wide and closed them tightly a few times, swaying slightly.

"I am very, very tired," he said.

Patricia realized he wasn't going to help her to her feet, so she pushed herself up off the floor.

"Let me clean this up," she said, reaching for the casserole dish. "I feel so stupid."

"No," he said. "You have to leave." He wavered, his head jerking in little shakes and nods.

"It'll only take a minute," she said.

"Please," he said. "Please, just go home. I need to be alone."

He ushered her out his bedroom door.

"I can get a cloth and make sure it doesn't leave a stain," Patricia said as he pushed her down the hall. "I feel awful for barging in when we haven't been introduced, but I could see you weren't breathing, and I was a nurse—I am a nurse—and I was so sure you were ill, and I feel like a nummy."

As she talked, he propelled her into the cluttered front room, and he had the front door open, and he stood behind it, squinting hard, eyes streaming water, and she knew he wanted her to go.

"Please," she said, standing with one hand on the handle of his screen door. "I'm so sorry. I didn't mean to disturb you like that."

"I need to get back to bed," he said, and his hand was on the small of her back, and then she was through the screen door, standing in the hot sun on his front porch, and the door closed firmly in her face. Patricia hoped that no one had seen her go inside. If anyone else knew about her stupidity, she would just die.

She turned and jumped as the front of a large tan sedan nosed up into the front yard, right on top of her. Behind the sun's glare on the windshield, she saw Francine, the woman who did for Ann Savage. Francine was older, with a face like a dried apple, and not many people still hired her in the Old Village because she had a vinegary nature.

She and Francine locked eyes through the glass. Patricia lifted one hand in the barest semblance of a greeting, then tucked her head down and scrambled up the street as fast as she could, mentally ticking off all the people Francine might tell.

CHAPTER 7

All the way home Patricia tasted Ann Savage's nephew on her lips: dusty spices, leather, unfamiliar skin. It made the blood fizz in her veins, and then, overcome with guilt, she brushed her teeth twice, found half of an old bottle of Listerine in the hall closet, and gargled it until her lips tasted like artificial peppermint flavoring.

For the rest of the day, she lived in fear that someone would drop by and ask what she'd been doing in Ann Savage's house. She was terrified she'd run into Mrs. Francine when she went to the Piggly Wiggly. She jumped every time the phone rang, thinking it would be Grace saying she'd heard Patricia tried to perform CPR on a sleeping man.

But night came and no one said anything, and even though she couldn't meet Carter's eyes at supper, by the time she went to bed she'd forgotten the way the nephew's lips had tasted. The next morning she forgot about Francine somewhere between figuring out where Korey needed to be dropped off and picked up all week, and making sure Blue was studying for his State and Local History exam instead of reading about Adolf Hitler.

She made sure Korey and Blue were enrolled in summer camp (soccer for Korey and science day camp for Blue), she called Grace to get the phone number of someone who could look at their air conditioner, and she picked up groceries, and packed lunches, and dropped off library books, and signed report cards (no summer school this year, thankfully), and barely saw Carter every morning as he dashed out the door ("I promise," he told her, "as soon as this is over we'll go to the beach"), and suddenly a week had passed and she sat at dinner, half listening to Korey complain about something she wasn't very interested in at all.

"Are you even listening to me?" Korey asked.

"Pardon?" Patricia asked, tuning back in.

"I don't understand how we can almost be out of coffee again," Carter said from the other end of the table. "Are the kids eating it?"

"Hitler said caffeine was poison," Blue said.

"I said," Korey repeated, "Blue's room faces the water and he can open his windows and get a breeze. And he's got a ceiling fan. It's not fair. Why can't I get a fan in my room? Or stay at Laurie's house until you get the air fixed?"

"You're not staying at Laurie's house," Patricia said.

"Why on earth would you want to live with the Gibsons?" Carter asked.

At least when their children said completely irrational things they were on the same page.

"Because the air conditioning is broken," Korey said, pushing her chicken breast around her plate with her fork.

"It's not broken," Patricia said. "It's just not working very well."

"Did you call the air-conditioner man?" Carter asked.

Patricia shot him a look in the secret language of parenting that said, *Stay on the same page with me in front of the children and we'll discuss this later.*

"You didn't call him, did you?" Carter said. "Korey's right, it's too hot."

Clearly, Carter didn't speak the same secret language of parenting.

"I've got a photograph," Miss Mary said.

"What's that, Mom?" Carter asked.

Carter thought it was important his mother eat with them as often as possible even though it was a struggle to get Blue to the table when she did. Miss Mary dropped as much food in her lap as made it into her mouth, and her water glass was cloudy with food she forgot to swallow before taking a sip.

"You can see in the photograph that the man . . . ," Miss Mary said, "he's a man."

"That's right, Mom," Carter said.

That was when a roach fell off the ceiling and landed in Miss Mary's water glass.

"Mom!" Korey screamed, jumping backward out of her seat.

"Roach!" Blue shouted, redundantly, scanning the ceiling for more.

"Got it!" Carter said, spotting another one on the chandelier, and reaching for it with one of Patricia's good linen napkins.

Patricia's heart sank. She could already see this becoming a family story about what a terrible house she kept. "Remember?" they would ask each other when they were older. "Remember how Mom's house was so dirty a roach fell off the ceiling into Granny Mary's glass? Remember that?"

"Mom, that is *disgusting*!" Korey said. "Mom! Don't let her drink it!"

Patricia snapped out of it and saw Miss Mary picking up her water glass, about to take a sip, the roach struggling in the cloudy water. Launching herself out of her seat, she plucked the glass from Miss Mary's hand and dumped it down the sink. She ran the water and washed the roach and the sludge of disintegrating food fragments down the drain, then turned on the garbage disposal.

That was when the doorbell rang.

She could still hear Korey giving a performance in the dining room and she wanted to make sure she missed that, so she shouted, "I'll get it," and walked through the den to the quiet, dark front hall. Even from there she could hear Korey carrying on. She opened the front door and shame flooded her veins: Ann Savage's nephew stood beneath the porch light.

"I hope I'm not interrupting," he said. "I've come to return your casserole dish."

She could not believe this was the same man. He was still pale, but his skin looked soft and unlined. His hair was parted on the left and looked thick and full. He wore a khaki work shirt tucked into new blue jeans, the sleeves rolled up to his elbows, exposing thick forearms. A faint smile played at the corners of his thin lips, like they shared a private joke. She felt her mouth twitching into a smile in return. In one large hand he held the glass casserole dish. It was spotless.

"I am so sorry for barging into your home," she said, raising her hand to cover her mouth.

"Patricia Campbell," he said. "I remembered your name and looked you up in the book. I know how people get about dropping off food and never getting their plates back."

"You didn't have to do that," she said, reaching for the dish. He held onto it.

"I'd like to apologize for my behavior," he said.

"No, I'm sorry," Patricia said, wondering how hard she could try to pull the dish out of his hands before she started to seem rude. "You must think I'm a fool, I interrupted your nap, I . . . I really did think you were . . . I used to be a nurse. I don't know how I made such a stupid mistake. I'm so sorry."

He furrowed his forehead, raised his eyebrows in the middle, and looked sincerely concerned.

"You apologize a lot," he said.

"I'm sorry," she said quickly.

She instantly realized what she'd done and froze, flustered, not sure where to go next, so she blundered ahead. "The only people who don't apologize are psychopaths."

The moment it came out of her mouth she wished she hadn't said anything. He studied her for a moment, then said, "I'm sorry to hear that."

They stood for a moment, face to face, as she processed what he'd said, and then she burst out laughing. After a second, he did, too. He let go of the casserole dish and she pulled it to her body, holding it across her stomach like a shield.

"I'm not even going to say I'm sorry again," she told him. "Can we start over?"

He held out one big hand, "James Harris," he said.

She shook it. It felt cool and strong.

"Patricia Campbell."

"I am genuinely sorry about that," he said, indicating his left ear.

Reminded of her mutilated ear, Patricia turned slightly to the left and quickly brushed her hair over her stitches.

"Well," she said, "I suppose that's why I've got two."

This time, his laugh was short and sudden.

"Not many people would be so generous with their ears."

"I don't remember being given a choice," she said, then smiled to let him know she was kidding.

He smiled back.

"Were the two of you close?" she asked. "You and Mrs. Savage?"

"None of our family are close," he said. "But when family needs, you go."

She wanted to close the door and stand on the porch and have an actual adult conversation with this man. She had been so terrified of him, but he was warm, and funny, and he looked at her in a way that made her feel seen. Shrill voices drifted from the house. She smiled, embarrassed, and realized there was one way to get him to stay.

"Would you like to meet my family?" she asked.

"I don't want to interrupt your meal," he said.

"I'd consider it a personal favor if you did."

He regarded her for a split second, expressionless, sizing her up, and then he matched her smile.

"Only if it's a real invitation," he said.

"Consider yourself invited," she said, standing aside. After a moment he stepped over her threshold and into the dark front hall.

"Mr. Harris?" she said. "You won't say anything about"—she gestured with the casserole dish she held in both hands—"about this, will you?"

His expression got serious.

"It'll be our secret."

"Thank you," she said.

When she led him into the brightly lit dining room, everyone stopped talking.

"Carter," she said. "This is James Harris, Ann Savage's grand-nephew. James, this is my husband, Dr. Carter Campbell."

Carter stood up and shook hands automatically, as if he met the nephew of the woman who'd bitten off his wife's ear every day. Blue and Korey, on the other hand, looked from their mother to this enormous stranger in horror, wondering why she'd let him into their house.

"This is our son, Carter Jr., although we call him Blue, and our daughter, Korey," Patricia said.

As James shook Blue's hand and walked around the table to shake Korey's, Patricia saw her family through his eyes: Blue staring at him rudely. Korey standing behind her chair in her Baja hoodie and soccer shorts, gawping at him like he was a zoo animal. Miss Mary chewing and chewing even though her mouth was empty.

"This is Miss Mary Campbell, my mother-in-law, who's staying with us."

James Harris held out a hand to Miss Mary, who kept sucking her lips while staring hard at the salt and pepper shakers.

"Pleased to meet you, ma'am," he said.

Miss Mary raised her watery eyes to his face and studied him for a moment, chin trembling, then looked back down at the salt and pepper.

"I've got a photograph," she said.

"I don't want to interrupt your meal," James Harris said, pulling his hand back. "I was just returning a dish."

"Won't you join us for dessert?" Patricia asked.

"I couldn't . . . ," James Harris began.

"Blue, clear the table," Patricia said. "Korey, get the bowls."

"I do have a sweet tooth," James Harris said as Blue passed him carrying a stack of dirty plates.

"You can sit here," Patricia said, nodding to the empty chair on her left. It creaked alarmingly as James Harris eased himself into it. Bowls appeared and the half gallon of Breyers found its place in front of Carter. He began to hack at the surface of the freezer-burned ice cream with a large spoon.

"What do you do for a living?" Carter asked.

"All kinds of things," James said as Korey placed a stack of ice cream bowls in front of her father. "But right now, I've got a little money put aside to invest."

Patricia reconsidered. Was he rich?

"In what?" Carter asked, scraping long white curls of ice cream into everyone's bowls and passing them around the table. "Stocks and bonds? Small business? Microchips?"

"I was thinking something more local," James Harris said. "Maybe real estate."

Carter reached across the table and put a bowl of ice cream in front of James, then fitted a thick-handled spoon into his mother's hand and led it to the bowl of vanilla in front of her.

"Not my area," he said, losing interest.

"You know," Patricia said. "My friend Slick Paley at book club? Her husband, Leland, they're into real estate. They might be able to tell you something about the situation here."

"You're in a book club?" James asked. "I love to read."

"Who do you read?" Patricia asked as Carter ignored them and fed his mother, and Blue and Korey continued to stare.

"I'm a big Ayn Rand fan," James Harris said. "Kesey, Ginsburg,

Kerouac. Have you read *Zen and the Art of Motorcycle Maintenance?*"

"Are you a hippie?" Korey asked.

Patricia felt pathetically grateful that James Harris ignored her daughter.

"Are you looking for new members?" he continued.

"Ugh," Korey said. "They're a bunch of old ladies sitting around drinking wine. They don't even actually read the books."

Patricia didn't know where these things came from. She'd chalk it up to Korey becoming a teenager, but Maryellen had said they became teenagers when you stopped liking them, and she still liked her daughter.

"What kind of books do you read?" James asked, still ignoring Korey.

"All kinds," Patricia said. "We just read a wonderful book about life in a small Guyanese town in the 1970s."

She didn't mention that it was *Raven: The Untold Story of the Rev. Jim Jones and His People.*

"They rent the movies," Korey said. "And pretend to read the books."

"There wasn't a movie for this book," Patricia said, forcing herself to smile.

James Harris wasn't listening. He had his eyes on Korey.

"Is there a reason you're being fresh to your mother?" he asked.

"She's not usually like this," Patricia said. "It's all right."

"Some people use literature to understand their lives," James Harris said, continuing to stare at Korey, who squirmed beneath the intensity of his gaze. "What are you reading?"

"*Hamlet,*" Korey said. "That's by Shakespeare."

"Assigned reading," James Harris said. "I meant, what are you reading that other people didn't pick out for you?"

"I don't have time to sit around reading books," Korey said. "I actually go to school and I'm captain of the soccer team and the volleyball team."

"A reader lives many lives," James Harris said. "The person who doesn't read lives but one. But if you're happy just doing what you're told and reading what other people think you should read, then don't let me stop you. I just find it sad."

"I . . . ," Korey began, working her mouth. Then stopped. No one had ever called her sad before. "Whatever," she said, and slumped back in her chair.

Patricia wondered if she should be upset. This was new territory for her.

"What book are y'all talking about?" Carter asked, tucking more ice cream into his mother's mouth.

"Your wife's book club," James Harris said. "I guess I'm partial to readers. I grew up a military brat, and wherever I went, books were my friends."

"Because you don't have any real ones," Korey mumbled.

Miss Mary looked up, right at James Harris, and Patricia could almost hear her eyes zoom in on him.

"I want my money," Miss Mary said angrily. "That's Daddy's money you owe."

There was silence at the table.

"What's that, Mom?" Carter asked.

"You came creeping back, you," Miss Mary said. "But I see you."

Miss Mary glared at James Harris, fuzzy gray eyebrows furrowed, the slack skin around her mouth pulled into an angry knot. Patricia turned to James Harris and saw him thinking, genuinely trying to puzzle something out.

"She thinks you're someone from her past," Carter explained. "She comes and goes."

Miss Mary's chair scraped backward with an ear-grinding shriek.

"Mom," Carter said, taking her arm. "Are you finished? Let me help you."

She jerked her arm out of Carter's grip and rose, eyes fixed on James Harris.

"You're the seventh son of a saltless mother," Miss Mary said, and took a step toward him. The wattles of fat beneath her chin quivered. "When the Dog Days come we'll put nails through your eyes."

She reached out and pressed her hand against the table, holding herself up. She swayed over James Harris.

"Mom," Carter said. "Calm down."

"You thought no one would recognize you," Miss Mary said. "But I've got your photograph, Hoyt."

James Harris stared up at Miss Mary, not moving. He didn't even blink.

"Hoyt Pickens," Miss Mary said. Then she spat. She meant for it to be a country hawker, something sharp that would slap the dirt, but instead a wad of white saliva thickened with vanilla ice cream and speckled with chicken oozed over her lower lip, then rolled down her chin and plopped onto the front of her dress.

"Mom!" Carter said.

Patricia saw Blue gag and clap his napkin over the lower half of his face. Korey leaned back in her chair, away from her grandmother, and Carter reached for his mother, napkin outstretched.

"I'm so sorry," Patricia said to James Harris as she got up.

"I know who you are," Miss Mary shouted at James Harris. "In your ice cream suit."

Patricia hated Miss Mary at that moment. Someone interesting had come into their home to talk about books, and Miss Mary wouldn't even let her have that.

She hustled Miss Mary out of the dining room, pulling her beneath the armpits, not caring if she was a little rough. Behind her, she was aware of James Harris rising as Carter and Korey both started talking at once, and she hoped he was still there when she got back. She hauled Miss Mary to the garage room and got her seated in her chair with the plastic bowl of water and her toothbrush and came back to the dining room. The only person left was Carter, sucking on his ice cream, hunched over his bowl.

"Is he still here?" Patricia asked.

"He left," Carter said, through a mouthful of vanilla. "Mom seemed weird tonight, don't you think?"

Carter's spoon clicked against the bottom of the bowl and he stood up, leaving his bowl on the place mat for her to clean up, not waiting to hear what she had to say. In that moment, Patricia hated her family with a passion. And she wanted to see James Harris again, badly.

CHAPTER 8

That was how she found herself a little after noon the next day, standing on the porch of Ann Savage's yellow-and-white cottage.

She knocked on the screen door and waited. In front of the new mansion across the street, a cement truck dumped gray sludge into a wooden frame for its driveway. James Harris's white van sat silently in the front yard, the sun spiking off its tinted windshield and making Patricia squint.

With a loud crack, the front door broke away from the sticky, sun-warmed paint and James Harris stood there, sweating, wearing oversize sunglasses.

"I hope I didn't wake you," Patricia said. "I wanted to apologize for my mother-in-law's behavior last night."

"Come in quickly," he said, stepping back into the shadows.

She imagined eyes watching her from every window up and down the street. She couldn't go into his house again. Where was Francine? She felt exposed and embarrassed. She hadn't thought this through.

"Let's talk out here," she said into the dark doorway. All she could see was his big pale hand resting on the edge of the door. "The sun feels so nice."

"Please," he said, his voice strained. "I have a condition."

Patricia knew genuine distress when she heard it, but she still couldn't make herself step inside.

"Stay or go," he said, anger edging his voice. "I can't be in the sun."

Looking up and down the street, Patricia quickly slipped through the door.

He brushed her aside to slam the main door, forcing her deeper into the middle of the room. To her surprise, it was empty. The furniture had been pushed up against the walls along with the old suitcases and bags and cardboard boxes of junk. Behind her, James Harris locked his front door and leaned against it.

"This looks so much better than yesterday," she said, making conversation. "Francine did a wonderful job."

"Who?" he asked.

"I saw her on my way out the other day," she said. "Your cleaner."

James Harris stared at her through his large sunglasses, completely blank, and Patricia was about to tell him she needed to leave when his knees buckled and he slid down to the floor.

"Help me," he said.

His heels pushed uselessly against the floorboards, his hands had no strength. Her nursing instincts kicked in and she stepped close, planted her feet wide, got her hands under his armpits, and lifted. He felt heavy and solid and very cool, and as his massive body rose up in front of her, she felt overwhelmed by his physical presence. Her damp palms tingled all the way up to her forearms.

He slumped forward, dropping his full weight onto her shoulders, and the intense physical contact made Patricia light-headed. She helped him to a pressed-back rocking chair by the wall, and he dropped heavily into it. Her body, freed of his weight, felt suddenly lighter than air. Her feet barely touched the floor.

"What's wrong with you?" she asked.

"I got bitten by a wolf," he said.

"Here?" she asked.

She saw his thigh muscles clench and relax as he began to un-consciously rock himself back and forth.

"When I was younger," he said, then flashed his white teeth in a pained smile. "Maybe it was a wild dog and I've romanticized it into a wolf."

"I'm so sorry," she said. "Did it hurt?"

"They thought I would die," he said. "I had a fever for several days and when I recovered I had some brain damage—just mild lesions, but they compromised the motor control in my eyes."

She felt relieved that this was starting to make sense.

"That must be difficult," she said.

"My irises don't dilate very well," he said. "So daylight is extremely painful. It's thrown my whole body clock out of whack."

He gestured helplessly around the room at everything piled up against the walls.

"There's so much to do and I don't know how to get a handle on any of it," he said. "I'm lost."

She looked at the liquor store boxes and bags lining the walls, full of old clothes and notebooks and slippers and medications and embroidery hoops and yellowed issues of *TV Guide*. Plastic bags of clothes, stacks of wire hangers, dusty framed photographs, piles of afghans, water-damaged books of Greenbax Stamps, stacks of used bingo cards rubber-banded together, glass ashtrays and bowls and spheres with sand dollars suspended in the middle.

"It's a lot to sort out," Patricia said. "Do you have anyone to come help? Any family? A brother? Cousins? Your wife?"

He shook his head.

"Do you want me to stay and talk to Francine?"

"She quit," he said.

"That doesn't sound like Francine," Patricia said.

"I'm going to have to leave," James Harris said, wiping sweat from his forehead. "I thought about staying but my condition makes it too hard. I feel like there's a train already moving and no matter how fast I run I can never catch up."

Patricia knew the feeling but she also thought about Grace, who would stay here until she had learned all she could about a good-looking, seemingly normal man who had found himself all alone in the Old Village with no wife or children. Patricia had never met a single man his age who didn't have some kind of story. It would probably prove to be small and anticlimactic, but she was so starved for excitement she'd take any mystery she could.

"Let's see if we can figure this out together," she said. "What's overwhelming you the most?"

He lifted a sheaf of mail off the cross-stretcher breakfast table next to him like it weighed five hundred pounds.

"What do I do about these?" he asked.

She went through the letters, sweat prickling her back and her upper lip. The air in the house felt stale and close.

"But these are easy," she said, putting them down. "I don't understand this letter from probate court, but I'll call Buddy Barr. He's mostly retired but he's in our church and he's an estate lawyer. The Waterworks is just up the street and you can be there and change the name on the account in five minutes. SCE&G has an office around the corner where you can get the electric bill put in your name."

"It all has to be done in person," he said. "And their offices are only open during the day when I can't drive. Because of my eyes."

"Oh," Patricia said.

"If someone could drive me . . . ," he began.

Instantly, Patricia realized what he wanted, and she felt the jaws of yet another obligation closing around her.

"Normally I'd be happy to," she said, quickly. "But it's the last week of school and there's so much to do . . ."

"You said it would only take five minutes."

For a moment, Patricia resented his wheedling tone, and then she felt like a coward. She'd promised to help. She wanted to know more about him. Surely she wasn't going to quit at the first obstacle.

"You're right," she said. "Let me get my car and pull it around. I'll try to get as close to your front door as I can."

"Can we take my van?" he asked.

Patricia balked. She couldn't drive a stranger's car. Besides, she'd never driven a van before.

"I—" she began.

"The tinted windows," he said.

Of course. She nodded, not seeing another option.

"And I hate to bother you when you're doing so much already . . ." he began.

Her heart sank, and then immediately she felt selfish. This man had come to her home last night and been sassed by her daughter and spat at by her mother-in-law. He was a human being asking for help. Of course she would do her best.

"What is it?" she asked, making her voice sound as warm and genuine as possible.

He stopped rocking.

"My wallet was stolen, and my birth certificate and all those kind of things are in storage back home," he said. "I don't know how long it'll take someone to hunt them down. How can I do any of this without them?"

An image of Ted Bundy with his arm in a fake cast asking Brenda Ball to help him carry his books to his car flashed across Patricia's mind. She dismissed it as undignified.

"That probate court letter is going to solve the problem of identification," she said. "That's all you need for the Waterworks, and when we're there we'll get a bill printed with your name and this address on it to show the electric company. Give me the keys and I'll get your car."

The tinted windows kept the front seats of his van dim and purple, which wasn't such a bad thing since they were covered in stains and rips. What Patricia didn't like was the back. He had screwed wood over the back windows to make it completely dark, and it made her nervous to drive with all that emptiness behind her.

At the Waterworks, they discovered that he had left his wallet at home. He apologized profusely, but she didn't mind writing the one-hundred-dollar check for the deposit. He promised to pay her back as soon as they got home. At SCE&G they wanted a two-hundred-fifty-dollar deposit, and she hesitated.

"I shouldn't have asked you to do this," James Harris said.

She looked at him, his face already reddening with sunburn, cheeks wet with the fluid streaming from beneath his sunglasses. She weighed her sympathy against what Carter would say when he balanced their checkbook. But it was her money, too, wasn't it? That was what Carter always said when she asked for her own bank account: this money belonged to both of them. She was a grown woman and could use it however she saw fit, even if it was to help another man.

She wrote the second check and tore it off with a brisk flick of her wrist before she could change her mind. She felt efficient. Like she was solving problems and getting things done. She felt like Grace.

Back at his house she wanted to wait on the front porch while he got his wallet, but he hustled her inside. By now it was after two o'clock and the sun pressed down hard.

"I'll be right back," he said, leaving her alone in his dark kitchen.

She thought about opening his refrigerator to see what he had inside. Or looking in his cupboards. She still didn't know anything about him.

The floor cracked and he came back into the kitchen.

"Three hundred fifty dollars," he said, counting it out on the table in worn twenties and a ten. He beamed at her, even though it looked painful to move his sunburned face. "I can't tell you how much this means to me."

"I'm happy to help," she said.

"You know . . . ," he said, and trailed off. He looked away, then shook his head briskly. "Never mind."

"What?" she asked.

"It's too much," he told her. "You've been wonderful. I don't know how I can repay you."

"What is it?" Patricia asked.

"Forget it," he said. "It's unfair."

"What is?" she asked.

He got very still.

"Do you want to see something really cool? Just between the two of us?"

The inside of Patricia's skull lit up with alarm bells. She'd read enough to know that anyone saying that, especially a stranger, was about to ask you to take a package over the border or park outside a jewelry store and keep the engine running. But when was the last time anyone had even said the word *cool* to her?

"Of course," she said, dry-mouthed.

He went away, then returned with a grimy blue gym bag. He swung it onto the table and unzipped it.

The dank stench of compost wafted from the bag's mouth and Patricia leaned forward and looked inside. It was stuffed with money: fives, twenties, tens, ones. The pain in Patricia's left ear disappeared. Her breath got high in her chest. Her blood sizzled in her veins. Her mouth got wet.

"Can I touch it?" she asked, quietly.

"Go ahead."

She reached out for a twenty, thought that looked greedy, and picked up a five. Disappointingly, it felt like any other five-dollar bill. She dipped her hand in again and this time pulled out a thick sheaf of bills. This felt more substantial. James Harris had just gone from a vaguely interesting man to a full-blown mystery.

"I found it in the crawl space," he said. "It's eighty-five thousand dollars. I think it's Auntie's life savings."

It felt dangerous. It felt illegal. She wanted to ask him to put it away. She wanted to keep fondling it.

"What are you going to do?" she asked.

"I wanted to ask you," he said.

"Put it in the bank."

"Can you imagine me showing up at First Federal with no ID and a bag of cash?" he said. "They'd be on the phone to the police before I could sit down."

"You can't keep it here," she said.

"I know," he said. "I can't sleep with it in the house. For the past week, I've been terrified someone's going to break in."

The solutions to so many mysteries began to reveal themselves to Patricia. He wasn't just sick with the sun, he was sick with stress. Ann Savage had been unfriendly because she wanted to keep people away from the house where she'd hidden her life savings. Of course she hadn't trusted banks.

"We have to open an account for you," Patricia said.

"How?" he asked.

"Leave that to me," she said, a plan already forming in her mind. "And put on a dry shirt."

They stood at the counter of First Federal on Coleman Boulevard half an hour later, James Harris already sweating through his fresh shirt.

"May I speak with Doug Mackey?" Patricia asked the girl across the counter. She thought it was Sarah Shandy's daughter but she couldn't be sure so she didn't say anything.

"Patricia," a voice called from across the floor. Patricia turned and saw Doug, thick-necked and red-faced, with his belly straining the bottom three buttons of his shirt, coming at them with his arms spread wide. "They say every dog has its day, and today's mine."

"I'm trying to help my neighbor, James Harris," Patricia said, shaking his hand, making introductions. "This is my friend from high school, Doug Mackey."

"Welcome, stranger," Doug Mackey said. "You couldn't have a better guide to Mt. Pleasant than Patricia Campbell."

"We have a slightly delicate situation," Patricia said, lowering her voice.

"That's why they let me have a door on my office," Doug said.

He led them into his office decorated in Lowcountry sportsman. His windows looked out over Shem Creek; his chairs were made of burgundy leather. The framed prints were of things you could eat: birds, fish, deer.

"James needs to open a bank account, but his ID has been stolen," Patricia said. "What are his options? He'd like to get it done today."

Doug leaned forward, pressing his belly into the edge of the desk, and grinned.

"Darlin', that's no problem a'tall. You can be the cosigner. You'd be responsible for any overdrafts and have full access, but it's a good way to start while he waits for his license. Those people at the DMV move like they get paid by the hour."

"Does it show up on our statement at all?" Patricia asked, thinking about how she'd explain this to Carter.

"Nah," Doug said. "I mean, not unless he starts writing bad checks all over town."

They all looked at each other for a moment, then laughed nervously.

"Let me get those forms," Doug said, leaving the room.

Patricia couldn't believe she'd solved this problem so easily. She felt relaxed and complacent, like she'd eaten a huge meal. Doug came back in and bent over the paperwork.

"Where are you from?" Doug asked, not looking up from his forms.

"Vermont," James Harris said.

"And what kind of initial deposit will you be making?" Doug asked.

Patricia hesitated, then said, "This."

She unfolded a two-thousand-dollar check and pushed it across Doug's desk. They'd decided depositing cash right away was a bad idea, especially given how seedy James Harris looked today. He'd already reimbursed her in cash, and it burned inside her purse. Her face burned, too. Her lips felt numb. She'd never written a check this big before.

"Excellent," Doug said, not hesitating for a second.

"Excuse me," James said. "How do you feel about cash deposits?"

"I feel good about them," Doug said, not looking up as he exhaled on a notary's stamp and smacked it across the bottom of the paperwork.

"I do a fair amount of landscaping," James Harris said, and Patricia almost gasped. He couldn't even go outside. "And a lot of my clients like to pay in cash."

"As long as it's under ten thousand we don't bat an eye," Doug said. "We like money around here. It's not like you're used to up north where they make you jump through hoops while singing 'The Star Spangled Banner' to do with what's yours."

"That sounds fine," James Harris said with a smile.

Patricia looked at his strong white teeth, gleaming and wet. The ease with which he'd lied made her doubt everything she'd done for him that morning and, for the briefest of moments, she felt like she'd gotten in over her head. On the ride home, James Harris's gratitude and praise came nonstop, even as he got weaker, and she ultimately had to let him lean on her to walk from the van to his front door. She helped him onto his bed, helped him take off his boots, and then he took her hand.

"I have never had someone help me like this," he said. "In my entire life, you are the kindest person I've ever met. You're an angel sent to me in my time of need."

He reminded her of Carter when they'd first gotten married, back when the slightest effort on her part—making coffee in the morning, baking a pecan pie for dessert—had elicited endless hymns of praise. His enthusiasm disarmed her so much that when he asked her what they were reading for book club that month, well, she couldn't help it: she invited him to join.

THE BRIDGES OF MADISON COUNTY

June 1993

CHAPTER 9

May had spun faster and faster, racing toward the finish line of school being out, and final exams, and report cards, and Korey was always studying at someone's house, getting picked up, dropped off, sleeping over, and Patricia had to fix snacks for Blue's homeroom end-of-the-year party, and teacher evaluations were due, and library fines had to be paid before report cards would be issued, and then on May 28 it all slammed to a stop. The kids were given summer reading lists, Albemarle Academy locked its doors, and June settled over the Old Village.

The days dawned noonday hot, and gas tanks hissed when you took off their caps. The sunlight fell hard and sharp, and insects roared in the bushes, only taking a break in the dead hour between three and four in the morning. Windows came down and doors shut tight. Every house became a hermetically sealed space station, central air hovering around a chilly sixty-eight, the ice maker rattling all day until around seven o'clock in the evening when it started making a grinding sound and just spat a few chips of watery ice into glasses, and physical exertion seemed like too much effort, and even thinking hard became exhausting.

Patricia really and truly meant to tell the book club that she'd invited James Harris to their next meeting, but the heat sucked the determination from her bones, and by the time the sun went down every day she barely had enough willpower left to cook supper, and she kept putting it off and putting it off, and finally it was the day of book club and she thought, *Well, maybe it's better this way.*

Everyone settled into her living room with their glasses of wine, and water, and iced tea, blotting the backs of their necks with Kleenex, fanning their faces, slowly reviving in the air conditioning, and Patricia thought this would be the perfect time to say something.

"Are you all right?" Grace asked. "You look like you're about to jump out of your skin."

"I just remembered the cheese tray," Patricia said, and went to the kitchen.

Mrs. Greene stood by the sink washing Miss Mary's supper dishes.

"I'm going to give Miss Mary a bath before bed," she said. "Just to cool her down some."

"Of course," Patricia said, taking her cheese tray out of the fridge and stripping the Saran Wrap from it. She balled it up and then stopped, wondering if she could use it again. She decided she could and left it beside the sink.

She took the cheese tray back into the living room and had just set it down on the wooden crate they used as a coffee table when the doorbell rang.

"Oh," Patricia said in the tone of someone who'd forgotten to buy half-and-half. "I forgot to mention that James Harris wanted to stop by and join us tonight. I hope no one minds."

"Who?" Grace asked, sitting bolt upright, neck stiff.

"He's here?" Kitty asked, flailing to sit up straighter.

"Great," Maryellen moaned. "Another man with his opinions."

Slick looked around wildly at everyone, trying to figure out how she should feel as Patricia scurried from the room.

"I'm so glad you could come," she said to James Harris, opening the front door.

He wore a plaid shirt tucked into blue jeans, white tennis shoes, and a braided leather belt. She wished he hadn't worn tennis shoes. It would bother Grace.

"Thank you so much for the invitation," he said, then stepped over her threshold and stopped. He made his voice so low she barely heard it over the screaming insects behind him in the yard. "I have over half in the bank. A little each week. Thank you."

It was more than she could bear to hear him talk about their shared secret with people right in the next room. Her arms prickled with goose bumps and her head felt light. She hadn't even deposited the two thousand three hundred and fifty dollars he'd given her into her and Carter's bank account. She knew she should have but instead it sat in her closet, tucked inside a pair of white gloves. She liked having it in her hands too much to let it go.

"Don't let the air conditioning out," she said.

She led James Harris into the living room and when she saw everyone's faces she realized she really should have made those phone calls and prepared them.

"Everyone, this is James Harris," Patricia said, putting on a smile. "I hope y'all don't mind if our new neighbor sits in tonight."

The room got quiet.

"Thank you all so much for letting me join you," James Harris said.

Grace coughed softly into a Kleenex.

"Well," Kitty said. "Having a man around will certainly liven things up. Welcome, tall dark stranger."

James Harris sat down on the sofa beside Maryellen, across from Kitty and Grace, and everyone pulled their legs together, tucked their skirts beneath their thighs, and straightened their spines. Kitty reached for the cheese tray, then pulled her hand back and held it in her lap. James Harris cleared his throat.

"Did you read this month's book, James?" Slick asked. She showed him the cover of her copy of *The Bridges of Madison County*. "We read *Helter Skelter* last month, and we're reading Ann Rule's *The Stranger Beside Me* next month, so this felt like a nice break."

"You ladies read a strange assortment of books," James Harris said.

"We're a strange assortment of broads," Kitty replied. "Patricia says you've decided to live here even after what your aunt did to her."

Patricia brushed her hair over her left ear and opened her mouth to say something nice.

"Great-aunt," James Harris said before Patricia could speak.

"That's cutting it a bit fine," Maryellen said.

"I'm surprised you don't mind the notoriety," Kitty said.

"I've been looking a long time for a community like this," James said with a smile. "Not a neighborhood, but a real community, away from all the chaos and change in the world, where people still have old-fashioned values, and kids can play outside all day until they're called in for supper. And just when I'd given up on ever finding someplace like that, I came to take care of my great-aunt and found what I'd been looking for all along. I'm a very lucky man."

"Did you already join a church?" Slick asked.

"And there's no Mrs. Harris joining you?" Kitty asked over her.

"No," James Harris said, addressing Kitty. "No children. No family, besides my great-aunt."

"That's peculiar," Maryellen said.

"What church do you belong to?" Slick asked again.

"Who do you read?" Kitty asked.

"Camus, Ayn Rand, Herman Hesse," James Harris said. "I'm a student of philosophy." He smiled at Slick. "I'm afraid I don't be-long to any organized religion."

"Then you haven't really thought it through," Slick said.

"Herman Hesse," Kitty said. "Pony read *Steppenwolf* in his En-glish class. It sounded like the kind of thing boys like."

James Harris turned the full force of his smile on Kitty.

"And Pony is your . . . ?" he asked.

"My oldest boy," Kitty said. "Everyone calls his father Horse, so we call him Pony. Then there's Honey, who's a year older, and Parish, who turns thirteen this summer and is driving all of us crazy. And Lacy and Merit, who can't stand to be in the same room together."

"What does Horse do?" James asked.

"Do?" Kitty said, and sputtered out a laugh. "I mean, he doesn't *do* anything. We live on Seewee, so he has to clear scrub, and do burns, and there's always something to fix. I mean, when you live at a place like that it's a full-time job just to keep the roof from falling in."

"I used to do property management out in Montana," James said. "I expect he could teach me a lot."

Montana? Patricia wondered.

"Horse? Teach someone?" Kitty laughed and turned to the rest of the room. "Did I tell y'all about Horse's pirate treasure? Someone came along looking for investors to hunt underwater pirate treasure, or Confederate artifacts, or something improbable like that. Well, they had this fancy slide presentation and real nice folders, and that's all it took for Horse to write them a check."

"Leland could have told him that was a scam," Slick said.

"Leland?" James asked.

"My husband," Slick said, and James Harris turned his attention to her. "He's a developer."

"I've been thinking of investing in real estate if I could find the right project," James Harris said.

Grace's face looked carved from stone and Patricia really, really wished they'd talk about anything besides money.

"Right now we're working on a project called Gracious Cay." Slick beamed. "It's a gated community we're building out by Six Mile. It's going to really elevate the surroundings. Gated communities let you choose your neighbors so the people around you are the kind of people you want around your children. By the time this century is over I expect just about everyone will live in a gated community."

"I'd be interested in hearing more about it," James said, which prompted Slick to go into her purse and hand him a business card.

"Where are you from, Mr. Harris?" Grace asked.

Patricia started to say that his father was in the military and he'd grown up all over when James Harris said, "I grew up in South Dakota."

"I thought your father was in the military?" Patricia asked.

"He was," James Harris said with a nod. "But he ended his career stationed in South Dakota. My parents got divorced when I was ten, so I was raised by my mother."

"If everyone's finished with the third degree," Maryellen said, "I'd like to get this month's book over with."

"Her husband's a police officer," Slick pointed out to James. "It's why she's so direct. By the way, maybe you want to join us this Sunday at St. Joseph's?"

Before he could answer, Maryellen said, "Can we please put this book out of my misery?"

Slick gave James Harris a *We'll continue this later* smile.

"Didn't y'all just love *The Bridges of Madison County*?" she asked. "I thought it was such a relief after last month. Just a good old-fashioned love story between a woman and a man."

"Who is clearly a serial killer," Kitty said, keeping her eyes on James Harris.

"I think the world is changing so quickly that people need a hopeful story," Slick said.

"About a lunatic who travels from town to town seducing women, then killing them," Kitty said.

"Well," Slick said. Thrown, she looked down at her notes and cleared her throat again. "We chose this book because it speaks about the powerful attraction that can exist between two strangers."

"We chose this book so you'd stop going on about it," Maryellen said.

"I don't think there's any actual evidence he's actually a serial killer," Slick said.

Kitty picked up her copy, bristling with bright pink Post-it notes, and waggled it in the air.

"He doesn't have any family ties, no roots, no past," Kitty said. "He doesn't even belong to a church. Very suspicious in today's world. Did you see the new driver's licenses? They have a little hologram on them. I remember when they were just a piece of cardboard. We are not a society that lets people roam around with no fixed address. Not anymore."

"He has a fixed address," Slick protested, but Kitty rolled on.

"Then he sails into town and do you notice he doesn't talk to anyone? But he targets this Francesca who's all alone, because that's what they do. These men find a vulnerable woman and arrange an 'accidental' meeting and they're so smooth and seductive that she invites him into her home. But when he visits he's *very* careful no one sees where he parks his truck. Then he takes her upstairs and *does things* to her for days."

"It's a romantic story," Slick said.

"I think he's feebleminded," Kitty said. "Robert Kincaid uses his cameras as hand weights, and he plays folk music on his guitar, and as a child he sang French cabaret songs and covered his walls with words and phrases he found 'pleasing to his ear.' Imagine his poor parents."

"What about you, James Harris?" Maryellen asked. "I've never met a man who doesn't have an opinion: is Robert Kincaid a romantic American icon or a drifter who murders women?"

James Harris flashed a bashful grin.

"Clearly I read a very different book from you ladies," he said. "But I'm learning a lot here tonight. Carry on."

At least he was trying, Patricia thought. Everyone else seemed bent on being as unpleasant as possible.

"The lesson of *Bridges*," Maryellen said, "is that the man gets to hog all the conversation. Francesca gets less than one page to summarize her entire life. She's had children and survived World War II in Italy, and all he's done is get divorced—and maybe kill people, according to Kitty—yet he goes on and on and on about his life for chapter after chapter."

"Well, he is the main character," Slick said.

"Why does the man always get to be the main character?" Mary-ellen asked. "Francesca's life is at least as interesting as his."

"If women have something to say they should just say it," Slick said. "You don't have to wait for an invitation. Robert Kincaid has hidden depths."

"Once you've washed a man's underwear you realize the sad truth about hidden depths," Kitty said.

"He's . . . ," Slick groped for words. "He's a vegetarian. I don't think I've ever met one of those."

Thanks to Blue, Patricia knew exactly what Kitty was about to say.

"Hitler was a vegetarian," Kitty said, proving her right. "Patricia, would you cheat on Carter with a stranger who showed up on your doorstep, with no people, and told you he was a vegetarian? You'd want to at least check his driver's license first, wouldn't you?"

Patricia saw Grace, facing her from the other side of the room, stiffen. Then she noticed Slick staring, too, and realized Grace's gaze was on the hall door behind her. Full of dread, she turned.

"I found your photograph, Hoyt," Miss Mary said, standing in the doorway, dripping wet and stark naked.

At first Patricia thought she wore some kind of flesh-colored sheet that hung in folds, and then her eyes focused on the angry purple varicose veins scrawled across Miss Mary's thighs, the livid veins in her sagging breasts, her slack, pendulous belly, and her sparse, gray pubic hair. She looked like a cadaver washed up on the beach.

No one moved for five long, terrible seconds.

"Where's Daddy's money?" Miss Mary shouted, voice cracking, staring furiously at James Harris. "Where's those children, Hoyt?"

Her voice echoed around the room, this shrieking hag from a nightmare, waving a small, white square of cardboard in front of her.

"You thought no one would recognize you, Hoyt Pickens!" Miss Mary howled. "But I have a photograph!"

Patricia heaved herself up out of her chair and scooped the fuzzy blue afghan from its back. She wrapped it around Miss Mary, who kept waving the photograph.

"Look!" Miss Mary crowed. "Look at him." And as the afghan closed around her, Miss Mary saw the photo in her hand and her face went slack.

"No," Miss Mary said. "No, that's not right. Not this one."

A horrified Mrs. Greene came running from the den.

"I'm so sorry," Mrs. Greene said.

"It's all right," Patricia said, shielding Miss Mary's nakedness from the room.

"I went to answer the phone," Mrs. Greene said, taking Miss Mary by her shoulders. "I was only gone for a second."

"Everything's all right," Patricia said, loud enough for everyone to hear as she and Mrs. Greene herded the old lady out of the living room.

"This isn't right," Miss Mary said, allowing herself to be led away, all her fight gone. "Not this one."

They got her to the garage room, Mrs. Greene apologizing all the way. Miss Mary clutched the photograph to her chest as they dried her with towels and Mrs. Greene got her into bed. Patricia went back into the living room but found everyone already in the hall. James Harris was making plans to visit Seewee Farms to meet Horse, and to attend St. Joseph's, and to meet Leland, and Patricia wanted to ask Grace why she'd been so quiet, but Grace slipped out the door while Patricia was apologizing for Miss Mary, and then everyone drained out the front door, leaving Patricia alone in the hall.

"What's going on?" Korey called down. Patricia turned and saw her on the upstairs landing. "Why was Granny Mary shouting?"

"It's nothing," Patricia said. "She was just confused."

Patricia went out onto the porch and watched Kitty's headlights reverse down the driveway. She made a mental note to call everyone the next day to apologize, then went back to the garage room.

Miss Mary lay in her hospital bed, clutching the photo to her chest. Mrs. Greene sat next to her, making up for her previous lapse with extra vigilance now.

"It's him," Miss Mary said. "It's him. I know I have it somewhere."

Patricia pried the photograph from between Miss Mary's fingers. It was an old black-and-white shot of the minister from Miss Mary's church in Kershaw surrounded by grim-faced children clutching Easter baskets.

"I'll find it," Miss Mary said. "I'll find it. I know. I will."

CHAPTER 10

She sat with Mrs. Greene, reassuring her that it wasn't her fault, while they waited for Miss Mary to fall back asleep. After the old lady began to breathe deep and regular, she stood in the driveway and watched Mrs. Greene's car back out and wondered how tonight had gone so wrong. It was partly her fault. She'd ambushed everyone with James Harris and they'd ambushed him back. Partly it was the book. Everyone felt irritated at having to read it, but sometimes they humored Slick because they all felt a little sorry for her. But mostly it was Miss Mary. She wondered if she was getting to be too much for them to handle anymore. If Carter got home from the hospital before eleven she'd bring it up with him.

An intolerably hot wind screamed off the harbor and filled the air with the hiss of bamboo leaves. The air felt heavy and thick and Patricia wondered if it might be making everyone restless. The live oaks whipped their branches in circles overhead. The lone streetlight at the end of the driveway cast a slender silver cone that made the night around it blacker, and Patricia felt exposed. She smelled the ghost of used incontinence pads and spilled coffee grounds, and she saw Mrs. Savage squatting in her nightgown, shoving raw meat in her mouth, and Miss Mary standing naked in the doorway, a skinned squirrel, hair streaming water, waving a useless photograph, and she ran for the front door and slammed it behind her, pushing it hard against the wind, and shot the deadbolt home.

Something small screamed in the kitchen, then all over the house. She realized it was the phone.

"Patricia?" the voice said when she picked up. She didn't recognize it over the interference at first. "Grace Cavanaugh. I'm sorry to call so late."

The phone line crackled. Patricia's heart still pounded.

"Grace, it's not too late at all," Patricia said, trying to slow down. "I'm so sorry about what happened."

"I called to see how Miss Mary is doing," Grace said.

"She's asleep."

"And I wanted you to know that we all understand," Grace said. "These things happen with the elderly."

"I'm sorry about James Harris," Patricia said. "I meant to tell everyone, I just kept putting it off."

"It's unfortunate he was there," Grace said. "Men don't know what it's like to care for an aging relative."

"Are you upset with me?" Patricia asked. In their five years of friendship it was the most direct question she'd ever asked.

"Why would I be upset with you?"

"About inviting James Harris," Patricia said.

"We're not schoolgirls, Patricia. I blame the book for the quality of the evening. Good night."

Grace hung up.

Patricia stood in the kitchen holding the phone for a moment, then hung up. Why wasn't Carter here? It was his mother. He needed to see her like this, and then maybe he'd understand that they needed more help. The wind rattled the kitchen windows and she didn't want to be alone downstairs anymore.

She went up and knocked gently on Korey's door while pushing it open. The lights were out and the room was dark, which confused Patricia. Why on earth was Korey asleep so early? The hall light spilled across Korey's bed. It was empty.

"Korey?" Patricia said into the darkness.

"Mom," Korey said from the shadows by her closet, her voice low and even. "There's someone on the roof."

Cold water flooded Patricia's veins. She stepped out of the hall light and into Korey's bedroom, standing to one side of the door.

"Where?" she whispered.

"Over the garage," Korey whispered back.

The two of them stood like that for a long moment until Patricia realized she was the only adult in the house, which meant she had to do something. She forced her legs to carry her to the window.

"Don't let him see you," Korey said.

Patricia made herself stand right in front of the window, expecting to see the dark shape of a man outlined against the night sky, but she only saw the sharp, black line of the roof's edge with thrashing bamboo behind it. She jumped when she heard Korey's voice beside her.

"I saw him," Korey said. "I promise."

"He's not there now," Patricia said.

She walked to the door and flipped on the overhead light. They both stood, dazzled, while their eyes adjusted. The first thing she saw was a half-empty bowl of old cereal on the windowsill, the milk and corn flakes dried into concrete. She'd asked Korey not to leave food in her room, but her daughter looked scared and vulnerable and Patricia decided not to say anything.

"There's going to be a storm," Patricia said. "But I'll leave your door open and the hall light on so your father remembers to say good night when he comes home."

She pulled Korey's comforter back. "Do you want to read your book?"

Her eye caught the top of the blue plastic milk crate Korey used for a bedside table. A copy of 'Salem's Lot by Stephen King lay on top of a stack of Sassy magazines. Suddenly it all made sense.

Korey saw her see the book. "I didn't make it up," she said.

"I don't think you did," Patricia said.

Disarmed by Patricia's refusal to argue, Korey got into bed and Patricia left the bedside lamp on, turned off the overhead light, and left the door open. In his bedroom, Blue was already in bed, covers pulled up.

"Good night, Blue," Patricia called to him across his dark room.

"There's a man in the backyard," Blue said.

"It's the wind," she said, picking her way between the clothes and action figures on his floor. "It makes the house sound scary. Do you want me to leave the light on?"

"He climbed up on the roof," Blue said, and right at that moment Patricia heard a footstep directly overhead.

It wasn't a limb falling or a branch scraping. It wasn't the wind making the house creak. Just a few feet over her head came a deliberate, quiet *thump*.

Her blood stopped in its veins. Her head craned back so far she put a crick in her neck. The silence hummed. Then another quiet *thump*, this time between her and Blue. Someone was walking on the roof.

"Blue," Patricia said. "Come."

He flew out of bed and grabbed her around the waist. She walked them in a straight line, stepping on his books and action figures. Plastic men snapped beneath their feet as they rushed to his bedroom door.

"Korey," she said, quiet and urgent from the hall. "Come on."

Korey flowed out of her bed and ran to the other side of her mother, and Patricia herded them both down the front stairs and sat them on the bottom step.

"I need you to wait here," Patricia whispered. "I'll check the doors."

She walked quickly through the dark downstairs den to the back door and turned the deadbolt, expecting to see the shadowy shape of a man through the door right before he smashed through the glass and yanked her out into the wild night. She made sure the sun porch door was deadbolted—they had too many doors—then went down the steps to Miss Mary's room, turning on the light as she went.

Miss Mary came to life on her bed, squirming and moaning, but Patricia kept on walking to the utility room, where she made sure the door to the garbage cans was deadbolted, too.

She went to the front hall and turned on the porch lights, then went to the sun porch and snapped on the floodlights that lit up the backyard.

"Korey," Patricia called from the sun porch, her eyes glued to the merciless white glare of the backyard, the floodlights picking out every blade of yellowed grass. "Bring me the portable phone."

She heard feet running from the front hall across the living room, and then her children were beside her. Korey pressed a hard plastic rectangle into her palm. She had the upper hand. The doors were locked, they could see everything around them, and they were secure. She could call the Mt. Pleasant police department in a flash. Maryellen said their response time was three minutes.

She kept her thumb over the dial button and they stood, eyes glued to the windows. The floodlights erased every shadow: the strange hollow depression in the center of the yard, the trunks of the oak trees with their bark stained yellow by the iron-rich Mt. Pleasant water, the geranium bushes against the fence separating their property from the Langs, the flower beds on the other side separating their yard from the Mitchells.

But beyond the reach of the lights, the night was a black wall. Patricia felt eyes out there looking into her house, watching her and the children through the glass. The scar tissue on her left ear began to crawl. The wind tossed the bushes and trees. The house creaked quietly to itself. They all watched, looking for something that didn't belong.

"Mom," Blue said, low and even.

She saw his gaze fixed on the top of the sun porch windows. The roof of the sun porch was a shingled overhang outside her bedroom windows, and along its edge Patricia caught something slowly and deliberately move and she knew immediately what it was: a human hand, letting go of the edge of the overhang and withdrawing back up out of sight.

She had the phone against her ear in an instant. Sharp static cracks made her yank it away.

"911?" she said. "Hello? My name is Patricia Campbell." The line *ZZZrrrrkkKKK*ed in her ear. "My children and I are at 22 Pierates Cruze." A series of hollow pops covered the faint sound of a human voice yabbering on the other end. "There is an intruder in our house and I'm here with my children alone."

That was when she remembered her bathroom window was wide open.

"Keep trying," Patricia said, thrusting the phone into Korey's hand, not giving herself a second to think. "Stay here and dial again." Patricia raced across the dark living room and heard Korey say behind her, "Please," to the operator as she turned the corner and ran up the dark stairs.

From the overhang over the sun porch it was just a short chin-up to the main roof, then up one side, down the other, and a short drop onto the porch roof right outside her bathroom, then in through the bathroom window. She'd opened it earlier to let out the smell of her hairspray.

She felt something dark and heavy above her on the roof racing her to the open window. Her legs pushed her weight hard up the stairs, chest heaving, breath burning in her throat, pulse cracking behind her ears, hurling herself around the banister at the top of the stairs and into her dark bedroom.

To her left she saw the harbor out the windows; to her right she felt hot air blowing in from the bathroom window, and she threw herself toward it, running down the dark tunnel of her bedroom and into the bathroom, closets on one side, smashing her stomach into the sharp edge of the counter, reaching for the window, slamming it shut, turning the latch, and something dark flashed past outside, cutting off the night sky. She yanked her hands back like the window was on fire.

They had to get out of the house. Then she remembered Miss Mary. She wasn't capable of running, or probably even leaving the house and walking across the backyard in the middle of the night. Someone would have to stay with her. She raced through her dark bedroom, back down the stairs, and into the living room.

"The phone doesn't work," Korey said, holding out the portable handset to her.

"We have to go," she told Korey and Blue. She took their hands and led them through the dining room and into the kitchen toward the back door.

Someone wanted to get into the house. She had no idea when Carter was coming home. They had no way to call for help. She needed to get to a phone, and she needed to get whoever it was away from her children.

"I want you to go into the garage room with Miss Mary," she told them. "And lock the door as soon as you're inside. Don't let anyone in."

"What about you?" Korey asked.

"I'm going to run to the Langs' and call the police," Patricia said. She looked out over the bright backyard. "I'll only be gone a minute."

Blue began to cry. Patricia unlocked the back door.

"Ready?" she asked.

"Mom?"

"No questions," she said. "Lock yourselves in with your grandmother."

Then she turned the handle and opened the door, and a man stepped into the house.

Patricia screamed. The man grabbed her by the arms.

"Whoa," James Harris said.

Patricia swayed and the floor rose to meet her. James Harris's strong arms held her up as her knees gave out.

"I saw the lights on back here," he said. "What's going on?"

"There's a man," Patricia said, relieved that help had arrived, speaking over her pounding heart. "On the roof. We tried to call the police. The phone isn't working."

"Okay," James Harris reassured her. "I'm here. There's no need to call the police. No one's hurt?"

"We're fine," Patricia said.

"I should check on Miss Mary," James Harris said, gently pushing Patricia back against the counter and stepping past her and the children. He moved away from them, going farther and farther into the den.

"I need to call the police," Patricia said.

"No need," James Harris told her from the middle of the den.

"They'll be here in three minutes," she said.

"Let me check on Miss Mary and then I'll look on the roof," James Harris said from the far end of the den.

Suddenly, Patricia didn't want James Harris in the room alone with Miss Mary.

"No!" she said, too loud.

He stopped, one hand on the garage room door, and turned slowly.

"Patricia," he said. "Calm down."

"The police?" she asked, stepping toward the kitchen phone.

"Don't," he told her, and she wondered why he was telling her not to call the police. "Don't do anything, don't call anyone."

Which was when a blue light flickered across the walls and strong white lights flooded the den windows.

Carter arrived forty-five minutes later while the police were still poking through the bushes with their flashlights. One of them was using his big car-mounted spotlight to light up two officers on the roof. Gee Mitchell and her husband, Beau, stood in their driveway next door and watched.

"Patty?" Carter called from the front hall.

"We're in here," she hollered, and a moment later he came down the steps into the garage room.

Patricia had decided they should all stay together in Miss Mary's room. James Harris had already spoken to the police and left. He'd returned to make sure Patricia was all right after her mother-in-law had broken up their book club meeting, and come around back when he saw the backyard lights on.

"Is everyone all right?" Carter asked.

"We're fine," Patricia said. "Right, everyone? Just scared."

Korey and Blue hugged their father.

"That guy saved us," Korey said.

"Someone got on the roof and they would have gotten us if he hadn't come," Blue said.

"Then I'm glad he was here," Carter said, and turned to Patricia. "Did you really have to call out the national guard? Christ, Patty, the neighbors are going to think I'm a wife beater or something."

"Hoyt," Miss Mary said from her bed.

"Okay, Mom," Carter said. "It's been a long night. I think we all just need to calm down."

Patricia didn't know if she would ever feel calm again.

CHAPTER 11

After they put Blue and Korey to bed, Patricia told Carter everything.

"I'm not saying it was your imagination," he said when she'd finished. "But you're always keyed up after your meetings. Those are morbid books y'all read."

"I want an alarm system," she told him.

"How would that have helped?" he asked. "Listen, I promise for the next little while I'll make sure I'm home before dark."

"I want an alarm system," she repeated.

"Before we go to all that trouble and expense, let's see how you feel after the next few weeks."

She stood up from the end of the bed.

"I'm going to check on Miss Mary," she told him, and left the room.

She checked the deadbolts on the front, back, and sun porch doors, leaving the lights on behind her, then went to Miss Mary's room. The room was lit by the orange glow of Miss Mary's night-light. She moved softly in case Miss Mary was asleep, then saw the night-light reflecting off her open eyes.

"Miss Mary?" Patricia asked. Miss Mary's eyes cut sideways at her. "Are you awake?"

The sheet moved and Miss Mary's claw struggled out, then ran out of energy and flopped down on her chest without getting where it was going.

"I'm." Miss Mary wetted her lips. "I'm."

Patricia stepped to the bed railing. She knew what Miss Mary meant.

"It's all right," she said.

The two women stayed like that for a long quiet moment, listening to the hot wind press on the windows behind the drawn curtains.

"Who's Hoyt Pickens?" Patricia asked, not expecting a reply.

"He killed my daddy," Miss Mary said.

That took the air out of Patricia's lungs. She'd never heard that name before. Besides which, Miss Mary usually forgot about the people who floated to the surface of her mind seconds after she'd spoken their names. Patricia had never heard her link the person and their importance together.

"Why do you say that?" she asked softly.

"I have a picture of Hoyt Pickens," Miss Mary rasped. "In his ice cream suit."

Her ragged voice made Patricia's scarred ear itch. The wind tried to open the hidden windows, rattled the glass, looked for a way in. Miss Mary's hand found some more energy and slithered across the blankets toward Patricia, who reached down and took the smooth, cold hand in her own.

"How did he know your father?" she asked.

"Before supper, the men and my daddy used to sit on the back porch passing a jar," Miss Mary said. "Us children had our supper early and played in the front yard, then we saw a man in a suit the color of vanilla ice cream come up the road. He turned into our yard and the men hid their jar because drinking was against the law. This man walked up to my daddy and said his name was Hoyt Pickens and he asked if my daddy knew where he could get himself some rabbit spit. That's what they called my daddy's corn whiskey, because it could make a rabbit spit in a bulldog's eye. He said he'd been on the Cincinnati train and his throat was dusty and it'd be worth two bits to him to wet it. Mr. Lukens brought out the jar and

Hoyt Pickens tasted it. He said he'd been from Chicago to Miami and that was the best corn liquor he ever had."

Patricia didn't breathe. It had been years since Miss Mary had put this many sentences together.

"That night Mama and Daddy argued. Hoyt Pickens wanted to buy some of Daddy's rabbit spit and sell it in Columbia, but Mama said no. It was ten-cent cotton and forty-cent meat back then. Reverend Buck told us the boll weevil had come because there were too many public swimming pools. The government taxed everything from cigarettes to bow legs, but Daddy's rabbit spit made sure we always had molasses on our cornbread.

"Mama told him the snake that stuck out its head usually got it chopped off, but Daddy was tired of scratching a living so he ignored Mama and sold twelve jars of rabbit spit to Hoyt Pickens and Hoyt went to Columbia and sold those right quick and came back for twelve more. He sold those, too, and soon Daddy had a second still and was gone from the house from sundown to sunup and sleeping all day.

"Hoyt Pickens sat regular at our table every Sunday and some Wednesdays and Fridays, too. He told Daddy all the things he should want. He told Daddy he could get more money if he laid up his rabbit spit in barrels until it turned brown. That meant Daddy had to lay out considerable and he wouldn't see his money back for six months until Hoyt took it to Columbia and got paid. But the first time Hoyt laid that thick stack of bills on the table we all got excited."

Something sharp tickled Patricia's palm. Miss Mary was scratching her nails against Patricia's skin, back and forth, back and forth, like insects creeping across the inside of her hand.

"Soon everything became about the rabbit spit. Once the sheriff saw what Daddy was doing he touched him for a taste of that money. Daddy needed other men to work the stills and he paid them in scrip while they waited for the rabbit spit to turn brown. Banks closed faster than you could remember their names so everyone held on to their money, but Daddy bought a set of encyclopedias, and a mangle for the wash, and the men all smoked store-bought cigars when they sat out back."

Patricia remembered Kershaw. They'd driven the hundred and fifty miles upstate many times to visit Carter's cousins, and Miss Mary when she lived alone. They hadn't been in a long while, but Patricia remembered a dry land populated by dry people, covered in dust, with filling stations at every crossroads selling evaporated milk and generic cigarettes. She remembered fallow fields and abandoned farms. She understood the appeal of something fresh, and clean, and green to people who lived in a small, hot place like that.

"Around then the Beckham boy went missing," Miss Mary said. Her throat rasped now. "He was a pale little redheaded thing, six years old, who'd follow anyone anywhere. When he didn't come home for supper we all went looking. We expected to find him curled up under a pecan tree, but no. Some people said the government inoculation men took him away, others said there was a colored gal in the woods who churned white children into a stew she sold as a love spell for a nickel a taste. Some folks said he fell in the river and got carried away, but it didn't matter what they said—he was gone.

"The next little boy to vanish was Avery Dubose. He was a tin bucket toter and Hoyt told everyone he must have fell in one of the machines at the mill and the boss lied about it. That stirred up bad feelings between the mill and the farmers, and with so much rabbit spit around tempers ran hot. Men started showing up at church with their arms in slings and bruises on their faces. Mr. Beckham shot himself.

"But we had presents under the tree that Christmas and Daddy convinced Mama sweet times were here. In January her belly got tight and round. I was their only baby who'd lived out of three, but now another baby had to root.

"They'd never have had Charlie Beckham if that combine

salesman hadn't stopped his horses at the Moores' old place and seen the water from their pump flow thick with maggots. They had to let that little boy's body sit in the icehouse for three days to let all the water drain before he'd fit in his coffin. Even then, they had to build it extra wide."

White spit formed gummy balls in the corners of Miss Mary's mouth, but Patricia didn't move. She worried that if she did anything to break the spell this thread might snap, and Miss Mary might never speak like this again.

"That spring, nobody could afford to plant nothing," Miss Mary went on. "Nobody had nothing in the ground so Daddy and Hoyt had to spend big to bring corn all the way from Rock Hill, and they had all their money tied up in the rabbit spit barrels. The banks didn't care about no scrip and they started taking everyone's tools, and their horses, and mules, and no one could do nothing. Everyone waited for those barrels.

"The third little boy to go missing was Reverend Buck's baby and the men got together on our back porch and I heard them speculate through my window about one person or another, and the jar kept getting passed, and then Hoyt Pickens said he'd seen Leon Simms around the Moore farm one night, and I wanted to laugh because only a stranger would say that. Leon was a colored fellow and something had happened to his head in the war. He sat in the sun outside Mr. Early's store, and if you gave him candy he'd play something for you on the spoons and sing. His mother took care of him and he got a government check. Sometimes he helped people carry packages and they always paid him in candy.

"But Hoyt Pickens said Leon liked to wander at night and had been creeping in places he shouldn't. He said this is what happens when people come down from up north and spread ideas in places that weren't ready for them. He said that Leon Simms sat outside Mr. Early's store and licked his lips over children and took them to secret places where he slaked his unnatural appetite.

"The more Hoyt Pickens talked, the more the men thought he sounded right. I must have nodded off because when I opened my eyes it was full dark and the backyard was empty. I heard the train pass, and a hoot owl carrying on out in the woods, and I was slipping back to sleep when the land lit up.

"A crowd of men came in following a wagon and they had lanterns and flashlights. They were quiet but I heard one hard voice talking loud, giving orders, and it was my daddy. Next to him stood Hoyt Pickens and his ice cream suit glowed in the dark. They pulled something off the back of the cart, a big burlap bag we used for picking cotton, and they lifted one end and something flowed out wet and black onto the dirt. It was Leon, all tied with rope.

"The men got shovels, and they dug a deep hole underneath the peach tree and dragged Leon to it and he must not have been dead because I heard him call my daddy 'boss' and say, 'Please, boss, I'll play you something, boss,' and they threw him down in that hole and piled dirt on top of him until his begging got muffled, and after a while you couldn't hear it anymore, but I still could.

"When I woke up early there was mist on the ground and I went out back to see if maybe I'd had a bad dream. But I could see the fresh-dug dirt and then I heard a noise and saw my daddy sitting real quiet in the corner of the porch and he had a jar of rabbit spit between his legs. His eyes were swollen red and when he saw me he gave me a grin that came straight out of Hell."

Patricia realized that was why Miss Mary let the peaches rot. The memory of the fruit's sweet juice running down her chin, its meat filling her stomach, now tasted sour with Leon Simms's blood.

"Hoyt Pickens left before the rabbit spit turned brown," Miss Mary croaked. "Daddy took the wagon to Columbia but he couldn't find who'd been buying from Hoyt. All our money was in those barrels but no one in Kershaw could buy the rabbit spit at the price Daddy needed and he drank up most of it himself over the next few years. Mama lost my brother child and Daddy sold his stills for eating money. He never worked another day, just sat out back, drinking that brown rabbit spit alone because no one would come by our place knowing what we had buried there. When he finally hanged himself in the barn it was a mercy. When hard times came a few years later some people say it was Leon Simms that poisoned the land, but I'll always know it was Hoyt."

In the long silence, water overflowed Miss Mary's twitching eyelids and ran down her face. She licked her lips, and Patricia saw that a white film coated her tongue. Her skin looked thin as paper, her hands felt cold as ice. Her breathing sounded like tearing cloth. Slowly, Patricia watched her bloodshot eyes lose their focus, and she realized telling the story had set Miss Mary adrift. Patricia started to pull her hand from Miss Mary's, but the old lady tightened her fingers and held firm.

"Nightwalking men always have a hunger on them," she croaked. "They never stop taking and they don't know about enough. They mortgaged their souls away and now they eat and eat and never know how to stop."

Patricia waited for Miss Mary to say something else, but her mother-in-law didn't move. After a while, she pulled her hand from Miss Mary's cold fingers and watched the old woman fall asleep with her eyes still open.

A black wind pressed down on her house.

THE STRANGER
BESIDE ME

July 1993

CHAPTER 12

Deep summer suffocated the Old Village. It hadn't rained all month. The sun cooked lawns to a crunchy yellow, baked sidewalks white-hot, made roof shingles soft, and heated telephone poles until the streets smelled like warm creosote. Everyone abandoned the outdoors except for the occasional midafternoon child darting across spongy asphalt streets. No one did yard work after ten in the morning, and they saved their errands until after six at night. From sunup to sundown, the whole world felt flooded in boiling honey.

But Patricia wouldn't run errands after the sun started to go down. When she had to go to the store or the bank, she raced to her sunbaked Volvo and blasted the air conditioner while sitting miserably on the scorching front seat until she could tolerate touching the burning hot steering wheel. She insisted that Blue take the garbage cans out to the street before dark, no matter how much he complained about dragging them to the end of the driveway under the relentless, burning sun.

After sundown Patricia stayed close to home. When Korey or Blue got picked up for sleepovers, she watched from the front porch until they got into the cars, closed the doors, and drove safely off the Cruze. Even when their central air conditioning finally broke and the air-conditioner man told them they should have called earlier and it would be two weeks before he could get parts, Patricia insisted on locking every window and door before they went to bed. No matter how many fans they had running, every night, everyone sweated through all their sheets, and every morning Patricia stripped every single bed and made them up again fresh. The dryer ran nonstop.

Finally, James Harris saved their lives.

The doorbell rang during supper one night and Patricia went to answer, not wanting Korey or Blue to open the door after dark. James Harris stood on her porch.

"I just wanted to check in and see how everyone was doing after the big scare," he said.

Patricia had thought she might not see him again after she'd overreacted the night the man got on their roof and shouted at him, as if he were the danger rather than the person trying to get into the house. She'd felt ashamed to think the worst of someone for no reason, so seeing him on their porch as if nothing had happened filled her with a profound sense of relief.

"I'm still kicking myself I wasn't here," Carter said, standing up from the table and shaking James's hand when she led him into the dining room. "Thank God you came by. The kids say you were the man of the hour. You're always welcome in our home."

James Harris took this literally, and Patricia soon found herself listening for his knock as Korey ate the last roll or Blue complained that he couldn't possibly finish his zucchini in this heat. Night after night she'd find James Harris on their front porch and they'd exchange comments about that month's book club book, or he'd ask what the latest update was on getting the air conditioner fixed, or how Miss Mary was doing, or he'd tell her he'd gone to church with Slick and Leland. Then she'd invite him inside for ice cream.

"How does he know exactly when dessert's going on the table?" Carter complained after James's fourth visit, hopping up and down on one foot while peeling off his sweaty socks in the bedroom. "It's like he can hear our freezer door open all the way down the street."

But Patricia liked having him there because Carter had only managed to keep his promise to be home before dark for two days before he started staying late at work again. Most nights she ate alone with the children, and because Korey was going to two-week soccer camp at the end of the month and apparently had to spend the night with every single one of her friends before she left, most nights it was just her and Blue at the supper table.

Around the fifth night James Harris stopped by Patricia started leaving the windows open later, and then she started leaving the upstairs windows open overnight, and then the downstairs windows, and before long she just left the screen doors on their latches, and the house throbbed softly with fans sitting in open windows all day and night.

The other reason she was glad James Harris came by was because she didn't know how to talk to Blue anymore. All Blue wanted to talk about was Nazis. She'd helped him get an adult library card and now he checked out photograph-packed Time-Life books about World War II. She found his old spiral notebooks covered in drawings of swastikas, SS lightning bolts, Panzer tanks, and skulls. Whenever she tried to talk to him about his summer Oasis program or going to the Creekside pool, he always countered with Nazis.

James Harris spoke fluent Nazi.

"You know," he said to Blue, "the entire American space program was built by Wernher von Braun and a bunch of other Nazis the Americans gave asylum to because they knew how to build rockets."

Or:

"We like to think that we beat Hitler, but it was really the Russians who turned the tide."

Or:

"Did you know the Nazis counterfeited British money and tried to destabilize their economy?"

Patricia enjoyed watching Blue hold his own in a conversation with an adult, even though she wished they would talk about something besides the Third Reich. But her mother had told her to appreciate what she had, not whine about what she didn't, and so she let them fill the space that had been left empty by Carter and Korey.

Those evenings over ice cream, sitting in the dining room with the windows open and a warm, salty breeze blowing through the house and Blue and James Harris talking about World War II, were the last time Patricia felt truly happy. Even after everything that came later, when everything in her life hurt, the memory of those nights wrapped her in a soft, sweet glow that often carried her away to sleep.

After almost three weeks, Patricia found herself actually looking forward to Grace's birthday party. She finally felt confident enough to go outside at night, even if it was just down the block, and Carter had promised to be home early and she felt like they could finally get back to normal.

The second Patricia and Carter were out the door, Mrs. Greene stepped out of her shoes and peeled off her socks and stuck them in her purse. It was too hot to have anything on her feet. Blue and Korey were spending the night out, and no one was home to care if she went barefoot or not.

The carpet felt hot beneath the soles of her feet. Every door and window in the house stood open, but the puny breeze that trickled in from the backyard was sticky and stunk of the marsh.

"You feel like eating something tonight, Miss Mary?" she asked.

Miss Mary hummed happily to herself. Mrs. Campbell had said she'd been going through her old photo albums all week, and if she hadn't lost so much weight Mrs. Greene would think she almost seemed like her old self.

"I found it," Miss Mary said, smiling. She rolled her boiled-egg eyes up to Mrs. Greene. "Do you want to see it?"

An old snapshot rested facedown on her knee. She stroked its back with trembling fingers.

"Who's it of?" Mrs. Greene asked, reaching for it.

Miss Mary covered it with the flat of her hand.

"Patricia first," she said.

"You want me to brush out your hair?" Mrs. Greene asked.

Miss Mary looked confused by the change of subject, considered it, then jerked her chin down once.

Mrs. Greene found the wooden hairbrush and stood behind Miss Mary's chair, and while the old lady looked at the TV and stroked her photograph, Mrs. Greene brushed her sparse gray hair, surrounded by the noise of the rushing fans.

Grace's parties were everything Patricia thought parties should be when she was a little girl. In the living room, Arthur Rivers had taken off his jacket and sat at the piano playing a medley of college fight songs, which were greeted with boos, cheers, and raucous singing along, depending on the college. He wouldn't stop as long as people kept bringing him bourbon.

The party spilled from the living room into the dining room, where it swirled in a circle around a table overflowing with miniature ham biscuits, cheese straws, pimento cheese sandwiches, and a tray of crudités that would be thrown out untouched tomorrow morning, and then it flowed through the kitchen and pooled on the sun porch with its panoramic view of the harbor. The white tablecloth-covered bar stood at the end of the room where the crowd was thickest, and two black men in white jackets made an endless stream of drinks behind it.

Every doctor and lawyer and harbor pilot in the Old Village had put on their seersucker and their bow ties and they held glasses and bellowed about what was wrong with Ken Hatfield this season, or if those businesses the hurricane had shut down along Shem Creek a few years ago would ever reopen, and when the Isle of Palms connector would be completed, and where all these damn marsh rats were coming from. Their wives clutched glasses of white wine and wore a veritable jungle of clashing prints—animal prints and floral prints and geometric prints and abstract prints—talking about their children's plans for the summer, their kitchen renovation projects, and Patricia's ear. This was the first social event she'd attended since the incident and she felt like everyone was staring at her.

"I can't tell unless I stand right in front of you so I can see both ears at the same time," Kitty reassured her.

"Is it that obvious?" Patricia asked, reaching up and smoothing her hair down over her scar.

"It just makes your face look a little cattywampus," Kitty said, and then she caught Loretta Jones's elbow as she shouldered past them in the crush. "Loretta, look at Patricia and tell me if you notice anything."

"Well, that man's grandmother bit off her ear," Loretta said, cocking her head to one side. "What do you mean? Did something else happen?"

Patricia wanted to slink away, but Kitty gripped her wrist.

"It was his great-aunt," Kitty said. "And she just took a nibble."

Loretta cocked her head and said, "Do you need a good plastic surgeon? I can get you a name. You look lopsided. Oh, there's Sadie Funche. Excuse me."

"Loretta always was a pill," Kitty said as Loretta disappeared into the crowd.

The big box fan stood in the door of the den where it was supposed to suck in hot air and blow it out cool in the garage room, but it barely stirred the sludge. It was intolerably hot. Ragtag lay, miserable, under Miss Mary's bed, panting.

Maybe she would give Miss Mary a cool bath, Mrs. Greene thought. The water would feel nice for both of them. She started to get up when she felt a living gaze on her. She looked to the den door and saw an enormous, wet, black rat sitting motionless beside the fan, staring at her. The air over its patchy, piebald back practically shimmered with disease. Mrs. Greene felt her bowels fill with ice water. She'd seen plenty of rats in her lifetime, but never one as big as this, and certainly not one sitting all cool and collected as if it owned the place.

"Shoo!" Mrs. Greene said, flicking her hands in its direction and stamping her foot. Ragtag lifted his head as if it weighed five hundred pounds and gave her a look, wondering if that "shoo" was directed at him.

"Go on, Ragtag," Mrs. Greene said, recognizing her natural ally. "Get that mean old rat. Get it!"

Ragtag's head tracked her gestures and saw the rat and, without moving a muscle, he began to growl from deep inside his throat. The rat oozed its body out long and flowed down onto the first step, and Mrs. Greene saw that it was as big as a man's shoe. Ragtag's growls went up in pitch, but they didn't seem to trouble the rat. Ragtag scrambled out from under the bed and faced the rat square on, his growl escalating, building toward a bark, and then it cut off with a yelp as three other, smaller, equally filthy rats poured down the steps on either side of the fat one and scurried across the carpet, coming for Mrs. Greene.

Ragtag ran at them without hesitation and seized one in his jaws and shook his head twice, once to break its neck, and again to fling its corpse against the wall. The second and third rats vanished beneath Miss Mary's hospital bed.

Mrs. Greene had pulled her bare feet up onto her chair, but now she realized she had to get involved. There would be a stick or a mop in the utility room behind her, and she needed to chase these rats out of the house before they bit someone.

"We got some rats in here, Miss Mary," Mrs. Greene said, standing up. "But me and Ragtag are going to get rid of them."

She went to the utility room door, then stopped when she saw the padlock they'd put on to secure it after that night Mrs. Campbell thought a man tried to get in the house. No one had given her a key.

BANG!

Something crashed behind her and she whirled to see Ragtag skip back in fear from the box fan that slid to a stop facedown at the bottom of the steps. Several new rats had joined the huge one on the steps, and they looked filthy, fur missing in patches, bodies encrusted in scabs, noses twitching. The box fan made a low, muffled moaning sound, unable to suck air from the carpet, and more rats jammed the doorway. Ragtag ran at them, barking, but they didn't budge.

"Get 'em, Ragtag!" Mrs. Greene said. "Get 'em!"

Mrs. Greene knew what to do. She would shut Miss Mary in the small bathroom across from the utility room, and then she'd get a blanket and she and Ragtag would drive these things back. As long as Ragtag stayed with her she could handle this.

"Miss Mary, I'm going to take you to the powder room for a minute," she said.

She leaned down and got her hands into Miss Mary's damp armpits and started to lift her up. Miss Mary gave a miserable groan and then Mrs. Greene smelled something rank. She looked up.

Rats covered the den, spilling from the door and falling clumsily onto the top step: wet and muddy, three-legged and four-legged, long-tailed and no-tailed and vile. Black eyes shone, whiskers twitched, tails squirmed, their seething bodies packed together in the doorway. None of them made a sound. A carpet of rats covered the floor of the den so thick, Mrs. Greene couldn't see the yellow linoleum, and more piled in from the dining room, from the back door, from the front hall, surging into the den, covering it like a seething pool of matted fur, crawling over each other, forming a packed, squirming mass.

How'd they get in here so fast? Where did they all come from?

Something bumped her leg and she looked down to see Ragtag, body stiff, facing the door, lips curled back to expose bared teeth, mouth open, tongue cramped in a fold, making a deep, nasty sound. The dirty smell of the rats rolled into the room, paralyzing Mrs. Greene with fear. She still remembered that night when she was a little girl, waking up with something squirming beneath the blankets, something bald and fleshy and cold slithering over her shins, and her sister screaming, high, long, and loud, like she'd never stop, until their mother came in running, pulling the covers back to find a hairy rat fixed to her sister's belly button, chewing its way in.

That childhood nightmare came screaming at her as the huge black rat on the steps went from stone still to a black blur, leaping off the stairs, racing at Miss Mary across the empty carpet, moving so fast she screamed.

And Ragtag was there, snapping the black rat up in his jaws and savagely shaking his head. She heard something snap, and a keening squeak muffled inside a furry throat, and then the enormous rat was on the ground, body contracting, going limp. But as its corpse twitched, the flood of rats bulged in the doorway, then broke and poured bonelessly down the steps, flowing around the box fan, coming for the three of them.

Mrs. Greene ran to Miss Mary's armchair but froze as the heavy rats skittered across her bare feet, their sharp nails scratching her skin, their hairless tails cold against her flesh. A few of them stopped and sank their claws into her pants leg and began pulling themselves up. She did a frantic, high-stepping dance to shake them free.

Razor blades shredded her toes. She reached down to pluck a gray rat out of her pants leg and it caught one of her fingers in its mouth. Sharp teeth met bone, and cold prickles of nausea flooded Mrs. Greene's gut.

Ragtag barked and raged, drowning in a living carpet of rats. One clawed its way onto his back, and another three hung from his ears. Mrs. Greene saw his tan fur go dark with blood. She threw the gray rat against the curtains, losing skin from her fingers as it went. Then she turned to Miss Mary.

"Ohuh, ughuh!" Miss Mary screamed, as a hairy river rose up her legs and pooled in her lap.

Rats came over the back of her chair, flowed down over her shoulders, got tangled in her hair. She raised one arm, holding the photograph she'd been pressing to her leg high up in the air, but the rats hauled themselves up her sleeves, went down the open collar of her nightgown, crawled up her neck, and covered her face.

Rats covered the carpet, the sofa, they crawled up the curtains, they darted across the white sheets of Miss Mary's hospital bed, they dashed along the windowsill, they filled the room. But the bathroom door was still closed. If she could get them both in there she would be safe.

Mrs. Greene felt hot needles pierce her belly button, and she looked down and saw a rat clinging to her waistband, nose beneath her shirt, and something inside her broke. She saw a squirming pile of rats where Miss Mary and Ragtag had been and she ran for the bathroom, grabbing the rat on her stomach with one hand and hurling it away, even as it sank its teeth into her belly button and she felt it tear with a sound she would never forget.

She hit the bathroom door with her body, turned the knob, and fell inside, then slammed the door on the rats behind her and leaned back, holding it closed as claws scrabbled against it from the other side. Covered in rat hair that made her sneeze and gag, she slid to the floor.

Sloshing came from the toilet and she heard the unmistakable sound of something losing purchase on the porcelain, sliding down, and thrashing in the toilet water. Mrs. Greene grabbed the shower head on its flexible hose and turned the knob to full hot. She stepped up onto the closed toilet lid just as dozens of rats began to push at it from below. She turned the steaming, hissing shower head on the scrabbling claws beneath the crack in the door, on the rats flattening their skulls and trying to squirm under, and their high-pitched screeches made her eardrums throb.

She squatted on top of the toilet lid in the tiny, hot bathroom, feeling the water beneath the lid boiling with rats as steam filled the bathroom, and after a while she couldn't hear Miss Mary's shrieks through the door anymore.

They sang "Happy Birthday" to Grace around 10:30 p.m., and then the party began to break up. Patricia suggested they stroll down to Alhambra Hall, just to get some fresh air, but Carter said he had to go in early so they went right home.

"What's that smell?" Carter asked as they opened the front door and stepped inside.

The house smelled so strongly of wild animals and urine that Patricia's eyes began to water. Even though she'd left the mushroom lamp on the hall table turned on, it was dark. She flipped the light switch and saw the mushroom lamp lying in pieces across the floor.

The smell got stronger in the den, the floor dotted with brown pellets and puddles of urine. The sofa was shredded, the curtains hung in tatters. Her first thought was that vandals had broken in. She and Carter walked fast for the garage room and stopped short in the doorway.

A giant had picked up the room and shaken it hard: chairs turned over, tables on their sides, medicine bottles scattered among dead rats, their corpses dotting the carpet. And in the middle of all this wreckage, Mrs. Greene knelt over Miss Mary, caked in blood, clothes torn to rags. She raised her head from the old woman's lips and pressed down hard on her chest, performing perfect CPR compressions, and then she saw them and cried out in a cracked and terrible voice, "The ambulance is on its way."

CHAPTER 13

Three of Miss Mary's fingers had been stripped to the bone. She would need reconstructive surgery to rebuild her lips. They weren't sure about her nose. They thought they could save her left eye.

"Uh-huh, uh-huh," Carter said, nodding rapidly. "But Mom'll be okay?"

"After we stabilize her she'll need several surgeries," the doctor said. "But at her age you may want to consider whether that's even wise. After that, with extensive rehab and physical therapy she should be able to return to her normal life, in a limited fashion."

"Good, good," Carter said, still nodding. "Good."

The doctor left and Patricia tried to take Carter's hand and reconnect him to reality.

"Carter," she said. "Do you want to sit down?"

"I'm good," he said, pulling his hand away and running it over his face. "You should go get some rest. It's been a long night."

"Carter," she said.

"I'm fine," he said. "I think I'll actually go by my office and catch up on some work. I'll see Mom when they bring her out of surgery."

Patricia gave up and drove home a couple of hours before dawn. When she pulled into the driveway her headlights swept across the yard and the shadows seethed and scattered, fading back into the dark bushes: hundreds and hundreds of rats. Patricia sat in her car for a minute, lights on bright, then got out and ran for the front door.

———————

Dead rats littered the den. There were even more in the garage room. She didn't know what to do. Bury them? Put them in the trash? Call Animal Control? She knew what to do if too many people showed up for supper, or if someone arrived early for a party, but what did you do when rats attacked your mother-in-law? Who told you how to cope with that?

She decided to start with the garage room. Her heart contracted painfully when she saw Ragtag's limp corpse stretched in the middle of the carpet. *Poor dog*, she thought as she bent over to pick him up.

He opened one eye and his tail thumped feebly against the carpet.

Patricia wrapped him in an old beach towel and drove to the vet's office at twenty-six miles per hour. She was waiting when he showed up to unlock his office door.

"He'll live," Dr. Grouse said. "But it won't be inexpensive."

"Whatever it takes," Patricia told him. "He's a good dog. You're a good dog, Ragtag."

She couldn't find an unlacerated part of him to pet, so she settled on thinking good thoughts about him as hard as she could all the way back home. When she got out of the car she heard the phone ringing inside the house. She took it in the kitchen.

"Mom died," Carter said, biting down hard on each word.

"Carter, I am so sorry. What can I do?"

"I don't know, Patty," he said. "What do people do? I was ten when Daddy died."

"I'll call Stuhr's," she said. "How's Mrs. Greene?"

"Who?" he asked.

"Mrs. Greene," she repeated, not sure how to better describe the woman who'd tried to save his mother's life.

"Oh," he said. "They put in some stitches and she'll have to get a rabies series, but she went home."

"Carter," she repeated. "I'm so sorry."

"Okay," he said, dazed. "You too."

He hung up. Patricia stood in the kitchen, not knowing what happened next. Who did she call? Where did she begin? Overwhelmed, she dialed Grace.

"How unusual," Grace said, after Patricia explained what had happened. "At the risk of sounding insensitive, we should get started."

Relief flooded Patricia as Grace took over. She called Maryellen, who arranged for Stuhr's to pick up Miss Mary's body from the hospital, and then she told Patricia what to do with the children.

"Korey will have to start soccer camp a few days late," Grace said. "I'll call Delta and change her ticket. As for Blue, he'll need to stay with friends. You don't want him seeing the house like this."

Grace and Maryellen searched for someone to clean the house, which was now crawling with fleas and reeking of rats, but they couldn't find anyone to take the job.

"So much for the professionals," Grace said. "I called Kitty and Slick and we're coming tomorrow. It'll take us a few days but we'll make sure it's done right."

"That's too much," Patricia said.

"Nonsense," Grace said. "The most important thing right now is to clean that house until it's safe. I'll make a list of furniture and drapes and carpets and all the things you'll need to replace. And of course you'll stay at the beach house with Carter and the children until we're finished."

On the other end of things, Maryellen organized the visitation, helped with Miss Mary's burial insurance, and got Miss Mary's obituary written and placed in the Charleston paper and in the *Kershaw News-Era*. The only thing she couldn't do was promise an open casket.

"I'm so sorry," she told Patricia, sitting in Johnny Stuhr's office. "Kenny does our makeup and he doesn't think there's enough left to work with."

Miss Mary's service followed upstate rules: no jokes, no laughter, and all the scripture from the King James Bible. Her coffin sat at the front of the church with no flowers on it, lid screwed down tight. They had to go back three hymnals to find the hymn Carter said was Miss Mary's favorite, "Come Thou Disconsolate."

Packed into the hard pews of Mt. Pleasant Presbyterian, Carter sat next to Patricia, hunched and miserable. She took his hand and squeezed, and he gave a limp squeeze back. For years, his mother had told him he was the smartest and most special boy in the world and he'd believed her. Having her die like this, in his house, in a way he couldn't even really explain to people, was a kind of failure he'd never experienced before.

Korey took things harder than Patricia expected, and tears ran down her cheeks throughout the service. Blue kept standing up to see the coffin, but at least he'd brought *A Bridge Too Far* to read and not a book with a swastika on the cover.

After the graveside service, Grace opened her home and took all the quiches, and ham biscuits, and Kitty's casseroles, and Slick's ambrosia, and all the cold-cut platters people had brought by and laid them out on her dining room table. There was no bar because that wasn't what you did for a funeral, and they made the children go down to Alhambra to play because having them horsing around in the front yard didn't look right.

As one old face from Carter's past after another brought him over to their children, told stories about him, made him smile, Patricia saw him coming back to life, assuming his natural place as the center of attention. After all, he was the small-town boy who'd worked hard and become a famous doctor in Charleston—that was his real identity, not the little boy whose mother died in his garage room in a way that made people do double takes when they were told.

Monday morning, Patricia drove Korey to the airport and was touched at how hard she clung to her for a moment before dashing out of the car, her huge red, white, and blue duffel bag knocking against her legs. Then she drove to the beach house, packed their bags, and moved them back into Pierates Cruze. The house smelled of bleach, and the downstairs looked empty and sounded hard. Anything with upholstery had been thrown out and would have to be replaced. But they were home. And the air conditioning finally worked.

Now Patricia had to do what she'd been dreading: she needed to check in on Mrs. Greene. She'd been hurt badly and hadn't attended the funeral, and Patricia felt guilty she hadn't gone to see her earlier.

The problem was getting someone to go with her.

"I couldn't possibly," Grace said. "I have to clean from the funeral party, and Ben needs me to drive up to Columbia with him for a meeting. I'm overwhelmed."

Next she tried Slick.

"We all love Mrs. Greene," Slick said. "She's such a wonderful cook, and she's strong in her faith, but Patricia, you would not believe how frantic we are with this new deal of Leland's. Did I tell you about it? Gracious Cay? He's been talking to investors and all those money people and things are just wild. Did I tell you . . ."

Finally, she tried Kitty.

"I'm just so busy . . . ," Kitty began.

"We wouldn't stay long, Patricia told her.

"It's Parish's birthday next week," Kitty said. "I've been run ragged."

Patricia tried guilt.

"What with Ann Savage, and now Miss Mary," Patricia said. "I don't feel comfortable driving so far alone."

It turned out that guilt worked. The next day Patricia drove down Rifle Range Road toward Six Mile with Kitty in the passenger seat, a pecan pie on her lap.

"I'm sure there are some very nice people who live out here," Kitty said. "But have you heard of super-predators? They're gangs who drive real slow at night and flash their headlights and if you flash back they follow you to your house and shoot you in the head."

"Doesn't Marjorie Fretwell live around here?" Patricia asked.

"Marjorie Fretwell once sucked a copperhead up in her vacuum cleaner because she didn't know what to do with it and then she had to throw the whole vacuum away," Kitty said. "Don't talk to me about Marjorie Fretwell."

They turned off Rifle Range Road onto the state road that led back into the woods around Six Mile. The houses got smaller and the yards got bigger—wide fields of dead weeds and yellowed finger-grass surrounding trailer homes mounted on cinder blocks and brick shoeboxes with crooked mailboxes out front. Electrical lines drooped across front yards crowded with too many cars that had too few tires.

Narrow roads, no wider than driveways, branched off the state road, plunging past chain-link fences, disappearing into groves of scrub oak and palmettos. Patricia saw the green-and-white reflective street sign for Grill Flame Road at the head of one of them, and she turned.

"At least lock your doors," Kitty said, and Patricia hit the door lock button, making a comforting *clunk*.

She drove slow. The road was potholed and its asphalt edges crumbled off into sand. Houses crowded around it at odd angles. A lot of them had been torn up during Hurricane Hugo and re-built by carpetbagging contractors who'd left before their work was complete. Some had heavy plastic stapled over their window frames instead of glass; others had framed rooms left unfinished and exposed to the weather.

No one's yards were landscaped. All the trees were encrusted in vines. A skinny black man in shorts with no shirt sat on the front steps of his trailer drinking water out of a plastic one-gallon jug. Some little children in diapers stopped running through a sprinkler and pressed up against a chain-link fence to watch them drive by.

"Look for number sixteen," Patricia said, concentrating on the potholed road.

They nosed forward beneath a scrub oak whose branches scraped the roof, then emerged into a big, sandy clearing. The road made a loop around a small, unpainted cinder-block church shaped like a shoebox. A sign out front proclaimed it to be Mt. Zion A.M.E. Neat little white and blue houses surrounded it. Down at the far end, some boys ran around a basketball court in the shade where the trees started, but here in front of the houses there was no shelter from the sun.

"Sixteen," Kitty said, and Patricia saw a clean white house with black shutters and white, pressed-tin porch columns. A sun-faded cardboard cutout of Santa's face sat inside a plastic holly wreath on the front door. Patricia parked at the end of the drive.

"I'll wait in the car," Kitty said.

"I'm taking the keys so you won't be able to run the air conditioner," Patricia said.

Kitty gathered her courage for a moment, then heaved herself up and followed Patricia outside. Instantly, the hot sun pierced the crown of Patricia's head like a nail and bounced off the Volvo, blinding her.

In the next sandy driveway over, three little girls skipped rope, double Dutch. Patricia stood for a minute, listening to their rhyme:

Boo Daddy, Boo Daddy
In the woods
Grabbed a little boy
'Cause he taste so good
Boo Daddy, Boo Daddy
In the sheets
Sucking all your blood
'Cause it taste so sweet

She wondered where they'd learned something like that. She walked around the hood of the car and headed for Mrs. Greene's, Kitty falling in beside her, and then she sensed movement behind them. She turned and saw a crowd of people coming their way, walking fast from the basketball courts, and before she or Kitty could move there were boys in front of them, boys behind them, boys leaning on the hood of her car, boys all around them, adopting lounging postures, fencing them in.

"What are you doing here?" one asked.

His white T-shirt was covered in random blue stripes and his hair was cut into a big wedge with straight lines shaved into one side.

"Nothing to say?" he said. "I asked you a question. What, the fuck, are you doing out here? 'Cause I don't think you live here. I don't think you got invited here. So what, the fuck?"

He performed for the boys around him and they made their faces hard, stepped in close, crowded Kitty and Patricia together.

"Please," Kitty said. "We're leaving right now."

A few of the boys grinned and Patricia felt a flash of anger. Why was Kitty such a coward?

"Too late for that," Wedgehead said.

"We're visiting a friend," Patricia said, clutching her purse tighter.

"You don't have any friends out here, bitch!" the boy exploded, pushing his face into hers.

Patricia saw her pale, frightened face reflected twice in his sunglasses. She looked weak. Kitty was right. They never should have come out here. She'd made a terrible mistake. She pulled her neck into her shoulders and got ready to be stabbed or shoved or whatever came next.

"Edwin Miles!" a woman's voice snapped through the sizzling air.

Everyone turned except Wedgehead, who kept his face so close to Patricia's she could count the sparse hairs in his mustache.

"Edwin Miles," the voice called again. This time he turned. "What are you playing at?"

Patricia turned and saw Mrs. Greene standing in the door to her house. She wore a red T-shirt and blue jeans and her arms were covered with white gauze pads.

"Who are these bitches?" the boy, Edwin Miles, called to Mrs. Greene.

"Don't you use that language with me," Mrs. Greene said. "I'll talk to your mother on Sunday."

"She don't care," Edwin Miles shouted back.

"You see if she doesn't once I'm through talking to her," Mrs. Greene said, walking toward them.

The boys faded before her, falling back in the face of her wrath. The last one standing was Edwin Miles.

"All right, all right," he said, stepping backward. "I didn't know they were with you, Mrs. G. You know us, we like to keep an eye on the comings and the goings."

"I'll comings-and-goings you," Mrs. Greene snapped. She reached them and gave Patricia and Kitty a sudden smile. "It's cooler in the house."

She walked toward her house without a backward glance, and Patricia and Kitty scampered along in her wake. Behind them they heard Edwin Miles's voice fading as he walked away with his friends.

"I'll just leave them here with you, Mrs. G.," he called. "It's all good. Didn't know you knew them, that's all."

The little girls started jumping rope again as they passed:

Boo Daddy, Boo Daddy
One, two, three
Sneaking in my window
And sucking on me.

Inside the house, Mrs. Greene closed the door and it took a moment for Patricia's eyes to adjust to the cool darkness.

"I am so grateful, Mrs. Greene," Kitty said. "I thought we were going to die. How do we get to Patricia's car? Do we need to call someone?"

"Like who?" Mrs. Greene asked.

"The police?" Kitty suggested.

"The police?" Mrs. Greene said. "What would they do? Jesse!" she hollered. A skinny little boy with a serious face appeared in the hall door. "Get some tea for our guests."

"Oh," Patricia said, almost forgetting. "I brought you something."

She held out the pecan pie.

"Jesse, put this in the refrigerator," Mrs. Greene said.

She passed it to him and he disappeared back down the hall and Mrs. Greene gestured to the sofa. This close, Patricia could see that her knuckles bristled with stitches.

Mrs. Greene limped stiffly to a La-Z-Boy recliner that bore the imprint of her body. Patricia's eyes had finally adjusted to the dim room and she realized it was full of Christmas. Red, green, and yellow Christmas tree lights ran around the ceiling. A large, artificial tree dominated one corner. Every lamp was made of an oversized nutcracker or a ceramic Christmas tree, and every lampshade sported a smiling Santa or a snowman. On the wall next to Patricia was a framed cross-stitch of Santa Claus holding the baby Jesus.

Patricia perched on the edge of the sofa, closest to Mrs. Greene. The bright white sterile dressings on Mrs. Greene's arms glowed in the dim room.

"You have to forgive those boys," Mrs. Greene said, settling into her chair. "Everyone out here has their nerves up about strangers."

"Because of super-predators," Kitty said, sitting gingerly on the other end of the sofa.

"No, ma'am," Mrs. Greene said. "Because of the children."

"Are they on drugs?" Kitty asked.

"No one out here's on drugs as far as I know," Mrs. Greene said. "Unless you count brown liquor or a little bit of rabbit tobacco."

Patricia felt like it was important to change the subject.

"How are you feeling?" she asked.

"They gave me pills," Mrs. Greene said. "But I don't like the way they make me do, so I stick with Tylenol."

"We are so grateful that you were there, and I know—and Dr. Campbell knows—that no one could have done more," Patricia said. "We feel responsible for leaving those windows open in the first place, so we wanted you to have this."

She put a check, folded in half, on the arm of Mrs. Greene's La-Z-Boy. Mrs. Greene picked up the check and opened it. Patricia was proud of the amount. It was almost twice what Carter had wanted to write. She felt disappointed when Mrs. Greene's expression didn't change. Instead she folded the check back up and tucked it into her breast pocket.

"Mrs. Campbell," she said, "I don't need charity from you. I need work."

Patricia saw the situation in a flash. With Mrs. Greene unable to do anything physical she had probably lost her other clients. Suddenly the amount of the check seemed woefully small.

"But you'll still work for us," Patricia said. "As soon as you're feeling better."

"I can't do much for another week," Mrs. Greene said.

"That's what the check is supposed to cover," Patricia said, happy to suddenly have a plan. "But after that I can use your help getting the house back together, and maybe cooking supper, too."

Mrs. Greene nodded once and closed her eyes, head leaned back against the chair.

"God provides for those who believe," she said.

"He does," Patricia said.

They sat silently in the glow of the Christmas tree lights, the colors changing quietly against the walls until Jesse entered the living room, walking slowly, holding a pressed-tin NFL tray in front of him bearing two glasses of iced tea. The ice chimed against the glasses as he walked across the room and lowered the tray to the coffee table.

"Go on, useless," Mrs. Greene said, and the boy looked at her.

She smiled at him; he smiled back and slipped out of the room.

Mrs. Greene watched Patricia and Kitty sip their iced tea. When she spoke again, her voice was low.

"I need to make that money fast," she said. "I'm sending my boys up to live with my sister in Irmo for the summer."

"On vacation?" Patricia asked.

"To keep them alive," Mrs. Greene said. "You heard those Nancy girls chanting out there. There's something in the wood's been taking our babies."

CHAPTER 14

"We really should get going," Kitty said, putting her iced tea back on the coffee table.

"Just a minute," Patricia said. "What's happening to the children?"

Kitty twisted around on the sofa and cracked the curtains, letting a slash of harsh sunlight into the living room.

"That boy is still hanging around your car," she informed Patricia, letting go of the curtains.

"It's nothing you ought to trouble yourself about," Mrs. Greene said. "I would just feel a whole lot safer with my babies away."

For two months, ever since she'd been bitten, Patricia had felt useless and scared. The Old Village she'd lived in for six years had always been someplace safe, where children left their bicycles in their front yards, and only a few people ever locked their front doors, and no one ever locked their back doors. It didn't feel safe now. She needed an explanation, something she could solve that would make everything go back to the way it was.

The check had been poorly judged and not nearly enough. She'd come out here to help and gotten into trouble with those boys and Mrs. Greene had had to help her out instead. But if there was some trouble with her children, she could maybe do something about that. Here was something tangible. Patricia felt victory at hand.

"Mrs. Greene," Patricia said. "Tell me what's wrong with Jesse and Aaron. I want to help."

"Nothing's wrong with them," Mrs. Greene said, pulling herself to the edge of her recliner, as close as she could get to Patricia so she could talk low. "But I don't want to have happen to them what happened to the Reed boy, or the others."

"What happened to them?" Patricia asked.

"Since May," Mrs. Greene said, "we've had two little boys turn up dead and Francine has gone missing."

The room stayed silent as the Christmas tree lights cycled through their colors.

"I haven't read anything about it in the newspaper," Kitty said.

"I'm a liar?" Mrs. Greene asked, and Patricia saw her eyes get hard.

"No one says you're lying," Patricia reassured her.

"She just did," Mrs. Greene said. "Came right out and said it."

"I read the paper every day," Kitty shrugged. "I just haven't heard anything about children going missing or getting killed."

"Then I guess I made up a story," Mrs. Greene said. "I guess those little girls you heard singing out there made up their rhymes, too. They call him the Boo Daddy because that's what they say's in the woods. That's why those boys were so nervous about strangers. We all know someone's out here sniffing after the children."

"What about Francine?" Patricia asked.

"She's gone," Mrs. Greene said. "No one's seen her car since May fifteen or so. The police say she's run off with a man, but I know she wouldn't leave without her cat."

"She left her cat?" Patricia asked.

"Had to get someone from the church to sneak open her window and get it out before it starved," Mrs. Greene said.

Next to her, Patricia felt Kitty turn and look through the curtains again, and she wanted to tell her to stop squirming but she didn't want to break Mrs. Greene's concentration.

"And what about the children?" Patricia asked.

"The little Reed boy," Mrs. Greene said. "He killed himself. Eight years old."

Kitty stopped wiggling.

"That's not possible," she said. "Eight-year-old children don't commit suicide."

"This one did," Mrs. Greene said. "Got hit by a tow truck while he was waiting for the school bus. The police say he was fooling around and stumbled in the road, but the other children in line with him say different. They say Orville Reed stepped right out in front of that truck deliberate. It knocked him clean out of his shoes, threw him fifty feet down the street. When they had his funeral he looked like he was just sleeping there in his coffin. Only thing different was a little tiny bruise on the side of his face."

"But if the police think it was an accident . . . ," Patricia began.

"The police think all kind of things," Mrs. Greene said. "Doesn't necessarily make them true."

"I haven't seen anything in the paper," Kitty protested.

"The paper doesn't talk about what happens in Six Mile," Mrs. Greene said. "We're not quite Mt. Pleasant, not quite Awendaw, not quite anyplace. Certainly not the Old Village. Besides, one little boy has an accident, an old lady runs away with some man, the police figure it's just colored people being colored. It'd be like reporting on a fish for being wet. The only one that looks unnatural is what happened to that other boy, Orville Reed's cousin, Sean."

Patricia felt caught up in a particularly lurid and unstoppable bedtime story and now it was her turn to prompt the teller.

"What happened to Sean?" she asked.

"Before he died, Orville's mother and auntie say he got real moody," Mrs. Greene said. "They say he was irritable and sleepy all the time. His mother says he took long walks out in the woods every day when the sun started to go down, and came back giggling, and then the next day he'd be sick and unhappy again. He wouldn't take food, would hardly drink water, he'd just stare at the television, whether it was cartoons or commercials, and it was like he was asleep while he was awake. He limped when he walked and cried when she asked him what the matter was. And she couldn't keep him out of those woods."

"What was he doing out there?" Kitty asked, leaning forward.

"His cousin tried to find out," Mrs. Greene said. "Tanya Reed didn't care for that boy, Sean. She put a padlock on her refrigerator because he kept stealing her groceries. He used to come over when she wasn't home from work and smoke cigarettes in her house and watch cartoons with Orville. She tolerated it because she thought Orville needed a male role model, even a bad one. She said Sean got worried about Orville going in the woods all the time. Sean told her he thought someone in the woods was doing something to Orville. Tanya wouldn't listen. Just threw him right out on his behind.

"One of the men who hangs around the basketball court has a few pistols and rents them to people. He says Sean couldn't afford to rent a gun, so he rented him a hammer for three dollars, and he says Sean told him he was going to follow his little cousin into the woods and scare off whoever was bothering him. But the next time they saw Sean he was dead. The man says he still had his hammer, too, for all the good it did. Says Sean was found by a big live oak back in the deep woods where someone had picked him up and mashed his face against the bark and scraped it right down to the skull. They couldn't have an open casket at Sean's funeral."

Patricia realized she wasn't breathing. She carefully let out the air in her lungs.

"That had to be in the papers," she said.

"It was," Mrs. Greene said. "The police called it 'drug-related' because Sean had been in that kind of trouble before. But no one out here thinks it was and that's why everyone's real skittish about strangers. Before he stepped in front of that truck, Orville Reed told his mother he was talking to a white man in the woods, but she thought maybe he was talking about one of his cartoons. No one thinks that after what happened to Sean. Sometimes other children say they see a white man standing at the edge of the woods, waving to them. Some people wake up and say they see a pale man staring in through their window screens, but that can't be true because the last one to say that was Becky Washington and she lives up on the second floor. How'd a man get up there?"

Patricia thought about the hand vanishing over the edge of the sun porch overhang, the footsteps on the roof over Blue's room, and she felt her stomach contract.

"What do you think it is?" she asked.

Mrs. Greene settled back in her chair.

"I say it's a man. One who drives a van and used to live in Texas. I even got his license plate number."

Kitty and Patricia looked at each other and then at her.

"You got his license plate number?" Kitty asked.

"I keep a pad by the front window," Mrs. Greene said. "If I see a car driving around I don't know, I write down the license plate number in case something happens and the police need it later for evidence. Well, last week, I heard an engine buzzing late one night. I got up and saw it turning, leaving Six Mile, heading back for the state road, but it was a white van and before it turned off I got most of its license plate number."

She put her hands on the arms of her chair, pulled herself up, and limped to a little table by the front door. She picked up a spiral notebook and opened it, scanning the pages, then she limped back to Patricia, turned the notebook around, and presented it to her.

Texas, it read. - - *X 13S.*

"That's all I had time to write," Mrs. Greene said. "It was turning when I caught it. But I know it was a Texas plate."

"Did you tell the police?" Patricia asked.

"Yes, ma'am," Mrs. Greene said. "And they said *thank you very much and we'll call if we have any further questions* but I guess they didn't because I never got a call. So you can understand why people out here don't have much patience with strangers. Especially white ones. Especially now with Destiny Taylor."

"Who's Destiny Taylor?" Kitty asked before Patricia could.

"Her mother goes to my church," Mrs. Greene said. "She came to me one day after services and wanted me to see her little girl."

"Why?" Patricia asked.

"People know I'm in the medical field," Mrs. Greene said. "They're always trying to get free advice. Now, Wanda Taylor doesn't work, just takes a government check, and I can't abide lazy people, but she's my cousin's best friend's sister, so I said I'd look at her little girl. She's nine years old and sleeping all hours of the day. Not eating, real lethargic, barely drinking water and this weather is hot. I asked Wanda if Destiny's going into the woods, and she says she doesn't know, but sometimes she'll find twigs and leaves in her shoes at night, so she reckons maybe."

"How long has this been going on?" Patricia asked.

"She says about two weeks," Mrs. Greene said.

"What did you tell her?" Patricia asked.

"I told her she needed to get her little girl out of town," Mrs. Greene said. "Get her someplace else by hook or by crook. Six Mile isn't safe for children anymore."

CHAPTER 15

Patricia only knew one person who owned a white van. She dropped Kitty off at Seewee Farms and with a heavy sense of dread drove to the Old Village, turned onto Middle Street, and slowed to look at James Harris's house. Instead of the white van in his front yard, she saw a red Chevy Corsica parked on the grass, glowing like a puddle of fresh blood beneath the angry late-afternoon sun. She drove by at five miles an hour, squinting painfully at the Corsica, willing it to turn back into a white van.

Of course, Grace knew exactly where to find her notebook.

"I know it's probably nothing," Patricia said, stepping into Grace's front hall, pulling the door shut behind her. "I hate to even bother you, but I have this terrible thought gnawing at me and I need to check."

Grace peeled off her yellow rubber gloves, opened the drawer of her hall table, and pulled out a spiral-bound notebook.

"Do you want some coffee?" she asked.

"Please," Patricia said, taking the notebook and following Grace into her kitchen.

"Let me just make some room," Grace said.

The kitchen table was covered in newspaper and in the middle stood two plastic tubs lined with towels, one filled with soapy water, the other filled with clean. Antique china lay on the table in orderly rows, surrounded by cotton rags and rolls of paper towel.

"I'm cleaning Grandmother's wedding china today," Grace said, carefully moving the fragile teacups to make room for Patricia. "It takes a long time to do it the old-fashioned way, but anything worth doing is worth doing well."

Patricia sat down, centered Grace's notebook in front of her, then flipped it open. Grace set her mug of coffee down, and bitter steam stung Patricia's nostrils.

"Milk and sugar?" Grace asked.

"Both, please," Patricia said, not looking up.

Grace put the cream and sugar next to Patricia, then went back to her routine. The only sound was gentle sloshing as she dipped each piece of china into the soapy water, then the clean. Patricia paged through her notebook. Every page was covered in Grace's meticulous cursive, every entry separated by a blank line. They all started with a date, and then came a description of the vehicle— *Black boxy car, Tall red sports vehicle, Unusual truck-type automobile*— followed by a license plate number.

Patricia's coffee cooled as she read—*Irregular green car with large wheels, Perhaps a jeep, Needs washing*—and then her heart stopped and blood drained from her brain.

April 8, 1993, the entry read. *Ann Savage's House—parked on grass—White Dodge Van with drug dealer windows, Texas, TNX 13S.*

A high-pitched whine filled Patricia's ears.

"Grace," she said. "Would you read this, please?"

She turned the notebook toward Grace.

"He killed her grass parking on it like that," Grace said, after she read the entry. "Her lawn is never going to recover."

Patricia pulled a sticky note from her pocket and placed it next to the notebook. It read, *Mrs. Greene—white van, Texas plate, - - X 13S.*

"Mrs. Greene wrote down this partial license plate number from a car she saw in Six Mile last week," Patricia said. "Kitty went with me to take her a pie and she scorched our ears with this story. One of the children at Six Mile committed suicide after he was sick for a long time."

"How tragic," Grace said.

"His cousin was murdered, too," Patricia said. "At the same time, they saw a white van driving around with this license plate number. It niggled at the back of my mind, thinking where else I'd seen a white van, and then I remembered James Harris had one. He's got a red car now, but these plates match his van."

"I don't know what you're implying," Grace said.

"I don't either," Patricia said.

James Harris had told her his ID was being mailed to him. She wondered if it had ever arrived, but it must have, otherwise how had he bought a car? Was he driving around without a license? Or had he lied to her about not having any ID? She wondered why someone wouldn't use their identification to open a bank or a utility account. She thought about that bag of cash. The only reason she thought it belonged to Ann Savage was because he said so.

They had read too many books about mafia hit men moving to the suburbs under assumed names and drug dealers living quietly among their unsuspecting neighbors for Patricia not to start connecting dots. You kept your name off public records if you were wanted for something by the government. You had a bag of money because that was how you had been paid, and people who got paid in cash were either hit men, drug dealers, bank robbers—or waiters, she supposed. But James Harris didn't seem like a waiter.

Then again, he was their friend and neighbor. He talked about Nazis with Blue and drew her son out of his shell. He ate with them when Carter wasn't home and made her feel safe. He had come around the house to check on them that night someone got on the roof.

"I don't know what to think," she repeated to Grace, who dipped a serving platter in the soapy water and tilted it from side to side. "Mrs. Greene told us that a Caucasian male is coming into Six Mile and doing something to the children that makes them sick. She thinks he might be driving a white van. And it's only been happening since May. That's right after James Harris moved here."

"You're under the influence of this month's book," Grace said, lifting the platter out of the soapy water and rinsing it in the tub of clean. "James Harris is our neighbor. He is Ann Savage's grand-nephew. He is not driving out to Six Mile and doing something to their children."

"Of course not," Patricia said. "But you read about drug dealers living around normal people, or sex abusers bothering children and getting away with it for so long, and you start to wonder what we really know about anyone. I mean, James Harris says he grew up all around, but then says he grew up in South Dakota. He says he lived in Vermont, but his van had Texas plates."

"You have suffered two terrible blows this summer," Grace said, lifting the platter and gently drying it. "Your ear has barely healed. You are still grieving for Miss Mary. This man is not a criminal based on when he moved here and the license plate of a passing car."

"Isn't that how every serial killer gets away with it for so long?" Patricia asked. "Everyone ignores the little things and Ted Bundy keeps killing women until finally someone does what they should have done in the first place and connects the little things that didn't add up, but by then it's too late."

Grace set the gleaming platter on the table. Creamy white, it featured brightly colored butterflies and a pair of birds on a branch, all picked out in delicate, near-invisible brushstrokes.

"This is real," Grace said, running one finger along its rim. "It's solid, and it's whole, and my grandmother received it as a wedding gift, and she gave it to my mother, and she passed it down to me, and when the time comes, if I deem her appropriate, I'll hand it down to whomever Ben marries. Focus on the real things in your life and I promise you'll feel better."

"I didn't tell you this," Patricia said, "but when I met him he showed me a bag of money. Grace, he had over eighty thousand dollars in there. In cash. Who has that just lying around?"

"What did he say?" Grace asked, dipping a tureen lid in the soapy water.

"He told me he'd found it in the crawl space. That it was Ann Savage's nest egg."

"She never struck me as the kind of woman who'd trust a bank," Grace said, rinsing the tureen lid in clean water.

"Grace, it doesn't add up!" Patricia said. "Stop cleaning and listen to me. At what point do we get concerned?"

"Never," Grace said, drying the tureen lid. "Because you are spinning a fantasy out of coincidences to distract yourself from reality. I understand that sometimes reality can be overwhelming, but it must be faced."

"I'm the one facing it," Patricia said.

"No," Grace said. "You stood right there on my front porch after book club two months ago and said you wished that a crime or something exciting would happen here because you couldn't stand your routine. And now you've convinced yourself something dangerous is happening so you can act like a detective."

Grace picked up a stack of saucers and began placing them in the soapy water.

"Can't you stop cleaning china for a second and admit that maybe I'm right about this?" Patricia asked.

"No," Grace said. "I can't. Because I need to be finished by 5:30 so I can clear off the table and set it for supper. Bennett's coming home at six."

"There are more important things than cleaning," Patricia said.

Grace stopped, holding the last two saucers in her hand, and turned on Patricia, eyes blazing.

"Why do you pretend what we do is nothing?" she asked. "Every day, all the chaos and messiness of life happens and every day we clean it all up. Without us, they would just wallow in filth and disorder and nothing of any consequence would ever get done.

Who taught you to sneer at that? I'll tell you who. Someone who took their mother for granted."

Grace glared at Patricia, nostrils flaring.

"I'm sorry," Patricia said. "I didn't mean to offend you. I'm just worried about James Harris."

Grace put the last two saucers in the soapy water bin.

"I'll tell you everything you need to know about James Harris," she said. "He lives in the Old Village. With us. There isn't anything wrong with him because people who have something wrong with them don't live here."

Patricia hated that she couldn't put into words this feeling gnawing at her guts. She felt foolish that she couldn't shift Grace's certainty even for a moment.

"Thank you for putting up with me," she said. "I need to start supper."

"Vacuum your curtains," Grace said. "No one ever does it enough. I promise it'll make you feel better."

Patricia wanted that to be true very badly.

"Mom," Blue said from the living room door. "What's for supper?"

"Food," Patricia said from the sofa.

"Is it chicken again?" he asked.

"Is chicken food?" Patricia replied, not looking up from her book.

"We had chicken last night," Blue said. "And the night before. And the night before that."

"Maybe tonight will be different," Patricia said.

She heard Blue's footsteps retreat to the hall, walk into the den, go into the kitchen. Ten seconds later he reappeared at the living room door.

"There's chicken defrosting in the sink," he said in an accusatory tone.

"What?" Patricia asked, looking up from her book.

"We're having chicken again," he said.

A pang of guilt twisted through Patricia. He was right—she'd made nothing but chicken all week. They'd order pizza. It was just the two of them and it was a Friday night.

"I promise," she said. "We're not having chicken."

He gave her a sideways look, then went back upstairs and slammed his bedroom door. Patricia went back to her book: *The Stranger Beside Me: The Shocking Inside Story of Serial Killer Ted Bundy*. The more she read, the more uncertain she felt about everything in her life, but she couldn't stop.

Not-quite-book-club loved Ann Rule, of course, and her *Small Sacrifices* had long been one of their favorites, but they'd never read the book that made her famous, and Kitty was shocked when she found out.

"Y'all," Kitty had said. "She was just a housewife who wrote about murders for crummy detective magazines, and then she got a deal to write about these coed murders happening all over Seattle. Well, she winds up finding out that the main suspect is her best friend at a suicide hotline where she works—Ted Bundy."

He wasn't Ann Rule's best friend, just a good friend, Patricia learned as she read, but otherwise everything Kitty said was true.

That just goes to show, Grace had pronounced, *whenever you call one of those so-called hotlines, you have no clue who's on the other end of that phone. It could be anyone.*

But the further she got into the book, the more Patricia wondered not how Ann Rule could have missed the clues that her good friend was a serial killer, but how well she herself actually knew the men around her. Slick had called Patricia last week, breathless, because Kitty had sold her a set of her Grandmother Roberts's silver but asked her not to mention it to anyone. It was William Hutton and Slick couldn't help herself—she needed someone to know that she'd gotten it for a song. She'd chosen Patricia.

Kitty told me she needed extra money to send the children to summer camp, Slick had said over the phone. *Do you think they're in trouble? Seewee Farms is expensive, and it's not like Horse works.*

Horse seemed so solid and dependable, but apparently he was spending all his family's money on treasure-hunting expeditions while Kitty snuck around selling off family heirlooms to pay camp fees. Blue would grow up to go to college and play sports and meet a nice girl one day who would never know he was once so obsessed with Nazis he couldn't talk about anything else.

She knew that Carter spent so much time at the hospital because he wanted to be head of psychiatry, but she wondered what else he did there. She was relatively sure he wasn't seeing a woman, but she also knew that since his mother had died he was spending fewer and fewer hours at home. Was he at the hospital every time he said he was? It shocked her to realize how little she knew about what he did between leaving the house in the morning and coming home at night.

What about Bennett, and Leland, and Ed, who all seemed so normal? She was starting to wonder if anyone really knew what people were like on the inside.

She ordered pizza and let Blue watch *The Sound of Music* after supper. He only liked the scenes with the Nazis and knew exactly when and where to fast-forward so the three-hour movie flew by in fifty-five minutes. Then he went upstairs to his room and closed the door, and did whatever it was he did in there these days, and Patricia's mood darkened while she washed the dishes. It was too late to run the vacuum cleaner and vacuum her curtains, so she decided to take a quick walk. Without meaning to, her feet took her right past James Harris's house. His car wasn't out front. Had he driven up to Six Mile? Was he seeing Destiny Taylor right this minute?

Her head felt dirty. She didn't like thinking these thoughts. She tried to remember what Grace had said. James Harris had moved here to take care of his sick great-aunt. He had decided to stay. He wasn't a drug dealer, or a child molester, or a mafia hit man in hiding, or a serial killer. She knew that. But when she got home she went upstairs, took out her day planner, and counted the days. She had taken the casserole to James Harris's house and seen Francine on May 15, the day Mrs. Greene said she went missing.

Everything felt wrong. Carter was never home. Mrs. Savage had bitten off a piece of her ear. Miss Mary had died terribly. Francine had run away with a man. An eight-year-old boy had killed himself. A little girl might do the same. This wasn't any of her business. But who looked out for the children? Even the ones who weren't their own?

She called Mrs. Greene and part of her hoped she wouldn't pick up. But she did.

"I'm sorry to call after nine," she apologized. "But how well do you know Destiny Taylor's mother?"

"Wanda Taylor isn't someone I spend a lot of time thinking about," Mrs. Greene said.

"Do you think we could talk to her about her daughter?" Patricia asked. "That license plate you saw, I think it belongs to a man who lives here. James Harris. Francine worked for him and I saw her at his house on May 15. And there are some funny things with him. I wonder if we could talk to Destiny, maybe she could tell us if she'd seen him out at Six Mile."

"People don't like strangers asking after their children," Mrs. Greene said.

"We're all mothers," Patricia said. "If something were happening to one of ours and someone thought they knew something, wouldn't you want to know? And if it turns out to be nothing, all we've done is bother her on a Friday night. It's not even ten."

There was a long pause, and then:

"Her light's still on," Mrs. Greene said. "Get out here quick and let's get this over with."

Patricia found Blue in his room, sitting on his beanbag chair, reading *The Rise and Fall of the Third Reich*.

"I need to run out for a little while," Patricia said. "Just to the church. There's a meeting of the deacons I forgot. Will you be okay?"

"Is Dad home?" Blue asked.

"He's on his way," Patricia said, although she didn't really know. "Will you answer the phone? I'm going to lock the front door. Your father has his key."

"Okay," Blue said, barely looking up from his book.

"I love you," Patricia said, but Blue didn't seem to hear.

Patricia hesitated in her bedroom for a moment. She had never lied about where she would be before, and it made her feel nervous. She decided to leave a note for Carter on their dresser telling him where she was and giving him Mrs. Greene's phone number. On it she wrote, *Need to give Mrs. Greene a check.* Then she got in her Volvo and hoped Grace was right and this was all just a product of the overactive imagination of a stupid little housewife with too much free time on her hands. If it was, she promised herself, tomorrow she would vacuum her curtains.

CHAPTER 16

There were no other cars on Rifle Range Road and the drive felt lonely. The streetlights stopped at the state road, and the narrow, crumbling one-lane road winding through the trees and chain-link fences felt too narrow. Patricia's headlights brushed across mobile homes and prefabricated sheds and she worried she might be waking people up. She checked her dashboard clock—9:35 p.m.—but the absolute dark of the country road made it feel much later.

She parked in front of Mrs. Greene's and, after looking around to make sure no one was on the basketball court, she stepped out of her Volvo and into a buzzing, razzing night, furious with insects. Scattered streetlights glowed orange over the cinder-block houses and trailers, but they were spaced so far apart the darkness felt even more vast and lonely. When Mrs. Greene opened her front door Patricia felt relieved to see a familiar face.

"Would you like something to drink?" Mrs. Greene asked.

"I think it's best if we see Mrs. Taylor before it's too late," Patricia said.

"Jesse?" Mrs. Greene called back into her house. "Look after your brother. I'm going across the way."

She closed and locked her door behind her, the plastic holly wreath scratching against the aluminum door as it swung from side to side.

"This way," Mrs. Greene said, leading her down the sandy path in front of her house.

They walked onto the dirt road that circled the little church, then stepped over the ankle-high railing in front of Mt. Zion A.M.E., cutting through the center of Six Mile. They crunched over the sandy soil, their footsteps loud in the night. No one sat outside on their porch, no one called to their friends, no one passed them on the way home. The dirt roads of Six Mile were deserted. Patricia saw curtains drawn over most of the windows. Others had cardboard or bedsheets tacked up over them instead. From behind all of them came the cold, blue shifting light of television.

"No one goes out after dark around here anymore," Mrs. Greene said.

"What should we say to Mrs. Taylor so we don't upset her?" Patricia asked.

"Wanda Taylor gets out of bed upset," Mrs. Greene said.

Patricia wondered how she'd react if someone showed up on her doorstep to tell her Blue was on drugs.

"Do you think she'll be angry?" she asked.

"Probably," Mrs. Greene said.

"Maybe this is a bad idea," Patricia said.

"It *is* a bad idea," Mrs. Greene said, turning to face her. "But you told me you were worried about her little girl and now I can't stop thinking about that. She may not roll out the welcome wagon, but you convinced me we're doing what's right. Don't convince me to come out halfway and then go back in."

A yellow bulb burned over the door of Wanda Taylor's trailer, and before Patricia could ask for a moment to gather herself, they had walked up the rotten front porch and Mrs. Greene was knocking on the rattling metal door. The rickety porch swayed back and forth beneath their feet. Moths tapped at the yellow lightbulb. Patricia could feel heat radiating off it, making her scalp and forehead prickle. Just when she couldn't stand the warmth anymore, the door opened and Wanda Taylor stared out at them. She wore a drug company T-shirt and stonewashed blue jeans and hadn't done her hair. Behind her, Patricia heard a TV playing.

"Evening, Wanda," Mrs. Greene said.

"It's late," Wanda said, then took in Patricia. "Who's that?"

She spoke to Mrs. Greene as if Patricia weren't there.

"Can we come inside?" Mrs. Greene asked.

"No," Wanda Taylor said. "It's almost ten o'clock. Some people have to get up in the morning."

"You came to me about Destiny and I thought you might have a few minutes to discuss the health of your little girl," Mrs. Greene said, her voice prickly.

Wanda screwed her face up in disbelief.

"I came to you about Destiny and you told me to go to the doctor if I was so worried," she said. "That's what I'm doing, first thing tomorrow morning, we're going to the clinic."

"Mrs. Taylor," Patricia said. "I'm a nurse from the clinic. I thought Destiny's condition might be urgent so I came to see you tonight. How old is she?"

Wanda and Mrs. Greene stared at Patricia, both for different reasons.

"Nine," Wanda finally said. "You have some ID?"

"She works at the clinic," Mrs. Greene said. "She's not the police. She's not from DSS. She doesn't have a badge."

Wanda studied Patricia, her face shadowed by the yellow light.

"All right," she finally said, used to doing what people in authority told her. She stepped backward into her trailer. "But she's sleeping right now, so keep your voices low."

They followed her inside. It felt crowded and smelled like cooked hamburger meat. A black plastic sofa sat across from a television with a built-in VCR resting on top of a cardboard box. A window-unit air conditioner chuffed out frozen air beneath the venetian blinds. Wanda gestured to a rickety table in the kitchen alcove and Patricia and Mrs. Greene sat down in its padded, thrift-store chairs.

"Do you want some Kool-Aid?" she asked. "Lite beer?"

"No, thank you," Patricia said.

Wanda turned to her kitchen cabinets, took out two snack packs of Fritos, pulled them open, and poured them into a Styrofoam cereal bowl.

"Help yourselves," she said, putting it on the table between them.

"We really should see Destiny for a minute," Patricia said. "I'd like to ask her some questions about her condition."

"You have to talk to her now?" Wanda asked.

"Wanda," Mrs. Greene said. "You need to do what the nurse tells you."

Wanda took three steps down the hall and scratched on a beige, plastic accordion door.

"Dessy," she whispered in a singsong.

The window-unit air conditioner froze the air. Patricia's skin prickled with goose bumps. The top of the table felt sticky. She kept her hands in her lap.

"Dessy, wakey wakey," Wanda sang, sliding open the partition.

She clicked on a lamp in the bedroom.

"Dessy?" Wanda said.

She stepped into the hall and opened another door, this one revealing the bathroom.

"Dessy? Where're you hiding?" Wanda said, and her voice had an edge to it.

Patricia and Mrs. Greene crowded into the little hall and stood in the door of Destiny's room.

"She was right here not half an hour ago," Wanda said, kneeling on the floor.

The bedroom was so tiny Wanda's legs stuck out into the hall as she leaned her head underneath the sleeping platform. On top lay a foam mattress cove ' with a My Little Pony fitted sheet and a folded plaid blanket. he little girl's toys and clothes were stacked up in clear plastic boxes in the corner. A window over the bed was an uncurtained black rectangle looking out at the night.

"Where's Dessy?" Wanda said, her voice starting to fray. "What did you do to her?"

"We just got here," Mrs. Greene said.

Wanda shoved past Patricia and ran into the living room like she was going to catch her invisible daughter at the door.

"Dessy?" she called.

"What do you think?" Mrs. Greene asked Patricia, voice low.

In the kitchen, Wanda yanked open every cabinet and moved every box and bag.

Patricia pulled on the window over Destiny's bed. Smooth and easy, it slid wide open. There was no screen. A wave of warm air and insect screams rolled into the tiny bedroom. Patricia and Mrs. Greene looked out the open window into the woods just a few feet away. Patricia knelt on the sleeping platform and looked down. Outside the window stood a large wooden spool that telephone cable came on. Someone standing on it could reach right through the window.

They walked back to the living room.

"We need to call the police," Mrs. Greene said.

"What?" Wanda Taylor asked. "What for?"

"Mrs. Taylor," Patricia said. "There is a man named James Harris who has been dealing drugs to children. You need to call the police and tell them that your daughter is missing, and you think he's taken her."

"Oh, Lord Jesus," Wanda said, and she belched loudly, filling the living room with the stench of her stomach acid.

"He has her in the woods," Mrs. Greene said. "He'll still be close by."

She got Wanda seated on the sofa and helped her light a menthol cigarette to settle her nerves. Wanda looked helplessly for an ashtray and finally just tapped her ashes on the carpet. Patricia stretched the kitchen phone into the room, dialed 911, and handed it to Wanda.

"Hello," Wanda Taylor said, smoke puffing out of her mouth to the rhythm of her words. "My name is Wanda Taylor and I live at 32 Grill Flame Road. My daughter is not in her bed." She paused. "No, she is not hiding in the house." Pause. "Because I looked all over and there isn't much house for her to hide in. Please send someone, please. Please."

She didn't know what else to say so she repeated "Please" until Mrs. Greene took the phone from her hand. Wanda looked helplessly from Patricia to Mrs. Greene like she was seeing them for the first time.

"Would you like Kool-Aid or lite beer?" she asked. "It's all I've got. The water out here smells like eggs."

"We're fine, thank you," Patricia said, kindly.

"We need to sit and wait for the police," Mrs. Greene said, patting Wanda's knee. "They'll be here soon."

"If you hadn't come I wouldn't know she was gone," Wanda said. "The police will be here soon?"

"Real soon," Mrs. Greene said, taking her hand.

"I should check her bedroom again," Wanda said.

They let her go. Patricia thought about the three-minute response time in Mt. Pleasant.

"How long until the police get here?" she asked.

"Could be a while," Mrs. Greene said. "This is the country."

Wanda came back into the room and stood in the kitchen.

"She isn't back," she said, then noticed them for the first time again. "Would you like something to drink? I have Kool-Aid and lite beer."

"Wanda," Mrs. Greene said. "You need to sit down and wait for the police."

Wanda pulled a chair out from the sticky table and went to take a drag on her cigarette, but it had burned down to the filter. She searched for her pack. Patricia thought about James Harris, somewhere out in the woods with a little girl in his arms, doing something unspeakable to her. She couldn't picture that part clearly, but she imagined it was Korey. She imagined it was Blue. She imagined the police would be a while.

"Do you have a flashlight?" she asked Wanda.

CHAPTER 17

Patricia went down the shaky front steps with a silver Boy Scout flashlight in one hand. Mrs. Greene stood in the doorway.

"I'm just going to look around the back of the trailer," Patricia said, but Mrs. Greene had already closed and locked the front door. Patricia heard her slide the chain into place.

All over Six Mile she heard the hum of air conditioners. The woods around her were a tornado of screaming insects. Every breath felt like it came through a towel soaked in warm water. She made her legs move, taking her around the dark corner of the trailer.

She clicked on the flashlight and played it over the big wooden spool, as if she might see an incriminating footprint outlined in black ink on its top. She shined her light down on the sandy soil and saw indentations and shadows and lumps but didn't know what any of them meant. She straightened and shined her light at the woods.

The pale yellow beam played over pine trees. They were spaced pretty far apart and she realized she could walk along the edge of them and still keep an eye on the trailer. Before she could think better of it she stepped around the first one, then the second, the flashlight beaming a lamplight circle on the ground in front of her, leading her into the woods step by step, as the screaming insects closed in around her.

Something grabbed her foot and yanked and her heart flooded with cold water before she saw that she'd snagged it on a rusty wire stretched along the ground. She looked back behind her, feeling confident, but the lit windows of the houses were farther away than she'd expected. She wondered if the police had arrived but knew she'd see their blue lights if they had.

The smell of warm sap surrounded her, and pine needles were thick underfoot. She knew this was the last moment when she could turn back. If she kept walking forward she wouldn't be able to see the lit windows at all anymore and then she was going to be out here alone with James Harris.

Hang on, Destiny, she thought as she started walking deeper into the woods. *I'm coming.*

With the flashlight beam bouncing before her, she concentrated on each tree trunk, not the entire dark mass of them crowding around and behind her. She went carefully, not wanting to step in a hole, conscious of the loud crashing sounds her body made as she brushed through the branches, bushes, and vines.

Something that wasn't her rustled to the right. She froze and clicked off her flashlight so it wouldn't give her away. The night rushed in around her. She strained to listen over the sound of blood throbbing in her ears. Her pulse thumped in her wrists. Her breath rasped in her nose. Then she realized: the insects had stopped screaming.

Blobs of dark color flashed across her vision. She heard something scurry through the trees, and suddenly the thought of standing still panicked her, and she needed to move, but without the flashlight she couldn't see her way forward so she clicked it back on and the trees and pine needles on the ground materialized in front of her again.

She moved fast, flashlight pointed down, looking for a little girl's leg clad in denim sticking out from behind a pine tree. Mixed in with the sound of her breath and her heartbeat and her pulse she heard things groaning in the trees all around her; any minute a big hand would settle on the back of her neck. Her pounding heart pulled her forward.

She should turn around and go home. She was nothing but a tiny speck in the forest. She was a fool to think she'd somehow stumble across Destiny Taylor this way, and what was she going to say when she saw James Harris? Was she going to knock him over the head with her little flashlight? She needed to go back.

Then the trees stopped and she stepped onto a dirt road. It wasn't very wide but the sandy soil was loose and she realized someone must be building something nearby because of the big tread marks pressed into its surface. She flashed the light in one direction and saw the little road disappearing into a dark tunnel of trees. She flashed the light in the other direction and saw the chrome grille of James Harris's white van.

She snapped off her light and stepped back into the pines, stumbling over a stump. He could've seen her. She'd snapped her light off in time, but she realized that he could've seen her beam bobbing through the trees as she approached, and then she'd stood there like a dummy looking the other way before shining her light at the van. She wanted to run but made herself hold still instead. The van didn't move.

It wasn't fifty feet away. She could walk over and touch it. She needed to walk over and touch it. She needed to know if he was inside.

She walked toward it, her shoes sinking into the sand, making no sound, her stomach churning. She waited for the headlights to scream on and pin her down, the engine to roar to life and run her over. The van's grille and windshield swam from side to side in her vision, bouncing up and down, getting closer, and then she was there. She realized that inside was darker than outside so she ducked down, knees popping, to make sure he didn't see her head outlined through his windshield against the night sky.

She put out one hand to steady herself. The curve of the hood felt cool. She wondered if the police were at Wanda's trailer yet. She wanted to go back. Didn't drug dealers have guns, and knives, and all kinds of weapons? She imagined Blue in the back of the van and knew she had to look. Destiny Taylor wasn't her child but she was still a child.

Patricia slowly rose, knees cracking, and leaned forward until the edges of her hands touched the cold windshield, and she cupped them around her eyes and peered inside. Beyond the thin crescent rim of the steering wheel it was pitch-dark. She narrowed her eyes until the muscles in them ached, but she couldn't see a thing.

Then she realized he wasn't in the van. He was still in the woods with Destiny, or he'd finished with her and was on his way back. Before he got there she could look inside quickly and see if there were any clues, any clothes from that other child, anything that belonged to Francine. She had seconds.

She walked to the back of the van, wrapped her hand around the door handle, and pulled. Then she raised her flashlight and turned it on.

A man's back bent over something on the floor, his rear end and the soles of his work boots turned toward her, and then his back reared up, and he turned into the flashlight's beam and she saw James Harris. But there was something wrong with the lower half of his face. Something black, shiny, and chitinous like a cockroach's leg, stuck several inches out of his mouth. His jaws hung open, stupefied, as he blinked blearily in the light, but otherwise his body didn't move as this long insectoid appendage slowly withdrew into his mouth, and when it had retreated fully, he closed his lips and she saw that his chin and cheeks and the tip of his nose were coated in slick, wet blood.

Beneath him, a young black girl lay sprawled on the floor, long orange T-shirt pushed up to her stomach, legs akimbo, an ugly dark purple mark on the inside of one thigh, oily with fluids.

James Harris slapped the palm of one hand against the metal side of the van and the vehicle shook from side to side as he hauled himself to his feet. He squinted and Patricia realized her flashlight had blinded him. He took an unsteady, lurching step toward her. She froze, not knowing what to do, and then he took another step, rocking the van more, and she realized there was only three feet between them. The little girl moaned and squirmed like she was asleep, whimpering like Ragtag in his dreams.

The van rocked as James Harris took another step. There were maybe two feet between them now and she had to do something to get that little girl out of there, and he still squinted into the flashlight beam. He reached for it slowly, fingers outstretched, inches from her face. Patricia ran.

The second the flashlight beam was off his face she heard his feet clang once on the van's floor and then hit the sand behind her. She ran into the woods, flashlight on, beam dancing crazily over stumps and trunks and leaves and bushes, and she shoved her way past branches that slapped her face and tree trunks that bruised her shoulders and vines that lashed her ankles. She didn't hear him behind her but she ran. She didn't know for how long, but she knew it was long enough for her flashlight's batteries to dim. She thought these woods would never end, and then the woods spat her out beside a chain-link fence and she knew she was back on one of the roads leading into Six Mile.

She shined her light around but it only made the shadows loom larger and dance crazily. She searched for something familiar and then everything exploded into bright white light and she saw a car coming her way slowly, jouncing up and down the bumpy road, and she cringed against a fence and it stopped, and a police officer's voice said, "Ma'am, do you know who called 911?"

She got in the back and had never been so grateful to hear anything as she was to hear the door slam shut behind her. The air conditioning instantly dried her sweat and left her skin gritty. She saw that the officer had a gun on his hip, and his partner in the passenger seat turned around and asked, "Can you show us the house where the child went missing?" They had a shotgun in a rack between them, and all of it made Patricia feel safe.

"He's got her right now," Patricia said. "He's doing something to her. I saw them in the woods."

The partner said something into a handset and they turned on their flashing lights but not their siren, and the car flew down the narrow road. Patricia saw the Mt. Zion A.M.E. church ahead of them.

"Where did you see them?" the officer asked.

"There's a road," Patricia said as the police car bounced into Six Mile. "A construction road back in the woods behind here."

"Over there," the officer in the passenger seat said, lowering the radio handset, pointing across the car.

The driver turned hard, and mobile homes reeled to the right in their headlights. Then the police car surged forward between two small homes and they left Six Mile behind. Trees surrounded them and the officer driving turned the wheel to the right and Patricia felt its tires slide on sand, heavy and slow, and then they were on the road she'd found.

"This is it," Patricia said. "He's in a white van up ahead."

They slowed, and the officer in the passenger seat used a handle to steer a spotlight mounted outside the car to shine into the woods on both sides of the road, panning across the trees. It was thousands of times brighter than Patricia's little flashlight. They rolled down their windows to listen for a little girl's cries.

Before they knew it, they'd reached the end of the road, coming to where it ran into the state road.

"Maybe we missed him?" one of the officers said.

Patricia didn't look at her watch but she felt like they drove up and down that soft, sandy road for an hour.

"Let's try the house," the driver said.

She directed them back to Six Mile and they parked outside Wanda's trailer. The partner let Patricia out of the back and she ran up the rickety front porch and banged on the door. Wanda practically threw herself outside.

"She hasn't come back," she said. "She's still out there."

"We need to see the child's room," one police officer said. "We have to see the last place you saw her."

"You don't need to do that," Patricia said. "His name is James Harris. He lives near me. He might have taken her back to his house. I can show you."

One officer stayed in the living room and wrote what she said on a pad while the other followed Wanda down the short hall to Destiny's bedroom, then a loud shriek filled the trailer. The officer lowered his pad and ran down the hall. Patricia couldn't squeeze past the officers so she stayed with Mrs. Greene until Wanda Taylor emerged from between them with Destiny in her arms.

The little girl looked sleepy and unconcerned about all the fuss. Wanda sat on the sofa, Destiny draped across her lap, limp body cradled in her mother's arms. The officers didn't say anything and their faces betrayed no expression.

"I saw him," Patricia told them. "His name is James Harris, he lives on Middle Street, his van is a white van with tinted windows. Something's wrong with his mouth, with his face."

"This happens sometimes, ma'am," one of the officers said. "A kid hides under the bed or sleeps in the closet and the parents call the police saying she's been abducted. Gets everyone worked up."

The enormity of what he was saying was too much. All Patricia could say was, "She doesn't have a closet."

Then she realized what she could do.

"Check her leg," she said. "Beneath her panties on the inside part of her thigh, there should be a mark there, like a cut."

Everyone looked at each other but no one moved.

"I'll look," Mrs. Greene said.

"No, ma'am," the officer said. "If you want us to check the child we need to call the ambulance and take her to the hospital so someone qualified can do it. Otherwise we can't use it as evidence."

"Evidence?" Patricia asked.

"If you want to bring charges against this man, you have to do it the right way," the officer said.

"If you're alleging that you saw a man molesting this child, it is imperative that a trained medical professional examine her," the other officer said.

"I'm a nurse," Patricia told him.

"No one's taking my little girl anywhere," Wanda said, holding Destiny, her limp head flopping against her mother's shoulder, eyes half closed, arms hanging down at her sides. "She's staying with me. She's not going out of my sight again."

"It's important," Patricia said.

"She's seeing the doctor in the morning," Wanda Taylor said. "She's not going anywhere until then."

Pounding came from the front door and they looked at each other, frozen. The aluminum door rattled in its frame until Mrs. Greene pushed past everyone. She flung the door open. Carter stood on the porch.

"Jesus Christ, Patty," he said. "What the hell is going on?"

"If my wife says she saw this man doing this, then that's what happened," Carter told the officers, standing in the middle of the trailer. He looked out of place to Patricia, and then she remembered he'd grown up poor, and if mobile homes had existed in 1948 he would almost certainly have been born in one.

"We searched everywhere she told us, sir," the officer repeated with a heavy emphasis on the *sir*. "But that doesn't mean we don't believe her. If they find anything wrong with this little girl tomorrow we'll have what your wife said tonight in the report."

"I'm sleepy," Destiny said, dreamy and soft, and Wanda began the process of getting everyone out of her home.

Outside, Carter made sure the two officers had his information, while Mrs. Greene walked over to Patricia.

"No point standing around outside when it's this hot," she said, and they started back to her house. Then she added, "They're going to take that little girl away."

"Not if there's nothing wrong with her," Patricia said.

"You saw how they looked at Wanda," Mrs. Greene said. "You saw how they looked at her home. They think she's trash, and she is, but not the kind of trash they think she is."

"She needs to get to the doctor," Patricia said. "No matter what."

"What'd you really see that man doing to her?" Mrs. Greene asked.

They stepped over the low railing around Mt. Zion A.M.E. and got all the way to its steps before Patricia said anything.

"It wasn't natural," she said.

It took Patricia two steps to realize Mrs. Greene had stopped walking. She turned around. In the church's porch light, Mrs. Greene looked very small.

"Everyone's hungry for our children," she said, and her voice cracked. "The whole world wants to gobble up colored children, and no matter how many it takes it just licks its lips and wants more. Help me, Mrs. Campbell. Help me keep that little girl with her mother. Help me stop that man."

"Of course," Patricia said. "I'll—"

"I don't want to hear *of course*," Mrs. Greene said. "When I tell someone what's happening out here they see an old woman living in the country who's never been to school. When you tell them, they see a doctor's wife from the Old Village and they pay attention. I don't like to ask for favors but I need you to make them pay attention to this. You know I did everything I could to save Miss Mary. I gave my blood for her. When you called me on the telephone tonight you said we're all mothers. Yes, ma'am, we are. Give me *your* blood. Help *me*."

Reflexively, Patricia almost said *of course* again, then wiped it from her mind. She didn't say a thing. She stood across from Mrs. Greene and spoke, soft and firm.

"We'll save them," she said. "We won't let them take Destiny, and we won't let that man take any more children. I will do everything in my power to stop him. I promise you."

Mrs. Greene didn't reply, and the two of them stood like that for a moment.

"Well, that's that," Carter said, coming up behind her. "They'll have her to the doctor tomorrow and if anything's wrong they have my information in the report."

The mood broke and the three of them walked toward Mrs. Greene's house.

"Carter," Patricia said. "You don't think DSS will do anything to that little girl, do you?"

"What?" he asked. "Like, take her?"

"Yes," Patricia said.

"No," he said. "The doctor who sees her is mandated to report signs of abuse, but we don't just snatch wailing babies out of their mothers' arms. There's a whole process. If you're worried, I'll ask around and see what kind of doc this guy is tomorrow."

"Thank you," Patricia said. "I'm just feeling nervous."

"Don't worry," Carter said. "I'll make sure."

Mrs. Greene went into her house and Patricia heard her lock the door. Carter opened Patricia's car door for her. She clicked in her seat belt and rolled down the window.

"Thank you for coming," she said.

"I got your note," he said. "Too many things have happened for you to be riding around all alone out here in the middle of the night. Why don't you follow me home and we'll get some rest and talk in the morning?"

She nodded, grateful that he wasn't trying to make her feel like a fool, and then she followed his red taillights all the way out of Six Mile, down Rifle Range Road, and back to the Old Village.

When they passed James Harris's house she saw Carter's brake lights flare briefly, probably because he also noticed James's Chevy Corsica parked in front of his house.

That night, for the first time in months, Carter held Patricia while she slept. She knew because she kept waking up from nightmares about a bloody red mouth chasing her through the woods and each time she felt his arms around her, and went back to sleep, reassured.

CHAPTER 18

Patricia woke up feeling like she'd fallen down the stairs. Her joints popped when she got out of bed, and her shoulders groaned like they were stuffed with broken glass when she reached for the coffee filters. When she undressed for her shower she noticed bruises on both hips from sliding back and forth across the back seat of the police car.

Carter had to go in to the hospital even though it was Saturday, and Patricia let Blue do whatever he wanted because it was light out.

"But be back before it starts to get dark," she said. "We're having early supper."

It wasn't safe to have Blue out of her sight after dark. She didn't know what James Harris was, she didn't care, she couldn't think straight, but she knew he wouldn't go out in the sun. She wanted to call Grace, to tell her what she'd seen, but when Grace didn't understand something she refused to believe it existed. She forced herself to calm down.

She couldn't bring herself to vacuum her curtains, so she did laundry. She ironed shirts and slacks. She ironed socks. She kept seeing James Harris with that thing on his face, his beard of blood, that little girl on the floor of his van, kept trying to figure out how to explain this to someone. She cleaned the bathrooms. She watched the sun slide across the sky. She felt grateful that Korey was still away at soccer camp.

The phone rang while she was throwing out expired condiments.

"Campbell residence," Patricia said.

"They took her daughter," Mrs. Greene told her.

"What? Who did?" Patricia asked, trying to catch up.

"This morning when Wanda Taylor took her to the doctor," Mrs. Greene said, "he found a mark on her leg, like you said, and he made Wanda wait outside while he talked to Destiny."

"What did she say?" Patricia asked.

"Wanda doesn't know, but then the DSS showed up and a policeman stood at the door," Mrs. Greene said. "They told her Destiny was on drugs and had marks where someone injected her. They asked her who the man was that Destiny referred to as 'Boo Daddy.' Wanda told them she wasn't seeing any man, but they didn't believe her."

"I'll call those officers from last night," Patricia said, frantic. "I'll call them and they can talk to DSS. And Carter can call her doctor. What was his name?"

"You promised this wouldn't happen," Mrs. Greene said. "Both of you promised."

"Carter will call," Patricia said. "He'll straighten this out. Should I come out to talk to Wanda?"

"I think it's best if you don't see Wanda Taylor right now," Mrs. Greene said. "She's not in a receptive frame of mind."

Patricia disconnected the call but held onto the receiver as the kitchen spun around her. She had seen Destiny. She'd been in her bedroom. She'd sat with her mother. She'd seen her tiny, limp body underneath James Harris, while he stood over her, his face covered in her blood.

"I'm bored," Blue said, coming into the den.

"Only boring people get bored," Patricia said, automatically.

"Everyone's at camp," Blue said. "There's no one to play with."

How had this happened? What had she done?

"Go read a book," she said.

She picked up the phone and dialed Carter's office.

"I've read all my books," he said.

"We'll go to the library later," she said.

The phone rang, Carter picked up, and she told him what had happened.

"I'm in the middle of a million things right now," he said.

"We promised her, Carter. We made a promise. That woman is covered in stitches from trying to help your mother."

"Okay, okay, Patty, I'll make some calls."

"Everyone thinks Hitler was bad," Blue said to the dinner table. "But Himmler was worse."

"Okay," Carter said, trying to wind him down. "Can you pass the salt, Patty?"

Patricia picked up the saltshaker but didn't hand it to Blue just yet.

"Did you call that doctor about Destiny Taylor today?" she asked.

Carter had been deflecting her ever since he got home.

"Can I get the salt before I'm interrogated?" he asked.

She made herself smile and passed it to Blue.

"He was the head of the SS," Blue said. "Which stands for *Schutzstaffel*. They were the secret police in Germany."

"That sounds pretty bad, buddy," Carter said, taking the salt from him.

"I'm not sure that's appropriate conversation for the dinner table," Patricia said.

"The Holocaust was all his idea," Blue continued.

Patricia waited until Carter had salted everything on his plate for what Patricia thought was a very long time.

"Carter?" she asked the second the saltshaker touched the table. "Did you call?" He put down his fork and gathered his thoughts before looking up at her, and Patricia knew this was a bad sign. "We *promised*, Carter."

"The second they form a search committee, any chance I have

of becoming department head is over," Carter said. "And they are so close to a decision that everything I do is scrutinized under a microscope. How do you think it would look if the candidate for chief of psych, who's a state employee, started calling up other state employees and telling them how to do their jobs? Do you know how bad that would look for me? The Medical University is a state institution. Things have to get done a certain way. I can't just run around asking questions and casting aspersions."

"We made a promise," Patricia said, and realized her hand was shaking. She put her fork down.

"They did medical experiments in the camps," Blue said. "They would torture one twin and see if the other one felt anything."

"If her doctor made a decision to remove her from her home, he had a good reason and I'm not going to second-guess him," Carter said, picking up his fork. "And frankly, after seeing that trailer, he probably made the right decision."

Which was when the doorbell rang, and Patricia jumped in her seat. Her heart started beating triple time. She had a sinking feeling she knew who it was. She wanted to say something to Carter, to show him how unfair he was being, but the doorbell rang again. Carter looked up over his forkful of chicken.

"Are you going to get that?" he asked.

"I'll get it," Blue said, sliding out of his chair.

Patricia stood up and blocked him.

"Finish your chicken," she said.

She walked toward the front door like a prisoner approaching the electric chair. She swung it wide and through the screen door she saw James Harris. He smiled. This first encounter would be the hardest, but with her family at her back and her house around her, standing on her private property, Patricia gave him her very best fake hostess smile. She'd had lots of practice.

"What a pleasant surprise," she said through the screen door.

"Did I catch you during a meal again?" he said. "I'm so sorry."

"It's no bother."

"You know," he said, "I got interrupted during a meal recently. It was very upsetting."

For a moment, she couldn't breathe. No, she told herself, it was an innocent comment. He wasn't testing her.

"I'm sorry to hear that," she said.

"It made me think about you," he said. "It made me realize how often I interrupt your family's meals."

"Oh, no," she said. "We enjoy having you."

She examined his face carefully through the screen. He examined her face right back.

"That's good to hear," he said. "Ever since you invited me into your home I just can't stay away. I almost feel like it's my house, too."

"How nice," she said.

"So when I found myself dealing with an unpleasant situation today I thought of you," he said. "You were so helpful last time."

"Oh?" Patricia said.

"The woman who cleaned for my great-aunt disappeared," he said. "And I heard that someone was spreading the story that the last place she was seen was my house. The insinuation is that I had something to do with it."

And Patricia knew. The police had been to see him. They hadn't said her name. He hadn't seen her last night. But he was suspicious and had come here to test her, to see if he could jolt her into revealing something. Clearly he had never been to a cocktail party in the Old Village before.

"Who would say something like that, I wonder?" Patricia asked.

"I thought you might have heard something."

"I don't listen to gossip."

"Well," he said. "The way I heard it, she took off with some fella."

"Then that settles that," she said.

"It hurts me to think that you or your kids might hear that I did something to her," he said. "The last thing I want is for anyone to be afraid of me."

"Don't you worry about that for a second," Patricia said, and she made herself meet his eyes. "No one in this house is afraid of you."

They held each other for a second, and it felt like a challenge. She looked away first.

"It's just the way you're talking to me," he said. "You won't open the door. You seem distant. Usually you invite me in when I drop by. I feel like something's changed."

"Not a thing," she said, and realized what she had to do. "We were about to have dessert. Won't you join us?"

She kept her breathing under control, kept a pleasant smile on her face.

"That would be nice," he said. "Thank you."

She realized she had to let him in now, and she forced her arm to reach out toward the door, and she felt the bones in her shoulder grating as she took the latch in one hand and twisted it clockwise. The screen door groaned on its spring.

"Come in," she said. "You're always welcome."

She stood to the side as he stepped past her, and she saw his chin covered with blood and that thing retracting into his mouth, and it was only a shadow, and she closed the door behind him.

"Thank you," he said.

He had gotten into her house the same as if he'd held a gun to her head. She had to stay calm. She wasn't helpless. How many times had she stood at a party or in the supermarket, talking about someone's child being slow, or their baby being ugly, and that person appeared out of nowhere and she smiled in their face and said, *I was just thinking about you and that cute baby of yours*, and they never had a clue.

She could do this.

". . . would drain the person of all their blood and then give them someone else's blood that was the wrong type," Blue was say-ing as she led James Harris back into the dining room.

"Mm-hmm," Carter said, ignoring Blue.

"Are you talking about Himmler and the camps?" James Harris asked.

Blue and Carter stopped and looked up. Patricia saw every detail in the room all at once. Everything felt freighted with importance.

"Look who stopped by." She smiled. "Just in time for dessert."

She picked up her napkin and sat down, gesturing to her left for James Harris to be seated.

"Thank you for inviting an old bachelor in for dessert," he said.

"Blue," Patricia said. "Why don't you clear the table and bring in the cookies. Would you like coffee, James?"

"It'll keep me up," he said. "I have enough trouble sleeping as it is."

"Which cookies?" Blue asked.

"All of them," Patricia said, and Blue scampered from the room, practically skipping.

"How're you enjoying summer?" Carter asked. "Where'd you live before here?"

"Nevada," James Harris said.

Nevada? Patricia thought.

"That's a dry heat," Carter said. "We got up to eighty-five per-cent humidity today."

"It's certainly not what I'm used to," James said. "It really ruins my appetite."

Was that what he'd been doing to Destiny Taylor, Patricia won-dered? Did he think he was eating blood? She thought about Richard Chase, the Vampire of Sacramento, who killed and partially ate six people in the seventies and literally believed he was an actual vampire. Then she saw that hard, thorny thing retreating into James Harris's mouth like a cockroach's leg, and she didn't know how to explain that. Her pulse sped up as she realized that it lay in his throat, behind a thin layer of skin, so close to her she could reach over and touch it.

So close to Blue. She took a breath and forced herself to calm down.

"I have a recipe for gazpacho," she said. "Have you ever had gazpacho, James?"

"Can't say I have," he said.

"It's a cold soup," Patricia said. "From Italy."

"Gross," Blue said, coming in with four bags of Pepperidge Farm cookies clutched to his chest.

"It's perfect for warm weather," Patricia smiled. "I'll copy the recipe down for you before you go."

"Look," Carter said, in his business voice, and Patricia looked at him, trying to convey in the secret language of married couples that they needed to stay absolutely normal because they were in more danger than he knew right this minute.

Carter made eye contact and Patricia flicked her eyes from her husband to James Harris and put everything inside her heart, everything they shared in their marriage, she put it all into her eyes in a way only he could see, and he got it. *Play it safe*, her eyes said. *Play dumb*.

Carter broke eye contact and turned to James Harris.

"We need to clear the air," he said. "You have to realize that Patty feels terrible about what she said to the police."

Patricia felt like Carter had cracked open her chest and dumped ice cubes inside. Anything she could say froze in her throat.

"What did Mom do?" Blue asked.

"I think it's better if you hear it from your mother," James Harris said.

Patricia saw James Harris and Carter both watching her. James Harris wore a sincere mask but Patricia knew that behind it he was laughing at her. Carter wore his Serious Man face.

"I thought Mr. Harris had done something wrong," Patricia told Blue, pushing the words through her constricted throat. "But I was confused."

"It wasn't much fun having the police stop by my house today," James Harris said.

"You called the police on him?" Blue asked, astounded.

"I feel awful about all this," Carter said. "Patty?"

"I'm sorry," Patricia said, faintly.

"We cleared it all up," James Harris said. "Mostly it was just embarrassing to have a police car parked in front of my house since I'm new here. You know how these small neighborhoods are."

"What did you do?" Blue asked James Harris.

"Well, it's a little adult," James Harris said. "Your mother should really be the one to tell you."

Patricia felt trapped by Carter and James Harris, and the unfairness of it all made her feel wild. This was her house, this was her family, she hadn't done anything wrong. She could ask everyone to leave, right this minute. But she had done something wrong, hadn't she? Because Destiny Taylor was crying herself to sleep without her mother right this minute.

"I . . . ," she began, and it died in the dining room air.

"Your mother thought he had done something inappropriate with a child," Carter said. "But she was absolutely, one hundred percent wrong. I want you to know, son, we would never invite someone into this house who might harm you or your sister in any way. Your mother meant well but she wasn't thinking clearly."

James Harris kept staring at Patricia.

"Yes," she said. "I was mixed up."

The silence stretched on and Patricia realized what they were waiting for. She looked hard at her plate.

"I'm sorry," she said in a voice so faint she barely heard it.

James Harris bit noisily into a Pepperidge Farm Mint Milano and chewed. In the silence, she could hear his teeth grinding it to pulp, and then he swallowed and she heard the wad of chewed-up cookie slide down his throat, past that thing.

"Well," James Harris said, "I have to run but don't worry—I can't be too mad at your mom. After all, we're neighbors. And you've been so kind to me since I moved in."

"I'll show you out," Patricia said, because she didn't know what else to say.

She walked through the dark front hall in front of James Harris and felt him leaning forward to say something. She couldn't take it. She couldn't handle one more word. He was so smug.

"Patricia . . . ," he began, voice low.

She snapped on the hall light. He flinched, squinting and blinking. A teardrop leaked from one eye. It was childish, but it made her feel better.

As they got ready for bed, Carter tried to talk to her.

"Patty," he said. "Don't get upset. It was better to get that out in the open."

"I'm not upset," she said.

"Whatever you think you saw, he seems like an okay guy."

"Carter, I saw it," she said. "He was doing something to that little girl. They took her from her mother today because they found a mark on her inner thigh."

"I'm not going to get into that again," he said. "At some point you have to assume the professionals know what they're doing."

"I saw him," she said.

"Even if you did look in his van that no one could find," Carter said, "eyewitness accounts are notoriously unreliable. It was dark, the light source was a flashlight, it happened fast."

"I know what I saw," Patricia said.

"I can show you studies," Carter said.

But Patricia knew what she had seen and she knew it was unnatural. From the way Ann Savage attacked her, to Miss Mary being attacked by rats, to the man on the roof that night, to James Harris and all his hints about eating and being interrupted, the way the Old Village no longer felt safe—something was wrong. She'd already removed their spare key from its hiding place outside in the fake rock, and she'd started deadbolting the doors whenever she left the house, even just to run errands. Things were changing too fast, and James Harris was at the center of it.

And something he'd said ate at her. She got up and went downstairs.

"Patty," Carter called behind her. "Don't storm off."

"I'm not storming," she called over her shoulder, but really didn't care if he heard her or not.

She found her copy of *Dracula* in the bookcase in the den. They'd read it for book club in October two years ago.

She flipped through the pages until the phrase she was looking for jumped out at her:

"He may not enter anywhere at the first," says Van Helsing in his *Dutch-tainted English, "unless there be some of the household who bid him to come; though afterwards he can come as he please."*

She had invited him inside her house months ago. She thought about Richard Chase, the Vampire of Sacramento, again, and then she thought about that thing in his mouth, and the next day after church she drove to The Commons shopping center and went into the Book Bag. She checked to make sure no one she knew was there before she walked over to the register.

"Excuse me," she said. "Could you tell me where your horror books are?"

"Behind Sci-fi and Fantasy," the kid grunted without looking up.

"Thank you," Patricia said.

She picked books by their covers, one after the other, and began piling them up by the cash register.

When she was ready to pay, the clerk rang them up, one cover of a hunky, smooth-shaven young man with spiked hair after another:

Vampire Beat, Some of Your Blood, The Delicate Dependency, 'Salem's Lot, Vampire Junction, Live Girls, Nightblood, No Blood Spilled, The Vampire's Apprentice, Interview with the Vampire, The Vampire Lestat, Vampire Tapestry, The Hotel Transylvania. If it had fangs, sharp teeth, or bloody lips on the cover, Patricia bought it. Her final total: $149.96.

"You must be really into vampires," the clerk said.

"Will you take a check?" she asked.

She hid the books in the back of her closet, and as she read them one by one behind her closed bedroom door she realized that she couldn't do this alone. She needed help.

CHAPTER 19

On book club night, Grace brought frozen fruit salad, Kitty brought two bottles of white wine, and they all sat in Slick's crowded living room, surrounded by Slick's collection of Lenox Garden bird figurines, and Beanie Babies, and wall plaques bearing devotional quotations, and all the things Slick bought off the Home Shopping Network, and Patricia prepared to lie to her friends.

"And so, in conclusion," Maryellen said, bringing her case against the author of *The Stranger Beside Me* to a close, "Ann Rule is a world-class dope. She knew Ted Bundy, she worked next to Ted Bundy, she knew the police were looking for a good-looking young man named Ted who drove a VW Bug, and she knew that her good-looking young friend Ted Bundy drove a VW Bug, but even when her buddy is arrested she says she'll 'suspend judgment.' I mean, what does she need? For him to ring her doorbell and say 'Ann, I'm a serial killer'?"

"It's worse when it's someone close to you," Slick said. "We want the people we know to be who we think they are, and to stay how we know them. But Tiger has a little friend named Eddie Baxley right up the street and we love Eddie but when we found out his parents let him watch R-rated horror movies, we had to tell Tiger that he was no longer allowed to play at their house. It was hard."

"That's not the point at all," Maryellen said. "The point is, if the evidence says your best friend Ted talks like a duck, and walks like a duck, and drives the same car as a duck, then he's probably a duck."

Patricia decided she wouldn't get a better opportunity. She stopped toying with her frozen fruit salad, put her fork on the plate, took a deep breath, and told her lie:

"James Harris deals drugs."

She'd thought long and hard about what to tell them, because if she told them what she really thought they'd send her to the funny farm. But the one crime guaranteed to mobilize the women of the Old Village, and the Mt. Pleasant police department, was drugs. There was a war on them, after all, and she didn't care how they got the police poking into James Harris's business. She just wanted him gone. Now she delivered the second part of her lie:

"He's selling drugs to children."

No one said a word for at least twenty seconds.

Kitty downed her entire glass of wine in a single gulp. Slick got very, very still, eyes wide. Maryellen looked confused, as if she couldn't tell if Patricia was making fun of her or not, and Grace slowly shook her head from side to side.

"Oh, Patricia," Grace said, in a disappointed voice.

"I saw him with a young girl," Patricia said, forging ahead. "In the back of his van in the woods at Six Mile. That girl has been taken from her mother by Social Services because of the mark they found on her inner thigh, a bruise with a puncture mark over her femoral artery, like what street drug users call a track mark from injecting. Grace, Bennett said Mrs. Savage had the same kind of mark on her inner thigh when she went to the hospital."

"That was confidential information," Grace said.

"You told it to me," Patricia said.

"Because she had bitten your ear," Grace said. "I thought you should know she was an IV drug user. I didn't mean for you to broadcast it all over the Village."

This wasn't going the way she wanted. Patricia had spent hours putting this story together, going through all the true crime books they'd read together, practicing how to lay out the facts. She needed to stop bickering with Grace and stick to her notes.

"When James Harris got here he had a bag in his house with eighty-five thousand dollars in it," Patricia said, talking fast. "The first afternoon I met him I helped him open his bank account because he didn't have ID. But he must have a driver's license, so why didn't he want to show it at the bank? Because maybe he's wanted for something. Maybe he's done this somewhere before. Also, Mrs. Greene copied down a partial license plate number of a van in Six Mile that shouldn't have been there, and it turned out to be his license plate. And I think I was the last person to see Francine before she disappeared, and she was going into his house."

None of their expressions had changed and she'd used up all her facts.

"His story changes about where he's from," she tried. "Nothing about him adds up."

She saw her friendships die, right there in front of her. She could see it clearly. They'd say they believed her, and end the book club meeting awkwardly. First, there would be the unreturned phone calls, the excuses to go talk to someone else when they ran into each other at parties, the canceled invitations for Korey or Blue to spend the night. One by one, they'd turn their backs.

"Patricia," Grace said. "I warned you when you came to see me. I begged you not to make a fool out of yourself."

"I know what I saw, Grace," Patricia said, although she felt less and less sure.

Patricia felt herself losing control of the conversation. She tried to find a place to put her frozen fruit salad plate, but the coffee table was crowded with a bowl of marble roses, glass pyramids of various sizes, two brass gamecocks frozen in combat, and a stack of oversize books with titles like *Blessings*. She decided to just hold it in her hand and focus on the person she thought she could best sway. If one of them would believe her, the rest would follow.

"Maryellen," she said. "You just called Ann Rule a dope because if the evidence says your best friend talks like a duck, and walks like a duck, and drives the same car as a duck, then he's probably a duck."

"There's a difference between a compelling chain of evidence and accusing someone of a crime based on a bunch of coincidences," Maryellen said. "So let me get your evidence straight. Mrs. Greene says there may or may not be a man in the woods molesting the children of Six Mile."

"Giving them drugs," Patricia corrected.

"Okay, giving them drugs," Maryellen said. "Mrs. Greene may or may not have seen a van with the license plate number, but not even the full number, of James Harris's van which no longer belongs to James Harris because he sold it to someone else."

"I don't know what happened to it," Patricia said.

"Putting the van aside," Maryellen continued, "you want us to believe that the simple fact he went out to Six Mile, even though he wasn't there at the time anyone died or anything happened, means he's somehow involved in something?"

"I saw him out there," Patricia said. "I saw him doing something to a little girl in the back of his van. I. Saw. Him."

No one said anything.

"What did you see him do?" Slick asked.

"I went out to visit one of the children who seemed sick," Patricia said. "Mrs. Greene went with me. The little girl was missing from her bedroom. We went looking for her in the woods, and I saw his white van. He was in the back with the child. He was . . ." She barely hesitated. ". . . injecting her with something. The doctor said she had a track mark on her leg."

"Then why don't you tell the police?" Slick asked.

"I did!" Patricia said, louder than she meant. "They couldn't find the van, they couldn't find him, and they think the mother gave her daughter the drugs. Or her boyfriend."

"So why aren't they looking at the boyfriend more closely?" Maryellen asked.

"Because she doesn't have a boyfriend," Patricia said, trying to keep calm.

Maryellen gave a shrug.

"This just goes to show that the North Charleston police and the Mt. Pleasant police have very different standards."

"It's not a joke!" Patricia shouted.

Her voice echoed harshly in the cramped living room. Slick jumped, Grace's spine stiffened, Maryellen winced.

"Do we have any more wine?" Kitty asked.

"I'm so sorry," Slick said. "I think it's all gone."

"A child is being hurt," Patricia said. "Don't any of you care?"

"Of course we care," Kitty said. "But we're a book club, not the police. What are we supposed to do?"

"We're the only ones who've noticed something might be wrong," Patricia said.

"You, not us," Grace said. "Don't lump me in with your foolishness."

"Ed would laugh this right out of court," Maryellen said.

"The police wrote me off," Patricia said. "I need your help to go to them again. I need y'all to think through this with me, to help me put it together. Maryellen, you know how the police work. Kitty, you were in Six Mile. You saw how it was. Tell them."

"I mean," Kitty said, trying to help, "something wasn't right out there. Everyone was on edge. We almost got jumped by a street gang. But accusing one of our neighbors of being a drug dealer . . ."

"Here's how I see it," Patricia said. "In Six Mile, they think that someone is doing something to the children, giving them something that makes them go crazy and hurt themselves. Now over here in the Old Village, we've had Mrs. Savage go crazy and attack me. And then there's Francine. I saw her go into his house, and then she disappeared. She may have stumbled on his drugs, or his money, or something, and he had to get rid of her. But everything is connected through him. It's all happening around him. How many coincidences do you need before you wake up?"

"Patricia," Grace said, speaking slowly. "If you could hear yourself you'd feel terribly embarrassed."

"What if I'm right?" Patricia said. "And he's out there giving drugs to these children and we're too scared of being embarrassed to do anything? It could be our children. Think about how many young women would still be alive today if people hadn't taken Ted Bundy at face value and started asking questions earlier. Think if Ann Rule had put the pieces together sooner. How many lives could she have saved? I mean, you have to agree, something strange is going on here."

"No, we don't," Grace said.

"Something strange is going on," Patricia continued. "Children in first grade are killing themselves. I got attacked in my own yard. Mrs. Savage has the same mark on her body Destiny Taylor did. Francine is missing. In every book we read, no one ever thought anything bad was happening until it was too late. This is where we live, it's where our children live, it's our home. Don't you want to do absolutely everything you can to keep it safe?"

Another silence stretched out, and then Kitty spoke.

"What if she's right?"

"Excuse me?" Grace asked.

"We've all known Patricia forever," Kitty said. "If she says she saw him in the back of his van doing something to a young girl, I believe her. I mean, come on, one thing I've learned from all these books: it pays to be paranoid."

Grace stood up. "I value our friendship, Patricia," she said. "And I am ready to be your friend when you come back to your senses. But anyone catering to this delusion is not being helpful."

Slick stood up and went to her bookcase filled with titles like *Satan, You Can't Have My Children* and pulled out a Bible. She flipped to a passage and read it out loud:

"'There are those whose teeth are swords, whose fangs are knives, to devour the poor from off the earth, the needy from among mankind. The leech has two daughters: Give and Give. Three things are never satisfied; four never say, "Enough."' Proverbs 30:15."

She turned more pages, then read, "Ephesians 6:12, 'For we do not wrestle against flesh and blood, but against the rulers, against the authorities, against the cosmic powers over this present darkness, against the spiritual forces of evil in the heavenly places.'"

Then she looked at them all with a wide smile on her face.

"I knew my test would come," she said. "I knew that one day my Lord would set me against Satan, and try my faith in a battle against his snares, and this is just so exciting, Patricia."

"Are you putting us on?" Maryellen asked.

"Satan wants our children," Slick said. "We have to believe the righteous and smite the wicked. Patricia is righteous because she is my friend. If she says James Harris is among the wicked, then it is our Christian duty to smite him.

"The only thing smited is your brains," Maryellen said, turning to Grace. "But she's not wrong."

Grace said, "Pardon?"

"New Jersey was the kind of place where no one watched out for each other," Maryellen said. "Our neighbors were nice but they would never write down the license plate number of a strange car. They would never tell you they saw a stranger watching your house. There are a lot of things that are different down here, but not once do I regret living in a community where we keep an eye out for each other. Let's see if we can make a more convincing argument than Patricia, and if so, I'll run it by Ed. If Ed thinks it holds up, then maybe we've done some good."

Patricia felt a wave of gratitude toward her.

"I will not be a part of some kind of lynch mob," Grace said.

"We're not a lynch mob, we're a book club," Kitty said. "We've always been there for each other. This is where Patricia is now? It's kind of weird, but okay. We'd do the same for you."

"If that situation ever occurs," Grace said, "don't."

And she walked out of Slick's house.

The next morning Patricia had just decided to clean the den closet before doing more research on vampires when the phone rang. She answered.

"Patricia. It's Grace Cavanaugh."

"I'm so sorry about what happened at book club," Patricia said, who hadn't realized until this moment how desperately she wanted to hear Grace's voice. "I won't talk about it with you anymore if you don't want me to."

"I found his van," Grace said.

The change to another page was so fast Patricia couldn't follow.

"What van?" she asked.

"James Harris's," Grace said. "You see, I remembered that in *Silence of the Lambs* that man hides his car containing a head in a mini-storage unit. And I remembered that I've known you for almost seven years and I should afford you the benefit of the doubt."

"Thank you," Patricia said.

"The only mini-storage establishment in Mt. Pleasant is Pak Rat over on Highway 17," Grace continued. "They spell *pack* wrong because they think it's cute. It's not. Bennett knows Carl, the man who runs it. So I called Carl's wife, Zenia, last night, I'm not sure you've ever met her but we're both in handbell choir. I told her what I was looking for and she was happy to call over and see what she could find and it turns out there is a James Harris who rents a unit, and the attendant said he'd seen him going in and out of it a few times in a white van. He saw him in it last week. So he still owns it."

"Grace," Patricia said. "That's wonderful news."

"Not if he's hurting children," Grace said.

"No, of course not," Patricia said, feeling chastised and triumphant at the same time.

"If you really think this man is up to no good," Grace said, "you need more than this before we go to Ed. We don't want to go off half-cocked."

"Don't worry, Grace," Patricia said. "When we go off, we'll be fully cocked."

PSYCHO

August 1993

CHAPTER 20

"But I said you could spend the night with Laurie," Patricia told Korey.

"Well, now I changed my mind," Korey said.

She stood in the doorway to Patricia's bathroom while Patricia finished doing her makeup. Korey had come home from soccer camp and increased Patricia's stress exponentially. It was hard enough to make sure Blue was always somewhere safe after dark, but Korey hung around the house aimlessly, watching TV for hours, and then she'd get a phone call and suddenly need to borrow the car to go see her friends in the middle of the night. Except for tonight, when Patricia actually wanted her out of the house.

"I'm hosting book club," Patricia said. "You haven't seen Laurie since you got back from camp."

One of the reasons they were having it at her house was because she'd exerted gentle pressure on Carter to take Blue out for supper at Quincy's Steak House and then to a movie (they decided on something called *So I Married an Axe Murderer*). Korey was supposed to be spending the night downtown.

"She canceled," Korey said. "Her parents are getting divorced and her dad wants to spend quality time. That skirt's too tight."

"I haven't decided what I'm wearing yet," Patricia said, even though her skirt was definitely not too tight. "If you have to be home you need to stay in your room."

"What if I have to go to the bathroom?" Korey asked. "Can I leave my room then, Mother? Most parents would think it was great that their child wanted to spend more time with them."

"I'm only asking you to stay upstairs," Patricia said.

"What if I want to watch TV?" Korey asked.

"Then go to Laurie Gibson's."

Korey slouched off and Patricia changed her skirt because it felt tight, and then she finished her makeup and sprayed her hair. She wasn't going to put out anything to eat, but she'd made coffee and put it in a thermal jug in case the police wanted some. What if they wanted decaf? She didn't have any and worried that might affect their mood.

She felt tense. Before this summer she had never interacted with the police, and now she felt like that was all she did. They made her nervous, but if she could get through tonight, James Harris would no longer be her problem. All she had to do was convince the police that he was a drug dealer, they'd start looking into his affairs, and all his secrets would come spilling out. And she wasn't doing it alone; she had her book club.

Patricia wondered what they would have said if she told them that she thought James Harris was a vampire. Or something like that. She wasn't sure of the exact terminology, but that would do until a better name came along. How else to explain that thing coming out of his face? How else to explain his aversion to going out in sunlight, his insistence on being invited inside, the fact that the marks on the children and on Mrs. Savage all looked like bites?

When she'd tried to perform CPR on him he had looked sick and weak and at least ten years older. When she saw him the following week he'd positively glowed with health. What had happened in between? Francine had gone missing. Had he eaten her? Sucked her blood? He'd certainly done something.

When she got rid of her prejudices and considered the facts, vampire was the theory that fit best. Fortunately, she'd never have to say it out loud to anyone because this was just about finished. She didn't care how they ran him out of town, she just wanted him gone.

She went downstairs and jumped when she saw Kitty waving at

her through the window by the front door. Slick stood behind her.

"I know we're a half hour early," Kitty said as Patricia let them in. "But I couldn't sit around at home doing nothing."

Slick had dressed conservatively in a knee-length navy skirt and a white blouse with a blue batik vest over it. Kitty, on the other hand, had apparently lost her mind right before she got dressed. She wore a red blouse bedazzled with red rhinestones and a huge floral skirt. Looking at her made Patricia's eyes hurt.

Patricia put them in the den, then went to make sure Korey had her bedroom door closed, then checked the driveway, and walked back into the den just as Maryellen opened the front door.

"Yoo-hoo? Am I too early?" Maryellen called.

"We're in the kitchen," Patricia hollered.

"Ed went to pick up the detectives," Maryellen said, coming in and putting her purse on the den table. She took two business cards out of her day planner. "Detective Claude D. Cannon and Detective Gene Bussell. He says Gene is from Georgia but Claude is local and they're both good. They'll listen to us. He can't promise how they'll react, but they'll listen."

They each examined the cards for lack of anything else to do.

Grace walked into the den.

"The door was open," she said. "I hope you don't mind?"

"Do you want some coffee?" Patricia asked.

"No, thank you," Grace said. "Bennett is at a heart association dinner. He won't be back until late."

"Horse is at the Yacht Club with Leland," Kitty said. "Again."

As July had gotten hotter, Leland had convinced Horse to put what money he could scrape together into Gracious Cay. Then the Dow had surged and Carter had cashed out some AT&T shares Patricia's father had given them as a wedding present and he'd put that money into Gracious Cay, too. The three men had all started going out for dinner together, or meeting for drinks at the back bar of the Yacht Club. Patricia didn't know where Carter found the time, but male bonding seemed to be the in thing these days.

"Patricia," Grace said, pulling a sheet of paper from her purse. "I wrote all your talking points down in an outline just in case you needed to jog your thoughts."

Patricia looked at the handwritten list, numbered and lettered in Grace's careful calligraphy.

"Thank you," she said.

"Do you want to go over it again?" Grace asked.

"How many times are we going to hear this?" Kitty asked.

"Until we have it right," Grace said. "This is the most serious thing we've ever done in our lives."

"I can't keep hearing about those children," Kitty moaned. "It's horrible."

"Let me see it," Maryellen said, reaching toward Patricia.

Patricia handed her the paper and Maryellen scanned it.

"Lord help us," she said. "They're going to think we're a bunch of crazies."

They sat around Patricia's kitchen table. The living room had fresh cut flowers in it, the furniture was new, and the lights were just right. They didn't want to go onstage until it was time. No one had much to say. Patricia went over her list in her head.

"It's eight o'clock," Grace said. "Should we move to the living room?"

People pushed back their chairs, but Patricia felt like she needed to say something, give some kind of pep talk, before they committed themselves to this.

"I want everyone to know," Patricia said, and they all stopped to listen. "Once the police get here there is no turning back. I hope everyone's prepared for that?"

"I just want to go back to talking about books," Kitty said. "I want this all to be over with."

"Whatever he's done," Grace said, "I don't think James Harris is going to want to call any more attention to himself after tonight.

Once the police start asking him questions, I'm sure he'll leave the Old Village quietly."

`"Let's hope you're right," Slick said.

"I just wish there were another way," Kitty said, shoulders slumping.

"We all do," Patricia said. "But there isn't."

"The police will be discreet," Maryellen said. "And this will all be over very quickly."

"Will y'all join me in a moment of prayer?" Slick asked.

They bowed their heads and joined hands, even Maryellen.

"Heavenly Father," Slick said. "Give us strength in our mission, and make us righteous in your cause. In thy name we pray, amen."

Single file, they walked through the dining room and into the living room, where they arranged themselves and Patricia realized her error.

"We need water," she said. "I forgot to put out ice water."

"I'll get it," Grace said, and disappeared into the kitchen.

She brought the water back at five after eight. Everyone adjusted and readjusted their skirts, their collars, their necklaces and earrings. Slick took her three rings off, then put them back on, then took them off again, and put them back on one more time. It was 8:10, then 8:15.

"Where are they?" Maryellen muttered to herself.

Grace checked the inside of her wrist.

"Ed doesn't have a car phone, does he?" Patricia asked. "Because we could call if he does and see where he is."

"Let's just sit tight," Maryellen suggested.

At 8:30 they heard a car pull up in the driveway, then another.

"That's Ed and the detectives," Maryellen said.

Everyone came awake, sat up straighter, touched her hair to make sure it was in place. Patricia walked to the window.

"Is it them?" Kitty asked.

"No," Patricia said, as they heard car doors slam. "It's Carter."

CHAPTER 21

"Did he forget something?" Maryellen asked behind her.

Patricia looked out the window and felt everything falling apart around her. She watched as Carter and Blue got out of the Buick and Leland's BMW parked behind them. She saw Bennett's little Mitsubishi pickup drive past the end of their driveway and park at his house, and then Bennett got out and came up her drive, joining Carter and Blue. Ed emerged from the back seat of Leland's gold BMW in a short-sleeved shirt tucked into his blue jeans, wearing a knit tie. Rumpled old Horse hauled himself out of the passenger side of Leland's car and hitched up his pants. Leland got out of the driver's seat and pulled on his summer-weight, polyester blazer.

"Who is it?" Kitty asked from the sofa.

Maryellen got up and stood next to Patricia, and Patricia felt her stiffen.

"Patricia?" Grace asked. "Maryellen? Who all's there?"

The men shook hands and Carter saw Patricia standing in the window and said something to the rest of them and they trooped up to the front porch in single file.

"All of them," Patricia said.

The front door opened, and Carter walked into the hall, Blue right behind him. Then came Ed, who saw Maryellen standing at the base of the stairs and stopped. The rest of the men piled up behind him, hot evening air billowing in around them.

"Ed," Maryellen said. "Where are Detectives Cannon and Bussell?"

"They're not coming," he said, fiddling with his tie.

He stepped toward her, to take her shoulder or stroke her cheek, and she jerked herself backward, stopping at the base of the banister, holding on to it with both hands.

"Were they ever coming?" she asked.

Keeping eye contact, he shook his head. Patricia put one hand on Maryellen's shoulder, and it hummed beneath her like a high-tension line. The two of them stood aside as Carter sent Blue upstairs and the men filed past them and crowded into the living room. Carter waited until they were all inside, then gestured to Patricia like a waiter ushering her to her table.

"Patty," he said. "Maryellen. Join us?"

They allowed themselves to be led inside. Kitty wiped tears from her cheeks, face flushed. Slick stared at the floor between her and Leland and he glared at her, both of them holding very, very still. Grace made a point of studying the framed photo of Patricia's family hanging over the fireplace. Bennett looked past them all, through the sun porch windows, out over the marsh.

"Ladies," Carter said. Clearly the other men had elected him their spokesman. "We need to have a serious talk."

Patricia tried to slow her breathing. It had gotten high and shallow and her throat felt like it was swelling closed. She glanced at Carter and saw how much anger he carried in his eyes. "There aren't enough chairs for everyone," she said. "We should get some of the dining room chairs."

"I'll get them," Horse said, and moved to the dining room.

Bennett went with him, and the men hauled chairs into the living room and there was only the clattering of furniture as everyone arranged themselves. Horse sat next to Kitty on the sofa, holding her hand, and Leland leaned against the door to the hall. Ed sat backward in a dining room chair, like someone playing a policeman on TV. Carter sat directly across from Patricia, adjusting the crease in his dress pants, the cuffs of his jacket, putting his professional face on over his real face.

Maryellen tried to regain the initiative.

"If the detectives aren't coming," she said, "I'm not sure why you're all here."

"Ed came to us," Carter said. "Because he heard some alarming things and rather than risk y'all embarrassing yourselves in front of the police and doing serious damage to both yourselves and to your families, he did the responsible thing and brought it to our attention."

"What you have to say about James Harris is libelous and slanderous," Leland cut in. "You could have gotten me sued into oblivion. What were you even thinking, Slick? You could have ruined everything. Who wants to work with a developer who accuses his investors of dealing drugs to children?"

Slick lowered her head.

"I'm sorry, Leland," she said to her lap. "But children—"

"'On the day of judgment,'" Leland quoted, "'people will give account for each careless word they speak.' Matthew 12:36."

"Do you even want to know what we have to say?" Patricia asked.

"We got the gist," Carter said.

"No," Patricia said. "If you haven't heard what we have to say, then you have no right to tell us who we can and can't speak to. We're not our mothers. This isn't the 1920s. We're not some silly biddies sitting around sewing all day and gossiping. We're in the Old Village more than any of you, and something is very wrong here. If you had any respect for us at all, you'd listen."

"If you've got so much free time, go after the criminals in the White House," Leland said. "Don't fabricate one down the street."

"Let's all slow down," Carter said, a gentle smile on his lips. "We'll listen. It can't hurt and who knows, maybe we'll learn something?"

Patricia ignored the calm, medical-professional tone of his voice. If this was his bluff, she'd call it.

"Thank you, Carter," she said. "I would like to speak."

"You're speaking for everyone?" Carter asked.

"It was Patricia's idea," Kitty said, from the safety of Horse's side.

"Yes," Grace said.

"So tell us," Carter said. "Why do you believe that James Harris is some master criminal?"

It took a moment for her blood to stop singing in her ears and settle to a duller roar. She inhaled deeply and looked around the room. She saw Leland staring at her with his face stretched taut, practically shimmering with rage, his hands jammed deep in his pockets. Ed studied her the way policemen on TV watched criminals dig themselves in deeper. Bennett stared out the windows behind her at the marsh, face neutral. Carter watched her, wearing his most tolerant smile, and she felt herself shrinking in her chair. Only Horse looked at her with anything approaching kindness.

Patricia released her breath and looked down at Grace's outline, shaking in her hands.

"James Harris, as you all know, moved here around April. His great-aunt, Ann Savage, was in poor health and he took care of her. When she attacked me, we believe that she was on whatever drugs he's dealing. We think he's selling them in Six Mile."

"Based on what?" Ed asked. "What evidence? What arrests? Have you seen him selling drugs there?"

"Let her finish," Maryellen said.

Carter held out a hand and Ed stopped.

"Patricia." Carter smiled. She looked up. "Put your paper down. Tell us in your own words. Relax, we're all interested in what you have to say."

He held out his hand, and Patricia couldn't help herself. She handed him Grace's outline. He folded it in thirds and tucked it into his jacket pocket.

"We think that he gave this drug," Patricia said, forcing herself to see Grace's outline in her head, "to Orville Reed and Destiny Taylor. Orville Reed killed himself. Destiny Taylor is still alive, for now. But before they died they claimed to have met a white man in the woods who gave them something that made them sick. There was also Sean Brown, Orville's cousin, who was involved in drugs, according to the police. He was found dead in the same woods where the children went, during the same period. In addition, Mrs. Greene saw a van with the same license plate as James Harris's in Six Mile during the time this was all happening."

"Did it have the exact same license plate number?" Ed asked.

"Mrs. Greene only wrote down the last part, X 13S, but James Harris's license plate is TNX 13S," Patricia said. "James Harris claims he got rid of that van, but he's keeping it in the Pak Rat Mini-Storage on Highway 17 and has taken it out a few times, mostly at night."

"Unbelievable," Leland said.

"Sean Brown was involved in the drug trade, and we think James Harris killed him in a horrible way to teach other drug dealers a lesson," Patricia said. "Ann Savage died with what you'd call track marks on the inside of her thigh. Destiny Taylor had something similar. James Harris must have injected something into them. We believe that if you examine Orville Reed's body you'll find the same mark."

"That's very interesting," Carter said, and Patricia felt herself getting smaller with every word he spoke. "But I'm not sure it tells us anything."

"The track marks link Destiny Taylor and Ann Savage," Patricia said, remembering Maryellen's advice during one of their rehearsals. "James Harris's van was seen in Six Mile even though he says he's never been to Six Mile. His van is no longer at his house, but he's keeping it in Pak Rat Mini-Storage. Orville Reed's cousin was killed because of what's going on. Destiny Taylor suffers from the same symptoms as Orville Reed did before he killed himself. We don't think you should wait for Destiny Taylor to follow his example. We believe that while this evidence is circumstantial, there is a preponderance of it."

Maryellen, Kitty, and Slick all looked from Patricia to the men, waiting for their reaction. They gave none. Thrown, Patricia took a sip of water, then decided to try something they hadn't rehearsed.

"Francine was Ann Savage's cleaning woman," she said. "She went missing in May of this year. The day she went missing, I saw her pull up in front of James Harris's house to clean."

"Did you see her go inside?" Ed asked.

"No," Patricia said. "She was reported missing and the police think she went somewhere with a man, but, well, you have to know Francine to realize that's—"

Leland's voice rang out loud and clear. "I'm going to stop you right there. Does anyone need to hear more of this nonsense?"

"But, Leland—" Slick began.

"No, Slick," Leland snapped.

"Would you ladies be open to hearing another perspective?" Carter asked.

Patricia hated his psychiatric voice and his rhetorical questions, but she nodded out of habit.

"Of course," she said.

"Ed?" Carter prompted.

"I ran that license plate number you gave me," Ed said to Maryellen. "It belongs to James Harris, Texas address, no criminal record except a few minor traffic violations. You told me it belonged to a man Horse and Kitty's girl was dating."

"Honey's dating this guy?" Horse asked in a shocked voice.

"No, Horse," Maryellen said. "I made that up to get Ed to run the plates."

Kitty rubbed Horse's back as he shook his head, dumbfounded.

"I'll tell you," Ed sa͟   ͟m always happy to help out a friend, but I was pretty damn embarrassed to meet James Harris thinking he was a cradle robber. It was a cock-up of a conversation until I realized I'd been played for a fool."

"You met him?" Patricia asked.

"We had a conversation," Ed said.

"You discussed this?" Patricia asked, and the betrayal made her voice weak.

"We've been talking for weeks," Leland said. "James Harris is one of the biggest investors in Gracious Cay. Over the past months he's put, well, I won't tell you how much money he's put in, but it's a substantial sum, and in that time he's demonstrated to me that he's a man of character."

"You never told me," Slick said.

"Because it's none of your business," he said.

"Don't be upset with him," Carter said. "Horse, Leland, James Harris, and I have formed a kind of consortium to invest in Gracious Cay. We've had several business meetings and the man we've gotten to know is very different from this murderous, drug-dealing predator you describe. I think it's safe to say that we know him significantly better than you do at this point."

Patricia thought she'd knitted a sweater, but all she held in her hands was a pile of yarn and everyone was laughing at her, patting her on the head, chuckling at her childishness. She wanted to panic. Instead, she turned to Carter.

"We are your wives. We are the mothers of your children, and we believe there is a real danger here," she said. "Does that not count for something?"

"No one said it didn't—" Carter began.

"We're not asking for much," Maryellen said. "Just check his mini-storage. If the van's there, you can get a search warrant and see if it links him to these children."

"No one's doing anything of the sort," Leland said.

"I asked him about that," Ed said. "He told us he did it because he thought all you Old Village ladies didn't like his van parked in his front yard, bringing down the tone of the neighborhood. Grace, he told me you said it was killing his grass. So he got the Corsica, and put the van in storage because he couldn't bear to let it go. He's spending eighty-five dollars a month because he wants to fit in better with the neighborhood."

"And for that," Leland said, "you want to drag his name through the mud and accuse him of being a drug dealer."

"We are men of standing in this community," Bennett said. His voice carried extra weight because he hadn't spoken yet. "Our children go to school here, we have spent our lives building our reputations, and y'all were going to make us laughingstocks because you're a bunch of crazy housewives with too much time on your hands."

"We're just asking you to go look at the mini-storage unit," Grace said, surprising Patricia. "That's all. Just because you've had some drinks with him at the Yacht Club doesn't mean he's hammered from purest gold."

Bennett fixed his eyes on her. His normally friendly face got red.

"Are you arguing with me?" he asked. "Are you arguing with me in public?"

The rage in his voice sucked the air out of the room.

"I think we need to calm down," Horse said, unsure of himself. "They're just worried, you know? Patricia's been through a lot."

"We're worried about the children," Slick said.

"It's true, Patricia has had some emotional blows recently," Carter said. "And they've shaken her more than even I realized. You may not know this, but just a few weeks ago she accused James Harris of being a child molester. You women have all got fine minds, and I know how hard it is to find intellectual stimulation in a place like this. Add in the morbid books you read in your book club and it's a perfect recipe for a kind of group hysteria."

"A book club?" Leland said. "They're in a Bible study group."

The room went silent, and then Carter chuckled.

"Bible study?" he said. "Is that what they call it? No, they meet once a month for book club and read those lurid true crime books full of gory murder photographs you see in drugstores."

Blood drained from the women's faces. Slick's hands twisted in her lap, knuckles white. Leland stared at her from across the room. Horse squeezed Kitty's hand.

"A covenant has been broken," Leland said. "Between husband and wife."

"What's going on?" Korey said from the living room door.

"I told you to stay upstairs!" Patricia snapped, all the humiliation she felt erupting at her daughter.

"Calm down, Patty," Carter said, then turned to Korey, playing the gentle father figure. "We're just having an adult conversation."

"Why's Mom crying?" Korey asked.

Patricia noticed Blue peering in from the dining room door.

"I'm not crying. I'm just upset," she said.

"Wait upstairs, honey," Carter said. "Blue? Go with your sister. I'll come explain everything later, okay?"

Korey and Blue retreated into the hall. Patricia heard them go up the stairs, too loudly and obviously, and in her head she counted the steps. They stopped before they reached the top and she knew they were sitting on the landing, listening.

"I think everything's been said that could possibly be said," Carter pronounced.

"You can't stop me from going to the police," Patricia said.

"I can't stop you, Patty," Carter said. "But I can inform them that I believe my wife is not in her right mind. Because the first person they'll call isn't a judge to get a search warrant; it'll be your husband. Ed's made sure of that."

"You can't keep sending the police on wild-goose chases," Ed said.

Carter checked his watch.

"I think the only thing that remains are apologies."

Patricia's spine turned to stone. This was something she could hold on to, this was ground on which she could stand.

"If you think I'm going down to that man's house and apologizing, you are deeply mistaken," she said, drawing herself up, speaking as much like Grace as she could. She tried to make eye contact with Grace, but Grace stared miserably into the cold fireplace, not making eye contact with anyone.

"You don't have to go anywhere," Carter said as the doorbell rang. "He's agreed to come here."

Right on cue, Leland stepped into the hall and came back with James Harris. Unbelievably, he was smiling. James wore a white button-up oxford shirt tucked into a new pair of khaki pants, and brown loafers. He looked like someone who belonged on a boat. He looked like someone from Charleston.

"I'm sorry about all of this, Jim," Ed said, standing and shaking his hand.

All the men exchanged firm handshakes and Patricia saw their shoulders relax, the tension in their faces dissolve. She saw that they thought of him as one of their own. James Harris turned to the women, studying each of their faces, stopping at Patricia.

"I understand I've been the source of a whole lot of fuss and worry," he said.

"I think the girls have something they want to say," Leland said.

"I feel terrible to have caused all this commotion," James said.

"Patricia?" Carter prompted.

She knew he wanted her to go first to set an example for the other women, but she was her own person, and she didn't have to do anything she didn't want to. He'd forced her to apologize once already. Not again.

"I have nothing to say to Mr. Harris," she said. "I think he's not who he says he is and I think all anyone would need to do is look inside his mini-storage unit to see I'm right."

"Patricia—" Carter started.

"I'm willing to let bygones be bygones if Patricia is," James said, and stepped toward her with one hand outstretched. "Forgive and forget?"

Patricia saw his hand and the whole room behind it blurred and she felt everyone's eyes on her.

"Mr. Harris," she said. "If you don't remove your hand from my face immediately, I'm going to spit on it."

"Patty!" Carter snapped.

James gave a sheepish grin and pulled his hand back.

"I thought we were friends," he said. "I'm sorry for whatever I've done to offend you."

"Shake hands with him right this minute like an adult," Carter said.

"Absolutely not," she said.

"You are embarrassing yourself and the children," Carter said. "I am asking you to apologize."

Then Grace saved the day.

"Mr. Harris," she said, standing and walking over to him. "Please accept my apologies. It seems our imaginations ran away with us."

He shook her hand and then, one after the other, each of the women stood and apologized, and shook his hand, and simpered, and curtsied, and kissed his ring, while Patricia sat there, at first simmering with hot rage, then going cold.

"I'd like to ask something, if it's not too much," James Harris said.

"At this point, I think we're all willing to do whatever it takes to put this behind us," Carter said.

"The more you get to know me," James Harris said, "the more you'll realize I'm not some kind of super criminal. I'm just an ordinary man who's fallen in love with this neighborhood and wants to be a part of it. We're only scared of what we don't know. I've been a source of a lot of anxiety for Patricia, and I'm sure she's not the only one. I don't want anyone to be afraid of me. I want to be your friend and your neighbor. So, if it's okay with everyone, I'd like to join your book club as a full-time member. You had me as a guest once, and I think it'd be a good place where you could get to know the real me."

Patricia could not believe what she was hearing.

"That is a generous and thoughtful suggestion," Carter said. "Patty? Girls? What do you think?"

Patricia didn't say a word. She knew it didn't matter what she thought anymore.

"I think that's a yes," Carter said.

CHAPTER 22

Patricia didn't want to talk that night, and Carter had the good sense not to push it. She went to bed early. Carter thought nothing was wrong? Let *him* worry about Korey and Blue. Let *him* feed them and keep them safe. Downstairs she heard him go out and bring back take-out Chinese for the kids, and the buzzing rise and fall of A Serious Conversation filtered up from the dining room. After Korey and Blue went to bed, Carter slept on the den sofa.

The next morning, she saw Destiny Taylor's picture in the paper and read the story with numb acceptance. The nine-year-old had waited until it was her turn in the bathroom of her foster home, then took dental floss, wrapped it around her neck over and over, and hanged herself from the towel rack. The police were investigating whether it might be abuse.

"I'd like to speak to you in the dining room," Carter said from the door to the den.

Patricia looked up from the paper. Carter needed to shave.

"That child killed herself," she said. "The one we told you about, Destiny Taylor, she killed herself just like we warned you she would."

"Patty, from where I'm standing, we stopped a lynch mob from running an innocent man out of town."

"It was the woman whose trailer you came to in Six Mile," Patricia said. "You saw that little girl. Nine years old. Why does a nine-year-old child kill herself? What could make her do that?"

"Our children need you," Carter said. "Do you see what your book club has done to Blue?"

"My book club?" she asked, off balance.

"The morbid things y'all read," Carter said. "Did you see the videotapes on top of the TV? He got *Night and Fog* from the library. It's Holocaust footage. That's not what a normal ten-year-old boy looks at."

"A nine-year-old girl hanged herself with dental floss and you won't even bother to ask why," Patricia said. "Imagine if that was your last memory of Blue—hanging from the towel rod, floss cutting into his neck—"

"Jesus Christ, Patty, where'd you learn to talk this way?"

He walked into the dining room. Patricia thought about not following, then realized that this wouldn't end until they'd played out every single moment Carter had planned. She got up and followed. The morning sun made the yellow walls of the dining room glow. Carter stood facing her from the other end of the table, hands behind his back, one of her everyday saucers in front of him.

"I realize I bear some of the responsibility for how bad things have gotten," he said. "You've been under a great deal of stress from what happened with my mother, and you never properly processed the trauma of being injured. I let the fact that you're my wife cloud my judgment and I missed the symptoms."

"Why are you treating me like this?" she asked.

He ignored her, continuing his speech.

"You live an isolated life," Carter said. "Your reading tastes are morbid. Both your children are going through difficult phases. I have a high-pressure job that requires me to put in long hours. I didn't realize how close to the edge you were."

He picked up the saucer, carried it to her end of the table, and set it down with a *click*. A green-and-white capsule rolled around in the center.

"I've seen this turn people's lives around," Carter said.

"I don't want it," she said.

"It'll help you regain your equilibrium," he said.

She pinched the capsule between her thumb and forefinger. *Dista Prozac* was printed on the side.

"And I have to take it or you'll leave me?" she asked.

"Don't be so dramatic," Carter said. "I'm offering you help."

He reached into his pocket and pulled out a white bottle. It rattled when he set it on the table.

"One pill, twice a day, with food," he said. "I'm not going to count the pills. I'm not going to watch you take them. You can flush them down the toilet if you want. This isn't me trying to control you. This is me trying to help you. You're my wife and I believe you can get better."

At least he had the good sense not to try to kiss her before he left.

After he was gone, Patricia picked up the phone and called Grace. Her machine picked up, so she called Kitty.

"I can't talk," Kitty said.

"Did you see the paper this morning?" Patricia asked. "That was Destiny Taylor, page B-6."

"I don't want to hear about those kind of things anymore," Kitty said.

"He knows we've gone to the police," Patricia said. "Think of what he's going to do to us."

"He's coming to our house," Kitty said.

"You have to get out of there," Patricia said.

"For supper," Kitty said. "To meet the family. Horse wants him to know there are no hard feelings."

"But why?" Patricia asked.

"Because that's how Horse is," Kitty said.

"We can't give up just because the rest of the men suddenly think he's their pal."

"Do you know what we could lose?" Kitty asked. "It's Slick and Leland's business. It's Ed's job. It's our marriages, our families. Horse has put all our money into this project he's doing with Leland."

"That little girl died," Patricia said. "You didn't see her, but she was barely nine."

"There's nothing we can do about it," Kitty said. "We have to take care of our families and let other people worry about theirs. If someone's hurting those children, the police will stop them."

She got Grace's machine again, then tried Maryellen.

"I can't talk," Maryellen said. "I'm right in the middle of something."

"Call me back later," Patricia said.

"I'm busy all day," Maryellen said.

"That little girl killed herself," Patricia said. "Destiny Taylor."

"I have to run," Maryellen said.

"It's on page B-6," Patricia said. "There's going to be another one after this, and another after that, and another, and another."

Maryellen spoke quiet and low.

"Patricia," she said. "Stop."

"It doesn't have to be Ed," Patricia said. "What were the names of those other two police detectives? Cannon and Bussell?"

"Don't!" Maryellen said, too loud. Patricia heard panting over the phone and realized Maryellen was crying. "Hold on," she said, and sniffed hard. Patricia heard her put the phone down.

After a moment, Maryellen picked it back up.

"I had to shut the bedroom door," she said. "Patricia, listen to me. When we lived in New Jersey, we came home from Alexa's fourth birthday party and our front door was standing wide open. Someone broke in and urinated on the living room carpet, turned over all our bookcases, stuffed our wedding pictures in the upstairs bathtub and left it running so it backed up and flooded the ceiling. Our clothes were hacked to shreds. Our mattresses and upholstery slashed. And in the baby's room they'd written *Die Pigs* on the wall. In feces."

Patricia listened to the line hum while Maryellen caught her breath.

"Ed was a police officer and he couldn't protect his own family," Maryellen continued. "It ate him alive. When he was supposed to be at work he parked across the street and watched our house. He missed shifts. They wanted to give him a few weeks off, but he needed the hours, so he kept going in. It wasn't his fault, Patty, but they sent him to pick up a shoplifter at the mall and the boy lipped off and Ed hit him. He didn't mean to, it wasn't even that hard, but the boy lost some of the hearing in his left ear. It was one of those freak things. We didn't come down here because Ed wanted some-place quieter. We came down here because this was all he could find. Ed used up all his favors getting transferred."

She blew her nose. Patricia waited.

"If anyone talks to the police," Maryellen said, "they're going to follow it back to Ed. That boy he hit was eleven years old. He will never find another job. Promise me, Patricia. No more."

"I can't," Patricia said.

"Patricia, please—" Maryellen began.

Patricia hung up.

She tried Grace again. The machine was still picking up so she called Slick.

"I saw it in the paper this morning," Slick said. "That poor girl's mother."

Patricia's heart unclenched.

"Kitty is too frightened to do anything," Patricia said. "She's buried her head in the sand. And Maryellen is in a bad position be-cause of Ed."

"That man is evil," Slick said. "Look how he twisted us up like pretzels and made us seem like fools. He knew exactly how to get Leland's trust."

"He says he got that money he put into Gracious Cay from Ann Savage," Patricia said. "But that's dirty money if I've ever seen it."

"I know, but he's Leland's business partner now," Slick contin-ued. "And I can't accuse him of this kind of thing without cutting my own family's throat. We've been there before, Patricia. I'm not going back there again. I will not do that to my children."

"This is about children's lives," Patricia said. "That matters more than money."

"You've never lost your house," Slick said. "You've never had to explain to your children why they have to move in with their grandmother, or why you have to take the dog to the pound because food stamps don't cover dog food."

"If you'd met Destiny Taylor you wouldn't be able to harden your heart," Patricia said.

"My family is my rock," Slick said. "You've never lost everything. I have. Let Destiny's mother worry about Destiny. I know you think this makes me a bad person, but I need to turn inward and be a good steward to my family right now. I'm sorry."

Grace's machine picked up again when she called back, so Patricia got her purse and went over to her house, stepping out into the blast furnace of the day. By the time she rang Grace's bell, sweat was already seeping through her blouse. She let the echoes of the chimes die inside the house, then rang again. The doorbell got louder as Mrs. Greene opened the door.

"I didn't know you were helping Grace today," Patricia said.

"Yes, ma'am," Mrs. Greene said, looking down at Patricia. "She's feeling poorly."

"I'm sorry to hear that," Patricia said, trying to step inside.

Mrs. Greene didn't move. Patricia stopped, one foot on the threshold.

"I'm just going to say hello for a quick minute," Patricia said.

Mrs. Greene inhaled through her nostrils. "I don't think she wants to see anyone," she said.

"I'll only be a minute," Patricia said. "Did she tell you what happened yesterday?"

Something confused and conflicted flickered through Mrs. Greene's eyes, and then she said, "Yes."

"I have to tell her we can't stop."

"Destiny Taylor died," Mrs. Greene said.

"I know," Patricia said. "I'm so sorry."

"You promised you'd get her back to her mother and now she's dead," Mrs. Greene said, then turned and disappeared into the house.

Patricia stepped into the cool, dark house. Her skin contracted and broke out in goose pimples. She'd never felt the air conditioning turned this low before.

She walked down the hall, into the dining room. The overhead chandelier was on but it only seemed to make the room darker. Grace sat at one end of the table in slacks and a navy turtleneck beneath a gray sweater. The table was covered in trash.

"Patricia," Grace said. "I'm not up to seeing visitors."

She had strawberry jam clotted in the corner of her mouth, and as Patricia came closer she saw it was a scab crusted around a split lip.

"What happened?" she asked, raising her fingers to the same place on the corner of her own mouth.

"Oh," Grace said, and made her face look happy. "The silliest thing. I was in a car accident."

"A what?" Patricia asked. "Are you all right?"

She'd just seen Grace last night. When had she had time to get in a car accident?

"I ran to Harris Teeter this morning," Grace said, smiling. It cracked the scab and Patricia saw wet blood gleaming in the wound. "I was backing out of my space and backed right into a man in a Jeep."

"Who was it?" Patricia asked. "Did you get his insurance?"

Grace was already dismissing her before she finished.

"No need," she said. "It was just a silly thing. He was more shaken up than me."

She gave Patricia another enthusiastic smile. It made Patricia feel ill, so she looked down at the table to gather her thoughts. A cardboard box sat at one end, and its dark wood surface was covered in jagged, white shards of broken porcelain. A delicate handle protruded from a ceramic curve and Patricia recognized an orange and yellow butterfly, and then her vision widened and took in the entire table.

"The wedding china," she said.

She couldn't help it. The words just fell out of her mouth. The entire set had been smashed. Shards were spread across the table like bone fragments. She felt horrified, as if she were seeing a mutilated corpse.

"It was an accident," Grace began.

"Did James Harris do this?" Patricia asked. "Did he try to intimidate you? Did he come here and threaten you?"

She tore her eyes away from the carnage and saw Grace's face. It was pinched with fury.

"Do not ever say that man's name again," Grace said. "Not to me, not to anyone. Not if you want our relations to remain cordial."

"It was him," Patricia said.

"No," Grace snapped. "You are not listening to what I am saying. I shook his hand and apologized because you made fools of us all. You humiliated us in front of our husbands, in front of a stranger, in front of your children. I tried to tell you before and you wouldn't listen, but I am telling you now. As soon as I've cleared up this . . . mess"—her voice cracked—"I am phoning every member of the book club and telling them in no uncertain language that this matter is at an end and will never, ever be mentioned again. And we will welcome this man into book club and do whatever it takes to put this behind us."

"What did he do to you?" Patricia asked.

"You did this to me," Grace said. "You made me trust you. And I looked like a fool. You humiliated me in front of my husband."

"I didn't—" Patricia tried.

"You caught me up in your playacting," Grace said. "You arranged this amateur theatrical event in your living room and somehow convinced me to participate—I must have been out of my mind."

The morning flowed into Patricia's limbs like black sludge, filling her up as Grace talked.

"This tawdry soap opera you've imagined between yourself and James Harris," Grace said. "I'd almost suspect you were . . . sexually frustrated."

Patricia couldn't stop herself. The anger wasn't hers. She was only a channel. It came from someplace else, it had to, because there was so much of it.

"What do you do all day, Grace?" she asked, and heard her voice echoing off the dining room walls. "Ben is off to college. Bennett is at work. All you do is look down your nose at the rest of us, hide in this house, and clean."

"Do you ever think how lucky you are?" Grace asked. "Your husband works himself to the bone providing for you and the children. He's kind, he doesn't raise his voice in anger. All your needs are catered to, yet you weave these lurid fantasies out of boredom."

"I'm the only person who sees reality," Patricia said. "Something is wrong here, something bigger than your grandmother's china, and your silver polish, and your manners, and next month's book, and you're too scared to face it. So you just sit in your house and scrub away like a good little wife."

"You say that like it's nothing," Grace wailed. "I *am* a good person, and I *am* a good wife, *and* a good mother. And, yes, I clean my house, because that is my job. It is my place in this world. It is what I am here to do. And I am satisfied with that. And I don't need to fantasize that I'm . . . I'm Nancy Drew to be happy. I can be happy with what I do and who I am."

"Clean all you want," Patricia said. "But whenever Bennett has a drink, he's still going to smack you in the mouth."

Grace stood, frozen in shock. Patricia couldn't believe she had said that. They stayed like that in the freezing cold dining room for a long moment, and Patricia knew their friendship would never recover. She turned and left the room.

She found Mrs. Greene dusting the banister in the front hall.

"You don't believe this, do you?" Patricia asked her. "You know who he really is."

Mrs. Greene made her face perfectly calm.

"I spoke with Mrs. Cavanaugh and she explained to me that y'all wouldn't be able to help anymore," Mrs. Greene said. "She told me everyone in Six Mile are on our own. She explained everything to me in great detail."

"It's not true," Patricia said.

"It's all right," Mrs. Greene said, smiling dimly. "I understand. From here on out, I don't expect anything from any of y'all."

"I'm on *your* side," Patricia said. "I just need some time for everything to settle down."

"You're on *your* side," Mrs. Greene said. "Don't ever fool yourself about that."

Then she turned her back on Patricia and kept dusting Grace's home.

Something exploded red and black inside Patricia's brain and the next thing she knew she was storming into her house, standing on the sun porch, seeing Korey slumped in the big chair staring at the TV.

"Would you please turn that off and go downtown or to the beach or somewhere?" Patricia snapped. "It is one o'clock in the afternoon."

"Dad said I didn't have to listen to you," Korey told her. "He said you were going through a phase."

It touched off a fire inside her, but Patricia had the clarity to see how carefully Carter had built this trap for her. Anything she did would prove him right. She could hear him saying, in his smooth psychiatric tones, *It's a sign of how sick you are, that you can't see how sick you are.*

She took a deep breath. She would not react. She would not participate in this anymore. She went into the dining room and saw the Prozac in its saucer and the bottle of pills next to it. She snatched them up and took them into the kitchen.

Standing by the sink, she ran the water and washed the pill down the drain. She unscrewed the bottle, and looked at it for a moment. Then she got out a glass, filled it, set it down, and began to take the entire bottle of pills, one by one.

CHAPTER 23

The sweet reek of boiled ketchup crawled up Patricia's nostrils, slid over her sinuses, and coated her throat. She ran her tongue around the inside of her mouth, and tasted a bitter film coating her teeth. Her skull lurched as her upper body jerked forward and she opened her eyes and saw a nurse cranking up her bed. It had white sheets and a beige rail. Carter stood at the end of her hospital bed.

"We don't need that," he told the nurse.

Patricia saw a burgundy plastic tray on a rolling table in front of her, and a covered dish stinking of boiled ketchup. The nurse lifted the lid and Patricia saw three gray meatballs sitting on a limp pile of yellow spaghetti covered in ketchup.

"I have to leave the meal," the nurse said.

"Then put it over there," Carter said, and the nurse placed it on a chair by the door and left.

"Tell me you mixed up the dosage," Carter said. "Tell me you made a mistake."

She didn't want to have this conversation right now. Patricia turned and stared out her window at the late-afternoon sunlight slashing across the upper floors of the Basic Sciences building and realized she was in the psych unit.

"Do I have brain damage?" she asked.

"Do you know who found you?" Carter asked, resting his hands on the bed rail. "Blue. He's ten years old and he found his mother having a seizure on the kitchen floor and you probably would have brain damage if he hadn't been smart enough to call 911. What were you thinking, Patty? *Were* you thinking?"

Hot tears squirted from her eyes, one at a time, tapping her nose, streaming over her lips.

"Is Blue here?" she asked.

"I don't know what's wrong with you, Patty, but I swear we're going to get to the bottom of it."

He made her feel like an essay question on one of the children's tests, but she didn't have a right to object. Blue must have been terrified when he found her twitching on the kitchen floor. It would haunt him for the rest of his life. The hot, gristly smell of meatballs made her stomach twist itself tight.

"I wasn't trying to kill myself," she said, her jaw clenched.

"No one's listening to you anymore," Carter said. "You made a serious suicide attempt, however you try to explain it away. They have you on a twenty-four-hour involuntary hold, but I'm going to check you out of here first thing in the morning. There's nothing wrong with you we can't solve at home. But before any of that happens, I need to know right now: was this about James Harris?"

"What?" she asked, and turned to look at her husband.

His face was stricken, open, and raw. His hands fidgeted hard on the bed rail.

"You're my whole life," he said. "You and the children. You and I have grown up together. And suddenly you're obsessed with Jim, you can't stop thinking about him, you can't stop talking about him, and then you do this. The woman I married would never try to kill herself. It wasn't in her character."

"I wasn't . . . ," she said, genuinely trying to explain, "I didn't want to die. I was just so angry. You wanted me to take those pills so badly, so I took them."

His face instantly closed up, and a steel door came down.

"Don't you dare put this on me," he said.

"I'm not. Please."

"Why are you fixated on Jim?" he asked. "What's between the two of you?"

"He's dangerous," she said, and Carter's shoulders slumped and he turned away from her bed. "I know you think he hangs the moon but he is a dangerous person, more dangerous than you know."

And for a moment, she thought about telling him what she'd read all those weeks ago. After she'd read that passage in *Dracula* about him needing to be invited into a home, she'd sat down and read the entire book again and halfway through she'd come across a sentence that brought her up short and made her hands turn cold.

He can command all the meaner things, Van Helsing told the Harkers, explaining the powers of Dracula. *The rat, and the owl, and the bat . . .*

The rat.

In that moment, she knew who was responsible for Miss Mary's death. Rarely had she known something with such certainty. Patricia thought about what Carter would say if he knew that his friend had put his mother into the hospital, one hand stripped of its skin, the soft tissues torn from her face. She also knew with certainty that if she said that to Carter he would never let her out of this room.

"I wish you were having an affair with him," Carter said. "It would make your fixation easier to understand. But this is sick."

"He's not who you think he is," she said.

"Do you know what is at stake here?" he asked. "Do you know the toll your obsession is taking on your family? If you continue down this path you will lose everything we have built together. *Everything.*"

She thought about Blue coming into the kitchen for a snack and seeing her convulsing on the yellow linoleum and all she wanted to do was hold on to her baby and reassure him she was all right. That everything would be all right. But it wasn't all right, not as long as James Harris lived down the street.

Carter walked to the door. He stopped when he got there and

made a big production out of talking to her without turning around.

"I don't know if you care," he said. "But they've put together a search committee to replace Haley."

"Oh, Carter," she croaked, genuinely upset for him.

"Everyone heard you were on a psychiatric hold," he said. "Haley came down this morning to tell me I need to focus on my family right now and not my career. Your actions affect other people, Patricia. The whole world doesn't revolve around you."

He left her alone in the room, and she watched the sun creep across the Basic Sciences building and tried to imagine life ever being normal again. She had ruined everything. Everything anyone knew about her had been destroyed by what she had done. From now on she would be *unstable* no matter what she did. How would her children ever trust her again? The smell of meatballs made her feel sick.

A clatter at the door and she turned back to see Carter ushering in Korey and Blue. Korey slumped forward, hair hanging in her face, wearing a tie-dyed T-shirt and her white jeans with rips over the knees. Blue wore his navy shorts and a red *Iraq-na-phobia* T-shirt. He carried a thick library book called *Auschwitz: A Doctor's Eyewitness Account*. Korey dragged the only chair across the floor and dropped it as far away from Patricia as she could get. Blue leaned against the wall beside her.

Patricia wanted to hold her babies so badly and she reached out to them and something yanked her wrists. She looked down, confused, and saw that her wrists were tied to the bed with thick black Velcro straps.

"Carter?"

"They didn't know if you were a flight risk," he said. "I'll ask to have them taken off when I see the doctor."

But Patricia knew he had done this on purpose. When she was unconscious, he had told them she was a flight risk, because this was how he wanted the children to see her. Fine, he could play his games, but she was still their mother.

"Blue," she said. "I'd like a hug if that's okay with you."

He opened his book and pretended to read, leaning against the wall.

"I'm sorry you saw me that way," Patricia said to him in a low, calm voice. "I did a stupid thing and I took too many of my pills and they made me sick. I might have gotten brain damage if you hadn't been brave enough to call 911. Thank you for doing that, Blue. I love you."

He opened his book wider, and then wider, pressing its covers toward each other, and from across the room, Patricia heard its spine crack.

"Blue," she said. "I know you're angry at me, but that's not how we treat books."

He dropped his book on the floor with a *thud*, and when he bent over to pick it up, he lifted it by the pages and several of them tore off in his hand.

"You're mad at me, son," Patricia said. "Not at the book."

Then he was screaming, face red, shaking the book by its pages, the covers flopping back and forth.

"Shut up!" he screamed, and Korey stuck her fingers in her ears and hunched lower. "I hate you! I hate you! You tried to kill yourself because you're crazy and now you're tied to the bed and you're going to be sent to a mental hospital. You don't love any of us! All you care about are your stupid books!"

He grabbed the pages of his book in one hand and frantically tore them out, letting them fall to the floor. They slid across the room, beneath the bed, under the chair. Then he threw the cover, now just cardboard, at Patricia. It hit her in the leg.

"That's *ENOUGH*!" Carter bellowed, and Blue stopped, stunned into silence, his face twisted with rage, cheeks mottled, snot running from his nose, fists clenched by his side, body vibrating.

Patricia needed to go to him and take him in her arms and take that anger from him, but she was tied to the bed. Carter stood by the door, not moving, arms folded, surveying the scene he had created, not going to comfort their son, not unstrapping her arms so she could do it instead, and Patricia thought, *I will never forgive you for this. Never. Never. Never.*

"Can I get money for the machines?" Korey mumbled.

"Sweetheart," Patricia asked. "Do you feel the same way as your brother?"

"Dad?" Korey repeated, ignoring Patricia. "Can I get a dollar for the vending machines?"

Carter looked away from Patricia and nodded, putting his hand in his back pocket and pulling out his wallet. The only sound in the room was Blue crying.

"Korey?" Patricia asked.

"Here," Carter said, holding out some bills. "Take your brother. I'll be there in a minute."

Korey hauled herself to her feet and left, leading Blue by the shoulder. She didn't look at Patricia once.

"There you have it, Patty," Carter said after they'd gone. "That's what you're doing to your children. So what's it going to be? Are you going to continue with this fixation on someone you hardly know? What's he done, exactly? Oh, I remember: nothing. He hasn't done one single, solitary thing. He's not accused of anything. The only person who thinks he's done something wrong is you, and you have no evidence, no proof, nothing except your *feelings*. So you can continue to be fixated on him, or you can put your attention where it belongs: on your family. It's up to you. I've lost my promotion, but it's not too late for the kids. This can still be fixed, but I need a partner, not someone who's going to keep making it worse. So that's the decision you have to make. Jim, or us? Which is it going to be, Patty?"

THREE YEARS LATER . . .

CLEAR AND PRESENT DANGER

October 1996

CHAPTER 24

It made Patricia nervous when Carter used his cellular phone while driving, but he was the better driver and they were already running late for book club, which meant it was going to be hard to find parking.

"And you'll upgrade me to a king," Carter said, letting go of the wheel with one hand to put on his turn signal.

Their dark red BMW took the turn into Creekside smooth and easy. Patricia didn't like it when he drove like this, but on the other hand this was one of the few times he didn't have Rush Limbaugh on the radio, so she took her blessings where she could.

"You can make the check out to Campbell Clinical Consulting," Carter said. "The address is on the invoice I faxed."

He snapped his phone shut and hummed a little tune.

"That's the sixth talk," he said. "It's going to be busy this fall. You're sure you're all right with me being gone so much?"

"I'll miss you," she said. "But college isn't free."

He steered them down the cool tunnels formed by Creekside's trees, dying sunlight flickering between the leaves, strobing over the windshield and hood.

"If you still want to remodel the kitchen, you can," Carter said. "We have enough."

Up ahead, Patricia saw the back of Horse's Chevy Blazer parked at the end of a long line of Saabs, Audis, and Infinitis. They were still a block from Slick and Leland's house, but the parked cars stretched all the way back here.

"Are you sure?" Patricia asked. "We still don't know where Korey's thinking of going."

"Or if she's even thinking," Carter said, pulling up behind Horse's Chevy but leaving a big buffer zone between their cars. It didn't pay to park too close to Horse these days.

"What if she picks somewhere like NYU or Wellesley?" Patricia said, undoing her seat belt.

"The chances of Korey getting into NYU or Wellesley, I'll take those odds," Carter said, giving her a peck on the cheek. "Quit worrying. You'll make yourself sick."

They got out of the car. Patricia hated getting out of cars. According to the bathroom scale, she'd gained eleven pounds and she felt them hanging from her hips and stomach, and they made her feel unsteady on her feet. She didn't think she looked bad with a fuller face as long as she sprayed her hair a little bigger, but getting in and out of cars made her feel graceless.

She waddled—*walked*—up the street with Carter, the October chill prickling her arms with goose bumps. She readjusted her grip on this month's book—why did Tom Clancy need more pages than the Bible to tell a story?—and Carter opened the gate in the literal white picket fence around Slick and Leland's front yard. Together, they went up the path of the Paleys' large, barn-red Cape Cod that looked like it belonged in New England, right down to the decorative millstone in the front yard.

Carter rang the bell and the door instantly swung open to reveal Slick. She was gelled and moussed and her mouth was too small for her lipstick, but she looked genuinely happy to see them.

"Carter! Patricia!" she cried, beaming. "You look fabulous."

Recently, Patricia had surprised herself when she realized that the main reason she kept coming to book club was to see Slick.

"You look wonderful, too," Patricia said, with a genuine smile.

"Isn't this vest adorable?" Slick spread her arms. "Leland bought it for me at Kerrison's for almost nothing."

It didn't matter how many Paley Realty signs sprang up all over Mt. Pleasant, or how much Slick talked about money, or showed off things Leland bought for her, or tried to gossip about Albemarle Academy now that Tiger had finally gotten in. To Patricia she was a person of substance.

"Come on back!" Slick said, leading them into the claustrophobic, overstuffed roar of book club.

People spilled out of Slick's dining room, and Patricia twisted her hips to avoid bumping into anyone as Slick led them past the stairs, past all the display cases for her collections—the Lenox Garden bird figurines, little ceramic cottages, miniature sterling silver furniture—past new wall plaques bearing even more devotional quotations, past the collectible wristwatches mounted in shadow boxes.

"Hello, hello!" Patricia said to Louise Gibbes as they went by.

"You look fabulous, Loretta," Patricia said to Loretta Jones.

"Your Gamecocks took a whupping Saturday," Carter said to Arthur Rivers, clapping him on one shoulder, never slowing down.

They emerged from the hall into the new addition at the back of the house and the ceiling suddenly shot up over their heads, soaring to a series of skylights. The addition stretched almost to the Paleys' property line, a massive barn for entertaining, and every inch was crammed with people. There must be forty members these days, and Slick was just about the only person with enough house for all of them.

"Help yourselves," Slick said over the roar of conversation bouncing off the high ceilings and the far walls, which were hung with picturesque farm implements. "I have to find Leland. Did you see this? He gave me a Mickey Mouse watch. Isn't it fun?"

She waved her sparkly wrist at Patricia, then slipped away into a forest of backs and arms holding rental glasses and hands holding rental plates and everyone with copies of *Clear and Present Danger* tucked beneath their elbows, or resting on the backs of chairs.

Patricia looked for someone she knew, and saw Marjorie Fretwell over by the buffet. They kissed on both cheeks, the way people did these days.

"You look wonderful," Marjorie said.

"Have you lost weight?" Patricia asked.

"Are you doing something different with your hair?" Marjorie asked back. "I love it."

Sometimes it bothered Patricia how much time they spent telling each other how good they looked, how wonderful they seemed, how fantastic they were. Three years ago she would have suspected Carter had called ahead and told everyone to make sure they kept Patricia's spirits up, but now she realized that all of them did it, all the time.

But what was wrong with enjoying their blessings? They had so many good things in their lives. Why not celebrate?

"Hey, man!" a loud voice said, and Patricia saw Horse's red face rising up over Marjorie's shoulder. "Is that husband of yours around?"

He leaned in unsteadily to peck Patricia on the cheek. He hadn't shaved, and a yeasty cloud of beer hovered around his head.

"A horse is a horse, of course, of course," Carter said, coming up behind Patricia.

"You won't believe it, but we're rich again," Horse said, putting one hand on Carter's shoulder to steady himself. "Next time we go to the club, drinks are on me."

"Don't forget, we've got four more who want to go to college," Kitty said, stepping into the circle and giving Patricia a one-armed hug.

"Don't be cheap, woman!" Horse bellowed.

"We signed the papers today," Kitty explained.

"When I see Jimmy H. I'm gonna kiss him," Horse said. "Right on the lips!"

Patricia smiled. James Harris had totally transformed Kitty and Horse's lives. He'd straightened out the management of Seewee

Farms, hired them a young man to run things, and convinced Horse to sell 110 acres to a developer. That was what had finally come through today.

It wasn't just them. All of them, including Patricia and Carter, had invested more and more money in Gracious Cay, and as outside investors kept coming in they'd all taken out credit lines against their shares. It felt like money just kept falling out of the sky.

"You got to come with me Saturday," Horse told Carter. "Do some boat shopping."

"How are the children?" Patricia asked Kitty, because that was the kind of thing you said.

"We finally convinced Pony to look at the Citadel," Kitty said. "I can't stand the idea of him up at Carolina or Wake Forest. He'd be so far away."

"It's better when they stay local," Marjorie nodded.

"And Horse wants another Citadel man in the family," Kitty said.

"That class ring opens doors," Marjorie said. "It really does."

As Marjorie and Kitty talked, the room began to close in around Patricia. She didn't know why everyone's voices sounded so loud, or why the small of her back felt cold and greasy with sweat, or why her underarms itched. Then she smelled the Swedish meatballs bubbling away in the silver chafing dish on the buffet table beside her.

Carter and Horse laughed uproariously over something and Horse put his beer down on the buffet table and he already had another one in his hand and Kitty said something about Korey, and the familiar reek of boiling ketchup filled Patricia's skull and coated her throat.

She forced herself to stop thinking about it. It was better not to think about it. Her life was back to normal now. Her life was better than normal.

"Did you see on the news about that school in New York?" Kitty asked. "The children have to get there at five a.m. because it takes them two and a half hours to go through the metal detectors."

"But you can't put a price on safety," Marjorie said.

"Excuse me," Patricia said.

She pushed her way past shoulders and backs, needing to get away from that smell, twisting her hips to the side, terrified she'd knock someone's drink out of their hands, forcing her way through scraps of conversation.

". . . taking him up to tour the campus . . ."

". . . have you lost weight . . ."

". . . divest into Netscape . . ."

". . . the president's just a Bubba, it's his wife . . ."

Kitty hadn't visited her in the hospital.

She didn't want to keep score like this but for the first time in years it just popped into her mind.

"You were in and out so quickly," Kitty had told Patricia over the phone. "I was going to come just as soon as I got organized but by the time that happened, you were already home."

She remembered Kitty begging for reassurance. "With all those pills, you just mixed up your prescription, didn't you?"

That was what had happened, she agreed, and Kitty had been so grateful it didn't have to go any further or get any messier and she had been so grateful that everyone had let it drop and never talked about it again that she hadn't realized how much it hurt that none of them came by the hospital. At the time, she was just grateful. She was grateful no one called her a suicide and treated her different. She was grateful it had been so easy to slip back into her old life. She was grateful for the new dock and the trip to London and the surgery to fix her ear and the backyard cookouts and the new car. She was grateful for so many things.

"Ice water, please," she said to the black man in white gloves behind the bar.

The only one who came to the hospital had been Slick. She showed up at seven in the morning and knocked gently on the open door and came in and sat down next to Patricia. She didn't say much. She didn't have any advice or insight, no ideas or opinions. She didn't need to be convinced it had all been an accident. She just sat there, holding Patricia's hand in a kind of silent prayer, and around seven forty-five she said, "We all need you to get better," and left.

She was the only one of them Patricia cared about anymore. She didn't hold anything too much against Kitty and Maryellen and they saw each other socially, but the only time she came near Grace now was at book club. When she saw Grace she thought about things she'd said that she didn't want to remember.

She turned, cold glass in one hand, grateful she couldn't smell the meatballs anymore, and saw Grace and Bennett standing behind her.

"Hello, Grace," she said. "Bennett."

Grace didn't move; Bennett stood motionless. No one leaned forward for a hug. Bennett had an iced tea in his hand instead of a beer. Grace had lost weight.

"It's quite a turnout," Grace said, surveying the room.

"Did you enjoy this month's book?" Patricia asked.

"I've certainly learned a lot about the war on drugs," Grace said.

I hated it, Patricia wanted to say. Everyone talked in the same terse, manly sentences you'd expect from an insurance salesman fantasizing about war. Every sentence dripped with DDOs and DDIs and LPIs and E-2s and F-15s and MH-53Js and C-141s. She didn't understand half of what she read, there were no women in it except fools and prostitutes, it had nothing to say about their lives, and it felt like a recruitment ad for the army.

"It was very illuminating," she agreed.

James Harris had turned their book club into this. He'd started getting the husbands to attend, and they'd started reading more and more books by Pat Conroy ("He's a local author.") and Michael Crichton ("Fascinating concepts"), and *The Horse Whisperer* and *All the Pretty Horses* and *Bravo Two Zero*, and sometimes Patricia despaired over what were they going to read next—*The Celestine Prophecy*? *Chicken Soup for the Soul*?—but mostly she marveled at how many people came.

It was better not to dwell on it. Everything changes, and was it really so bad that more people wanted to discuss books?

"We need to find seats," Grace said. "Excuse us."

Patricia watched them retreat into the crowd. The track lighting got brighter as the sky outside got darker, and she made her way back to her group. As she got nearer she smelled sandalwood and leather. People parted and she saw Carter talking excitedly to someone, and then she passed the last person blocking her view and saw James Harris, dressed in a blue oxford shirt with the sleeves rolled up just so, and his khakis pressed exactly right, his hair tousled by experts, and his skin glowing with health.

"You wouldn't believe the schedule they have me on this fall," Carter was telling him. "Six talks before January. You'll have to keep an eye on the old homestead."

"You know you love it," James Harris said, and they both laughed.

Patricia's steps faltered and she cursed herself for not wanting to see James Harris, who had done so much for all of them, and she forced herself to walk toward him with a big smile. James Harris was Leland's business advisor these days. He called himself a consultant. He made up for not being able to go outside during the day by working through the night. He pored over the plans for Gracious Cay, he wooed outside investors at catered dinners he hosted at his home, and sometimes when Patricia walked down Middle Street early in the morning she could still smell cigar smoke lingering in the street outside his house. He worked the phones, he encouraged people to get outside their comfort zones, he convinced Leland to grow a ponytail. He carried them into the future.

"We're going to have to get you married so you can know what it's like to be tied down," Carter said to James Harris.

"I still haven't met someone worth giving up my freedom for," James said.

He and Carter were almost like brothers these days. He was the one who'd convinced Carter to go into private practice. He was the one who'd talked Carter into getting on the lecture circuit, where he extolled the virtues of Prozac and Ritalin to doctors on paid vacations in Hilton Head, and Myrtle Beach, and Atlanta, courtesy of Eli Lilly and Novartis. He was the one responsible for all the money piling up in their bank account that would let them send Korey to college, and remodel the kitchen, and pay off the BMW. And yes, sometimes the phone rang after Carter came back from one of his trips and a young woman would ask for Dr. Campbell, or sometimes they'd call him Carter, but Patricia always gave them his office number, and when she asked who they were Carter always said, "Damn secretaries," or "That effing girl at the travel agency," and it made him so angry that Patricia finally stopped asking, and just kept giving out his office number when they called, and she tried not to think about it because she knew how easily ideas could get into her head and grow into twisted shapes.

"Patricia!" James Harris beamed. "You look wonderful!"

"Hello, James," she said as he pulled her into a hug.

She still wasn't used to all this hugging, so she held still and let him squeeze her.

"This one was just telling me I'm going to be having supper with y'all all fall," James Harris said. "To keep an eye on you while he's out of town."

"We're looking forward to it," Patricia said.

"Did you understand any of this month's book?" Kitty asked. "All that military language left my head whirling."

"Whirlybird!" Horse cheered, loudly, raising his beer.

And the men started to talk about the war on drugs, and the inner cities, and metal detectors in schools, and James Harris said something about crack babies, and for a moment Patricia saw him, chin dripping black blood, something inhuman retracting back into his mouth, and then she hustled that image away and saw him the way she saw him so often—waving as he walked through the neighborhood in the evenings, at book club, at their table when Carter invited him over for supper. It had been dark in the back of his van. It had been so long ago. She wasn't even exactly sure of what she'd seen. It had probably been nothing. He had done so much for them.

It was better not to think about it.

CHAPTER 25

"So what did he say?" Carter asked.

He stopped slapping undershirts and dress socks into his suitcase on the end of their bed.

"Major said Blue has Saturday school for the next two months," Patricia said. "And he has to do twelve hours of volunteering at an animal shelter before the end of the year."

"That's almost an hour a week between now and then," Carter said. "On top of Saturday school. Who's going to take him to all that?"

His suitcase slipped off the end of the bed and clattered to the floor. Cursing, Carter started to bend down, but Patricia got there first, squatting awkwardly, knees popping. He was always frantic before he left on one of his trips, and she needed him calm if he was going to help with Blue. She picked up the suitcase and put it back on the bed.

"Slick and I are going to carpool the boys," Patricia said, refolding his spilled undershirts.

Carter shook his head.

"I don't want Blue around that Paley boy," he said. "To be honest, I don't want you around Slick. She's a loudmouth."

"That's just not practical," Patricia said. "Neither of us has time to drive them back and forth separately every Saturday."

"You're both housewives," he said. "What else do you do all day?"

She felt her veins tighten, but didn't say anything. She could find the time if it was that important to him. She felt her veins relax. What bothered her more were his comments about Slick.

She pressed the last refolded undershirt on top of the pile in Carter's suitcase.

"We need to talk to Blue," she said.

Carter let out a soul-deep sigh.

"Let's get this over with," he said.

She knocked on Blue's door. Carter stood behind her. No answer. Patricia whisked her knuckles against it again, listening for any sound that could be a "yeah" or an "uh-huh" or even the rare "what?" and then Carter reached past her and rapped on the door sharply, twisting the handle, pushing it open while still knocking.

"Blue?" he said, stepping past Patricia. "Your mother and I need to talk to you."

Blue jerked his head up from his desk like he'd been caught in the middle of something. When he'd gone to camp last summer they'd gotten him a blond wood Scandinavian bedroom unit that wrapped around the walls, with cabinets built into the window seat, a desk built into the bookshelves, and a bed built in beside the desk. Blue had decorated it with horror movie ads cut out from the newspaper: *Make Them Die Slowly, I Eat Your Skin, I Drink Your Blood.* The ceiling fan made the ads pulse and flutter like pinned butterflies. Books lay in piles on the floor, most of them about Nazis, but also something called *The Anarchist's Cookbook* on top of one stack, and her copy of *The Stranger Beside Me,* which she'd been looking for.

On his bed lay a library copy of *Nazi Human Experiments and Their Outcomes* and on the window seat were the mutilated remains of his Star Wars action figures. She remembered buying those for him years ago and their adventures through the house and in the car had played in the background of her life for years. Now, he'd taken his Boy Scout knife and whittled their faces into pink, multi-faceted lumps. He'd melted their hands with the hot glue gun. He'd scorched their bodies with matches.

And it was her fault. He'd found her convulsing on the kitchen floor. He'd dialed 911. He'd live with that memory for the rest of his life. She told herself he was too old for action figures anyway. This was just how teenage boys played.

"What do you want?" Blue asked, and his voice honked a little at the end.

Patricia realized his voice was changing, and her heart gave a small pinch.

"Well," Carter said, looking around for a place to sit. He hadn't been in Blue's room recently enough to know that was impossible. He perched on the edge of the bed. "Can you tell me what happened at school today?"

Blue huffed, throwing himself backward in his desk chair.

"God," he said. "It wasn't a big deal."

"Blue," Patricia said. "That is not true. You abused an animal."

"Let him speak for himself," Carter said.

"Oh, my God," Blue said, rolling his eyes. "Is that what you're going to say? I'm an animal abuser. Lock me up! Look out, Ragtag."

This last was directed at the dog, who was sleeping on a pile of magazines beneath his bed.

"Let's all calm down," Carter said. "Blue, what do you think happened?"

"It was just a dumb joke," Blue said. "Tiger took some spray paint and said it would be funny to put it on Rufus and then he wouldn't stop."

"That is not what you told us in Major's office," Patricia said.

"Patty," Carter warned, not taking his eyes off Blue.

She realized that she was pushing and stopped, hoping it wasn't too late. She had pushed before and it wound up with Blue having a meltdown on a flight to Philadelphia, with Korey throwing the dish rack and breaking a whole set of plates, with Carter massaging the bridge of his nose, with her taking those pills. She pushed and things always got worse. But it was already too late.

"Why are you always taking everyone's side except mine?" Blue said, throwing himself forward in his chair.

"Everyone needs to calm down—" Carter began.

"Rufus is a dog," Blue said. "People die every day. People abort little babies. Six million people died in the Holocaust. No one cares. It's just a dumb dog. They'll wash it off."

"Everyone needs to take a breath," Carter said, palms out in the calming gesture to Blue. "Next week you and I are going to sit down and I'm going to give you a test called a Conners Scale. It's just to determine if paying attention is harder for you than it is for other people."

"So what?" Blue asked.

"If it is," Carter explained, "then we give you something called Ritalin. I'm sure a lot of your friends take it. It doesn't change anything about you, it's just like eyeglasses for your brain."

"I don't want eyeglasses for my brain!" Blue screamed. "I'm not taking a test!"

Ragtag lifted his head. Patricia wanted to stop this. Carter hadn't talked about this with her before. This was the kind of decision they needed to make together.

"That's why you're the child and I'm the adult," Carter said. "I know what you need better than you do."

"No, you don't!" Blue screamed again.

"I think we should all take a few minutes," Carter said. "We can talk again after supper."

He guided Patricia out of the room by one elbow. She looked back at Blue, hunched over his desk, shoulders shaking, and she wanted to go to him so badly she felt it in her blood, but Carter steered her into the hall and closed the door behind them.

"He's never—" Carter began.

"Why's he screaming?" Korey asked, practically leaping out at them from her bedroom door. "What'd he do?"

"This has nothing to do with you," Carter said.

"I just thought you'd want the opinion of someone who actually sees him sometimes," Korey said.

"When we want your opinion we'll ask for it," Carter said.

"Fine!" Korey snapped, slamming her bedroom door. It smacked sharply into its frame. From behind it came a muffled, "Whatever."

Korey had been so easy for so many years, going to step aerobics after school, staying out on Wednesday nights to watch *Beverly Hills, 90210* with the same group of girls from her soccer team, going to Princeton soccer camp in the summer. But this fall she'd started spending more and more time in her room with the door closed. She'd stopped going out and seeing her friends. Her moods ranged from virtually comatose to explosive rage, and Patricia didn't know what set her off.

Carter told her he saw it all the time in his practice: it was her junior year, the SATs were coming, she had to apply for colleges, Patricia shouldn't worry, Patricia didn't understand, Patricia should read some articles about college stress he'd give her if she felt concerned.

Behind Korey's door, the music got louder.

"I need to finish cleaning the kitchen," Patricia said.

"I'm not going to take the blame for the way he's acting," Carter said, following Patricia down the stairs. "He has zero self-control. You're supposed to be teaching him how to handle his emotions."

He followed Patricia into the den. Her hands ached to hold a vacuum cleaner, to have its roar blot out everyone's voices, to make it all go away. She didn't want to think about Blue acting out because she knew it was her fault. His behavior had changed from the minute he found her on the kitchen floor. Carter followed her into the kitchen. She could hear Korey's music coming through the ceiling, all muffled harmonicas and guitars.

"He's never acted like this before," Carter said.

"Maybe you're just not around him enough," Patricia said.

"If you knew things were this bad, why didn't you say something before?" he asked.

Patricia didn't have an answer. She stood in the middle of the kitchen and looked around. She'd been measuring it for the remodel when school called for her to come see Major about Blue and Tiger spray-painting that dog, and there was so much in the cabinets they needed to throw out: the row of cookbooks she never used, the ice cream maker still in its box. The air popper they couldn't find the plug for. She undid the rubber bands on the dog food cabinet handles and looked inside. There was a shoebox of gas station road maps in one corner. Did they really need all these?

"You can't go around with your head in the sand, Patty," Carter said.

She'd have to go through the junk drawer. She pulled it open. What were all these bits and pieces for? She wanted to dump them all in the trash, but what if one of them was an important part of something expensive?

"Are you even listening to me?" Carter asked. "What are you doing?"

"I'm cleaning out the kitchen cabinets," Patricia said.

"This is not the time," Carter said. "We need to figure out what's going on with our son."

"I'm leaving," Blue said.

They turned. Blue stood in the doorway to the den with his backpack on. It wasn't his school backpack but the other one with the broken strap that he kept in his closet.

"It's after dark," Carter said. "You're not going anywhere."

"How're you going to stop me?" Blue asked.

"We're having supper in an hour," Patricia said.

"I can handle this, Patty," Carter said. "Blue, go upstairs until your mother calls you for supper."

"Are you going to padlock my bedroom door?" Blue asked. "Because if not, I'm leaving. I don't want to be in this house anymore. You just want to give me a bunch of pills and make me a zombie."

Carter sighed and stepped forward to better explain things. "No one's making you a zombie," he said. "We're—"

"You can't stop me from doing anything," Blue snarled.

"If you step out that door I'll call the police and report you as a runaway," Carter said. "They'll bring you home in handcuffs and you'll have a criminal record. Is that what you want?"

Blue glowered at them.

"You suck!" Blue screamed, and stormed out of the den.

They heard him run up the stairs and slam his bedroom door. Korey turned her music up louder.

"I did not realize things had gotten this bad," Carter said. "I'm going to change my flight and come back a day early. Obviously, this has to be dealt with."

He continued talking as Patricia began organizing the old cookbooks. He was explaining the Ritalin options to her—time release, dosages, coatings—when Blue came back into the den holding his hands behind his back.

"If I leave the house you're calling the police?" he asked.

"I don't want to do that, Blue," Carter said. "But you'll be leaving me with no choice."

"Good luck calling the police without any phone cords," Blue said.

He pulled his hands out and for a moment Patricia thought he held spaghetti noodles, and then she realized he was holding the cords to their telephones. Before the sight had fully registered, he ran out of the den and she and Carter trotted after him, getting to the front hall just as the door slammed. By the time they were on the porch, Blue had vanished into the twilight murk.

"I'll get the flashlight," Patricia said, turning to go back inside.

"No," Carter said. "He'll come home the minute he's cold and hungry."

"What if he gets to Coleman Boulevard and someone offers him a ride?" Patricia asked.

"Patty," Carter said. "I admire your imagination, but that's not going to happen. Blue is going to wander around the Old Village and sneak back home in an hour. He didn't even take a jacket."

"But—" she began.

"I do this for a living, remember?" he said. "I'm going to run to Kmart and pick up some new phone cords. He'll be back before I am."

He wasn't. After supper, Patricia kept clearing out the kitchen cabinets, watching the numbers on the microwave clock crawl from 6:45, to 7:30, to a minute after eight.

"Carter," she said. "I really think we need to do something."

"Discipline takes discipline," he said.

She pulled the garbage cans around to the front porch and dropped the air popper and the old ice cream maker into them, and unhooked everything from the saltwater fish tank and put it in the laundry room sink to dry. Finally, the microwave clock read 10:00.

I won't say anything until 10:15, Patricia promised herself, stuffing old cookbooks into plastic Harris Teeter bags.

"Carter," she said, at 10:11. "I'm going to get in the car and drive around."

He sighed, and put down the paper.

"Patty—" he began, and the phone rang.

Carter got there before Patricia.

"Yes?" he said, and she saw his shoulders relax. "Thank God. Of course . . . uh-huh, uh-huh . . . if you don't mind . . . of course . . ."

He showed no sign of hanging up, or even telling her what was happening, so Patricia ran to the living room and picked up the extension.

"Korey, get off the phone," Carter said.

"It's me," Patricia said. "Hello?"

"Hello, Patricia," a smooth, low voice said.

"James," she said.

"I don't want you to worry," James Harris told them. "Blue's with me. He came by a couple of hours ago and we've been talking. I told him he could chill here but he had to tell his mom and dad where he was. I know you guys must be tearing your hair out."

"That's . . . very kind of you," Patricia said. "I'll be right there."

"I'm not sure that's a good idea," James Harris said. "I don't want to meddle in your home life, but he's asked to spend the night. I have a guest bedroom."

James Harris and Carter had drinks at the back bar of the Yacht Club once a week. They went dove hunting with Horse. They'd taken Blue and Korey night shrimping at Seewee Farms. He'd even had supper with them five or six times when Carter was out of town, and every time she saw him, Patricia didn't think about what she'd seen. She made herself remote, and cool, but pleasant. The children adored him, and he had given Blue a computer game called *Command* something for Christmas, and Carter talked to him about his career, and he had opinions about music that Korey actually tolerated, so Patricia tried. But she still didn't want Blue in James Harris's house alone overnight.

"We don't want to impose," Patricia said, her voice high and hard in her chest.

"Maybe it's for the best," Carter said. "We could use the time to let the air clear."

"It's no worry," James Harris said. "I'm happy to have the company. Hold on a minute."

There was a pause, a thump in her ear, and then Patricia heard her son breathing.

"Blue?" she asked. "Are you all right?"

"Mom," Blue said. She heard him swallow hard. "I'm sorry."

Tears spiked Patricia's eyes. She wanted him in her arms. Now.

"We're just glad you're okay," she said.

"I'm sorry I yelled at you and I'm sorry for what I did to Rufus," Blue said, swallowing, breathing hard. "And, Dad, if you want me to take the test, James says I should."

"I want what's best for you," Carter said. "Your mom and I both do."

"I love you," Blue said in a rush.

"Listen to your Uncle James," Carter said, and then James Harris was back on the phone.

"I don't want to do anything you're not one hundred percent comfortable with," he said. "You're both sure this is fine?"

"Of course it is," Carter said. "We're very grateful."

Patricia took a breath to say something, and then stopped.

"Yes," she said. "Of course it's fine. Thank you."

This was better for her family. James Harris had proven himself so many times. He'd talked her son around from quivering with rage to telling her he loved her. She had to stop dwelling on something she thought she maybe remembered from so many years ago.

It's not such a big thing, she said to herself, *to ignore some crazy, terrible idea you were once convinced was once true in exchange for all this, for the dock, and the car, and the trip to London, and your ear, and college for the children, and step aerobics for Korey, and a friend for Blue, and for so much of everything. It isn't such a bad trade at all.*

CHAPTER 26

Carter picked up Blue from James Harris's house in the morning.

"It's all going to be fine, Patty," he said.

She didn't argue. Instead she made Toaster Strudel, and told Korey she couldn't wear a choker to school, and had to listen while Korey told her she was practically a nun, and then her daughter was gone, and Patricia stood in her house, alone.

Even though it was October, the sun warmed the rooms and made her sleepy. Ragtag found a patch of sunlight in the dining room and collapsed onto it, ribs rising and falling, eyes closed.

Patricia had so many projects—finish with the kitchen cabinets, pick up all the newspapers and magazines on the sun porch, do something with the saltwater tank in the laundry room, vacuum the garage room, clean out the closet in the den, change the sheets—she didn't know where to begin. She had a fifth cup of coffee and the silence in the house pressed down on her, and the sun kept getting hotter and warmer, thickening the air into a sleep-inducing fog.

The phone rang.

"Campbell residence," she said.

"Did Blue get to school all right?" James Harris asked.

A thin sheen of sweat broke out across Patricia's upper lip and she felt stupid, like she didn't know what to say. She took a breath. Carter trusted James Harris. Blue trusted him. She had kept him at arm's length for three years and what had that achieved? He was important to her son. He was important to her family. She needed to stop pushing him away.

"He did," she said, and made herself smile so he could hear it in her voice. "Thank you for taking him in last night."

"He was pretty upset when he showed up," James Harris said. "I'm not even sure why he chose to come here."

"I'm glad he thinks of it as a place he can go," she made herself say. "I'd rather him be there than out wandering the streets. It's not as safe in the Old Village as it used to be."

James Harris's voice took on the relaxed quality of someone who had plenty of time to chat. "He said he was scared you'd gone next door and called the police, so he hid in the bushes behind Alhambra for a while. I didn't know if he'd eaten, so I heated up some of those French bread pizzas. I hope that's okay."

"It's fine," she said. "Thank you."

"Is there something going on at home?" James Harris asked.

The sun coming through the kitchen windows made Patricia's eyes ache, so she looked into the cool darkness of the den instead.

"He's just turning into a teenager," she said.

"Patricia," James Harris said, and she heard his voice shade earnest. "I know you got a bad impression of me when I moved here, but whatever you think, believe me when I say that I care about your children. They're good kids. Carter works so much and I worry about you doing this mostly by yourself."

"Well, his private practice keeps him busy," Patricia said.

"I've told him he doesn't have to make every dollar in the world," James Harris said. "What's the point of working if you miss out on your kids growing up?"

She felt disloyal talking about Carter behind his back, but it was also a relief.

"He puts a lot of pressure on himself," she said.

"You're the one with pressure on you," James Harris said. "Raising two teenagers practically by yourself, it's too much."

"It's hardest on Blue," she said. "He has such a hard time keeping up at school. Carter thinks it's attention deficit disorder."

"His attention is fine when it comes to World War II," James Harris said.

The familiarity of discussing Blue with someone who understood him relaxed Patricia.

"He spray-painted a dog," she said.

"What?" James Harris laughed.

After a moment, she laughed, too.

"Poor dog," she said, feeling guilty. "His name is Rufus and he's the school's unofficial mascot. Blue and Slick Paley's youngest spray-painted him silver and now they've both got Saturday school for the rest of the year."

Just saying it out loud sounded absurd. She imagined it becoming a funny family story next year.

"Will the dog be okay?" James Harris asked.

"They say he will," she said. "But how do you clean spray paint off a dog?"

"I just bought a new CD changer," James Harris said. "I'll ask Blue over to help me hook it up. If it comes up, I'll ask him what happened and let you know what he says."

"Would you?" Patricia asked. "I'd be grateful."

"It's good talking this way again," James said. "Would you like to come over for some coffee? We can catch up."

She almost said yes because her first instinct in every situation was to be agreeable, but she smelled something clean and cool and medical and it took her out of her bright, sunny kitchen for a moment and suddenly it was four years ago and the garage door was open and she could smell the plastic incontinence pads they used for Miss Mary. For a moment she felt like the woman she had been all those years ago, a woman who didn't have to constantly apologize for everything, and she said, "No, thank you. I have to finish cleaning out the kitchen cabinets."

"Another day, then," he said, and she wondered if he'd heard the change in her voice.

They hung up and Patricia looked at the locked garage room door. She smelled the carpet shampoo she used to use in Miss Mary's room, and the pine-scented Lysol Mrs. Greene sprayed after Miss Mary had an accident. Any minute she expected to see the door swing open and Mrs. Greene come up the steps in her white pants and blouse, a balled-up bundle of sheets in her arms.

She made herself stand up and walk to the door, the smell of Miss Mary's room getting stronger with every step. She took the key off the hook by the door and watched her hand float out on the end of her arm and insert the key into the deadbolt. She twisted and the door popped open and it swung wide and the garage room stood empty. She smelled nothing but cool air and dust.

Patricia locked the door and decided to clean all the newspapers off the sun porch and then finish the kitchen cabinets. She walked through the dining room, where Ragtag lay sunbathing, twitching one ear as she passed. On the sun porch, light bounced off newspapers and glossy magazine covers, dazzling her. She picked up the papers Carter had left on the ottoman and walked back through the dining room to the kitchen. As she stepped into the den, a voice behind the dining room door said:

patricia

She turned. No one was there. And then, through the crack along the hinges of the dining room door, she saw a staring blue eye crowned by gray hair, and then nothing but the yellow wall behind the door.

Patricia stood for a moment, skin crawling, shoulders twitching. She felt a muscle tremble in one cheek. There was nothing there. She'd had some kind of olfactory hallucination and it made her believe she'd heard Miss Mary's voice. That was all.

Ragtag sat up, eyes focused on the open dining room door. Patricia put the papers in the garbage and made herself walk back through the dining room to the sun porch.

She picked up copies of *Redbook* and *Ladies' Home Journal* and

Time and hesitated briefly, then walked back through the dining room to the den. As she passed the open dining room door again, Miss Mary whispered from behind it:

patricia

Her breath stopped in her throat. Her knuckles cramped around the magazines. She could not move. She felt Miss Mary's eyes boring into the back of her neck. She felt Miss Mary standing behind the dining room door, staring madly through the crack, and then came a torrent of whispers.

he's coming for the children, he's taken the child, he's taken my grandchild, he's come for my grandchild, the nightwalking man, hoyt pickens suckles on the babies, on the sweet fat babies with their fat little legs, he's dug in like a tick, he's dug in like a tick and he's sucking everything out of you patricia, he's come for my grandchild, wake up patricia, wake up, the nightwalking man is in your house, he's on my grandchild, wake up patricia, patricia wake up, wake up, wake up . . .

Dead words, a lunatic river of syllables hissing from between cold lips.

"Miss Mary?" Patricia said, but her tongue felt thick and her words were barely a whisper.

he's the devil's son the nightwalking man and he's taking my grandchild, wake up wake up wake up, go to ursula, she has my photograph, it's in her house, go to ursula . . .

"I can't," Patricia said, and this time she had enough strength to make her voice echo off the den walls.

The whispers stopped. Patricia turned and the crack in the door stood empty. She jumped at the sound of fingernails tapping, but it was only Ragtag getting up and trotting out of the room.

Patricia didn't believe in ghosts. She had always considered Miss Mary's kitchen-table magic something that might be interesting to a sociologist from a local college. When women she knew said Grandmama appeared in their dreams and told them where to find a lost wedding ring or that Cousin Eddie had just died, she got irritated. It wasn't real.

But this was real. More real than anything she'd experienced over the past three years. Miss Mary had been in this room, standing behind the dining room door and whispering a warning that James Harris wanted her children, that James Harris wanted Blue. Ghosts weren't real. But this was real.

She worried for a moment that she was confused again. Her judgment was thin ice and she hesitated to trust it. But this had been real. It wouldn't hurt to make sure. After all, she was only a housewife. What else did she have to do?

wake up, patricia

"How?"

wake up, patricia

"How?"

go to ursula

"Who?"

ursula greene

CHAPTER 27

Patricia didn't know her palms could sweat so much, but they left wet marks all over her steering wheel as she drove up Rifle Range Road toward Six Mile. She had sent Mrs. Greene Christmas cards, and the phone worked both ways, and maybe Mrs. Greene hadn't wanted to see her, and maybe she was just respecting her personal space. She hadn't done anything wrong. Sometimes you just didn't talk to someone for a while. She wiped her palms on her slacks, one at a time, trying to get them dry.

Mrs. Greene probably wasn't even home because it was the middle of the afternoon. She was probably at work. *If her car isn't in the driveway, I'll just turn around and go home*, she told herself, and felt a huge wave of relief at the decision.

Rifle Range Road had changed. The trees along the side of the road had been cut back and the shoulders were bare. A shining new black asphalt turnoff led past a green-and-white plywood sign bearing a picture of a nouveau plantation house and *Gracious Cay— coming 1999—Paley Realty*. Beyond it, the raw, yellow skeletons of Gracious Cay rose up from behind the few remaining trees.

Patricia turned onto the state road and began winding her way back to Six Mile. Houses sat empty; a few were missing doors, and most had *For Sale* signs in the front yard. No children played outside.

She found Grill Flame Road and rolled down it slowly until she emerged into Six Mile. Not much of it survived. A chain-link fence hugged the back of Mt. Zion A.M.E., and beyond it lay a massive dirt plain full of bright yellow earthmoving equipment and construction debris. The basketball courts had been plowed up, the surrounding forest thinned to an occasional tree, and all the trailers over by where Wanda Taylor had lived were gone. Only seven houses remained on this side of the church.

Mrs. Greene's Toyota was in the drive.

Patricia parked and opened her car door and immediately her ears were assaulted by the high-pitched scream of table saws from Gracious Cay, the rumbling of trucks, the earsplitting clatter of bricks and bulldozers. The construction chaos staggered her for a moment and left her unable to think. Then she gathered herself and rang Mrs. Greene's front bell.

Nothing happened, and she realized Mrs. Greene probably couldn't hear her over the din, so she rapped on the window. No one was home. Maybe her car had broken down and she'd gotten a ride to work. Relief flooded Patricia and she turned and walked back to her Volvo.

The construction was so loud that she didn't hear it the first time, but she heard it the second: "Mrs. Campbell."

She turned and saw Mrs. Greene standing in the door to her house, hair in a wrap, wearing an oversized pink T-shirt and a pair of dungarees. Patricia's stomach hollowed out and filled with foam.

"I thought—" Patricia began, then realized her words were lost under the construction noise. She walked over to Mrs. Greene. As she got closer she saw that she had a gray tinge to her skin, her eyes were crusted with sleep, and she had dandruff in the roots of her hair. "I thought nobody was home," she shouted over the construction noise.

"I was taking a nap," Mrs. Greene shouted back.

"That's so nice," Patricia shouted.

"I clean in the morning and I do overnight stocking at Walmart in the evening," Mrs. Greene shouted. "Then I go right back to work in the morning."

"Pardon?" Patricia said.

Mrs. Greene looked around, then looked into her house, then back at Patricia, and nodded sharply. "Come on," she said.

She closed the door behind them, which cut the construction noise by half, but Patricia still heard the high, excited whine of a saw ripping through wood. The house looked the same except the Christmas lights were dark. It felt empty and smelled like sleep.

"How're the children?" Mrs. Greene asked.

"They're teenagers," Patricia said. "You know how they are. How are yours?"

"Jesse and Aaron are still living with my sister up in Irmo," Mrs. Greene said.

"Oh," Patricia said. "Do you get to see them enough?"

"I'm their mother," Mrs. Greene said. "Irmo is a two-hour drive. There is no *enough*."

Patricia winced at a massive crashing bang from outside.

"Have you thought about moving?" she asked.

"Most people already have," Mrs. Greene said. "But I'm not leaving my church."

From outside came the *beep-beep-beep* of a truck backing up.

"Are you taking on any more houses?" Patricia asked. "I could use some help cleaning if you're free."

"I work for a service now," Mrs. Greene said.

"That must be nice," Patricia said.

Mrs. Greene shrugged.

"They're big houses," she said. "And the money's good, but it used to be you'd talk to people all day long. The service doesn't like you to speak to the owners. If you have a question they give you a portable phone and you call the manager and he calls the owners for you. But they pay on time and take out the taxes."

Patricia took a deep breath.

"Do you mind if I sit?" she asked.

Something flashed across Mrs. Greene's face—disgust, Patricia thought—but she gestured to the sofa, unable to escape the burden of hospitality. Patricia sat and Mrs. Greene lowered herself into her easy chair. Its arms were more worn than the last time Patricia had seen it.

"I wanted to come see you earlier," Patricia said. "But things kept coming up."

"Mm-hmm," Mrs. Greene said.

"Do you think about Miss Mary much?" Patricia asked. She saw Mrs. Greene rearrange her hands. Their backs were covered with small, shiny scars. "I'll always be grateful you were with her that night."

"Mrs. Campbell, what do you want?" Mrs. Greene asked. "I'm tired."

"I'm sorry," Patricia said, and decided she would leave. She put her hands on the edge of the sofa to push herself up. "I'm sorry to have bothered you, especially when you're resting before work. And I'm sorry I haven't been out to see you earlier, only things have been so busy. I'm sorry. I just wanted to say hello. And I saw Miss Mary."

A distant clatter of boards falling to the ground crashed through the window panes. Neither of them moved.

"Mrs. Campbell . . . ," Mrs. Green began.

"She told me you had a photograph," Patricia said. "She said it was from a long time ago and you had it. So I came. She said it was about the children. I wouldn't have bothered you if it was about anything else. But it's the children."

Mrs. Greene glared. Patricia felt like a fool.

"I wish," Mrs. Greene said, "that you would get back in your car and drive home."

"Pardon?" Patricia asked.

"I said," Mrs. Greene repeated, "that I wish you would go home. I don't want you here. You abandoned me and my children because your husband told you to."

"That's . . . ," Patricia didn't know how to respond to the unfairness of the accusation. "That's dramatic."

"I haven't lived with my babies in three years," Mrs. Greene said. "Jesse comes home from football games hurt, and his mother isn't there to take care of him. Aaron has a trumpet performance and I'm not there to see it. No one cares about us out here except when they need us to clean up their mess."

"You don't understand," Patricia said. "They were our husbands. Those were our families. I would have lost everything. I didn't have a choice."

"You had more choice than me," Mrs. Greene said.

"I wound up in the hospital."

"That's your own fault."

Patricia choked, somewhere between a laugh and a sob, then pressed her palm over her mouth. She had risked all her certainty, all her comfort, everything they'd carefully rebuilt over the last three years to come out here and all she had found was someone who hated her.

"I'm sorry I came," she said, standing, blind with tears, grabbing her purse, and then not knowing which way to go because Mrs. Greene's legs blocked her passage to the front door. "I only came because Miss Mary stood behind my dining room door and told me to come, and I realize now how foolish that sounds, and I'm sorry. Please, I know you hate me but please don't tell anyone I was here. I couldn't bear for anyone to know I came out here and said these things. I don't know what I was thinking."

Mrs. Greene stood up, turned her back on Patricia, and left the room. Patricia couldn't believe Mrs. Greene hated her so much she wouldn't even walk her to the door, but of course she did. Patricia and the book club had abandoned her. She stumbled to the door, knocking one hip into Mrs. Greene's chair, and then she heard the voice behind her.

"I didn't steal it," Mrs. Greene said.

Patricia turned and saw Mrs. Greene holding out a glossy square of white paper.

"It was on my coffee table one day," Mrs. Greene said. "Maybe I brought it back here after Miss Mary passed and forgot I had it, but when I picked it up my hair stood on end. I could feel eyes staring into me from behind. I turned around and for a moment I saw the poor old lady standing behind that door there."

Their eyes met in the gloomy living room air, and the construction noises got very far away, and Patricia felt like she had taken off a pair of sunglasses after wearing them for a very long time. She took the photograph. It was old and cheaply printed, curling up around the edges. Two men stood in the center. One looked like a male version of Miss Mary but younger. He wore overalls and had his hands buried in his pockets. He wore a hat. Next to him stood James Harris.

It wasn't someone who looked like James Harris, or an ancestor, or a relative. Even though the haircut was slicked with Brylcreem and had a razor-edge part, it was James Harris. He wore a white three-piece suit and a wide tie.

"Turn it over," Mrs. Greene said.

Patricia flipped the photograph with shaking fingers. On the back someone had written in fountain pen, *162 Wisteria Lane, Summer, 1928.*

"Sixty years," Patricia said.

James Harris looked exactly the same.

"I didn't know why Miss Mary gave me this photo," Mrs. Greene said. "I don't know why she didn't give it to you direct. But she wanted you to come here, and that must mean something. If she still cares about you, then maybe I can put up with you, too."

Patricia felt scared. Miss Mary had come to both of them. James Harris didn't age. Neither of these things could possibly be true, but they were and that terrified her. Vampires didn't age, either. She shook her head. She couldn't start thinking that way again. That kind of thinking could ruin everything. She wanted to live in the same world as Kitty, and Slick, and Carter, and Sadie Funche, not over here on her own with Mrs. Greene. She looked at the photo again. She couldn't stop looking at it.

"What do we do now?" she asked.

Mrs. Greene went to her bookshelf and took a green folder off the top. It had been used and reused and had different headings written on it and scratched out. She laid it open on the coffee table and she and Patricia sat back down.

"I want my babies to come home," Mrs. Greene said, showing Patricia what was inside. "But you see what he does."

Patricia paged through the folder, clipping after clipping, and she got cold.

"It's all him?" she asked.

"Who else?" Mrs. Greene said. "My service cleans his house twice a month. One of his regular girls is gone. I volunteered to fill in this week."

Patricia's heart slowed to a crawl.

"Why?" she asked.

"Mrs. Cavanaugh gave me a box of those murder books y'all read. She said she didn't want them in her house anymore. Whatever Mr. Harris is, he's not natural, but I think he's got something in common with those evil men from your books. They always take a souvenir. They like to hold on to a little something when they hurt someone. I only met the man a few times but I could tell he was real full of himself. I bet he keeps something from each of them in his house so he can pull them out and feel like a bigshot all over again."

"What if we're wrong?" Patricia said. "I thought I saw him doing something to Destiny Taylor years ago, but it was dark. What if I was wrong? What if her mother did have a boyfriend and lied about it? We both think we saw Miss Mary, we both believe this is a picture of James Harris, but what if it's just someone who looks like him?"

Mrs. Greene pulled the picture over to her with two fingers and looked at it again.

"A no-good man will tell you he's going to change," she said. "He'll tell you whatever you want to hear, but you're the fool if you don't believe what you see. That's him in this picture. That was Miss Mary who whispered to us. Everybody may be telling me different, but I know what I know."

"What if he doesn't keep trophies?" Patricia asked, trying to slow things down.

"Then there's nothing there to find," Mrs. Greene said.

"You'll get arrested," Patricia said.

"It'd go faster with two of us," Mrs. Greene said.

"It's against the law," Patricia said.

"You turned your back on me once before," Mrs. Greene said, and her eyes blazed. Patricia wanted to look anywhere else but she couldn't move. "You turned your back on me and now he's come for your children. You're out of time. It's too late to find excuses."

"I'm sorry," Patricia said.

"I don't want your sorry," Mrs. Greene said. "I want to know if you'll come in his house and help me look."

Patricia couldn't say yes. She had never broken a law in her life. It went against everything in her body. It went against everything she'd lived for forty years. If she got caught she would never be able to look Carter in the eye again, she'd lose Blue, and she'd lose Korey. How could she raise the children and tell them to obey the law if she didn't?

"When?" she asked.

"This coming weekend he's going to Tampa," Mrs. Greene said. "I need to know if you're serious or not."

"I'm sorry," Patricia said.

Mrs. Greene's face screwed itself shut.

"I need to get my sleep," she said, starting to stand up.

"No, wait, I'll go," Patricia said.

"I don't have time for you to play," Mrs. Greene said.

"I'll go," Patricia said.

Mrs. Greene walked her to the front door. At the door, Patricia stopped.

"How could we have seen Miss Mary?" she asked.

"She's burning in Hell," Mrs. Greene said. "I asked my minister and he says that's where ghosts come from. They burn in Hell and they can't go into the cool, healing waters of the River Jordan until they let go of this world. Miss Mary suffers the torments of Hell because she wants to warn you. She burns because she loves her grandchildren."

Patricia's blood felt heavy in her veins..

"I think it's her, too," Patricia said, and she tried one last time to stop all this talk of ghosts, and men who didn't age, and to erase the image of James Harris in the back of the van, that inhuman thing coming out of his mouth, hunched over Destiny Taylor. "Maybe we're making this too difficult. Maybe if we go and ask him to stop . . . tell him what we know . . ."

"Three things are never satisfied," Mrs. Greene said, and Patricia recognized the quotation from somewhere. "And four is never enough. He'll eat up everyone in the world and keep on eating. The leech has two daughters and their names are Give and Give."

Patricia had an idea.

"If two of us make it go faster," she said, "it'll go even faster with three."

CHAPTER 28

"Patricia!" Slick cried. "Thank goodness!"

"I'm sorry to drop by without calling—" Patricia began.

"You're always welcome," Slick said, pulling her in off the doorstep. "I'm brainstorming my Halloween party and maybe you can unstick my logjam. You're so good at these things!"

"You're having a Halloween party?" Patricia asked, following Slick back to her kitchen.

She held her purse close to her body, feeling the folder and photograph burning through its canvas sides.

"I'm against Halloween in all its forms because of the Satanism," Slick said, pulling open her stainless-steel refrigerator and taking out the half-and-half. "So this year, on All Hallows' Eve, I will be holding a Reformation Party. I know it's last minute, but it's never too late to praise the Lord."

She poured coffee, added her half-and-half, and handed Patricia a black-and-gold Bob Jones University mug.

"A what party?" Patricia asked.

But Slick had already burst through the swinging door that led to the back addition. Patricia followed, mug in one hand, purse in the other. Slick sat on one of the sofas in what she called the "conversation area," and Patricia sat across from her and looked for a place to set her mug. The coffee table between them was covered in photocopies, clipped-out magazine articles, three-ring binders, and pencils. The end table next to her was crowded with a collection of snuffboxes, several marble eggs, and a bowl of potpourri. Along with the dried flower petals, leaves, and wood shavings, Slick had added a few golf balls and tees to pay tribute to Leland's passion for the sport. Patricia decided to just hold her mug in her lap.

"You catch more flies with sugar than vinegar," Slick said. "So on Sunday I'll throw a party that will make everyone forget about Halloween: my Reformation Party. I'm going to present the idea to St. Joseph's tomorrow. See, we'll take the children to the Fellowship Hall—and of course Blue and Korey will be welcome—and we'll make sure there are activities for the teenagers. They're the ones most at risk, after all, but instead of monster costumes they dress up like heroes of the Reformation."

"The who?" Patricia asked.

"You know," Slick said. "Martin Luther, John Calvin. We'll have medieval line dancing and German food, and I thought it would be fun to have themed snacks. What do you think? It's a Diet of Worms cake."

Slick handed Patricia a picture she'd cut out of a magazine.

"A worm cake?" Patricia asked.

"A *Diet* of Worms cake," Slick corrected. "When the Holy Roman Empire declared Martin Luther a fugitive for nailing his ninety-five theses to the church door? The Diet of Worms?"

"Oh," Patricia said.

"You decorate it with gummy worms," Slick said. "Isn't that hilarious? You have to make these things entertaining *and* educational." She plucked the clipping out of Patricia's hand and studied it. "I don't think it's sacrilegious, do you? Maybe not enough people know who John Calvin is? We're also going to try reverse trick-or-treating."

"Slick," Patricia said. "I hate to change the subject, but I need help."

"What's the matter?" Slick asked, putting down the clipping and scooting to the edge of her seat, eyes fastened on Patricia. "Is it about Blue?"

"You're a spiritual person?" Patricia asked.

"I'm a Christian," Slick said. "There's a difference."

"But you believe there's more to this world than what we can see?" Patricia asked.

Slick's smile got a little thin.

"I'm worried about where all this is going," she said.

"What do you think about James Harris?" Patricia asked.

"Oh," Slick said, and she sounded genuinely disappointed. "We've been here before, Patricia."

"Something's happened," Patricia said.

"Let's not go back there again," Slick said. "All that's behind us now."

"I don't want to do this again, either," Patricia said. "But I've seen something, and I need your opinion."

She reached into her purse.

"No!" Slick said. Patricia froze. "Think about what you're doing. You made yourself very sick last time. You gave us all a scare."

"Help me, Slick," Patricia said. "I genuinely don't know what to think. Tell me I'm crazy and I'll never mention it again. I promise."

"Just leave whatever it is in your purse," Slick said. "Or give it to me and I'll put it through Leland's shredder. You and Carter are doing so well. Everyone's so happy. It's been three years. If anything bad was going to happen, it would have happened by now."

A feeling of futility washed over Patricia. Slick was right. The past three years had been forward progress, not a circle. If she showed Slick the photo she'd be right back where she started. Three years of her life reduced to running in place. The thought made her so exhausted she wanted to lie down and take a nap.

"Don't do it, Patricia," Slick said, softly. "Stay here with me in reality. Things are so much better now than they were. Everyone's happy. We're all okay. The children are safe."

Inside her purse, Patricia's fingers brushed the edge of Mrs. Greene's folder, worn soft by handling.

"I tried," Patricia said. "I really did try for three years, Slick. But the children *aren't* safe."

She pulled her hand out of her purse with the folder.

"Don't," Slick moaned.

"It's too late," Patricia said. "We've run out of time. Just look at this and tell me if I'm crazy."

She laid the folder on top of Slick's papers and placed the photograph on it. Slick picked up the photo and Patricia saw her fingers tighten and her face get still. Then she laid it back, facedown.

"It's a cousin," she said. "Or his brother."

"You know it's him," Patricia said. "Look at the back. 1928. He still looks the same."

Slick drew in one shuddering breath, then blew it out.

"It's a coincidence," she said.

"Miss Mary had that photograph," Patricia said. "That's her father. James Harris came through Kershaw when she was a little girl. He called himself Hoyt Pickens and he got them involved in a financial scheme that made them a lot of money, and then bankrupted the whole town. And he stole their children. When people turned on him he blamed a black man and they killed him, and he disappeared. I think it was so long ago, and Kershaw's so far upstate, he didn't imagine he'd be recognized if he came back."

"No, Patricia," Slick said, pressing her lips together, shaking her head. "Don't do this."

"Mrs. Greene put these together," Patricia said, opening the green folder.

"Mrs. Greene is strong in her faith," Slick said. "But she doesn't have the education we have. Her background is different. Her culture is different."

Patricia laid out four printed letters from the Town of Mt. Pleasant.

"They found Francine's car in the Kmart parking lot back in 1993," she said. "Remember Francine? She did for James Harris when he moved here. I saw her go into his house, and apparently no one ever saw her again. They found her car abandoned in the Kmart parking lot a few days later. They sent her letters telling her to come pick it up from the towing company, but they just sat in her mailbox. That's where Mrs. Greene found them."

"Stealing the mail is a federal crime," Slick said.

"They had to break into her house to feed her cat," Patricia said. "Her sister wound up declaring her dead and selling the house. They put the money in escrow. They say she has to be gone for five years before that money gets paid."

"Maybe she was carjacked," Slick suggested.

Patricia pulled out the sheaf of newspaper clippings and laid them out like playing cards, the way Mrs. Greene had done. "These are the children. You remember Orville Reed? He and his cousin Sean died right after Francine disappeared. Sean was killed and Orville stepped in front of a truck and killed himself."

"We did this before," Slick said. "There was that other little girl—"

"Destiny Taylor."

"And Jim's van, and all the rest," Slick gave her a sympathetic look. "Taking care of Miss Mary put you under a terrible strain."

"It didn't stop," Patricia said. "After Destiny Taylor came Chivas Ford, out in Six Mile. He was nine years old when he died in May 1994."

"Children die for all kinds of reasons," Slick said.

"Then came this one," Patricia said, tapping a police blotter clipping. "One year after that, in 1995. A little girl named Latasha Burns in North Charleston cut her own neck with a butcher knife. How would a nine-year-old do that if there weren't something terrible she was trying to get away from?"

"I don't want to hear this," Slick said. "Is every child who passes in some terrible way Jim's fault? Why stop at North Charleston? Why not go all the way to Summerville or Columbia?"

"Everyone started leaving Six Mile because of the Gracious Cay development getting built," Patricia said. "Maybe it wasn't easy to find children who wouldn't be missed anymore."

"Leland paid fair prices for those homes," Slick said.

"Then this year," Patricia continued, "Carlton Borey up in Awendaw. Eleven years old. Mrs. Greene knows his aunt. She says they found him dead in the woods of exposure. Who freezes to death in the middle of April? She said he'd been sick for months, the same as the other children."

"None of this adds up," Slick said. "You're being silly."

"It's a child a year, for three years," Patricia said. "I know they're not our children, but they're children. Are we not supposed to care about them because they're poor and black? That's how we acted before and now he wants Blue. When will he stop? Maybe he'll want Tiger next, or Merit, or one of Maryellen's?"

"This is how witch hunts happen," Slick said. "People get all worked up over nothing and before you know it someone gets hurt."

"Are you a hypocrite?" Patricia asked. "You're using your Reformation Party to protect your children from Halloween, but are you lifting a finger to protect them from this monster? Either you believe in the Devil or you don't."

She hated the bullying tone in her voice, but the more she talked the more she convinced herself that she needed to ask these questions. The more Slick denied what was right in front of her eyes, the more she reminded Patricia of how she'd acted all those years ago.

"*Monster* is a very strong word for someone who's been so good to our families," Slick said.

Patricia turned Miss Mary's photograph over.

"How is he not aging, Slick?" she said. "Explain that to me and I'll stop asking questions."

Slick chewed her lip.

"What are you going to do?" she asked.

"The men are all out of town this weekend," Patricia said. "The cleaning company Mrs. Greene works for cleans his house on Saturday and Mrs. Greene is going to be there and she's going to let me in, and while she cleans, I'm going to see if I can find some answers."

"You can't break into someone's house," Slick said, horrified.

"If we don't find anything," Patricia said, "then I'll stop and it's all over. Help me finish this. We'll either find something or we won't, but either way it'll be over."

Slick pressed her fingertips to her mouth and studied her bookshelves for a long time, then picked up the photograph and considered it again. Finally, she put it back down.

"Let me pray on this," she said. "I won't tell Leland, but let me keep the photograph and the folder and pray on them."

"Thank you," Patricia said.

It never occurred to her not to trust Slick.

CHAPTER 29

Slick called on Thursday at 10:25 in the morning.

"I'll come," she said. "But I'll only look. I won't open anything that's closed."

"Thank you," Patricia said.

"I don't feel right about this," Slick said.

"I don't either," Patricia said, and then she hung up and called Mrs. Greene to tell her the good news.

"This is a big mistake," Mrs. Greene said.

"It'll go faster with three of us," Patricia said.

"Maybe," Mrs. Greene said. "But all I'm telling you is that it's a mistake."

She kissed Carter good-bye on Friday morning at 7:30, and he left for Tampa on Delta flight 1237 from the Charleston airport, with a layover in Atlanta. On Saturday morning at 9:30 she drove Blue to Saturday school. She told Korey they could work on her list of colleges together, but by noon, when she had to go pick up Blue from Saturday school, Korey had barely glimpsed at the catalogs.

When she pulled up in front of Albemarle at 12:05, the only other car there was Slick's white Saab. She got out and tapped on the driver's-side window.

"Hi, Mrs. Campbell," Greer said, rolling down the window.

"Is your mother all right?" Patricia asked.

"She had to take something over to the church," Greer said. "She said she might be seeing you later?"

"I'm helping her plan her Reformation Party," Patricia said.

"Sounds fun," Greer said.

She and Blue got home at 12:40. Korey had left a note on the counter saying she was going downtown to step aerobics and then to a movie with Laurie Gibson. At 2:15, Patricia knocked on Blue's bedroom door.

"I'm going out for a little while," she called.

He didn't answer. She assumed he'd heard.

She didn't want anyone to see her car, and it was a warm afternoon anyway, so she walked up Middle Street. She saw Mrs. Greene's car parked in James Harris's driveway, next to a green-and-white Greener Cleaners truck. James Harris's Corsica was gone.

She hated his house. Two years ago, he'd torn down Mrs. Savage's cottage, split the lot in half, and sold the piece of it closest to the Hendersons to a dentist from up north someplace, then built himself a McMansion that stretched from property line to property line. A massive Southern lump with concrete pineapples at the end of the drive, it stood on stilts with an enclosed ground floor for parking. It was a white monstrosity painted white with all its various tin roofs painted rust red, encircled by a huge porch.

She'd been inside once for his housewarming party last summer, and it was all sisal runners and enormous, heavy, machine-milled furniture, nothing with any personality, everything anonymous and done in beige, and cream, and off-white, and slate. It felt like the embalmed and swollen corpse of a ramshackle Southern beach house, tarted up with cosmetics and central air.

Patricia turned onto McCants then turned again and looped back until she stood on Pitt Street directly behind James Harris's house. She could see its red roofs looming over the trees at the end of a little drainage ditch that ran between two property lines from this side of the block to the other. When it rained, the ditch carried the overflow water off Pitt down to the harbor. But it hadn't rained in weeks and now it was a swampy trickle, with a worn path the children used as a shortcut between blocks running alongside it.

She stepped off the root-cracked sidewalk and walked to his house along the path, as fast as possible, feeling like eyes were watching her the entire way. James Harris's backyard lay in the heavy shadow of his house, and it was as chilly as the water at the bottom of a lake. His grass didn't get enough light and the yellowed blades crunched beneath her feet.

She walked up the stairs to his back porch and paused, looking back to see if she could spot Slick, but she hadn't gotten there yet. She kept moving, wanting to get out of sight as soon as possible. She knocked on the back door.

Inside, she heard a vacuum cleaner whirl down and a minute later the weather seal cracked and the door opened to reveal Mrs. Greene in a green polo shirt.

"Hello, Mrs. Greene," Patricia said, loudly. "I came to see if I could find my keys. That I left here."

"Mr. Harris isn't home," Mrs. Greene responded loudly, which let Patricia know that the other woman working with her was nearby. "Maybe you should come back later."

"I really need my keys," Patricia said.

"I'm sure he won't mind if you look for them," Mrs. Greene said.

She stepped out of the way, and Patricia came inside. The kitchen had a large island in the middle, half of it covered by some kind of stainless-steel grill. Dark brown cabinets lined the walls, and the refrigerator, dishwasher, and sink were all stainless steel. The room felt cold. Patricia wished she'd brought a sweater.

"Is Slick here yet?" Patricia asked quietly.

"Not yet," Mrs. Greene said. "But we can't wait."

A woman in the same green polo shirt as Mrs. Greene came in from the hall. She wore yellow rubber dishwashing gloves and a shiny leather fanny pack.

"Lora," Mrs. Greene said. "This is Mrs. Campbell from down the street. She thinks she left her keys here and is going to look for them."

Patricia gave what she hoped looked like a friendly smile.

"Hi, Lora," she said. "Pleased to meet you. Don't let me get in your way."

Lora turned her large brown eyes from Patricia to Mrs. Greene, then back to Patricia. She reached down to her belt and unclipped a mobile phone.

"There's no need," Mrs. Greene said. "I know Mrs. Campbell. I used to clean for her."

"I'll just be a minute," Patricia said, pretending to scan the granite countertops. "I know those keys are somewhere."

Her huge brown eyes still on Mrs. Greene, Lora flipped the phone open and pressed a button.

"Lora, no!" Patricia said, too loudly.

Lora turned and looked at Patricia. She blinked once, holding the open phone in her yellow rubber hand.

"Lora," Patricia said. "I really do need to find my keys. They could be anywhere and it might take me a while. But you won't get in any trouble for what I'm doing. I promise. And I'll pay you for the inconvenience."

She had left her purse at home, but Mrs. Greene had told her to bring money, just in case. She reached into her pocket and pulled out four of the five ten-dollar bills she'd brought and placed them on the kitchen island closest to Lora, then stepped away.

"Mr. Harris won't be coming back until tomorrow," Mrs. Greene said.

Lora stepped forward, took the bills, and made them disappear into her fanny pack.

"Thank you so much, Lora," Patricia said.

Mrs. Greene and Lora left the kitchen and the vacuum cleaner roared back to life, and Patricia looked out the back window to see if she could spot Slick coming up the path, but it was empty. She turned and walked through the wide front hall and looked out the window by the door. The glass was artfully rippled to make it seem as if it were antique. Slick's Saab wasn't in the driveway. It wasn't like her to be late, although if she'd lost her nerve at the last minute maybe that wasn't the worst thing in the world. She didn't know how Lora would react to two of them searching the house.

Besides, there wasn't much in it. The kitchen drawers were empty. The cabinets barely contained any food. No junk drawer. No magnetized advertisements from the exterminator or the pizza delivery people on the fridge door. No toaster on the countertops, no blenders, no waffle irons, no George Foreman grills. It was the same all over the house. She decided to go upstairs. If he had anything personal it was more likely to be hidden there.

She started up the carpeted stairs, the vacuum cleaner noise falling away below her. She stood in the upstairs hall lined with closed doors and suddenly felt like she was on the verge of making a terrible mistake. She shouldn't be here. She should turn around and leave. What had she been thinking? She thought about *Bluebeard* where the bride was told not to look behind a certain door by her husband and of course she did and discovered the corpses of his previous brides. Her mother had told her the moral of the story was that you should trust your husband and never pry. But wasn't it better to know the truth? She headed for the master bedroom.

The master bedroom smelled of hot vinyl and new carpet, even though the carpet must be two years old by now. The bed was made neatly and had four posts, each one crowned with a carved pineapple. An armchair and table sat by the window. On the table was a notebook. Every page was empty. Patricia looked in the walk-in closet. All the clothes hung in dry-cleaner bags, even his blue jeans, and they all smelled like cleaning chemicals.

She searched the bathroom. Combs, brushes, toothpaste, and floss, but no prescriptions. Band-Aids and gauze but nothing that told her anything about the occupant. It smelled like sealant and Sheetrock. The sink and the shower were dry. Patricia went back to the hall and tried again.

She went from room to room, opening empty closets, looking inside empty drawers. Everything smelled like fresh paint. Every room echoed emptily. Every bed was carefully made up with pristine pillow shams and decorative pillows. The house felt abandoned.

"Find anything?" a voice said, and Patricia leapt into the air.

"Ohmygoodness," she gasped, pressing her hand to the middle of her chest. "You scared me half to death."

Mrs. Greene stood in the doorway.

"Did you find anything?" she repeated.

"It's all empty," Patricia said. "Slick hasn't come by, has she?"

"No," Mrs. Greene said. "Lora is having lunch in the kitchen."

"There's nothing here," Patricia said. "This is pointless."

"There's nothing in this entire house?" Mrs. Greene said. "Nowhere? Are you sure you looked?"

"I looked everywhere," Patricia said. "I'm going to leave before Lora changes her mind."

"I don't believe that," Mrs. Greene said.

Her stubbornness provoked a flash of irritation from Patricia. "If you can find something I missed, by all means, feel free," she said.

The two of them stood, glaring at each other. The disappointment made Patricia irritable. She'd come this far, and now nothing. There was no path forward.

"We tried," she finally said. "If Slick comes, tell her I came to my senses."

She walked past Mrs. Greene, heading for the stairs.

"What about that?" Mrs. Greene said from behind her.

Wearily, Patricia turned and saw Mrs. Greene with her neck craned back, staring at the hall ceiling. More specifically, she was staring at a small black hook in the hall ceiling. Using it as a landmark, Patricia could just make out the rectangular line of a door around it, the hinges painted white. She got a broom from the kitchen and used the eyelet in its handle to snag the hook. They both pulled and, with a groan of springs and a cracking of paint, the rectangular edges got bigger, darker, and the attic door dropped down and the metal stairs attached to it unfolded.

A dry, abandoned smell rolled down into the hall.

"I'll go up," Patricia said.

She gripped the edges hard, and the ladder rattled as she climbed. She felt too heavy, like her foot was going to break the steps. Then her head passed through the ceiling and she was in the dark.

Her eyes adjusted and she realized it wasn't completely dark. The attic ran the length of the house and there were louvers on either end. Daylight filtered through. It felt hot and stuffy. The end of the attic facing the street was bare, just joists and pink insulation. The back was a jumble of dim shapes.

"Do you have a flashlight?" she called down.

"Here," Mrs. Greene said.

She unclipped something from her keychain and Patricia came down a few steps and took it: a small, turquoise rubber rectangle the size of a cigarette lighter.

"You squeeze the sides," Mrs. Greene said.

A tiny bulb on the end emitted a weak glow.

It was better than nothing.

Patricia went up into the attic.

The floor was gritty, covered in a layer of cockroach poison, mouse droppings, dried guano, pigeon feathers, dead cockroaches on their backs, and larger piles of excrement that looked like they came from raccoons. Patricia started walking toward the clutter. Cool air formed a cross breeze blowing from the vents at either end. The white powder ground against the plywood beneath her feet.

It smelled like dead insects up here, like rotten fabric, like wet cardboard that had dried and mildewed. Everything downstairs had been meticulously cleaned and polished, scoured of anything organic. Up here, the house lay exposed: splintery joists, filthy plywood flooring, construction measurements penciled onto the exposed plywood beneath the shingles. Patricia played the flashlight beam over the mound of items at the rear and realized that this was the graveyard of Mrs. Savage's life.

Blankets and quilts and sheets were draped over all the boxes and trunks and suitcases she'd once seen in the old lady's front room. Studded with cockroach eggs, sticky with spiderwebs stretched between every open space, the filthy sheets and blankets were stiff and rank.

Patricia lifted one tacky corner of a pink quilt and released a puff of rotten wood pulp. Beneath it, on the floor, lay a cardboard box of water-damaged paperback romances. Mice had chewed one corner to shreds and brightly colored paperback guts spilled onto the floor. Why had he brought all this garbage into a new house? It felt wrong. In his entire, new, meticulously blank home, this stood out like a mistake.

Her skin seethed in revulsion wherever she touched the blankets. They were covered in grime, white cockroach poison, and mouse droppings. She walked around the boxes to where the blankets ended, where the brick chimney rose through the floor and then the ceiling. She recognized the row of old suitcases sitting next to it, surrounded by furniture she remembered from the old house: standing lamps completely obscured by spiderwebs that were thick with eggs, the rocking chair with its seat chewed into a mouse nest, the cross-stretcher table whose veneer top had warped and split.

Not knowing where to start, Patricia lifted each of the suitcases. They were empty except for the second-to-last one. It didn't budge. She tried again. It felt rooted to the floor. She slid the brown, hard-sided Samsonite bag out, sweat dripping from her nose. She undid its first latch, stiff with disuse, then the second, and the weight of whatever was inside popped it open.

The chemical stench of mothballs exploded into her face, making her eyes water. She squeezed the light Mrs. Greene had given her and saw that it was crammed with black plastic sheeting speckled with white mothballs that rolled onto the floor. She pulled aside some of the plastic and a pair of milky eyes reflected the light back at her.

Her fingers went numb and the flashlight went dark as she dropped it into the plastic. She stepped back, missed the edge where the plywood flooring ended, and her foot came down on the empty space between two of the joists. She started to fall backward, arms pinwheeling, and only just managed to grab a rough beam on the ceiling and catch herself.

Reaching into the suitcase, barely controlling her panic, her fingers found the flashlight and squeezed. She saw the eyes again, and now she made out the face around them. It was wrapped in a clear, plastic dry-cleaning bag and Patricia saw white grains in it that had turned yellow and brown over time. She realized they were salt. The mothballs were there to kill the smell. The salt was to preserve the body. The skin on the face of the corpse was dark brown and stretched tight, pulling the lips away from the teeth in a terrible grin. But even then, Patricia recognized Francine.

Heart cracking hard inside her chest, hands tingling with blood, she forced herself to let the penlight go out. She slid it into her pocket and struggled with the Samsonite until she had it closed again. She twisted the stiff latches, grabbed the handle with both hands, and dragged it toward the stairs. It made a loud, gritty sound as she slid it across the floor.

She pulled on the suitcase, took a step, pulled it again, took a step, and step by step she dragged it halfway to the attic stairs. Her shoulders burned, the base of her spine felt broken, but eventually she got it to the lip of the trapdoor and felt relief course through her body when she saw the clean room down below.

She'd leave the bag here, get Mrs. Greene, and they'd get this out of the house together. She wouldn't hesitate. She'd drive it right to the police station. She turned around and stepped onto the first step down. That was when she heard voices downstairs and automatically pulled her foot back.

"Mrs. Greene," a distant man's voice said. She missed the next part and then: ". . . a surprise."

She heard Mrs. Greene say something she couldn't make out, and then she heard the end of James Harris's reply: ". . . come home early."

CHAPTER 30

Electricity raced down Patricia's arms and legs, rooting her to the spot.

". . . can wrap up," she heard James Harris say. ". . . want to go upstairs and get some rest."

A horrible thought gripped Patricia's brain: any minute Slick was going to stroll up to the back door and knock. Slick couldn't lie to save her life. She'd say she was there to meet Patricia.

A voice she couldn't hear spoke, and then James Harris said, "Lora here today?"

Patricia looked down and her heart banged so hard it left a bruise against her ribs. Lora stood in the door of the guest room, a dust rag in one hand, looking up at Patricia.

"Lora," Patricia whispered.

Lora blinked, slowly.

"Close the stairs," Patricia begged. Lora just stared. "Please. Close the stairs."

James Harris was saying something to Mrs. Greene that Patricia couldn't hear because everything in her body was directed at Lora, willing her to understand. Then Lora moved: she held out one yellow gloved hand, palm up in a universal gesture. Patricia remembered the other ten-dollar bill. She jammed her hand into her pocket, bending the nail of her forefinger backward, and pulled it out. She dropped it and it fluttered down slowly, right into Lora's hand.

Downstairs, she heard James Harris say, "Has anyone stopped by?"

Lora leaned down, grabbed the bottom of the stairs, and pushed them up. The springs didn't groan this time but they were closing too fast and she squatted, extending her hands, catching the trap-door, bringing it to a gentle close with a quiet *bump*.

She had to replace the suitcase before he came upstairs. She stood and wedged her right foot beneath it, feeling its weight crush her bones, and lifted, stepping her foot forward, using her shoe as a bumper when she brought the suitcase down, swinging it forward a step at a time. It was loud, but not as loud as dragging. Limping wildly, bruising her shin with every step, her pulse snapping in her wrists, the suitcase scraping the top of her foot raw, she slowly made it to the end of the attic and slid the Samsonite back into place. Then she saw that there were mothballs scattered all over the floor, glowing like pearls in the dim attic light.

She scooped them up and, with nowhere else to put them, dropped them into her pockets. Her head spun; she thought she might faint. She had to know where he was. Stepping from joist to joist, she made her way back to the trapdoor, brushed three dead cockroaches out of her way and knelt on the floor, bringing her ear close to the gritty plywood.

She heard the muffled thumps of bedroom doors opening and closing. She prayed that Lora had closed the one with the attic stairs in it, and then she heard it open, and footsteps right beneath her, and her heart clenched. She wondered if the marks from the ladder could be seen in the carpet's pile. Then more footsteps and the door closed.

Everything went quiet. She pushed herself up. Every joint in her body ached. How could she get out of here? And why had he traveled in daylight? She knew he was capable of doing it but would only take the risk in desperation. What had happened to make him hurry home? Did he know she was here? And what was going to happen when Slick showed up?

She heard faint voices floating up from downstairs:

". . . come again next . . ."

He was sending them home. She heard a distant, final thump and realized it was the front door closing. She was in the house alone.

With James Harris. Everything was silent for a few minutes and then, from right beneath the trapdoor, a singsong voice drifted up.

"Patricia," James Harris sang. "I know you're in here."

She froze. He was going to come up. She wanted to scream but caught it before it could slip out between her lips.

"I'm going to find you, Patricia," he singsonged.

He would come up the ladder. Any second she would hear the springs stretch and see the light around the edges get brighter, she'd hear his heavy steps on the rungs, and she'd see his head and shoulders emerge into the attic, looking right at her, mouth splitting wide into a grin, and that thing, that long black thing boiling up out of his throat. She was trapped.

Below her, a bedroom door opened, then another. She heard closet doors rattling open and shut, nearer and farther away, and then a bedroom door slammed with a bang and she jumped a little inside her skin. Another bedroom door opened.

It was only a matter of time before he remembered the attic. She had to find a hiding place.

She squeezed the penlight and looked at the floor, trying to see if she'd given herself away. The white cockroach poison had her tracks all through it as well as drag marks from the suitcase. Squatting, forcing herself to move slowly and carefully, she used her palms to whisk the poison smooth, leaving the gritty white layer thinner, but undisturbed. She walked backward, hunched over, brushing the floor lightly, the small of her back on fire until she reached the suitcases and stood. She used the penlight to check her work and was pleased.

She examined the suitcase and realized the one with Francine's body in it was rubbed clean. She scooped up roach powder and mouse droppings and used them to dirty the suitcase. It would do the job if he didn't look closely.

Standing made her feel exposed, so she forced herself to lie down behind the draped mound of Mrs. Savage's things. With her ear pressed to the filthy plywood floor, she heard the house vibrating beneath her. She heard doors opening and closing. She heard foot-steps. Then she heard nothing. The silence made her nervous.

She checked her wristwatch: 4:56. The silence lulled her into a trance. She could stay here, he wouldn't look for her here, she'd wait as long as she needed, and she'd listen, and when it got dark he'd leave the house and she could sneak out. She would be strong. She would be smart. She would be safe.

She heard the springs groan as the trapdoor opened, and light flooded the far end of the attic.

"Patricia," James Harris said loudly, coming up the steps, springs screaming crazily beneath his feet. "I know you're up here."

She looked at the filthy blankets draped over the boxes and real-ized that even getting under them wouldn't help. The furniture was too sparse to hide her. If he walked around to this side of the stacks he'd see her. There was nowhere to go.

"I'm coming for you, Patricia," he called, happily, as he got to the top of the ladder.

Then she saw the pile of clothes on the edge of the attic where the plywood flooring ended. Several boxes had split open and dis-gorged their contents into a huge mound.

If she could burrow into that pile she would be hidden. She crawled closer, staying low, the reeking stench of rotting fabric scraping her sinuses raw. Her gorge slapped against the back of her throat. The footsteps coming up the ladder stopped.

"Patty," James's voice said from the middle of the attic. "We need to talk."

She heard the plywood creak beneath his weight.

She raised the stiff edge of the pile and began to slither under, head first. Spiders fled from the disturbance, and roach eggs loos-ened from the fabric and rained down on her face. Centipedes fell out and squirmed against the hollow of her throat. She heard James Harris coming across the attic floor and she forced herself to fight down her gorge and slither in, moving carefully so she didn't disturb the blankets draped overhead. His feet came closer; they were at the edge of the boxes now, and she pulled her feet in under the rotting pile of clothes and lay there, trying not to breathe.

Insects seethed across her body, and she realized she'd disturbed a mouse nest. Clawed feet squirmed over her stomach, writhed over her hip. She wanted to scream. She kept her mouth clamped shut, taking small shallow breaths through her nose, feeling the stinking fabric around her crawling with mites, roaches, and mice.

Desiccated insect husks lay on her face, but she didn't dare brush them away. Spiders crept across her knuckles. She made herself hold very still. She heard another step and she could tell he was lifting the blankets draped over Ann Savage's boxes, looking underneath, and she pretended she was invisible.

"Patricia," James Harris said, conversationally. "Why are you hiding in my attic? What are you looking for up here?"

She thought about how he'd gotten Francine's body into the suitcase, how he'd probably had to take his big hands and break her arms, shatter her shoulders, crush her elbows, pull her legs out of their sockets and twist them into splinters to make them fit. He was so strong. And he was standing directly over her.

The pile of rotten fabric shifted and moved, and she willed herself to become smaller and smaller until there was nothing left. Something extended a delicate, gentle leg onto her chin, then moved over her lips, delicately scraping them with its hairy legs, and she felt the roach's antenna brush the rim of her nostrils like long, waving hairs. She wanted to scream but she pretended she was made of stone.

"Patricia," James Harris said. "I can see you."

Please, please, please don't go up my nose, she silently begged the cockroach.

"Patricia," James Harris said from right beside her. What if her feet were sticking out? What if he could see them? "It's time to stop playing. You know how much it hurts me to go outside during the day. I don't feel very good right now, and I'm not in the mood for games."

The roach stepped past her nose, brushed over her cheekbone, and she squeezed her eyes shut, gritty in their sockets with all the rotting fabric flaking into them, and the roach's progress across her face tickled so badly she had to brush her cheek or she would go insane. The roach crawled down the side of her face, over her ear, probing inside her ear canal with its antenna, then, drawn by the warmth, its legs began to scrabble into her ear.

Oh, God, she wanted to moan.

Please, please, please, please . . .

She felt the antenna waving, exploring deep inside her ear, and it sent cold shivers down her spine, and bile boiled up her throat, and she pressed her tongue against the roof of her mouth, and felt the bile fill her sinuses, and the legs were inside her ear now, and its wings were fluttering delicately against the top of her ear canal, and she felt it crush its body into her ear.

"Patricia!" James Harris shouted, and something moved violently, and crashed over, and she almost screamed but she held on, and the roach forced its way deeper into her ear, three quarters in, its legs scrabbling deeper, and soon she wouldn't be able to get it out, and James Harris kicked over furniture, and she felt the blankets move.

Then loud stomps moved away from her, and she heard the springs moan, and the roach fluttered its wings, trying to force itself deeper, but it was jammed, and she felt like it was fluttering its front legs against the side of her brain, and she knew James Harris was only pretending to go down, and then there was a bang and the floor jumped, and silence, and she knew he was waiting for her.

She got her left hand ready to catch the back legs of the roach before it disappeared into her ear, and she listened, waiting to hear James Harris give himself away, but then, far away, deep down inside the house she heard a door slam.

Patricia scrambled out from under the pile of clothes, feeling mouse droppings shower from her body, tearing at her ear, and she couldn't catch the roach, and it panicked and squirmed, pushing its way into her ear, and she grabbed her soft tissue all around it, and crumpled her ear closed. Something crunched and popped and warm fluid oozed deep inside her ear canal, and she pulled out the mangled corpse of the roach, and scraped the hot gunk out with her little finger.

Spiders crawled from her hair onto her neck. She slapped at them, praying they weren't black widows.

Finally, she stopped. She looked at the pile of old clothes and knew that even if he came back, there was no way she could make herself go under them again.

She watched the louvers get dimmer on the side of the attic facing the back of the house, and get brighter behind the louvers facing the harbor, and then the light turned rose, then red, then orange, and then it was gone. She began to shiver. How was she going to get out? What if he stayed in the house all night? What if he came back up after she'd fallen asleep? What if Carter called home? Did Blue and Korey know where she was?

She checked her watch. 6:11. Her thoughts chased themselves around and around inside her head as the sun went down and the heat leached out of the attic. She felt thirsty, hungry, scared, and filthy. Eventually she put her feet back under the moldering pile of clothes to keep them warm.

Occasionally, she dropped off to sleep and would wake up with a jerk of her head that made her neck snap. She listened for James Harris, shivered uncontrollably, and stopped looking at her watch because she'd think an hour had passed and each time discovered it had only been five minutes.

She wondered what had happened to Slick, and she wondered why he had come back early, and why he had risked going out in daylight, and inside her cold, gummy head, these thoughts went slower and slower and melted together and suddenly she knew it was Slick.

Slick had told him she was here. That was why Slick hadn't come. She had called James Harris in Florida because her Christian values couldn't stand to bend the rules, and Patricia had found something, she'd found *the* something, she'd found Francine, but Slick didn't care about that, she didn't care that Patricia had told her James Harris was dangerous, she just cared about her precious, lily-white soul.

She looked at her watch. 10:31. She'd been up here for seven hours. She had at least that many more to go. Why had Slick betrayed her? They were supposed to be friends. But Patricia realized she was on her own again.

It took a few minutes to identify the noise beneath her, coming through the floor, repeating itself again and again. Patricia wiped her nose and listened, but she couldn't tell what it was. Then it stopped.

"What?!?" James Harris yelled. Even far away and muffled by the walls, it still made her jump.

The sound had been the phone ringing. She heard footsteps running downstairs, she heard the front door open and slam, then silence.

She sat, heart pounding, teeth chattering. Then her skin crawled: someone was scratching at the other side of the trapdoor. He was coming up again, finding the eyelet, pulling the trapdoor down. She was too tired, too cold, she couldn't move, she couldn't hide. Then came a noise like the end of the world as the trapdoor cracked, the springs screamed, and James Harris came up the ladder.

CHAPTER 31

"Patricia?" Kitty whispered.

Patricia couldn't understand what Kitty was doing with James Harris.

"Patricia?" Kitty called louder.

Patricia pushed herself up on her elbows, then onto her hands, and looked over the top of the boxes. Kitty stood halfway inside the attic. Alone.

"Kitty?" Patricia said, her dry tongue sticking to the syllables.

"Oh, thank God," Kitty said. "You scared me half to death. Come on."

"Where is he?" Patricia asked, thoughts coming thick and slow.

"He left," Kitty said. "Now mush. We need to be gone before he comes back."

Patricia pushed herself up off the floor and reeled toward Kitty, knees popping, spine cracking, feet screaming with pins and needles as the blood poured back into them.

"How?" Patricia asked.

"Gracious Cay caught on fire," Kitty said. "Mrs. Greene called and told me I needed to come get you out."

"Where is she?" Patricia slurred, reaching the trap door.

Kitty grabbed Patricia's waist and held her steady.

"First thing I did was take Blue and Korey out to Seewee," she said, helping Patricia place her foot on the top step. "We told them you had to visit a sick cousin upstate. They've been crabbing all day with Honey and we rented a stack of movies. I've got beds made up for them. They're having a high old time."

She got both Patricia's feet onto the top step, then helped her turn around and come down the stairs. Halfway down, Patricia's head emerged into the hallway and it smelled so clean she wanted to weep.

"How is Gracious Cay on fire?" she asked, clinging to the ladder as the room spun slowly around her. "Where's Mrs. Greene?"

"Same answer to both questions," Kitty said. "I think it's the first time she's ever broken the law. Keep moving."

"No," Patricia said. "You have to see this."

She made herself climb back up the ladder.

"I've seen attics before," Kitty called up after her. "Patricia! We don't have time."

Patricia knelt on the attic floor and faced Kitty through the hatch.

"If you don't see this, it's all for nothing," she said. "You'll all say I'm crazy again."

"No one thinks you're crazy," Kitty said.

Patricia disappeared into the darkness. After a minute, she heard the stairs creaking and Kitty emerged from the trap door.

"It's pitch-black," Kitty said.

Patricia pulled the penlight from her pocket and used it to light Kitty's way to the chimney where she heaved out the Samsonite bag and laid it on one side.

"I've seen luggage before," Kitty said.

"Hold this." Patricia handed her the penlight. "Point here and squeeze."

Kitty held the light as Patricia twisted the locks open. She opened the suitcase and pulled back the black plastic. Francine's wide-open eyes and exposed teeth didn't scare her this time, they just made her sad. She'd been alone up here for a long time.

"Ah!" Kitty screamed in surprise and the penlight went dark. Patricia heard her dry heave once, twice, and then Kitty burped something thick and meaty. After a moment, the light came back on and played over the contents of the suitcase.

"It's Francine," Patricia said. "Help me get her down."

She closed the lid and locked it again.

"We can't move evidence," Kitty said, and immediately Patricia felt stupid. Of course. The police needed to find Francine here.

"But you saw her, right?" Patricia asked.

"I saw her," Kitty said. "I most definitely saw her. I'll testify to that in court. But we have got to go."

They put the suitcase back and Kitty helped Patricia out of the attic. But it wasn't until they'd closed the attic, made their way through the upstairs hall, and reached the bottom of the front stairs that Patricia had a sudden sinking thought and turned. She was filthy from the attic. The carpeted stairs were white.

"Oh, no," she moaned, and the strength went out of her legs and she sank to the floor.

"We don't have time for this," Kitty said. "He's going to be back any minute."

"Look!" Patricia said, and pointed to the carpet.

It showed the dirt clearly. They weren't footprints, but they were close. There was one on every step, leading all the way up and, Patricia knew, right back to where the attic door opened.

"He's going to know it was me, and that I've been in his attic," she said. "He'll get rid of the suitcase before we can get back here with the police. It'll all be for nothing."

"We don't have time," Kitty said, pulling her toward the kitchen and the back door.

Patricia imagined hearing a key in the front door, the door swinging open, and the frozen moment while they all looked at each other before James Harris rushed down the hall at them. She imagined the three empty suitcases in the attic next to the one holding Francine, waiting for their broken bodies, and she let Kitty drag her to the back door.

But what if the police wouldn't search his attic? What if Kitty was too scared to back up her story? What if breaking into his house violated some technicality and no one could get a search warrant because of that? It happened all the time in true crime books. What if it cost Mrs. Greene her job? There had to be a better way.

Her mind flipped through one idea after another and then stopped on a pattern that looked familiar. She tested it, quickly, and it held. She knew what they had to do.

"Wait," Patricia said, and dug in her heels.

Kitty kept pulling her arm, but Patricia twisted out of her grip and stood her ground right outside the kitchen.

"I'm not fooling," Kitty said. "We got to go."

"Get the broom, and the vacuum cleaner," Patricia said, heading for the stairs. "I think they're in the closet under the stairs. We need carpet shampoo, too. I'm going back up."

"*For what???*" Kitty asked.

"If he comes back and sees that someone's been in his attic he's going to take that suitcase, drive it out to Francis Marion National Forest, and bury it where it will never be found," Patricia said. "We need someone to find it in his attic and that means we have to cover our tracks. We have to clean the stairs."

"Nuh-uh," Kitty said, shaking her head furiously, waving her hands back and forth, shaking her bracelets. "No, sir. We are gone."

Patricia came back down the hall until she stood in Kitty's face.

"We both saw what was in that attic," she said.

"Don't make me do this," Kitty begged. "Please, please, please."

Patricia squeezed her eyes shut. She felt a headache try to claw its way out through her forehead.

"He murdered her," she said. "We need to stop him. This is the only way."

Without giving Kitty a chance to protest, she turned and went back upstairs.

"Patricia," Kitty whined from the downstairs hall.

"The cleaning closet is under the stairs," Patricia called over the banister.

She pulled the attic steps down again and went up. The more she did this the more it didn't bother her when she opened the suitcase. She rustled around in the sticky plastic, occasionally feeling the back of her hand brush against something light, or her fingers grip an emaciated leg or forearm, but after a minute she found what she was looking for: Francine's pocketbook. She worked it out of the plastic, smelling cinnamon and old leather.

She took out Francine's wallet, removed her driver's license, and carefully packed everything back into the suitcase.

"We'll be back for you," she whispered to Francine, and snapped the latches closed again.

Downstairs, she found Kitty with the broom, vacuum cleaner, and carpet shampoo. She'd also taken out a roll of paper towels and some Lysol counter spray.

"If we're going to do this, let's go," Kitty said.

They swept the loose dirt off the carpet and sprayed it with foaming shampoo all the way back up the stairs, through the hall, to the trapdoor. They let the shampoo sit for five minutes, while Kitty muttered, "Come on . . . come on . . ." then vacuumed it up. Running the vacuum cleaner was the hardest part because it covered up the sound of a car pulling into the drive, the front door opening, James Harris coming into the house. She made Kitty stand by the front door as a lookout while she roared up and down the steps.

Finally, she shut off the vacuum cleaner, made sure the marks from the trapdoor's ladder weren't visible in the carpet pile, and lugged the vacuum back downstairs. She had just started wrapping the vacuum cleaner cord when Kitty hissed:

"Car!"

They froze.

"It's pulling in," Kitty said, racing back to Patricia. "Let's go! Let's go!"

Headlights swept the front hall, and Patricia wrapped faster, wrists aching. They got the broom and vacuum cleaner into the hall closet and closed the door. Outside, they heard a car door slam.

They bumped into each other going through the kitchen door, making for the back door, lit by the kitchen's under-the-cabinet lights. Footsteps clunked up the front porch steps.

"Paper towels!" Patricia said, and froze.

She looked back down the hall and saw the roll of paper towels sitting out at the end of the banisters on the newel post. They looked very, very far away. Footsteps came across the front porch. Patricia didn't think, she just ran for them. Down the hall, hearing footsteps stop on the other side of the door, keys rattling, she grabbed the paper towels, a clinking *thump* as James Harris dropped his keys, Patricia running back down the hall, hearing the keys slide into the front door, replacing the towels on their holder, Kitty holding the back door open, racing through it as they both heard the front door open, then closing the back door softly behind them and going down the back steps as quietly as they could.

Behind them, lights began to turn on all over the house.

Once they reached his backyard, they ran, racing down the path by the drainage ditch, so dark that Patricia almost fell in, reaching Kitty's Cadillac parked on Pitt Street. They slid into the front seats, and the roar of the engine sparking to life made Patricia jump. She reassured herself there was no way for James Harris to hear it.

Coming down from the adrenaline high, sticky, shaky, and feeling sick, she burrowed her hand into her front pocket and pulled out Francine's driver's license. She held it in front of her.

"We won," she said. "We finally won."

CHAPTER 32

"He'd been overserved," Patricia said breathlessly into the telephone receiver, eyes wide, voice full of astonished innocence. "And he was doing how men do at a party, talking big, showing off. I didn't mean to get so far away from my husband, but he just kept sort of pushing me farther and farther away."

Patricia stopped and swallowed, caught up in her own performance. She pulled Francine's driver's license out of her pocket and turned it over in her hand. She heard Mrs. Greene listening hard on the other end of the line.

"When he kind of got me over in a corner," she continued, "he told me, real low so no one else could hear, that years ago he'd gotten angry at the woman who did for him. She'd stolen some money, I think, I wasn't real clear on that point, Detective. But he said he 'fixed her.' I definitely remember that. Well, I didn't understand what he meant at first and I said I'd have to ask her about it when I saw her again, and he said I wouldn't be seeing her again, unless I went up in his attic and looked inside his suitcases. Well, I couldn't help it, it just sounded so absurd, and I laughed. I don't need to tell you how men get when you laugh at them. His face turned red, and he reached into his wallet and pulled out something and stuck it in my face and said if he was lying then how did I explain *that*. And, Detective, that's when I got scared. Because it was Francine's driver's license. I mean, who carries around a thing like that? If he hadn't hurt her, then where did he get it?" She paused, as if listening. "Oh, yes, sir. He put it right back in there. He'd had so much to drink he might not even remember showing it to me."

She stopped and waited.

"You think that'll work?" Mrs. Greene asked.

"They don't have to get a warrant or anything like that. All they have to do is stop by his house and ask to look inside his wallet. He'll have no clue it's in there, so of course he'll show them. Once they see it, they'll ask for permission to search his attic, he'll refuse, they'll leave someone with him while they go get a warrant, and then they'll find Francine."

"When?" Mrs. Greene asked.

"The Scruggs are having an oyster roast this coming Saturday out at their farm," Patricia said. "It's six days away but it will be crowded, it will be public, people will be drinking. It's our best chance."

Patricia didn't know how she'd get into his wallet—she didn't even know if he carried one—but she'd keep her eyes open and stay on her toes. Kitty's oyster roast started at 1:30. If she got it into his wallet early enough, she could call the police that afternoon; they could even come to the oyster roast and ask to see inside his wallet there, and this could all be over in less than a week.

"A lot could go wrong," Mrs. Greene said.

"We're running out of time," Patricia said.

It was already the end of the month. That night was Halloween.

The doorbell started ringing around four on Halloween evening, and Patricia oohed and ahhed over an endless stream of Aladdins and Jasmines and Teenage Mutant Ninja Turtles, and fairies in tutus with wings bouncing up and down on their backs.

She had fun-sized Butterfingers and small boxes of Sun-Maid raisins for the children, and Jack Daniel's for their fathers, who stood behind them, red Solo cups in hand. It was an Old Village tradition: moms stayed home and gave out candy on Halloween while dads took the kids trick-or-treating. Everyone kept a bottle of something behind their front door to top off whatever the dads were drinking. The dads got progressively louder and happier as the shadows got longer and the sun went down on the Old Village.

Carter wasn't among them. When Patricia had asked Korey if she wanted to go trick-or-treating she'd been treated to a withering glare and a single contemptuous snort. Blue said trick-or-treating was for babies so, Carter said, if neither of his children wanted him to take them, he'd go right from the airport to his office and get ahead on some work for Monday.

Around seven, Blue came downstairs, opened the dog food cabinet, and took out a paper shopping bag.

"Are you going trick-or-treating?" Patricia asked.

"Sure," he said.

"Where's your costume?" she asked, trying to reach him.

"I'm a serial killer," he said.

"Don't you want to be something more fun?" she asked. "We could put something together in just a few minutes."

He turned and walked out of the den.

"Be back by ten," she called as the front door slammed.

She had just run out of Butterfingers and given the first box of raisins to a deeply disappointed Beavis and Butthead when the phone rang.

"Campbell residence," she said.

No one answered. She figured it was a prank call and was about to hang up when someone inhaled, wet and sticky, and a ruined voice said:

". . . I didn't . . ."

"Hello?" Patricia said. "This is the Campbell residence?"

"I didn't . . . ," the voice said again, dazed, and Patricia realized it was a woman.

"If you don't tell me who this is, I'm going to hang up," she said.

"I didn't . . ." the woman repeated. ". . . I didn't make a sound . . ."

"Slick?" Patricia asked.

"I didn't make a sound . . . I didn't make a sound . . . I didn't make a sound," Slick babbled.

"What's going on?" Patricia asked.

Slick hadn't called—not to apologize for abandoning her, not to see if she was all right—and that was all the evidence Patricia needed to know that Slick had told James Harris she was breaking into his house. Slick was why he had come home early. As far as she was concerned, Slick could go hang.

Then Slick began to cry.

"Slick?" Patricia asked. "What's wrong?"

". . . I didn't make a sound . . ." Slick whispered over and over, and gooseflesh crawled up Patricia's arms.

"Stop it," she said. "You're scaring me."

"I didn't," Slick moaned. "I didn't . . ."

"Where are you?" Patricia asked. "Are you at home? Do you need help?"

Patricia couldn't hear Slick wheezing into the earpiece anymore. She hung up and dialed her back and got a busy signal. She thought about not doing anything, but she couldn't. Slick's voice had scared her, and something dark stirred in her gut. She grabbed her purse and found Korey on the sun porch, eyes glued to the TV, which was showing a commercial for Bounce Gentle Breeze dryer sheets.

"I have to run out to Kitty's," Patricia said, and realized that lies came easier the more she told them. "Can you get the door?"

"Mm," Korey said, not turning around.

Patricia supposed that was *yes* in seventeen-year-old language.

The Old Village streets were packed with a parade of kids and parents, and Patricia wove through them too slowly. The fathers looked pleasantly loaded, their steps getting heavier, their dips into the candy bags becoming more frequent. She couldn't imagine what had happened to Slick. She needed to get to her house. She crawled through the crowds at fifteen miles per hour, passing James Harris's house with its two jack-o'-lanterns flickering on the front porch, then turned up McCants and hit the brakes.

The Cantwells lived on the corner of Pitt and McCants, and every Halloween they filled their front yard with fake corpses hanging from the trees, Styrofoam headstones, and skeletons wired to their shrubberies. Every half hour, Mr. Cantwell emerged from the coffin on the front porch dressed as Dracula, and the family performed a ten-minute show. The Wolfman grabbed at the kids in front; the Mummy stumbled toward little girls who ran away shrieking; Mrs. Cantwell, wearing a fake warty nose, stirred her cauldron full of dry ice and offered people ladles of edible green slime and gummy worms. It ended with all of them dancing to "The Monster Mash" followed by mass candy distribution.

The crowd around their house spilled off the sidewalk and blocked the street. Patricia's face twitched. Was it just Slick? What about the rest of Slick's family? Something was wrong. She needed to go. She took her foot off the brake and rolled onto the edge of the Simmonses' front yard on the far side of McCants, flashing her lights to make people clear the way. It took her five minutes to get through the intersection, and then she picked up speed as she headed to Coleman Boulevard, and hit fifty on Johnnie Dodds. Even that wasn't fast enough.

She pulled into Creekside and wove around trick-or-treaters as fast as she dared. Both cars were parked in the Paleys' driveway. Whatever had happened had happened to the entire family. A flickering white candle sat on a kitchen stool on the front porch. Next to it sat a bowl of pamphlets emblazoned with orange type reading: *Trick? Yes. Treat? Only Through the Grace of God!*

Patricia reached for the doorbell and stopped. What if it was James Harris? What if he was still inside?

She tried the handle and the latch popped and the door swung silently open. Patricia took a breath and stepped inside. She closed the door behind her and stood, eyes and ears straining, listening for any sign of life, looking for a single telltale detail: a drop of blood on the hardwood floor, a picture knocked askew, a crack in one of the display cabinets. Nothing. She crept down the front hall's thick runner and pushed open the door to the back addition. People started screaming.

Every muscle in Patricia's body snapped into action. Her hands flew up to protect her face. She opened her mouth to scream. Then the screaming dissolved into laughter and she looked past her hands and saw Leland, LJ, their oldest, Greer, and Tiger sitting around the long dinner table halfway across the room, their backs to her, all laughing. Greer was the only one facing Patricia.

She caught sight of Patricia and stopped laughing. LJ and Tiger spun around.

"Ohmygosh," Greer said. "How'd you get in?"

A Monopoly board sat in the middle of the table. Slick wasn't there.

"Patricia?" Leland said, standing, genuinely baffled, trying to smile.

"Don't get up," she said. "Slick called and I thought she was home."

"She's upstairs," Leland said.

"I'll just pop right up," Patricia said. "Keep playing."

She left the room before they could say anything and went up the carpeted stairs fast. In the upstairs hall she didn't have a clue which way to go. The door to the master bedroom sat ajar. The bedroom light was off but the master bathroom light was on. Patricia walked in.

"Slick?" she called softly.

The shower curtain rattled and Patricia looked down and saw Slick lying in the tub, her lipstick smeared, her mascara running down her face in trails, her hair sticking out in clumps. Her skirt had been torn and she only wore one dangling sand dollar earring.

Everything between them evaporated and Patricia knelt by the bathtub.

"What happened?" she asked.

"I didn't make a sound," Slick rasped, eyes wide with panic.

Her mouth moved soundlessly, straining to form words. Her hands opened and closed.

"Slick?" Patricia repeated. "What happened?"

"I didn't . . . ," Slick began, then licked her lips and tried again. "I didn't make a sound."

"We need to call the ambulance," Patricia said, standing up. "I'll go get Leland."

"I . . . ," Slick said, and it trailed off to a whisper. "I didn't . . ."

Patricia walked to the bathroom door and heard hollow flailing in the tub behind her, and then Slick rasped, "No!"

Patricia turned around. Slick gripped the edge of the tub with both hands, knuckles white, shaking her head, her single sand dollar earring flopping from side to side.

"They can't know," she said.

"You're hurt," Patricia said.

"They can't know," Slick repeated.

"Slick!" Leland called from downstairs. "Everything all right?"

Slick locked eyes with Patricia and slowly shook her head back and forth. Patricia eased out into the bedroom, eyes still on Slick.

"We're fine," she called back.

"Slick?" Leland said, and from his voice Patricia could tell he was coming up the stairs.

Slick shook her head harder. Patricia held out one hand, then raced to the hall and headed off Leland at the top of the stairs.

"What's happening?" he asked, stopping two steps below her.

"She's ill," Patricia said. "I'll sit with her and make sure she's okay. She didn't want to break up your party."

"That doesn't make any sense," Leland said. "You didn't need to come all this way. We're right downstairs."

He tried to take a step but Patricia moved to block him.

"Leland," she said, smiling. "Slick wants you to have fun with the children tonight. It's important to her that they have . . . Christian associations with Halloween. Let me handle this."

"I want to see how she is," he said, sliding one hand up the banister, letting her know he was going to go right through her if necessary.

"Leland." She dropped her voice low. "It's a female problem."

She wasn't sure what a female problem meant to Leland, but his body sagged.

"All right," he said. "But if she's really not well, you'll tell me?"

"Of course," Patricia said. "Go back to the kids."

He turned and went back downstairs. She waited until he passed into the addition, and then sprinted back to the bathroom. Slick hadn't moved. Patricia knelt beside the tub, leaned forward, and got her arms around Slick. She stood, pulling Slick up with her, amazed at how weak her legs were. She helped her out of the tub, one foot at a time.

"They can't know," Slick said.

"I didn't say a word," Patricia said.

She took off Slick's one earring and laid it on the bathroom counter.

"The other one'll turn up," she reassured her.

Patricia locked the bathroom door, then pulled Slick's sweater over her head and unfastened her brassiere. Slick's breasts were small and pale and the way she was hunched over, the way her ribs stuck out, the way her breasts hung lifeless, she reminded Patricia of a plucked chicken.

She sat Slick down on the toilet and put her fingers in the waist of her skirt. It was torn down the back so there was no need to unzip it. The tear went right through the suede, not down the seam. Patricia didn't know what was strong enough to do that.

GRADY HENDRIX

As she started to pull off her skirt, Slick recoiled, pulling her hands up over her groin.

"What's wrong?" Patricia asked. "Slick, what's wrong?"

Slick shook her head back and forth, and Patricia's heart hitched. She focused on keeping her voice steady and slow.

"Show me," she insisted, but Slick shook her head faster. "Slick?"

"They can't know," Slick moaned.

She took Slick's thin wrists and pulled them away. Slick resisted at first, then went slack. Patricia pulled her skirt down. Slick's panties were torn. She pulled them off, lifting Slick's buttocks. Slick clamped her thighs closed.

"Slick," Patricia said, using her nurse's voice. "I need to see."

She pried Slick's knees apart. At first, Patricia didn't know what was coming through Slick's sparse, blond pubic hair, and then she saw Slick's abdominal muscles convulse and a runnel of black jelly oozed out of her vagina. It smelled rank, like something lying rotten on the side of the road in summer. And it kept coming, an endless ooze of fetid slime pooling in a quivering black puddle on the toilet seat lid.

"Slick?" Patricia asked. "What happened?"

Slick met her eyes, tears trembling along her lower lids, and she looked so haunted that Patricia leaned forward and embraced her. Slick stayed stiff in her arms.

"I didn't make a sound," Slick insisted.

Patricia sprayed enough air freshener in the bathroom to make her eyes burn, and then she ran the shower. She took off her blouse and helped Slick back into the tub, holding her under the hot, strong spray. She cleaned the makeup off Slick's face with a washcloth, rubbing until Slick's skin turned pink, then used as much soap as she could to clean between Slick's legs.

"Bear down," she told Slick over the spray. "Like you're going to the bathroom."

She saw the last remaining black drops fall into the water, stretch into tendrils, and swirl down the drain. She used an entire bottle of St. Ives shampoo to wash Slick's hair, and when they were finished the bathroom smelled steamy and floral. She dried herself and put her top back on while Slick stood naked and shivering, and then she wrapped Slick in her robe and tucked her into bed. She put a glass of water on her bedside table.

"Now," she told Slick, "I need you to tell me what happened."

Slick looked up at her with wide eyes.

"Talk to me, Slick," Patricia said.

"If he did this to me," Slick whispered, "what's he going to do to you?"

"Who?" Patricia asked.

"James Harris."

CHAPTER 33

"I prayed over your photograph," Slick whispered. "I sat with those clippings and your photograph, and I prayed for guidance. That man put so much money into Gracious Cay, and he made himself Leland's friend, and he came to church with my family, but I saw that picture, and read those clippings, and I didn't know what to do. That photograph is him. You look at it and you know."

Her chin started to shake, and a single teardrop streaked fast down one cheek, shining silver in the light of the bedside lamp.

"I called him in Tampa," Slick said. "I thought that was what God wanted me to do. I thought that if he knew I had these clippings and the photograph he would be scared and I could get him to leave the Old Village. I was a fool. I tried to threaten him. I told him that if he didn't leave right away, I would show everyone the photograph and the clippings."

"Did he know it was me, Slick?" Patricia asked.

Slick shot her eyes to the glass of water and Patricia handed it to her. She took two loud gulps and handed it back, then squeezed her eyes shut and nodded.

"I'm sorry," Slick said. "I'm so sorry. I called him yesterday morning and told you were going into his house. I said you'd find whatever he was hiding. I told him his only choice was to never come back. I told him he could let me know where he went and I'd mail him his checks when Gracious Cay returned on its investment, but he had to leave from Tampa and never come back. I thought he wanted money, Patricia. I thought he cared about his reputation.

I told him the photo and clippings were my insurance so he could never come back. I thought you'd be so happy I'd solved this. I was full of pride."

Without warning, Slick slapped herself in the face. Patricia grabbed for her hand, missed, and Slick hit herself again. Patricia caught her hand this time.

"Pride goeth," Slick hissed, eyes furious, face white. "The church didn't want to do my Reformation Party, so we kept the kids home tonight to have family time. We were playing Monopoly, Tiger and LJ weren't fighting for once, and I was about to put a hotel on Park Place. It all felt so safe. I got up to be excused, and I took my money with me because I pretended I thought Leland would steal it if I left it behind. The kids loved that. I came upstairs to use the bathroom because the downstairs toilet keeps running."

She looked around the room, reassuring herself the door was closed, the windows were shut, the curtains were drawn. She struggled to get her hands free and Patricia gripped her wrists harder.

"My Bible," Slick said.

Patricia saw it on the bedside table and handed it to her. Slick clutched her Bible to her chest like a teddy bear. It took her a minute before she could speak again.

"He must have come in the upstairs window and waited for me," Slick said. "I didn't know what happened. I was walking down the hall and then I was facedown on the carpet, and something heavy sat on my back, pressing me down, and a voice in my ear said if I made a sound, a single solitary sound he would . . . who is he? He said he would kill my entire family. Who is he, Patricia?"

"He's worse than we can imagine," Patricia said.

"I thought my back would break. It hurt so much." Slick put a hand to her lips and pressed her fingers against them, hard. Her forehead broke into deep furrows. "I've never been with anyone except Leland."

She gripped her Bible in both hands and closed her eyes. Her lips moved silently in prayer for a moment before she started talking again. Her voice was little more than a whisper.

"My Monopoly money went all over the carpet when he hit me," she said. "And I just kept looking at that orange five-hundred-dollar bill in front of my nose. That's what I focused on the entire time. And he kept telling me not to make a sound, and I didn't make a sound, but I was so scared one of them would come looking for me that I wanted him to finish so he would leave. I just wanted it to be over. That's why I didn't fight. And he did. He finished inside me."

Slick clutched her Bible so hard her knuckles turned red and white and her face crumpled. Patricia hated herself for asking the next question but she had to know.

"The picture?" she asked. "The clippings?"

"He made me tell him where they were," Slick said. "I'm sorry. I'm so sorry. My pride. My stupid, stupid pride."

"It's not your fault," Patricia said.

"I thought I could do this alone," Slick said. "I thought I was stronger than him. But none of us are."

The tips of Slick's bangs were wet with sweat. Her cheeks shook. She inhaled sharply.

"Where does it hurt?" Patricia asked.

"My privates," Slick said.

Patricia lifted the duvet. There was a dark stain on the robe over Slick's groin.

"We need to get you to a hospital," Patricia said.

"He'll kill them if I tell," Slick said.

"Slick . . . ," Patricia began.

"He'll kill them," Slick said. "Please. He will."

"We don't know what he did to you," Patricia said.

"If I'm still bleeding in the morning, I'll go," Slick said. "But I can't call an ambulance. What if he's outside watching? What if he's waiting to see what I do? Please, Patricia, don't let him hurt my babies."

Patricia went and got a warm washcloth and cleaned Slick as best she could, found some pads beneath the sink, and helped her into a nightgown. Downstairs, she took Leland aside.

"What's going on?" he asked. "Is she okay?"

"She's having bad cramps," Patricia said. "But she says she'll be fine tomorrow. You may want to sleep in the guest room, though. She needs some privacy."

Leland put a hand on Patricia's shoulder and looked into her eyes.

"I'm sorry I bit your head off earlier," he said. "But I don't know what I'd do if anything ever happened to Slick."

Outside, it was still and dark. The candle on the porch had burned out and all the Creekside trick-or-treaters must have long since gone home. Patricia walked briskly around the side of the house and threw Slick's underwear, robe, and ruined clothes into the trash, stuffing them all the way down under the bags. Then she ran to the Volvo and locked all the doors behind her. Slick was right. He might still be outside.

Once she had the car moving she felt safer and the anger rose up inside her, making her skin feel too tight. Her movements felt rushed and hurried. She couldn't contain herself. She needed to be somewhere else.

She needed to see James Harris.

She wanted to stand in front of him and accuse him of what he'd done. It was the only place to be that felt like it made any sense to her right now. She drove carefully through Creekside, using all her self-control to make wide circles around the few remaining trick-or-treaters, and then she was on Johnnie Dodds and she put the pedal to the floor.

In the Old Village she slowed again. The streets were almost empty. Burned-out jack-o'-lanterns sat on front porches. A cold wind whistled through her Volvo's air-conditioning vents. She stopped at the corner of Pitt and McCants. The Cantwells' front yard was empty, all its lights dark. As she turned toward James Har-

ris's house the wind set the corpses hanging from their trees twisting, following her, reaching for her with their bandaged arms as she
drove past.

The massive, malignant lump of James Harris's house loomed
on her left, and Patricia thought about his dark attic with its suitcase containing the lonely corpse of Francine. She thought about the
wild, hunted look in Slick's eyes. She remembered what Slick had
hissed:

If he did this to me, what's he going to do to you?

She needed to know where her children were, right that minute.
The overwhelming need to know they were safe flooded her body
and sent her flying home.

She pulled into the driveway and ran to the front door. One
jack-o'-lantern had burned out and someone had smashed the other
one against their front steps. She slipped in its slime as she raced
up her porch steps. She opened the door and ran to the sun porch.
Korey wasn't there. She raced upstairs and threw open Korey's bedroom door.

"What?" Korey shouted from where she sat, cross-legged on her
bed, hunched over a copy of *SPIN*.

She was safe. Patricia didn't say a word. She ran into Blue's
room. Empty.

She checked every room downstairs, even the dark garage room,
but Blue was still out. She felt frantic. She checked that the back
door was locked, she grabbed her car keys, but what if she went
out looking for him, and he came home? And how could she leave
Korey alone with James Harris out there?

She had to call Carter. He needed to come home. Two of them
could deal with this. She jumped at the noise of the front door
opening and ran to the hall. Blue was just closing it behind him.

She grabbed him and pressed him to her body. He froze for
a moment, then squirmed out of her arms.

"What?" he asked.

"I'm just glad you're safe," she said. "Where were you?"

"I was at Jim's," he said. It took her a moment to process.

"Where?" she asked.

"At Jim's," he said, defensively. "Jim Harris's house. Why?"

"Blue," she said. "It is very important you tell me the truth right now. Where have you been all evening?"

"At. Jim's. House," Blue repeated. "With Jim. Why do you care?"

"And he was there?" she asked.

"Yes."

"All night?"

"Yes!"

"Did he leave at any point, or was he out of your sight for even a single minute?" she asked.

"Only when a trick-or-treater rang the bell," Blue said. "Wait, why?"

"I need you to be honest with me," she said. "What time did you go over there?"

"I don't know," he said. "Right after I left. I was bored. No one was giving me good candy because they said I didn't have a real costume. And he saw me and said it didn't look like I was having much fun so he invited me inside to mess around on his Playstation. I'd rather hang out with him anyway."

What he was saying couldn't possibly have happened because of what James Harris had done to Slick.

"I need you to think," she said. "I need to know exactly what time you went into his house."

"Like around seven-thirty," he said. "Jesus, why do you care? We played *Resident Evil* all night."

He was lying, he didn't understand the severity of the situation, he thought it was just another spray-painted dog. Patricia tried to make her voice understanding.

"Blue," she said, focusing on him intently. "This is extremely important. Probably the most important thing you've ever said in your life. Don't lie."

"I'm not lying!" he shouted. "Ask him! I was there. He was there. Why would I lie? Why do you always think I'm lying? Jesus!"

"I don't think you're lying," she said, making herself breathe slow. "But I think you're confused."

"I'm! Not! Confused!" he shouted.

Patricia felt tangled in string, like every word she spoke only made things worse.

"Something very serious happened tonight," she said. "And James Harris was involved and I do not believe for a minute that he was with you the entire time."

Blue exhaled hard and turned to the front door. She grabbed his wrist.

"Where are you going?"

"Back to Jim's!" he shouted, and grabbed her wrist in return. "He doesn't scream at me all the time!"

He was stronger than she was and she could feel his fingers bearing down, pressing into her skin, against her bone, leaving a bruise on her forearm. She made herself unclench her fingers from his wrist, hoping he would do the same.

"I need you to tell me the truth," she said.

He let go of her wrist and stared at her with utter contempt.

"You're not going to believe anything I say anyway," he said. "They should put you back in the hospital."

His hatred radiated off his skin like heat. It made Patricia take a small step back. Blue stepped forward and she shrank from him. Then he turned and started up the stairs.

"Where are you going?" she asked.

"To finish my homework!" he yelled over his shoulder.

She heard his bedroom door slam. Carter still wasn't home. She checked the time—almost eleven. She checked all the doors and made sure all the windows were locked. She turned on the yard lights. She tried to think of something else she could do, but there wasn't anything. She looked in on Korey and Blue again, then she got into bed and tried to read November's book club book.

Books can inspire you to love yourself more, it said. *By listening to, writing out, or verbally expressing your feelings.*

She realized she'd been reading for three pages without remembering a word she'd read. She missed reading books that were actually about something. She tried again.

Take a time-out to center yourself, it said. *So that you can then come together again with greater understanding, acceptance, validation, and approval.*

She threw the book across the room and found her copy of *Helter Skelter*. She turned to the back section about the trials, and read about Charles Manson getting sentenced to death over and over again as if it were a bedtime story. She needed to reassure herself that not all men got away with it, not every time. She read about Charles Manson's sentencing until her eyes got grainy and she fell asleep.

MEN ARE FROM MARS, WOMEN ARE FROM VENUS

November 1996

CHAPTER 34

They took Slick to the Medical University on Tuesday. On Wednesday, they started making visitors wear paper gowns and masks.

"We don't know precisely what's going on," her doctor said. "She's got an autoimmune disease but it's developing faster than we'd expect. Her immune system is attacking her white blood cells, and more red blood cells than we'd like are hemolytic. But we're keeping her oxygenated and screening for everything. It's too early to hit the panic button."

The diagnosis simultaneously excited and horrified Patricia. It confirmed that whatever James Harris was, he wasn't human. He'd put a part of himself inside Slick, and it was killing her. He was a monster. On the other hand, Slick wasn't getting better.

Leland visited every day around six, but always seemed like he needed to leave the moment he arrived. When Patricia followed him out into the hall to ask how he was doing, he stepped in close.

"You haven't told anyone her diagnosis?" he asked.

"She doesn't have one as far as I know," Patricia said.

He stepped in closer. Patricia wanted to back up but she was already standing against the wall.

"They say it's an autoimmune disease," he whispered. "You can't repeat that. People are going to think she has AIDS."

"No one's going to think that, Leland," Patricia said.

"They're already saying it at church," he said. "I don't want it coming back on the kids."

"I haven't said anything to anyone," Patricia said, unhappy to be forced to participate in something that felt wrong.

Friday morning, they taped a sign to Slick's door that had been photocopied so many times it was covered with black dots saying that if you had a temperature, or been exposed to anyone with a cold, you were not allowed in the room.

Slick looked pale, her skin felt papery, and she didn't want to be left alone, especially at night. The nurses brought blankets and Patricia slept in the chair by her bed. After Leland went home, Patricia held the phone so Slick could say bedtime prayers with her kids, but most of the time Slick lay still, the sheets pulled up almost to her chin, her doll-sized arms wrapped in white tape, pricked with IV needles and tubes. She sweated out fevers most of the afternoon. When she seemed lucid Patricia tried to read to her from *Men Are from Mars, Women Are from Venus*, but after a paragraph she realized Slick was saying something.

"What's that?" Patricia asked, leaning over.

"Anything . . . else . . . ," Slick said. ". . . anything . . . else."

Patricia pulled the latest Ann Rule out of her purse.

"'September 21, 1986,'" she read, "'was a warm and beautiful Sunday in Portland—in the whole state of Oregon, for that matter. With any luck the winter rains of the Northwest were a safe two months away . . .'"

The facts and firm geography soothed Slick, who closed her eyes and listened. She didn't sleep, just lay there, smiling slightly. The light outside got dimmer and the light inside got stronger, and Patricia kept reading, speaking louder to compensate for her paper mask.

"Am I too late?" Maryellen said, and Patricia looked up to see her pushing open the door.

"Is she awake?" Maryellen whispered from behind her paper mask.

"Thank you for coming," Slick said without opening her eyes.

"Everyone wants to know how you're feeling," Maryellen said. "I know Kitty wanted to come."

"Are you reading this month's book?" Slick asked.

Maryellen pulled a heavy brown armchair to the foot of the bed.

"I can't even open it," she said. "*Men Are from Mars*? That's giving them too much credit."

Slick started coughing, and it took Patricia a moment to realize she was laughing.

"I made . . . ," Slick whispered, and Patricia and Maryellen strained to hear her. "I made Patricia stop reading it."

"I miss the books we used to read where at least there was a murder," Maryellen said. "The problem with book club these days is too many men. They don't know how to pick a book to save their lives and they love to listen to themselves talk. It's nothing but opinions, all day long."

"You sound . . . sexist," Slick whispered.

She was the only one not in a mask, so even though her voice was weakest, it sounded loudest.

"I wouldn't mind listening if any of them had an opinion worth a damn," Maryellen said.

With three of them in Slick's little hospital room, Patricia felt the absence of the other two more acutely. They felt like some kind of survivors' club—the last three standing.

"Are you going to Kitty's oyster roast on Saturday?" she asked Maryellen.

"If she has one," Maryellen said. "The way she's acting they might call it off."

"I haven't spoken to her since before Halloween," Patricia said.

"Give her a call when you have a chance," Maryellen said. "Something's wrong. Horse says she hasn't left the house all week and yesterday she barely left her room. He's worried."

"What does he say is wrong?" Patricia asked.

"He says it's nightmares," Maryellen said. "She's drinking, a lot. She wants to know where the children are every second of the day. She's scared something might happen to them."

Patricia decided it was time more people knew.

"Do you want to talk to Maryellen about anything?" she asked Slick. "Do you have something you need to tell her?"

Slick shook her head deliberately.

"No," she croaked. "The doctors don't know anything yet."

Patricia leaned down.

"He can't hurt you here," she said, quietly. "You can tell her."

"How is she?" a gentle, caring male voice said from the door.

Patricia hunched as if she'd been stabbed between the shoulder blades. Slick's eyes widened. Patricia turned, and there was no mistaking the eyes above the mask or the shape beneath the paper gown.

"I'm sorry I didn't come earlier," James Harris said through his mask, moving across the room. "Poor Slick. What's happened to you?"

Patricia stood and put herself between James Harris and Slick's bed. He stopped in front of her and placed one large hand on her shoulder. It took everything she had not to flinch.

"You're so good to be here," he said, and then gently brushed her aside and loomed over Slick, one hand resting on her bed rail. "How are you feeling, sweetheart?"

What he was doing was obscene. Patricia wanted to scream for help, she wanted the police, she wanted him arrested, but she knew no one would help them. Then she realized Maryellen and Slick weren't saying anything, either.

"Do you not feel up to talking?" James Harris asked Slick.

Patricia wondered who would break first, which one of them would cave in to niceties and make conversation, but they all stood firm, and looked at their hands, at their feet, out the window, and none of them said a word.

"I feel like I'm interrupting," James Harris said.

The silence continued and Patricia felt something bigger than her fear: solidarity.

"Slick's tired," Maryellen finally said. "She's had a long day. I think we should all leave her to get some rest."

As everyone shuffled around each other, trying to say good-bye, trying to get to the door, trying to get their things, Patricia worked spit into her dry mouth. She didn't want to do what she was about to do, but right before she said good-bye to Slick, she spoke as loudly as she could.

"James?"

He turned, his eyebrows raised above his mask.

"Korey took my car," she said. "Could you give me a ride home?"

Slick tried to push herself up in bed.

"I'll be back tomorrow," she told Slick. "But I need to go home and get some groceries in the fridge and make sure the children are still alive."

"Of course," James Harris said. "I'll be happy to give you a ride."

Patricia bent over Slick.

"I'll see you soon," she said, and kissed her on the forehead.

Maryellen insisted on walking with her to James Harris's car, which was on the third level of the parking garage. Patricia appreciated the gesture, but then came the moment when she had to go.

"Well," Maryellen said, like a bad actor on television. "I thought I was parked up here but I guess I was wrong again. You go on, I'll have to figure out where I put my car."

Patricia watched Maryellen walk to the stairwell until all she could hear were her heels, and then those faded, and the parking garage was silent. The door locks chunked up and Patricia jumped. She pulled the handle, slid self-consciously into the front seat, pulled the door closed, and clicked her seat belt on. The car engine came to life, idled, and then James Harris reached for her head. She flinched as he put his hand on the back of her headrest, looked over his shoulder, and reversed out of his space. They drove down the ramps in silence, he paid the attendant, and they pulled out onto the dark Charleston streets.

"I'm glad we can have this time together," he said.

Patricia tried to say something, but she couldn't force air through her throat.

"Do they have any idea what's wrong with Slick?" he asked.

"An autoimmune disorder," she managed.

"Leland thinks she has AIDS," James Harris said. "He's terrified people will find out."

His turn signal clicked loudly as he made a left onto Calhoun Street, past the park where the columns from the old Charleston Museum still stood. They reminded Patricia of tombstones.

"You and I have been making a lot of assumptions about each other," James Harris said. "I think it's time we got on the same page."

Patricia dug her nails into her palms to make herself keep quiet. She had gotten into his car. She didn't need to talk.

"I would never hurt anyone," he said. "You know that, right?"

How much did he know? Had they cleaned his stairs completely? Did he know she'd been in his attic, or did he just suspect? Had she missed a spot, left something behind, given herself away?

"I know," she said.

"Does Slick have any idea how she got this?" he asked.

Patricia bit the inside of her cheeks, feeling her teeth sink into their soft, spongy tissue, making herself more alert.

"No," she said.

"What about you?" he asked. "What do you think?"

If he had attacked Slick, what would he do to her now that they were alone? The position she'd put herself in began to sink in. She needed to reassure him that she was no danger.

"I don't know what to think," she managed.

"At least you're admitting it," he said. "I find myself in a similar position."

"What's that?" she asked.

They mounted the Cooper River Bridge, rising in a smooth arc over the city, leaving the land below, soaring over the dark harbor. Traffic was light, with only a few cars on the bridge.

The moment Patricia dreaded was coming soon. At the end of the bridge, the road forked. Two lanes curved toward the Old Village. The other two veered left and became Johnnie Dodds Boulevard, running out past strip malls, past Creekside, out into the country where there were no streetlights or neighbors, deep into Francis Marion National Forest where there were hidden clearings and logging roads, places where occasionally the police found abandoned cars with dead bodies in the trunk, or babies' skeletons wrapped in plastic bags and buried under the trees.

Which road he took would tell her if he thought she posed a threat.

"Leland did this to her," James Harris said. "Leland made her sick."

Patricia's thoughts fragmented. What was he saying? She tried to pay attention, but he was already talking.

"It all started with those damn trips," he said. "If I'd known, I never would have suggested them. It was that one last February to Atlanta, do you remember? Carter had that Ritalin conference and Leland and I went on Sunday to take some of the doctors out golfing and talk to them about investing in Gracious Cay. At dinner, this psychiatrist from Reno asked if we wanted to see some girls. He told us there was a place called the Gold Club owned by a former New York Yankee, so it must be on the level. It wasn't my kind of thing, but Leland spent almost a thousand dollars. That was the first time. After that, it seemed to get easier for him."

"Why are you telling me this?" Patricia asked.

"Because you need to know the truth," he said, and they were coming down the last rise of the bridge. Up ahead, the road branched: right or left. "I became aware of the girls last summer.

Leland would be with a different one almost every trip. Sometimes, when it was places like Atlanta or Miami where we went a few times, he would see the same girl. Some of them were professionals, some weren't. You know what I mean by that?"

He waited. She nodded stiffly in acknowledgment, eyes on the road. He drove in the middle lane, which could go either way. She wondered if this was a full and final confession because he knew she wouldn't be able to tell anyone soon.

"He got a disease from one of them and gave it to Slick," James Harris said. "There's no way to know what it is. But I know that's what happened. I asked him once if he used protection and he just laughed and said, 'Where's the fun in that?' Someone needs to tell her doctor.

He didn't put on his turn signal to change lanes; his car just came down off the bridge and then drifted, so slightly she almost didn't notice, and they were on the road to the Old Village. The muscles in her back unclenched.

"What about Carter?" she asked, after a moment.

They rode Coleman Boulevard's gentle curves toward the Old Village, passing houses, streetlights, then stores, restaurants, people.

"Him, too," he said. "I'm sorry."

She hadn't expected it to hurt so much.

"What do you want from me?" she asked.

"He's treated you like a fool," James Harris said. "Carter doesn't see what a wonderful family he has, but I do. I have all along. I was there when your mother-in-law passed, and she was a good woman. I've watched Blue grow up and he's having a hard time but he's got so much potential. You're a good person. But your husband has thrown it all away."

They passed the Oasis gas station in the middle of the road and entered the Old Village proper, the interior of the car getting darker as the streetlights became spaced farther apart.

"If Leland gave Slick something," he said, "Carter could do the same to you. I'm sorry to be the one to tell you, but you need to know. I want you to be safe. I care about you. I care about Blue and Korey. Y'all are a big part of my life."

He looked earnest as a suitor asking someone to be his bride as he turned from Pitt Street onto McCants.

"What are you saying?" she asked, lips numb.

"You deserve better," he said. "You and the children deserve someone who knows your true value."

Her stomach slowly turned inside out. He passed Alhambra Hall and she wanted to shove open the door and jump out of the car. She wanted to feel the asphalt slap and cut and scrape her. It would feel real, not like this nightmare. She made herself look at James Harris again, but she didn't trust herself to speak. She kept quiet until he pulled up in front of her driveway.

"I need time to think," she said.

"What are you going to tell Carter?" he asked.

"Nothing," Patricia said, and made her face a mask. "Not yet. This is between us."

She fumbled with the door handle, and as she did, she dropped Francine's license onto the floor of his car and slipped it beneath the passenger seat with her foot.

It wasn't his wallet, but it was the next best thing.

She woke up in the dark. She must have turned off the bedside light at some point and didn't remember. Now she lay there, scared to move, stiff as a board, listening. What had woken her? Her ears strained, scanning the darkness. She wished Carter were here, but he was on another drug company trip to Hilton Head.

Her ears wandered through the dark house. She heard the higher-pitched heat coming through the air registers, the ticking sound it made deep in the tin ducts. Behind the ticking came the high-pitched rush of warm air, and the drip from the bathroom faucet.

She thought about Blue. She needed to reach him, somehow, before James Harris got him further under control. He'd lied about a rape, but she didn't think it was too late. She needed to give him something he'd want more than he wanted James Harris's approval.

Then she heard it, behind all the house sounds, the deliberate sound of a window sliding open. It came from down the dark hall, from behind Korey's closed bedroom door, and in a flash Patricia realized Korey was sneaking out of the house.

She kicked herself. No wonder Korey acted so exhausted in the morning. No wonder she seemed so fuzzy headed. She was sneaking out of the house every night to see some boy. Patricia had been so caught up with Slick and James Harris and all these other things that she'd ignored the fact that she had two teenagers in the house, not just Blue. And there were plenty of normal, everyday risks to worry about.

She threw back her comforter, slid her feet into her slippers, and padded down the hall. There was a furtive, rhythmic sound coming from behind Korey's door and she realized that maybe Korey wasn't sneaking out, but this boy was sneaking in. She snapped on the hall light and threw open Korey's bedroom door.

At first she didn't understand what she was looking at in the spill of light from the hall.

Two pale, naked bodies lay on the bed, and she realized the one closest to her was James Harris, his muscled back and buttocks moving slightly, rhythmically, pulsing like a heartbeat. He knelt between the smooth long legs of a girl with a flat stomach and firm, upturned, underdeveloped teenaged breasts. His mouth was affixed to a place on her inner thigh, right next to her pubis. Her hair was spread out across the pillow, her eyes were half-closed in ecstasy, and she smiled with abandon, a smile Patricia had never seen before on Korey's face.

CHAPTER 35

Patricia fell on her daughter, shaking her shoulders, slapping her cheeks.

"Korey!" she screamed. "Korey! Wake up!"

Obscenely, they kept going, latched together, pulsing like an engorged sack of blood. Korey gave a small mew of pleasure and one hand drifted down, ghosting lightly across her stomach, toward her pubic hair, and Patricia grabbed her wrist and yanked it away and Korey began to squirm, and Patricia had to get James's head out from between her daughter's legs, and she looked down at him, and her stomach gave a warning flop. She was going to throw up.

She clamped her lips together, let go of Korey's feverish wrist, and tried to haul James away by the shoulders, but he struggled to stay latched to her daughter. Feeling like an idiot, Patricia grabbed a soccer cleat from the floor and hit him in the head with its heel. Her first blow was a silly, ineffectual tap, but the second was harder, and the third made a knocking sound when the cleats hit bone.

As she struck him in the head with Korey's shoe over and over again she heard herself repeating, "Get off! Get off! Get off my little girl!"

A sucking slobbering noise ripped through the quiet of the room, the sound of raw steak being torn in two, and James Harris looked up at her like a country cousin, mouth hanging open, something black and inhuman hanging from the hole in the bottom of his face, dripping viscous blood, eyes glazed. He tried to focus on Patricia, the shoe held back by her ear, ready to bring it down again.

"Uh," he said, dully.

He belched and a line of bloody drool dribbled from the corner of the proboscis hanging beneath his chin. Then it began to curl back up on itself, retracting slowly into his gore-slimed mouth.

My God, Patricia thought, *I've gone insane*, and she brought the cleat down again. James Harris rose, seizing her wrist in one hand, her throat in the other, and he threw her against the far wall. She took the impact between her shoulder blades. It punched all the air out of her lungs. It loosened the root of her tongue. Then he was on her, breath hot and raw, forearm across her throat, stronger than her, faster than her, and she went limp in his grip like prey.

"This is all your fault," he said, voice thick and slurred with liquid.

Blood coated his lips, and hot specks of it sprinkled her face. And she knew he was right. This. Was. All. Her. Fault. She had exposed her children to this danger, she had invited it into her house. She had been so obsessed with the children in Six Mile and Blue that she hadn't seen the danger to Korey. She had driven both her children right into James Harris's arms.

She saw a lump move down, down, down his throat as he swallowed whatever apparatus it was he used to suck their blood. Then he said, "You said this was between us."

She remembered saying that in the car earlier, and she had only meant to stall him, to buy more time, to keep his guard down, but she had said it, and to him it had been another invitation. She had led him on. She deserved this. But her daughter didn't.

"Korey," was the best she could manage through her constricted windpipe.

"Look what you're doing to her," he hissed, and wrenched her head to the side so she could see the bed.

Korey had pulled her arms and legs in on themselves, retracting into a fetal position, muscles twitching, going into shock. Blood spread on the mattress beneath her. Patricia closed her eyes to let the nausea pass.

"Mom?" Blue called from the hall.

She and James Harris locked eyes, him totally nude, his front a bib of blood, her in her nightgown, not even wearing a brassiere, the door standing a quarter of the way open. Neither of them moved.

"Mom?" Blue called again. "What's going on?"

Do. Something, James Harris mouthed at her.

She reached up and touched her fingertips to the back of the hand that held her throat. He let go.

"Blue," she said, stepping through the door and into the hall. She prayed that the flecks of Korey's blood she felt on her face wouldn't show. "Get back into bed."

"What's wrong with Korey?" he asked, standing in the hall.

"Your sister's sick," Patricia said. "Please. She'll be better later. But she needs to be alone right now."

Having determined that this was nothing that required his attention, Blue turned without speaking, went back into his bedroom, and closed the door. Patricia stepped back into Korey's room and turned on the overhead light just in time to see James Harris, naked, squatting on the windowsill. He held his clothes balled up against his belly like a lover fleeing an angry husband in some old farce.

"You asked for this," he said, and then he was gone and the window was just a big black rectangle of night.

Korey whimpered on the bed. It was the sound of her having a nightmare that Patricia had heard so many times before, and in sympathy she made the same sound back. She went to her daughter and examined the wound on her inner thigh. It looked swollen and infected, and it wasn't the only one. All around it were overlapping bruises, overlapping punctures, all their edges torn and ragged. Patricia realized this had happened before. Many times.

Her head was full of bats, shrieking and bumping into each other, tearing all coherent thought to tatters. Patricia didn't even know how she found the camera or took the pictures, how she got to the bathroom, how she stood in front of the sink running warm water onto a washcloth, how she bathed Korey's wound and put on bacitracin. She wanted to bandage it, but she couldn't, not without letting Korey know she'd seen this obscene thing. She couldn't cross that line with her daughter. Not yet.

Everything seemed too normal. She expected the house to explode, the backyard to fall into the harbor, Blue to walk out the door with a suitcase to move to Australia, but Korey's room was as messy as usual, and when she went downstairs the sailboat lamp burned on the front hall table like normal, and Ragtag raised his head from where he napped on the den couch, tags jingling, like normal, and the porch lights clicked off when she flipped the switch like normal.

She went into her bathroom and washed her face, hard, with a washcloth, scrubbing and scouring, and she tried not to look in the mirror. She scrubbed until it was red and raw. She scrubbed until it hurt. Good. She reached up and pinched her left ear until it hurt, twisting it, and that felt good, too. She got into bed and lay in the dark, staring at the ceiling, knowing she would never sleep.

It was all her fault. It was all her fault. It was all her fault.

Guilt, and betrayal, and nausea churned in her gut and she barely made it to the bathroom before she threw up.

She made every effort not to treat Korey differently the next morning, and Korey seemed no different than she was every morning: sullen and uncommunicative. Patricia's hands felt numb as she packed Korey and Blue off to school, and then she sat by the phone and waited.

The first call came at nine, and she couldn't bring herself to pick up. The machine took it.

"Patricia," James Harris's voice said. "Are you there? We need to talk. I have to explain what's going on here."

It was a cloudless, sunny October day. The bright blue sky protected her. But he could still call. The phone rang again.

"Patricia," he said to the machine. "You have to understand what's happening."

He called three more times, and on the third, she picked up.

"How long?" she asked.

"Come down and listen to me," he said. "I'll tell you everything."

"How long?" she repeated.

"Patricia," he said. "I want you to be able to see my eyes, so you know I'm being honest with you."

"Just tell me how long?" she asked, and to her own surprise her voice broke and her forehead cramped and she felt tears in the hinge of her jaw. She couldn't close her mouth; there was a howl inside that wanted to get out.

"I'm glad you finally know," he said. "I'm so tired of hiding. This doesn't change anything I said last night."

"What?"

"I value you," he said. "I value your family. I'm still your friend."

"What have you done to my daughter?" she managed.

"I'm sorry you had to see that," he said. "I know you must be confused and frightened but it's no different than my eyes—it's just a condition I have. Some of my organs don't work properly and from time to time I need to borrow someone's circulatory system and filter my blood through theirs. I'm not a vampire, I don't drink it, it's not any different than using a dialysis machine, except it's more natural. And I promise you there's no pain. In fact, from what I can tell it feels good to them. You have to understand, I would never do anything to hurt Korey. She agreed to do this. I want you to know that. After I told her about my condition she came to me and volunteered to help. You have to believe I would never make her do something against her will."

"What are you?" she asked.

"I'm alone," he said. "I've been alone for a very long time."

Patricia realized it wasn't repentance in his voice, it was self-pity.

She'd heard Carter feeling sorry for himself too often to mistake it for anything else.

"What do you want from us?"

"I care for you," he said. "I care for your family. I see how Carter treats you and it makes me furious. He throws away what I would treasure. Blue thinks the world of me already, and Korey has already done so much to help me that she has my eternal gratitude. I'd like to think we could come to an understanding."

He wanted her family. It came to her in an instant. He wanted to replace Carter. This man was a vampire, or as close to one as she would ever see. She remembered Miss Mary talking in the dark all those years ago.

They have a hunger on them. They never stop taking. They mortgaged their souls away and now they eat and eat and eat and never know how to stop.

He'd found a place where he fit in, with a nearby source of food, and he'd become a respected member of the community, and now he wanted to have a family because he didn't know how to stop. He always wanted more. That knowledge opened a door inside her mind and the bats flew out in a ragged black stream, leaving her skull empty and quiet and clear.

He had wanted old Mrs. Savage's house, so he took it from her. Miss Mary had endangered him with her photograph, and he'd destroyed her. He had attacked Slick to protect himself. He would say anything to get what he wanted. He had no limits. And she knew that the moment he suspected she knew what he wanted, her children would be in danger.

"Patricia?" he asked in the silence.

She took a shuddering breath.

"I need time to think," she said. If she got off the phone fast he wouldn't hear the change in her voice.

"Let me come there," he said, his tone sharper. "Tonight. I want to apologize in person."

"No," she said, and gripped the phone in her suddenly sweaty hand. She forced her throat to relax. "I need time."

"Promise you forgive me," he said.

She had to get off the phone. With a thrill of joy she realized she had to call the police right away. They would go to his house and find the license and search his attic and this would all be over by sundown.

"I promise," she said.

"I'm trusting you, Patricia," he said. "You know I wouldn't hurt anyone."

"I know," she said.

"I want you to know all about me," he said. "When you're ready, I want to spend a lot of time with you."

She was proud of the way she kept her voice calm and steady.

"Me, too," she said.

"Oh," he said. "Before I go, the damnedest thing happened this morning."

"What?" she asked, numb.

"I found Francine Chapman's driver's license in my car," he said, his voice full of wonder. "Remember Francine? Who used to clean for me? I don't know how it got there, but I took care of it. Strange, right?"

She wanted to dig her nails into her face, and rake them down, and rip off her skin. She was a fool.

"That is strange," she said, no life left in her voice.

"Well," he said. "Lucky I found it. That could have been hard to explain."

"Yes," she said.

"I'll wait to hear from you," he said. "But don't make me wait too long."

He hung up.

Her one job as a parent was to protect her children from monsters. The ones under the bed, the ones in the closet, the ones hiding in the dark. Instead, she'd invited the monster into her home and been too weak to stop it from taking whatever it wanted. The monster had killed her mother-in-law, seduced her husband, taken her daughter, and her son.

She was too weak to stop him alone, but he had to be stopped. There weren't many people left she could turn to.

She picked up the phone and called Mrs. Greene.

"Yes?" Mrs. Greene said.

"Mrs. Greene," Patricia said, and cleared her throat. "Can you make it downtown Monday night?"

"Why?" Mrs. Greene asked.

"I need you to come to my book club."

CHAPTER 36

On Monday, temperatures plunged around noon and dark clouds started piling up overhead. Leaves skimmed the Old Village's empty streets. On the bridge, sudden gusts blew cars sideways, forcing them to abruptly shift lanes. It got dark by four, and windows rattled in their frames, doors blew open suddenly, and the wind tore limbs from live oaks and smashed them down in the middle of the street.

The black wind pushed hard on the windows in Slick's hospital room and the glass creaked, while inside, the air felt as cold as the inside of a refrigerator.

"Is this going to take long?" Maryellen asked. "Monica has a Latin project due tomorrow and I need to help her build a Parthenon out of toilet paper tubes."

"I don't like being away from home," Kitty said, tucking her hands beneath her paper gown to keep them warm.

Kitty's gown was tied sloppily, and Patricia could see her brown sweater with two silver sequined handprints on its chest through the paper. Maryellen wore a gingham blouse and a neatly tied paper gown. The overhead fixture had been turned off and the only light came from fluorescent bars over Slick's headboard and over the sink, filling the room with shadows. Slick sat up in bed, a navy cardigan covered in aquamarine triangles draped over her shoulders. Patricia had done the best she could with her makeup, but Slick looked like a skull wearing a fright wig.

Someone tapped on the door, and Mrs. Greene came in.

"Thank you for coming," Patricia said.

"Hello . . . Mrs. Greene." Slick smiled.

It took Mrs. Greene a moment to recognize her, and Patricia saw her eyes become stricken with horror, and then she wrestled them into a pleasant expression.

"How are you, Mrs. Paley?" she said. "I'm sorry you're feeling poorly."

"Thank you," Slick said.

Mrs. Greene perched on a chair, purse in her lap, and a silence fell over the room. The wind thumped at the windows.

"Slick," Maryellen said. "You wanted us to come see you, but I'm getting a sinking feeling you have a secret agenda."

"I'm sorry, y'all," Kitty said. "But can we hurry this up?"

The door opened again, and they all turned and saw Grace. Everything inside Patricia squirmed and twisted away.

Grace nodded to Slick, then saw Mrs. Greene and Patricia.

"You called and asked me to drop by," she told Slick. "But it seems a little crowded right this minute. I'll come back another time."

She turned to go and Patricia shouted, "No!"

Grace looked back, eyes blank.

"Don't go," Slick wheezed from where she sat. "Please . . ."

Caught between making a scene and doing something she didn't want to do, Grace did something she didn't want to do. She threaded her way between Maryellen and Kitty and took the only open seat, which was the one closest to the bed. Slick and Patricia had decided it would be harder for her to leave that way.

"Well," Grace said in the long silence.

"You know," Maryellen said, "it's like the old book club's back together again. Any minute someone's going to pull an Ann Rule out of her bag."

Patricia leaned over and pulled *Dead by Sunset* out of her bag. Everyone laughed stiffly, except Grace and Mrs. Greene, who didn't get the joke. Slick's laughter turned into a coughing fit.

"I assume there's a reason we're here," Kitty said to Slick.

Slick nodded to Patricia, giving her the floor.

"We need to talk about James Harris," Patricia began.

"I just remembered someplace I need to be," Grace said, standing.

"Grace, I need you to hear this," Patricia said.

"I came because Slick called," Grace said, looping her purse over one shoulder. "I will not do this again. Now, excuse me."

"I was wrong," Patricia said. That stopped Grace. "I was wrong about James Harris. I thought he was a drug dealer and I misled all of you. And I'm sorry."

Grace's body relaxed slightly, and she leaned back toward her chair.

"That's big of you," Maryellen said. "But we were all responsible. We let those books get to our head."

"He isn't a drug dealer," Patricia said. "He's a vampire."

Kitty looked like she was about to throw up. Grace's face turned dark and ugly. Maryellen uttered a single bark of laughter and said, "What?"

"Slick," Patricia said. "Tell them what happened."

"I was . . . attacked," Slick said, and instantly her eyes turned red and wet. "By James Harris . . . Patricia and Mrs. Greene . . . had a photograph that . . . belonged to Carter's mother . . . It showed James Harris . . . in 1928 . . . looking exactly the same . . . as he does now."

"I do have to go," Grace said.

"Grace," Slick said. "If we were . . . ever friends . . . I need you to hear me now."

Grace didn't say anything, but she stopped edging toward the door.

"I had . . . the photograph and clippings . . . Mrs. Greene collected," Slick continued. "Patricia came to me . . . because she and Mrs. Greene thought it proved . . . he was Satan's agent . . . They wanted to go into his house . . . find evidence that he'd hurt children . . . but my pride was great . . . and I went to him and tried to bargain . . . I told him if he left town . . . I'd destroy the photograph and keep his secret . . . he attacked me . . . he forced himself on me . . . His . . . I'm sorry." She tilted her head back so her tears didn't cause her makeup to run. Patricia handed her a crumpled tissue and Slick dabbed it beneath her eyes. "His discharge . . . made me sick. No one knows what it's doing inside me . . . the doctors don't know . . . I didn't tell anyone what he did . . . because . . . he said as long as I kept quiet . . . he wouldn't hurt my children."

"Mrs. Greene and I went into his house," Patricia said, picking up from Slick. "We found Francine's corpse packed in a suitcase and shoved in his attic. I'm sure he's gotten rid of it by now."

"This is in poor taste," Grace said. "Francine was a human being. To use her death as part of your fantasy is grotesque."

Patricia pulled out the snapshot she'd taken the night before. It showed Korey's thigh. The flash made the bruise and puncture mark livid against her washed-out skin. She held it out to Grace.

"He did this to Korey," she said.

"What'd he do to her?" Kitty asked, softly, trying to see.

"He seduced her behind my back," Patricia said. "For months he's been seducing my daughter, grooming her, feeding on her, and making her think she liked it. He says he has a condition where he has to use a person to clean his blood, like dialysis. Apparently it creates a euphoric feeling in the person. They become addicted."

"It's the same mark they found on the children in Six Mile," Mrs. Greene said.

"It's the same mark Ben said they found on Ann Savage after she died," Patricia said.

"I thought he would leave our children alone if I kept quiet," Slick said. "But he took Korey. He could come after any one of us next. His hunger knows no limits."

"Before we just had suspicions," Patricia said. "Francine was gone. Orville Reed killed himself, Destiny Taylor killed herself. But Kitty and I saw Francine's body in his attic. He attacked Slick. He attacked my daughter. He's grooming Blue. He wants me."

"Did you really see Francine's body in his attic?" Maryellen asked Kitty.

Kitty looked down at her paper-shrouded knees.

"Tell her," Patricia said.

"He'd broken her arms and legs to stuff her inside a suitcase," Kitty said.

"How much more evidence do we need that none of us are safe?" Patricia asked. "The men all think he's their best friend, but he's taken everything he wanted right out from under our noses. How long do we wait before we do something? He is preying on our children."

"Call me old-fashioned," Grace snapped. "But first you tell the police he's a child molester. Then you tell us he's a drug dealer. Now you say he's Count Dracula. Your fantasies have come at a great cost to the rest of us, Patricia. Do you know what happened to me?"

"I know," Patricia said through gritted teeth. "I know, I messed up. Oh, God, Grace, I know I messed up and I am being punished for it, but we ran away when things got hard. And now we've waited so long that I don't think there's a normal way to get rid of him. I think he's ingrained himself too deeply into the Old Village."

"Spare me," Grace said.

"I am crawling on my knees begging for your help," Patricia said.

"Don't tell me the rest of you believe this nonsense?" Grace asked.

Maryellen and Kitty wouldn't meet her eyes.

"Kitty," Patricia said. "You and I saw what he did to Francine. I know how scared you are but how long do you think it will be until he figures out you were in his attic, too? How long do you think it will be before he comes after your family?"

"Don't say things like that," Kitty said.

"It's true," Patricia said. "We can't hide from it anymore."

"I'm not sure what you're asking us to do," Maryellen said.

"You said you wanted to live where people watched out for each other," Patricia told her. "But what's the good of watching if we're not going to act?"

"We're a book club," Maryellen said. "What are we supposed to do? Read him to death? Use strong language? We can't go to Ed again."

"I think . . . we're beyond that," Slick said.

"Then I don't know what we're talking about," Maryellen said.

"The last time we did this we learned one thing," Patricia said. "The men stick together. Their friendship with him is stronger now than it was then. There's only us."

Grace hitched her purse's shoulder straps higher over her shoulder and regarded the room.

"I am leaving now before this becomes even more absurd," she said, nodding to Kitty and Maryellen. "And I think you should both come with me before you do something you'll regret."

"Grace," Kitty said, low and calm, staring at her knees. "If you keep acting like I'm feebleminded, I'm going to smack you. I'm a grown woman, the same as you, and I saw a dead body in that attic."

"Good night," Grace said, heading for the door.

Patricia nodded to Mrs. Greene, who stepped into Grace's path, blocking her.

"Mrs. Cavanaugh," she said. "Am I trash to you?"

Grace did a double take, the first one any of them had ever seen.

"I beg your pardon?" Grace asked, all frozen hauteur.

Frozen hauteur didn't cut much ice with Mrs. Greene.

"You must think I'm trash," Mrs. Greene said.

Grace swallowed once, so outraged she couldn't even get the

words lined up on her tongue.

"I said no such thing," she managed.

"Your actions aren't the actions of a Christian woman," Mrs. Greene said. "I came to you years ago as a mother and as a woman, and I begged for your help because that man was preying on the children in Six Mile. I begged for you to do something simple, to come with me to the police, and tell them what you knew. I risked my job and the money that puts food on my table, to come to you. Do you even know my children's names?"

It took a minute for Grace to realize Mrs. Greene was waiting for an answer.

"There's Abraham," Grace said, searching for their names. "And Lily, I think . . ."

"The first Harry," Mrs. Greene said. "He passed. Harry Jr., Rose, Heanne, Jesse, and Aaron. You don't even know how many children I've got, and I don't expect you to. But you owe me. You protected yourself, but you didn't do a thing for the children of Six Mile because they weren't worthwhile to you. Well, now he's coming after your children. Mrs. Campbell's daughter is one of you. Mrs. Paley is supposed to be your friend. Mrs. Scruggs saw Francine's body in his house. What are you made of, Mrs. Cavanaugh, that lets you walk away from your friends?"

They watched Grace cycle through a dozen different emotions, a hundred possible responses, her jaw working, her chin clenching, the cords in her neck twitching. Mrs. Greene stared back at her, jaw outthrust. Then Grace pushed past her, threw open the door, and slammed it behind her.

In the silence, none of them moved. The only sound was wind whistling through a chink in the window's weatherstripping.

"She's right," Slick said. "All of us . . . got scared and sacrificed the children of Six Mile . . . for our own. We were . . . embarrassed and frightened. Proverbs says . . . 'Like a muddied spring or a polluted fountain . . . is a righteous man who gives way . . . before the wicked.' We gave way . . . We wanted to believe . . . that Patricia was wrong because it meant we didn't have to do . . . anything hard."

Patricia decided it was safe to push them to the next step.

"I don't know if the word is *vampire* or *monster*," Patricia said. "But I've seen him like this twice and Slick has seen it once. He's not like us. He can live for a very long time. He's strong. He can see in the dark."

"His willpower can make animals do his bidding," Mrs. Greene said.

Patricia looked over at her, both of them thinking about the rats, about the way the house smelled for days after, about Miss Mary in the hospital, unconscious, her wounds stained with iodine, breathing through a tube. Patricia nodded.

"I think you're right," she said. "And he needs to put his blood through people to live. They get addicted to him. Right now, Korey would stab me in the back for him to suck on her again. That's how good it feels. He's gotten everything he wants, so why would he stop by himself? We need to stop him."

"Again," Maryellen said, "we're a book club, not a bunch of detectives. If he's so much stronger than us, this is futile."

"You think . . . we can't match him?" Slick asked from her bed. "I've had three children . . . And some man who's never felt . . . his baby crown is stronger than me? Is tougher than me? He thinks he's safe . . . because he thinks like you . . . He looks at Patricia and thinks we're all a bunch of Sunshine Suzies . . . He thinks we're what we look like on the outside: nice Southern ladies. Let me tell you something . . . there's nothing nice about Southern ladies."

There was a long pause, and then Patricia spoke.

"He has one weakness," Patricia said. "He's alone. He's not connected to other people, he doesn't have any family or friends. If one of us so much as misses a car pool pickup everyone starts dropping by the house to make sure we're okay. But he's a loner. If we can make him disappear, totally and completely, there's no one to ask questions. There may be a hard day or two but they will pass, and it will be like he never existed."

Maryellen turned her face to the ceiling, arms out in a shrug. "How are you sitting here talking like this is normal? We're six women. Five women, because I don't think Grace is coming back. I mean, Kitty, your husband has to open jars for you."

"It's not . . . about that," Slick said, eyes blazing. "It's not about . . . our husbands or anyone else . . . it's about us. It's about whether . . . we can go the distance. That's what matters . . . not our money, or our looks, or our husbands . . . Can we go the distance?"

"Not with killing a man," Maryellen said.

"He's not a man," Mrs. Greene said.

"Listen to me," Slick said. "If there were . . . a toxic waste dump in this city . . . that caused cancer . . . we would not stop until we closed it down. This is no different. This is our families' safety we're talking about . . . our children's lives. Are you willing to gamble . . . with those?"

Maryellen leaned forward and touched Kitty's leg. Kitty looked up from studying her knees.

"You really saw Francine in his attic?" Maryellen asked. "Don't lie to me. You're sure it was her and not a shadow or a mannequin or some Halloween decoration?"

Kitty nodded, miserable.

"When I close my eyes I see her in that suitcase, wrapped in plastic," she moaned. "I can't sleep, Maryellen."

Maryellen studied Kitty's face, then leaned back.

"How do we do it?" she asked.

"Before we go any further," Slick said. "We have to see it through . . . and then never talk about it again . . . I have to hear it from each of you . . . After this there's no . . . changing your mind."

"Amen," Mrs. Greene said.

"Of course," Patricia agreed.

"Kitty?" Slick asked.

"God help me, yes," Kitty exhaled in a rush.

"Maryellen?" Slick asked.

Maryellen didn't say anything.

"He'll come for Caroline next," Patricia said. "Then Alexa. Then Monica. He'll do to them what he's done to Korey. He's just hunger, Maryellen. He'll eat and eat until there's nothing left."

"I won't do anything illegal," Maryellen said.

"We're beyond that," Patricia said. "We're protecting our families. We will do whatever it takes. You're a mother, too."

Everyone watched Maryellen. Her back was stiff and then the fight went out of her and her shoulders slumped.

"All right," she said.

Patricia, Slick, and Mrs. Greene exchanged a look. Patricia took it as her cue.

"We need a night when everyone's distracted," she said. "Next week is the Clemson-Carolina game. The entire population of South Carolina is going to be glued to their television sets from kickoff until the last down. That's when we do it."

"Do what?" Kitty asked in a very small voice.

Patricia took a black-and-white Mead composition book from her purse.

"I read everything I could about them," she said. "About things like vampires. Mrs. Greene and I have been making a list of the facts they agree on. There are as many superstitions about how to stop one as there are how to create one: exposure to sunlight, drive a stake through its heart, decapitation, silver."

"We can think he's evil and not an actual vampire," Maryellen said. "Maybe he's like that Richard Chase, the Vampire of Sacramento, and he just thinks he's a vampire."

"No," Patricia said. "We can't fool ourselves anymore. He's unnatural and we have to kill him the right way or he's just going to keep on coming back. He's underestimated us. We can't underestimate him."

Her words sounded bizarre in the sterile hospital room with its plastic cups and sippy straws, its television hanging from the ceiling, its Hallmark cards on the windowsill. They looked at each other in their practical flats with their roomy purses by their feet, with their reading glasses, and their notepads, and their ballpoint pens, and realized they had crossed a line.

"We have to drive a stake through his heart?" Kitty asked. "I don't think I'm up for that."

"No stakes," Patricia said.

"Oh, thank God," Kitty said. "Sorry, Slick."

"I don't think that would kill him," Patricia said. "The books say vampires sleep during the day, but he's awake in daylight. The sun hurts his eyes and makes him uncomfortable, but he doesn't have to sleep in a coffin when it's out. We can't take the stories literally."

"So what do we do?" Kitty asked.

"Miss Mary gave me an idea how we kill him," Patricia said. "But the hard part's going to be getting to the point where we can do it."

"I don't mean to sound difficult," Maryellen said. "But if he's everything Patricia says he is—suspicious, sharp senses, fast, strong—how do we even get close enough to do anything?"

Fear made Patricia's voice strong and clear, "I have to give him what he wants," she said. "I have to give him me."

CHAPTER 37

Patricia told Carter that Korey was on drugs. Korey was so sick and confused from James Harris that Carter believed her immediately. It helped that this was one of his biggest nightmares.

"This is from your side," he said as they threw Korey's clothes into an overnight bag. "No one on my side of the family has ever had this kind of problem."

No, Patricia thought. *They just murdered a man and buried his body in the backyard.*

She prayed for forgiveness. She prayed hard. Then they took Korey to Southern Pines, the local psychiatric and substance abuse treatment center.

"You'll make sure she's monitored twenty-four hours a day?" Patricia asked the intake administrator.

Her nightmare was that Korey would do what the other children had done. She thought of Destiny Taylor and the dental floss, Orville Reed stepping in front of the car, Latasha Burns and the knife. They had the money to weigh the odds in their favor, but she didn't want odds when it came to her daughter. She wanted a guarantee.

She tried to talk to Korey, she tried to say she was sorry, she tried to explain things, she tried hard, but whether it was because of James Harris or because of what they were doing to her, Korey didn't even acknowledge she was in the room.

"Some of them do this," the intake administrator said. "I saw one kid break his mother's nose during intake. Others just shut down."

When they got home the quiet in the house ate at Patricia, reminding her of the damage she had done to her family. She felt a sense of urgency. She had to finish this. She had to get her family back and glue the pieces together before it got any worse. It was only a matter of time before they hit a point beyond which nothing could be fixed.

That night, Carter left to bury himself in work at his office. Half an hour later, the phone rang. She answered.

"Where's Korey?" James Harris asked.

"She's sick," Patricia said.

"She wouldn't be sick if she were still with me," he said. "I can make her better."

"I need time," she said. "I need time to figure things out."

"What am I supposed to do while you dither?" he asked.

"You have to be patient," she said. "This is hard for me. It's my entire life. My family. It's everything I know."

"Think fast," he said.

"Until the end of the month," she said, trying to buy time.

"I'll give you ten days," he said, and hung up.

She tried to be around Blue as much as possible. She and Carter asked if he had any questions, they told him it wasn't his fault, they said that he could see Korey in a week or two, whenever her doctors said it was all right, but Blue barely spoke. She sat next to him while he played games on the computer in the little study. He clattered away on the keyboard, moving colored shapes and lines onscreen.

"What does this one do?" she asked about a button, and then pointed to a number at the top of the monitor. "Does that mean you're winning? Look at your score, it's so high."

"That's the amount of damage I've taken," he said.

She wanted to tell him she was sorry she hadn't protected him and his sister better. But whenever she began, it sounded like a farewell speech and she stopped. Let him have one more untroubled week.

Before she was ready, Saturday arrived and Patricia woke up scared. She cleaned Korey's room to keep herself busy, stripped her bed, collected all her clothes off the floor and washed them, folded them, put them back into drawers in neat stacks, ironed her dresses and hung them up, stacked her magazines, found the cases for all her CDs. She recovered $8.63 in change from the carpet and put it in a jar for when Korey came home.

Around four, Carter stood in the door and watched her work.

"We have to go soon if we want to see the pregame," he said.

They had made plans to watch the Clemson-Carolina game downtown near the hospital with Leland and Slick's children.

"You go on," Patricia said. "I have things to do."

"You sure you don't want to come?" he asked. "It'll be good to do something normal. It's morbid to sit around the house alone."

"I need to be morbid," she said, and gave him her "brave soldier" smile. "Have a nice time."

"I love you," he said.

It took her by surprise and she faltered for a moment, thinking of everything James Harris had told her about Carter's out-of-town trips and wondering how much of it was true.

"I love you, too," she made herself say back.

He left and she waited until she heard his car back out of the driveway, and then she got ready to die.

Patricia's stomach felt empty. Her whole body felt drained. She felt sick, light-headed, fluttery. Everything felt hollow, like it was all about to float away.

In her bathroom, she put on her new black velvet dress. It felt tight and awful and hugged her in all the wrong places and made her self-conscious of her new curves, and then she adjusted it and pulled it down and cinched and strapped and smoothed. It clung to her like a black cat's skin. She felt more naked with it on than off.

The phone rang. She answered it.

"Finally," he said.

"I want to see you," she said. "I made my decision."

There was a long pause.

"And," he prompted.

"I decided that I want someone who values me," she said. "I'll be at your place by 6:30."

Eyeliner, a bit of eyebrow pencil, mascara, some blush. She blotted her lipstick with Kleenex and dropped red balls of tissue into the trash. She brushed her hair, curled it just a touch to give it body, then sprayed it with Miss Brecks. She opened her eyes and they stung from the falling mist of hairspray droplets. She looked at herself in the mirror and saw a woman she didn't know. She didn't wear earrings or jewelry. She took off her wedding ring. She fed Ragtag, left a note for Carter saying she'd had to run downtown to see Slick in the hospital and she might spend the night, and left home.

Outside, a cold wind thrashed the trees. Cars lined the block, all of them there to watch the Clemson-Carolina game at Grace's. Bennett was a hardcore Clemson alum, and he hosted the big get-together for the game every year. Patricia wondered how he would deal with everyone drinking. She wondered if he'd start again.

The wind came black and bleak off the harbor, tossing the waves into whitecaps. She passed Alhambra Hall and looked at the far end of the parking lot, close to the water, and saw the minivan parked there. She could just see a few huddled shapes inside. They looked pathetically small.

Friends, Patricia thought. *Be with me now.*

James Harris's house was dark. His porch lights were off and only a single lamp shone from his living room window. She realized he'd done it so no one would see her come to his front door. Cars filled every single driveway, and as she walked, a swelling of cheers erupted from all the houses. Kickoff. The game had begun.

She knocked on the front door, and James Harris opened it, lit from behind by the dim glow of the living room lamp, the only light in the house. The radio purred classical music, a piano riding gentle orchestral surges. Her heart danced inside her rib cage as he locked the door behind her.

Neither moved, they just stood in the hall, facing each other in the soft spill of light from the living room.

"You've hurt me," she said. "You've scared me. You've hurt my daughter. You've made my son a liar. You've hurt the people I know. But the three years you've been here feel more real than the entire twenty-five years of my marriage."

He raised his hand and traced the side of her jaw with his fingers. She didn't flinch. She tried not to remember him screaming in her face, spattering it with her daughter's blood, her daughter who would hurt forever because of his hunger.

"You said you made up your mind," he said. "So. What do you want, Patricia?"

She walked past him into the living room. She left a trace of perfume in the air. It was a bottle of Opium she'd found while cleaning Korey's room. She almost never wore perfume. She stopped in front of the mantel and turned to face him.

"I'm tired of my world being so small," she said. "Laundry, cooking, cleaning, silly women talking about trashy books. It's not enough for me anymore."

He sat in the armchair across from her, legs spread, hands on its arms, watching her.

"I want you to make me the way you are," she said. Then she lowered her voice to a whisper. "I want you to do to me what you did to my daughter."

He looked at her, his eyes crawling across her body, seeing all of her, and she felt exposed, and frightened, and just a little bit aroused. And then James Harris stood up and walked over to her and laughed in her face.

The force of his laughter slapped her, and sent her stumbling a half step back. The room echoed with his laughter, and it bounced crazily off the walls, trapped, doubling and redoubling, battering at her ears. He laughed so hard he flopped back down in his chair, looked at her with a crazy grin on his face, and burst out laughing, again.

She didn't know what to do. She felt small and humiliated. Finally, his laughter rolled to a stop, leaving him short of breath.

"You must think," he said, gasping for air, "that I'm the stupidest person you've ever met. You come here, all dolled up like a hooker, and give me this breathless story about how you want me to make you one of the bad people? How did you get to be so arrogant? Patricia the genius, and the rest of us are just a bunch of fools?"

"That's not true," she said. "I want to be here. I want to be with you."

This brought another wave of ugly laughter.

"You're embarrassing yourself and you're insulting me," James Harris said. "Did you think I'd believe any of this?"

"It's not an act!" she shouted.

He grinned.

"I wondered when you'd get to righteous indignation." He smiled. "Look at you: Patricia Campbell, wife of Dr. Carter Campbell, mother of Korey and Blue, debasing herself because she thinks she's smarter than someone who's lived four times as long as her. See, Patricia, I never underestimated you. If you told Slick you planned to come into my house, I knew you came into my house. And if you got into my house, I knew you'd gotten into my attic and found everything there was to find. Was her license supposed to be bait? Leave it in my car and go to the police and tell them you found it and they'd pull me over and find it and get a search warrant? In what sad housewife's dream does something like that work? Those books you girls read have really rotted your brains."

She couldn't make her legs stop shaking. She sat down on the raised brick hearth. The velvet dress rode up and bunched around her stomach and hips. She felt ridiculous.

"Then again, I moved here because you people are all so stupid," he said. "You'll take anyone at face value as long as he's white and has money. With computers coming and all these new IDs I needed to put down roots and you made it so easy. All I had to do was make you think I needed help and here comes that famous Southern hospitality. Y'all don't like talking about money, do you? That's low class. But I waved some around and you all were so eager to grab it you never asked where it came from. Now your children like me more than they like you. Your husband is a weakling and a fool. And here you are, dressed up like a clown, with no cards left to play. I've been doing this for so long I'm always prepared for the moment when someone tries to run me out of town, but you've truly surprised me. I didn't expect the attempt to be so sad."

A rhythmic, wet huffing sound filled the room as Patricia bent double and tried to breathe. She attempted to start a sentence a few times, but kept running out of breath. Finally she said, "Make it stop."

From far away, she heard a chorus of faint voices shouting with disappointment.

"I tried once," he said. "But an artist is only as good as his materials. I thought for sure the humiliation I inflicted on you three years ago would make you kill yourself, but you couldn't even do that right."

"Make it stop," Patricia said. "Just make it all stop. I can't do this anymore. My son hates me. For the rest of his life I'll be the crazy woman who tried to kill herself, the one he found convulsing on the kitchen floor. I put my daughter in a mental hospital. I have ruined my family. I couldn't protect them from you."

She sat, hunched over, spitting her words at the floor, her hands were claws digging into her knees, her voice scouring her ears like acid.

"I thought you were filth. I thought you were an animal," she said. "But I'm worse. I'm nothing. I was a good nurse, I really was,

and I walked away from the one thing I loved because I wanted to
be a bride. I wanted to get married because I was terrified of being
alone. I wanted to be a good wife and a good mother, and I gave
everything I had, and it wasn't enough. I'm not enough!"

She shouted the last words, then looked up at James Harris, her
face a grotesque mask of streaked makeup.

"My husband has no more consideration for me than a dog,"
she said. "He goes off and screws little girls with the other men and
we sit home like good little women and wash their shirts and pack
their bags for their sex trips. We keep their houses warm and clean
for when they're ready to come home and shower off some other
woman's perfume before tucking their children into bed. For years
I've pretended I don't know where he goes, or who those girls are
on the phone, but every time he comes home, I lie there in bed
beside my husband, who doesn't touch me, who doesn't talk to me,
who doesn't love me, and I pretend I can't smell some twenty-year-
old's body on him. Our children hate us. Look at mine. It would
have been better if a dog raised them."

She hooked her fingers into claws and pulled them through
her hair, harrowing it into a crazed haystack, jutting out in every
direction.

"So here I am," she said. "Giving you the last thing I have of
value and begging you to spare my daughter. Take me. Take my
body. Use me until you throw me away, but leave Korey alone.
Please. Please."

"You think you can bargain with me?" he asked. "This is some
kind of sad seduction, trading your body for your daughter's?"

She nodded, meek and small.

"Yes."

She sat, a long runnel of snot dangling from her nose, dripping
onto her dress. And finally, James Harris said:

"Come."

She pushed herself up, and walked to him on shaky legs.

"Kneel," he said, pointing to the floor.

Patricia lowered herself onto the floor at his feet. He leaned forward and took her jaw in one big hand.

"Three years ago you tried to make a fool of me," he said. "You don't get any more dignity. We're going to finally be honest with each other. First, I'm going to replace Carter in your life. Is that what you want?"

She nodded, then realized he needed more. "Yes," she whispered.

"Your son loves me already," he said. "And your daughter belongs to me. I'll take you now, but she's next. Will you do that? Will you give me your body to buy her another year?"

"Yes," Patricia said.

"One day it will be Blue's turn," he said. "But for now, I'm the family friend who helps put your life back together after your husband dies. Everyone will think that we just naturally felt a powerful attraction, but you'll know the truth: you gave up your pathetic, miserable, broken failure of a life to accept your place at my feet. I'm not some doctor, or lawyer, or rich mommy's boy trying to impress you. I am singular in this world. I am what you people make legends from. And now I've turned my attention on you. When I'm done, I'll adopt your children and make them mine. But you've bought them one more year of freedom. Do you understand?"

"Yes," she said.

James Harris stood and walked up the stairs without looking back.

"Come," he said over his shoulder.

After a moment, Patricia followed, only pausing on the way to unlock the deadbolt on his front door.

In the darkness of the upstairs hall, she saw white solid walls all around her, each one a closed door, and then she saw a black hole like the entrance to a tomb. She walked into the master bedroom. James Harris stood in the moonlight. He had taken off his shirt.

"Strip," he said.

Patricia stepped out of her shoes and inhaled sharply. Standing barefoot on the cool wooden floor made her feel naked. She couldn't do this, but before she could stop herself her hands were already moving to her back.

She unzipped the dress and let it fall to the floor and stepped out of it. Blood rushed and flowed to parts of her body that were dry, leaving her light-headed. Her head spun and she wondered if she would faint. The darkness seemed very close around her and the walls seemed very far away. A fever seized her as she unsnapped her bra and shucked it off, then kicked her clothes into one corner and threw her brassiere on top.

She felt the cool air of a stranger's house on her bare breasts and hips and belly. Through the window she heard some family let out a mindless cheer, barely audible, like the shore roaring in a seashell or something half imagined carried on the wind.

He pointed to the bed, and she walked over to it and sat down. He stood before her, outlined dark in the moonlight. His broad shoulders and narrow waist, his thick thighs and long legs, the strong jaw, the full head of hair. She found where his eyes would be and saw a faint shimmer of white in the darkness. She maintained eye contact with him as she leaned back on his bed, feet still on the floor, and spread her legs for him and felt the cool air of his house kiss her sex. The air caressed her curls and made them unkink. He knelt between her legs.

Everything in her life funneled down to this moment.

She watched as his jaw moved in a way she'd never seen before. He looked up from between her legs and put his hand over the bottom of his face.

"Don't look," he said.

"But . . . ," she said.

"You don't want to see this," he said.

She reached out and gently moved his hand away. She wanted

to see everything. Their eyes met and it felt like the first honest moment they'd ever shared. Then he dipped his head down, and his face opened all the way, and she saw darkness come crawling from his mouth.

He was right. She didn't want to see this. She leaned back and looked up at the smooth, white painted ceiling, and his breath tickled her pubic hair and then she felt the worst pain she'd ever experienced. Followed by the greatest pleasure.

CHAPTER 38

"Do you think Patricia's all right?" Kitty asked, looking in the rear-view mirror.

They were parked in Maryellen's minivan at the far end of the Alhambra Hall parking lot. Maryellen sat in the driver's seat with Kitty riding shotgun. Mrs. Greene sat in the back.

"She's fine," Maryellen said. "You're fine. I'm fine. Mrs. Greene, are you fine?"

"I'm fine," Mrs. Greene said.

"We're all fine," Maryellen said. "Everyone's fine."

Kitty let the silence last a full five seconds this time.

"Except Patricia," she said.

No one had an answer to that.

"It's seven," Mrs. Greene said in the dark. No one moved. "Either Mrs. Campbell has done it by now, or it's too late."

Clothes rustled, and the back door thunked open.

"Come on," she said.

She got out of the minivan and the other two followed. Mrs. Greene took the red-and-white Igloo cooler out of the back, and Kitty carried the Bi-Lo grocery bag. The cooler clanked softly as their tools slid around inside. They wore dark clothes and walked quickly, turning onto Middle Street, preferring to take the risk of someone spotting them walking rather than have an extra car parked outside James Harris's house for three hours. People in the Old Village had a habit of writing down license plate numbers, after all.

Middle Street was a long, black tunnel leading straight to his house, lined with cars spilling out of driveways. The cold wind tugged at their coats. They put their heads down and forged forward, walking fast beneath the leafless trees and dead palmettos rattling in the wind.

"Have you bought your Christmas presents yet?" Kitty asked.

Mrs. Greene perked up at the mention of Christmas. Maryellen gave Kitty a sideways look.

"I get the big things during the after-Thanksgiving sales," Kitty said. "But I start planning people's gifts in August. This year I've still got more blanks than I normally do. Honey is easy, she needs a briefcase for job interviews. I mean, it's not that she needs it but I thought it would be the kind of thing she'd want. And Parish wants a tractor and Horse says we need a new one anyway, so that's taken care of. Lacy, I'm going to take to Italy as a graduation present next year so she'll get something small for now and she's fun to shop for anyhow, and as long as whatever I give Merit is bigger than what I get for Lacy she's thrilled. But I do not know what to buy for Pony. It's different to shop for a man, and he's got this new girl he's seeing, and I don't know if I have to get her a present or not. I mean, I want to, but does that make me seem overbearing?"

Maryellen turned to her.

"What on earth are you talking about?" she asked.

"I don't know!" Kitty said.

"Hush," Mrs. Greene said, and they passed the last house before James Harris's and they all fell silent.

The huge white house loomed over them, dark and still. The only light came from the living room window. They stepped off the street into his driveway then sat on the bottom step of his front stairs, took off their shoes, and hid them underneath. With Mrs. Greene leading the way, they stepped onto the cold boards and quietly climbed up to his porch.

He'd left his porch lights off so they were concealed by darkness, but Kitty still looked around nervously, trying to see if anyone was watching them from their windows. A cheer drifted to them on the wind, and they all froze for a moment. Then Kitty put down the paper Bi-Lo bag around the corner of the porch away from the living room light, and Mrs. Greene carefully placed the cooler in the shadows next to it. Kitty pulled an aluminum baseball bat out of the grocery bag and gave the sheathed hunting knife to Maryellen, who didn't know how to hold it. She decided it was just like a kitchen knife and that made it easier.

"My feet are freezing," Kitty whispered.

"Shhh," Mrs. Greene said.

The rushing wind helped hide the sounds they made as Maryellen carefully opened the screen door then tried the door handle while Kitty held the bat down by her leg, just in case. Mrs. Greene stood on Kitty's other side, holding a hammer.

The door popped open, silently and easily.

They stepped inside fast. The wind wanted to slam the door shut, but Maryellen eased it gently into its frame. They stood in the quiet downstairs hall, listening, worried that the howling wind rushing through the door had alerted James Harris. Nothing moved. All they heard was a piano concerto surging softly from a radio in the living room to their left.

Mrs. Greene pointed to the stairs leading up into darkness, and Kitty took the lead, palms sweating on the rubberized grip of her baseball bat. She held it straight up by her right shoulder and walked sideways, left foot first, right foot coming behind, one carpeted step at a time. Mrs. Greene walked in the middle, Maryellen in the rear. They needed to get him down before she could use the knife.

Every footstep was soft, soundless. Mrs. Greene jumped when a plummy man's voice started announcing the next selection from WSCI's *Classical Twilight* down below them in the living room.

Every step took an hour, and any second they expected to hear James Harris's voice from the top of the dark stairs.

They regrouped in the darkness of the upstairs hall. All around them were closed doors. A *CRACK* echoed through every room in the house and Maryellen almost screamed before realizing it was the wind shifting the window frames.

The master bedroom doorway stood dark in front of them and from it they heard a soft, wet suckling sound. They crept toward it, until they stood full in the doorway and the bright moonlight showed what lay on the bed.

Patricia lay back, arms flung over her head, a carnal half-smile on her lips, naked, her legs spread, and between them, blocking their view, crouched a shirtless James Harris, back muscles pulsing. His shoulder blades spread and retracted like wings as he fed on Patricia, his head by the join of her thighs, one large hand on her left thigh, gently pushing it open, the other on her stomach, fingers squirming on her pale flesh.

The sheer ravenous hunger of the sight paralyzed them. They could smell it, thick and carnal, filling the cramped room.

Kitty recovered before either of the other two women. She adjusted her grip, took three steps forward, ending with her left foot almost on James Harris's right ankle, and brought the bat straight off her shoulder, swinging hard in a powerful line drive.

The bat caught him in the side of the head with a metallic *TONK*, like a sledgehammer hitting stone, and Kitty let go with her lead hand and let the bat come around in a full arc, almost popping Mrs. Greene in the chin. A gout of regurgitated blood pulsed once out of James Harris's mouth and splattered across Patricia's pubic hair and belly, but otherwise he kept sucking, uninterrupted.

Patricia moaned once in sexual ecstasy, in heat, in pain, and Kitty brought the bat around again, even though her left shoulder ached. This time she swung for the fences.

The second blow got his attention, too much of it, in fact, and he whirled in a crouch, eyes feral, blood pouring down his face and dripping off something that hung from his chin. Blood poured from the wound in Patricia's thigh. Kitty saw the muscles in James Harris's stomach and shoulders tense and the planes of his face moved impossibly, and the thing hanging there disappeared, and Kitty thought, *He's going to*, and even though she wasn't a left-handed hitter she didn't have a choice—that was the side the bat was on and he wasn't going to give her time to get her stance back or even finish her thought. She brought the bat back at him as hard as she could but she knew it wasn't hard enough.

James Harris caught the bat on his ribs with a meaty *THWACK*. He brought his arm down and clamped it against his body, then spun and sent it clattering into the corner. Patricia moaned in pleasure, mindlessly grinding her thighs together, and James Harris was up, both hands grabbing Kitty's shoulders so hard she felt bone grind against bone. He drove her backward into the open bedroom door, brushing past Mrs. Greene and Maryellen, sending them spinning aside, slamming Kitty into the door so hard the knob embedded itself in the wall. Then he hurled her across the bedroom, sending her staggering toward the corner by the window, sprawling over an armchair on her way, tipping it over backward, as Mrs. Greene brought the hammer down on his head.

It glanced off his skull, and he plucked it easily out of her hand. She screamed and stepped backward, panicking, getting out of the room, wanting to get away from him as fast as possible, shoulder-checking Maryellen, getting turned around and winding up standing in the open doorway to the master bath instead.

Maryellen stood between James Harris and Mrs. Greene. She met his eyes and wet her pants. Her numb hands seemed to belong to someone else, someone far away, and her urine and the sheathed hunting knife hit the floorboards at the same time.

James Harris shoved Maryellen out of the way and advanced on Mrs. Greene. His powerful chest muscles stood out against his body like white armor, his thick forearms flexing as his fingers formed claws, and Mrs. Greene turned fast and tried to get into the bathroom. If she could get the heavy porcelain lid off the toilet tank she stood a chance. Instead, she tripped over the threshold where the tile began and sprawled forward, cracking both knees on the floor.

Blood drooled from James Harris's mouth and formed patterns on his chest and flat belly, and Mrs. Greene scrabbled onto tile so cold it burned, and then he had her right ankle in what felt like an iron band. With no effort at all, he pulled her back into the bedroom. Mrs. Greene rolled onto her back and brought her arms up to defend herself. When he got close she'd go for his eyes, but then she saw the fury in his face and knew that her arms were twigs in the face of this hurricane with teeth.

He leaned down, clawed fingers outstretched, and Kitty hit him from behind like a freight train, plowing into the small of his back, legs pumping, pushing him ahead of her all the way into the bathroom, both of them stepping on Mrs. Greene, feet bruising her stomach, one of them kicking her in the chin.

There was a loud *SMASH* and an *oomph* as James Harris took the edge of the sink in his stomach and went face-first into the tile wall. Kitty rode his back all the way to the floor. He landed with his arms beneath him. He was stronger but she outweighed him by fifty pounds.

He tried to flip over but she rolled her hips and pressed him into the floor. She grabbed his ears and smeared his face into the tiles. He tried to get an arm beneath him but she slapped it away.

"The knife! The knife!" she screamed, but Maryellen just stood numbly in the bedroom over a puddle of her cooling urine.

Mrs. Greene dragged herself out of the bathroom and into the safety of the bedroom. She watched as James Harris and Kitty wrestled, dark shapes on cold tiles. James Harris got both legs under him, lifting Kitty up on his hunched back as he stood.

"The knife, Maryellen! The knife!" Kitty shrieked, her voice hysterical.

Mrs. Greene looked and saw Maryellen staring down at the knife by her feet and realized she was too far away to grab it and James Harris was too close to standing up.

"Maryellen!" Mrs. Greene shouted, using her first name. "Throw me the knife!"

Maryellen looked up, saw her, looked down, saw the knife, and suddenly squatted. She tossed it underhanded to Mrs. Greene, who, for the first time in her life, caught something thrown to her. She unsnapped the button of the strap that held it in its sheath.

In the bathroom, Kitty wrapped a leg around James Harris's right leg, hooked his ankle, and kicked out. He went down on one knee, cracking it hard against the tile with Kitty's full weight on top of him. She bore down on her hips, pressing them into his buttocks. He had his left arm beneath him now, elbow braced against his ribs, so she used her left hand to try to pull it out of position, but it was like stone. In a desperate move, she drove her fingertips up hard into his wide-open left armpit and the shock made him lose his hold and drop to the floor with the sound of a side of beef hitting the slab.

She couldn't do this for much longer.

Kitty wriggled from side to side up his body, trying to keep her center of gravity over his as he thrashed, and she reached out for anything that might give her an advantage. She felt him mustering his strength again and suddenly she was a piece of paper riding a wave that was about to break and she knew this time it would take her under.

Something hard knocked the back of her hand and she understood what it was without the thought even consciously entering her mind. She grabbed it and turned it around, and there was one still, perfect moment when she saw the bowed back of James Harris's white neck and the ridges of his spine sticking out through his skin, perfectly outlined in the moonlight coming through the master bathroom skylight. She held the hunting knife with both hands and pushed the tip down.

He screamed, a sound so loud in the tiny, echoing bathroom that her right eardrum vibrated. She felt the knife grind bone. She dragged the point up and felt tissue give and she pressed down on the handle again. He threw his head back and trapped the blade between his vertebrae but she raised up her body so all her weight came down on her wrists, pushing the hilt down, and the steel tip of the blade gritted and squealed and crunched slowly, inch by inch, as she forced it deeper and deeper through his spine.

He tried to throw her off but his legs weren't kicking as hard as before, and he began squirming on the floor as she rode the handle, bearing down on the blade, and then his screams turned to gurgles, and he renewed his wriggling. She used her elbows to force his shoulders down and she slammed her chest down into the center of his back, and the knife took a sick crunching drop, and hit tile on the other side, and his body went slack.

She had done it.

In the silence she only heard him gargling and herself breathing as she rolled off and looked behind her. Mrs. Greene had one of his feet and Maryellen held the other, both of them pressing his legs to the floor. From downstairs drifted the jaunty sound of a symphony orchestra.

"You bitches haven't even slowed me down," James Harris gurgled.

Why is it always bitches, Kitty thought. As if men believed that word had some kind of magic power. She tried to stand but it was Maryellen who helped her to her feet, while Mrs. Greene kept kneeling on James Harris's legs in case he fought back. Kitty snapped on the bathroom light to make things feel more real.

All their pupils dilated at once and then adjusted to the bright-ness. They looked down at the vampire, facedown, lungs pumping, helpless on the bathroom floor.

Now came the hard part.

CHAPTER 39

"We should get the cooler," Kitty said from the bathroom door.

What she wanted was for Grace to be there, giving orders in her cool, condescending way. If Grace were in charge, things would be getting done the right way. But Grace had abandoned them, and they had to get moving. Maryellen pushed past her into the bedroom, snapping on the lights.

"She's not breathing," she called.

Kitty didn't know who she was talking about. Now that her adrenaline was beginning to fade, bruises were blossoming all over her body. Her neck hurt. She felt like she had a black eye.

"Who?" she asked, stupidly, then realized that of course Maryellen was talking about Patricia.

She turned and limped into the bedroom, leaving Mrs. Greene alone with the thing on the bathroom floor. The only sign that something had happened was the easy chair tipped over on its back in the corner, and Patricia, naked, blood soaking through the duvet beneath her thighs.

"I came in to put something over her," Maryellen said, hand flat on Patricia's forehead, lifting one eyelid.

All she could see beneath it was the white. Patricia was inert, lifeless, dead weight. Kitty tried to see if her chest rose and fell, but she knew that didn't tell you anything. She prodded at Patricia's throat without really knowing what she was doing.

"How do you know if she's breathing?" she asked.

"I listened to her chest and there's no sound," Maryellen said.

"Don't you know CPR?" she asked.

Patricia's shoulders hitched and her body began soft, boneless convulsions.

"Don't you?" Maryellen asked. "I've only seen it in movies."

"You've killed her," a voice echoed from the bathroom. It had a rasp in it but it still sounded strong and clear. "She's dying."

Maryellen looked full into Kitty's face, mouth slack, eyebrows raised in the middle like she was about to cry. Kitty felt lost.

"What do we do?" she asked. "Do we call 911?"

"No, roll her on her . . ." Maryellen took her hands and tried different approaches, fluttering over Patricia's twitching body. "Maybe raise her head. She might be in shock? I don't know."

Of course it was Mrs. Greene who knew CPR. One moment, Kitty watched Maryellen helplessly running through everything she knew and the next Mrs. Greene gently pushed her aside, placed her hands underneath Patricia's shoulders and said, "Help me get her on the floor."

Kitty took her feet and they half-dragged, half-dropped Patricia onto the throw rug next to the bed. Then Mrs. Greene put one hand under the back of Patricia's neck, the other on her chin, and popped Patricia's mouth open like the hood of a car.

"Check the blinds," Mrs. Greene said. "Make sure no one can see."

Kitty almost wept with gratitude at being told what to do. She looked in the bathroom and saw James Harris still on the floor where they'd left him. At first she thought he was convulsing, then realized he was laughing.

"I'm starting to feel much better," he said. "Every second I'm feeling better and better."

She made sure the blinds were closed all over the house. She wanted to switch off the symphony music on the radio downstairs, but finding the on/off switch took too much time and she needed to be back upstairs. There weren't enough of them to do all this.

In the bedroom, Mrs. Greene applied four perfect chest compressions, then four identical breaths into Patricia's mouth, as methodically and calmly as if she were blowing up a raft by the pool. Patricia's mouth hung slack. She had stopped convulsing. Was that a good sign?

Mrs. Greene stopped the CPR and Kitty's heart stopped, too.

"Is she . . ." she began, then found her throat was too dry to speak.

Mrs. Greene pulled a Kleenex from her pocket and wiped her mouth, checked the Kleenex, and dabbed at the corners of her lips.

"She's breathing," she said.

Kitty could see Patricia's chest lifting and falling. They both looked at Maryellen.

"I panicked," Maryellen said. "I'm sorry."

"I need you to put pressure on that wound," Mrs. Greene said, pointing to Patricia's thigh.

The place where James Harris had been torn away from Patricia's leg looked ragged and ugly. Blood oozed from it like sap.

"You haven't changed a thing," James Harris said from the bathroom. "She'll die later rather than sooner. So what?"

"Don't speak to him," Mrs. Greene said. "He's going to talk, try to convince us of something, but that's all he can do now. We need to remember our jobs and do them. Get a washcloth and hold it on her leg."

Kitty went into the bathroom, stepping over James Harris, avoiding his hands, and brought back all the hand towels and washcloths she could find. Maryellen folded one of the washcloths into a square and pressed it to Patricia's thigh. Mrs. Greene and Kitty went back into the bathroom.

"What's your big plan?" James Harris asked, as they rolled him over. His arms flopped uselessly. "You're going to book club me to death? Not invite me to your next meeting?"

They each gripped him beneath an armpit, raised him to a sitting

position, and then Mrs. Greene and Kitty exchanged glances and
nodded. *One . . . two . . .*

"Lift from your legs," Mrs. Greene said.

. . . *three.* They heaved James Harris up to sit on the edge of his
huge whirlpool tub.

"Drowning won't work," he said, grinning. "It's been tried."

They didn't care what happened to him now; he was as good as
dead, so they let go and he toppled backward and smashed into the
bottom of the fiberglass tub in a jumble of limbs.

"You'll have to do better than that," he said.

Kitty arranged him so that he lay full length, his back propped
up against one end of the tub, while Mrs. Greene moved everything
out of the way. Then she left the room and came back in with the
cooler and the grocery bag.

They unfolded a blue tarp over the floor and taped it down with
painter's tape. Kitty had taken several of Horse's deer hunting books
and photocopied the relevant pages. When they taped them up on
the wall over the bathtub for reference, James Harris got a good look.

"You can't," he said, eyes dilating with shock. "You can't do
that to me. I'm one of a kind. I'm a miracle."

Mrs. Greene laid out the tools from the cooler. Bow saws, ten
identical hunting knives with crossguards, a hacksaw with two packs
of extra blades, a squashed coil of blue nylon rope. Chain-mail
gloves to prevent cuts if they slipped. She and Kitty put on green
gardening knee pads.

"Listen to me," James Harris said. "I'm unique. There are bil-
lions of people and I'm the only one like me. Do you really want
to destroy that? It'd be like smashing a stained-glass window or . . .
or burning a library of books. You're a book club. You aren't book
burners."

They pulled off James Harris's shoes and socks, then his pants,
and let him lie naked on the bottom of the whirlpool. His nipples
were pale, and his penis flopped upside down on his blond pubic

thatch. Mrs. Greene turned on the water and made sure it was drain-
ing. She put in a drain catcher so no big pieces went down the pipes
to cause problems later. She handed Kitty a hunting knife.

Kitty got on her knees next to James Harris's head. She looked
at the diagram with its dotted lines and reached for James Harris's
arm. The first cut was supposed to be all the way around his elbow,
slicing through the ligaments, and then she was supposed to twist
and pull it off. She told herself it would be just like dressing a deer.

"Didn't Patricia tell you about me?" he said, trying to make eye
contact. "I've lived for four hundred years. I know the secret to
eternal life. I can tell you how to stop getting old. Don't you want
to stay this age forever?"

Kitty touched the tip of the knife to the soft skin on his inner
arm, hardly daring to breathe. The point dimpled the inside of his
elbow.

"This is the one time in your life you are face-to-face with
something bigger than yourselves," he said. "I am a mystery of the
universe. Is this really how you're going to respond?"

In the bright light, with James Harris lying helpless in the tub,
and everyone watching, in the calm rational white-tiled bathroom,
Kitty froze.

"Exactly," James Harris said. "You haven't done anything permanent yet. Just give me a few minutes and I'll be as good as new.
Then I'll show you how to live forever."

"Here," Mrs. Greene said, putting one hand on Kitty's shoulder
and holding out her hand. "You wait in the next room. Keep an eye
on Patricia."

Gratefully, Kitty handed the knife to Mrs. Greene and got up,
then stripped off the warm chain-mail glove and handed it to her.
Mrs. Greene closed her eyes in silent prayer.

"I'm the one thing in this world that's bigger than all of you,"
James Harris called after Kitty. "I can make you stronger than anyone you know, I can make you live longer; you have come face-to-

face with something truly amazing."

"What would that be?" Mrs. Greene asked, opening her eyes and kneeling by the side of the deep tub. She pulled on the glove.

"Me!" he said.

"We'll have to agree to disagree," she said.

Those would be the only words she spoke to James Harris for the next hour. Without giving herself a chance to hesitate, Mrs. Greene stuck the knife into the inside of James Harris's elbow. It hit bone right beneath the surface but she worked it around, and the more she imagined she was trimming the fat from a Christmas ham, the easier it became to dissociate herself from what she was doing as he screamed.

She hacked away at his elbow, giving up on clean, neat cuts and just chopping at the ligaments and tendons. She sawed, she sliced, she scraped at his skin with her hunting knife.

"Listen to me," James Harris gibbered. "You're confronted with the secret to eternal life and you're just flushing it away. This is insane."

Mrs. Greene ignored him and finally got his elbow carved down to the bone.

"Maryellen?" she called. "Let Kitty take care of Patricia. I need a hand."

"Yes, ma'am," Maryellen said, coming in from the bedroom.

Maryellen held James Harris's forearm in both hands and twisted it back and forth while Mrs. Greene held his shoulder and cut anything that looked like it was still connected. With a cartilage-tearing crunch and a series of small, fast pops, his forearm came free. A few strings of meat and gristle connected it to his body but Mrs. Greene cut the ones Maryellen couldn't pull apart. Maryellen dropped the forearm into a black plastic garbage bag and carefully tied a knot in the top. Immediately, the bag began to writhe as the arm tried to get out.

"I can feel my spine healing." James Harris grinned at Mrs. Greene. "You'd better hope you can cut faster than I can heal."

Mrs. Greene worked fast, with Maryellen assisting. They took off the rest of his left arm at the shoulder, then his right foot, his right leg at the knee, then at the hip. The black plastic bags piled up in the corner of the bathroom in a squirming heap. As his muscle and bone dulled each hunting knife, Mrs. Greene dropped it into a plastic bag and picked up a new one. Maryellen cleaned the chainmail gloves when they became too clotted with gore to keep a firm grip on his flesh anymore.

"Where are your boys living?" James Harris said to Mrs. Greene. "Irmo, isn't it? Jesse and Aaron. When I get out of here I'm going to pay them a visit."

Even when she turned him onto his stomach to work on his left arm and leg, James Harris kept up a running monologue that became less and less coherent as they cut more and more of him away.

"I never went where I wasn't invited," he rambled. "The farm, the widow's house, Russia, I only went where they wanted me. Lup asked me to use him, he asked me with his eyes, he knew I could keep him alive, but he had to keep me alive first. I'll always remember that beautiful boy. That soldier wanted it, his face was so burned, and I did him a favor. I only did what people asked for. Even Ann wanted what I had to offer."

They took a break. Mrs. Greene's arms throbbed and ached. The threat of James Harris's spinal column knitting itself back together loomed over her. They didn't have much time, but all she wanted to do was take a hot bath and go to sleep. The night felt endless.

"How's Patricia?" she asked Kitty.

"Asleep," Kitty said, still pressing the towel to Patricia's thigh.

Maryellen looked at the stiff way Kitty held her neck. A purple shiner circled her left eye.

"What'll you tell Horse?" Maryellen asked.

Kitty's face fell.

"I hadn't even thought of that," she said.

"We'll figure it out when we're through here," Mrs. Greene

said. Her confidence calmed Kitty. "Put some ice on your eye for now."

Back in the bathroom, James Harris's torso greeted her again. It was time for his head. She dreaded this moment although she also hoped it would finally shut him up. One thing she'd learned about men: they liked to talk.

As she worked her knife through the tough tendons and what remained of his spinal column, James Harris kept talking.

"The Wide Smiles Club will come looking for me," he said, eyes trying to find hers. "That's what we do. They'll come looking for me and when they find out what you've done, there will be hell to pay for you and your children and your families. This is your last chance. You can stop now and I'll tell them to leave you alone."

"No one is going to come looking for you," Mrs. Greene said, unable to resist. "You are all alone. You have no one in the world, and when you die no one will notice. No one will care. You leave nothing behind."

"That's where you're wrong," he said, and gave a bloody grin. "I'm leaving you all a present. Just wait until your friend Slick gets ripe."

He started to giggle and Mrs. Greene crunched her knife through his windpipe and she and Maryellen gripped him by the hair and pulled off his head with a loud pop.

Then they did what Miss Mary had told Patricia to do all those years ago at the supper table the night she spat at James Harris. Maryellen held his head and Mrs. Greene took a hammer and drove two thick twenty-penny nails into each of his eyes. His mouth finally stopped moving. Then they dropped his head into a bag and tied it shut.

They gutted him and packed his organs and entrails into different bags. She was too tired to saw through his rib cage, so they simply removed as much meat from it as they could and wrapped pound after pound of flesh and muscle in different plastic bags. They double- and triple-bagged them, reducing James Harris to a pile of tightly sealed trash bags that could fit into an ordinary sized garbage can.

When they were finished, the bathroom looked like an abattoir. Mrs. Greene and Maryellen went into the bedroom.

"Finished?" Kitty asked.

"We are," Mrs. Greene said.

"I need to get the car," Maryellen said, then sat down heavily on the floor, making sure she stayed off the throw rug. "I just need to sit for a minute."

They all ached, right down to the bone, but they weren't even close to finished. Mrs. Greene looked around the bathroom and the bedroom, and Maryellen followed her gaze. Kitty did, too.

"Jesus, Mary, Mother of God," Kitty said softly.

Blood was everywhere. Despite the tarp, the bathroom was painted red. The countertops, the walls, the door frame, the toilet. There was blood on the dark oak planks in the bedroom, blood on the duvet cover where Patricia lay, bloody handprints on the doors and walls. Seeing how much they had to clean drained them of their spirits, hammered them down to nothing. It was almost ten. The Clemson-Carolina game would be over in less than an hour.

"We don't have enough time," Maryellen said.

Something whispered in the bathroom. They looked at each other, then pushed themselves up off the floor and stood in the bathroom door. The pile of black plastic packages containing pieces of James Harris's body twisted like snakes. Their motion was muscular and angry.

"We put the nails through his eyes," Mrs. Greene said.

"He's not stopping," Kitty wailed. "It didn't work. He's still alive."

The doorbell rang.

CHAPTER 40

"They'll go away," Maryellen whispered.

It rang again, twice in a row.

Mrs. Greene's hands and feet went cold. Maryellen felt a headache start at the base of her skull. Kitty whimpered.

"Please go away," she whispered. "Please go away . . . please go away . . . please go away . . ."

The black plastic packages crackled in the bathroom. One of them rolled off the pile and hit the floor with a *THUMP*. It began to squirm towards the door.

"The lights are on," Maryellen said. "We forgot to turn out the lights. You can see them through the shutters. They'll know he's home."

The doorbell rang, three times in a row.

"Who's the least of a mess?" Maryellen asked. They looked at each other. She and Mrs. Greene were encrusted in blood. Kitty only had some bruises.

"Oh, merciful Jesus," Kitty moaned.

"It's probably one of the Johnsons," Maryellen said. "They must've run out of beer."

Kitty took three deep breaths, on the verge of hyperventilating, then walked out into the hall, down the stairs, and over to the front door. Everything was silent. Maybe they'd gone away.

The doorbell rang, so loudly that she squeaked. She grabbed the handle, flipped the deadbolt, and opened it a crack.

"Am I too late?" Grace asked.

"Grace!" Kitty shouted, dragging her inside by the arm.

They heard her all the way up in the bedroom and came running downstairs. Grace's face went slack when a blood-splattered Mary-ellen and Mrs. Greene appeared. She looked at them in horror.

"That's a white carpet," she said.

They froze and looked back at the stairs. Their bloody footprints came right down the middle of the carpet. They turned back around and saw Grace stepping back from them, taking in everything.

"You didn't . . ." she began, but couldn't finish.

"Go see for yourself," Maryellen said.

"I'd prefer not to," Grace said.

"No," Mrs. Greene said. "If you have doubts, you need to see. He's in the upstairs toilet."

Grace went reluctantly, fastidiously avoiding the bloodstains on the stairs. They heard her footsteps cross the bedroom and stop in the bathroom doorway. There was a long silence. When she came back down, her steps were shaky and she had one hand on the wall. She looked at the three women, covered in blood.

"What's wrong with Patricia?" she asked.

They filled her in on what had happened. As they talked, her face got firm, her shoulders squared, she stood straighter. When they finished, she said, "I see. And what's the plan to dispose of him?"

"Stuhr's has a contract with Roper and East Cooper Hospital," Maryellen said. "To burn their medical waste in the crematorium early in the morning and late at night. I put a big box of biohazard burn bags in my car, but . . . they're moving. We can't take them in like this."

They all watched as Grace tapped her fingers against her lips.

"We can still use Stuhr's," she said, then checked the inside of her wrist. "There's less than half an hour left in the game."

"Grace," Maryellen said, the dried blood crackling on her face. "We can't take moving bags of body parts to Stuhr's. They'll see them. They'll open them up and I can't explain what they are."

"Bennett and I have two columbarium niches for our ashes," Grace said. They're in the back of the cemetery, on the eastern side, facing the sunrise. We'll simply put his head in one and the rest of his remains in the other."

"But there's a record," Maryellen said. "On the computer. And what happens when the two of you pass?"

"Surely you can alter the records," Grace said. "As for Bennett and myself, hopefully it will be years before we have to cross that bridge. Now, let's see if he has some boxes somewhere. Maryellen, you and Mrs. Greene shower in the guest room. Use dark towels and leave them in the tub. Tell me you at least brought changes of clothes?"

"In the car," Maryellen said.

"Kitty," Grace said, "bring her car here. I'll look for boxes. You two clean yourselves up. We can only count on forty or so minutes before that street is full of people, so let's be purposeful."

Kitty brought the car around and helped Grace pack the squirming, plastic-wrapped body parts into boxes, and lugged them down to the front door. Mrs. Greene and Maryellen didn't clean themselves perfectly, but at least they didn't look like they worked in a slaughterhouse anymore.

"How much longer is left in the game?" Grace asked as they dropped the final cardboard box onto the stack by the front door.

Kitty turned on the TV.

". . . and Clemson has called a time-out hoping to run out the clock . . ." an announcer brayed.

"Less than five minutes," Kitty said.

"Then let's load the car while the streets are still clear," Grace said.

They almost ran, shambling up and down the dark front stairs, tossing the boxes into Maryellen's minivan. They could feel James Harris moving inside, like they were carrying boxes full of rats.

When they were finished, they stood in the front hall and realized that they had failed. The plan had been to wipe James Harris off the face of the earth, leaving his house pristine, as if he'd simply disappeared into thin air, or packed his things and walked out the door. But blood had pooled by the front door where they'd stacked the boxes, the white carpeted stairs were a mess of streaked gore, there were blood smears up and down the walls, bloody fingerprints were drying on the banister, and even from downstairs they could see that the mess covered the upstairs hall. And then there was the master bath.

A huge roar rose up from the surrounding houses. Someone activated an airhorn. The game was over.

"We can't do this," Maryellen said. "Someone will come looking for him and they'll know he was killed the second they open that door."

"Stop whining," Grace snapped. "You're looking for columbariums C-24 and C-25, Maryellen. I'm sure you can find those. You and Kitty are the least messy, so you're driving to Stuhr's."

"What are you going to do?" Maryellen asked. "Burn this place down?"

"Don't be absurd," Grace said. "Mrs. Greene and I will stay behind. We've been cleaning up after men our entire lives. This is no different."

Headlights snapped on up and down the street as drunk football fans stumbled to their cars, hollering and calling to one another in the dark. A ground mist lay low on the road.

"But—" Maryellen began.

"If ifs and buts were candy and nuts it would be Christmas every day," Grace said. "Now scoot."

Kitty and Maryellen limped for the minivan. Grace closed the door behind them and turned to Mrs. Greene.

"It's a lot of work," Mrs. Greene said.

"Between us we've been cleaning houses for eighty years," Grace said. "I believe we're up to the challenge. Now, we'll need baking soda, ammonia, white vinegar, and dishwashing detergent. We'll need to get the sheets and towels in the washer, and spray the carpets first so they can soak while we work."

"We should wash the towels and that duvet in the shower," Mrs. Greene said. "Get it real hot and take a hard bristle brush to them with some salt paste. Then put it in the dryer with plenty of fabric softener."

"Let's see if we can find some hydrogen peroxide for these bloodstains in the carpet," Grace said.

"I prefer ammonia," Mrs. Greene said.

"Hot water?" Grace asked.

"No, cold."

"Interesting," Grace said.

Around midnight, Maryellen called them from a gas station pay phone.

"We're done," Maryellen said. "C-24 and C-25. They're sealed tight and I'll clean up the database in the morning."

"Mrs. Cavanaugh is just ironing the sheets," Mrs. Greene said. "Then we have to shampoo the carpets, put things away, and we're done."

"How does it look?" Maryellen asked.

"Like no one ever lived here," Mrs. Greene said.

"How's Patricia?"

"Sleeping," Mrs. Greene said. "She hasn't made a sound."

"Do you want me to come pick you up?"

"Go home," Mrs. Greene said. "We don't want people to think this is a public parking lot. I'll get a ride."

"Well," Maryellen said. "Good luck."

Mrs. Greene hung up the phone.

She and Grace finished ironing the sheets, put the duvet back on the bed, and inspected the house for any bloodstains they'd missed.

Then Grace walked home and got her car while Mrs. Greene hauled Patricia downstairs, switched off the radio, turned off the lights, and used James Harris's keys to lock the front door behind her.

Bennett had passed out on the downstairs sofa, so they put Patricia in Grace's guest bedroom, and then Grace called Carter.

"She wound up watching the game over here after visiting Slick at the hospital," she told him. "She fell asleep. I think it's better not to wake her."

"Probably for the best," Carter said. He'd had a lot to drink so it came out *prollyferthebersh*. "I'm glad you girls are friends again."

"Good night, Carter," Grace said, and hung up.

She drove Mrs. Greene home and let her out in front of her dark house.

"Thank you for all your help," Grace said.

"Tomorrow," Mrs. Greene said, "I'm going to drive up to Irmo and bring my babies home."

"Good," Grace said.

"You were wrong three years ago," Mrs. Greene said. "You were wrong, and you were a coward, and people died."

They stood, considering each other in the glow of the car's ceiling light, as the engine idled. Finally Grace said something she'd almost never said before in her life.

"I'm sorry."

Mrs. Greene gave a small nod.

"Thank you for coming tonight," she said. "We couldn't have done it alone."

"None of us could have done this alone," Grace said.

Grace sat by Patricia's bed, dozing in her chair. Patricia woke up around four in the morning with a gasp. Grace smoothed her sweaty hair back from her face.

"It's over," Grace said.

Patricia burst into tears, and Grace took off her shoes and crawled into bed next to her and rocked Patricia while she cried herself out. The pain hit next, and Grace helped her to the bathroom and stood outside the door while Patricia sat on the toilet, her bowels turned to water. She'd barely got the toilet flushed before she had to kneel in front of it and vomit.

Grace helped her back to bed and sat with her while she tossed and turned. Finally, she found her copy of *In Cold Blood*.

"'The village of Holcomb stands on the high wheat plains of western Kansas,'" she read to Patricia in her soft Southern accent. "'A lonesome area that other Kansans call "out there." The land is flat, the views are awesomely extensive; horses, herds of cattle, a white cluster of grain elevators rising as gracefully as Greek temples are visible long before a traveler reaches them.'"

She read to her until the sun came up.

CHAPTER 41

Patricia saw Miss Mary one last time.

Her fever lasted for two days, so maybe it was only a dream. But when Patricia got older she forgot what she was wearing the day Carter proposed, she forgot whether Blue's high school graduation was outdoors on a sunny day or in the gym because it rained, and she even forgot the date of her wedding anniversary, but she never forgot opening her eyes one bright November afternoon and feeling a dry, smooth hand stroke her cheek, and seeing a pair of black shoes standing beside her bed.

They were ugly shoes, practical, and low—schoolteacher's shoes. The legs in them wore nude pantyhose, and they rose up to the hem of a plaid cotton dress, but she was too weak to lift her head and see the rest. Then the shoes turned, and walked out of her bedroom, and what Patricia would always remember about Miss Mary wasn't those hard meals, or the shock of finding her that night after Grace's party, or the roach falling into her water glass, but it was how much you had to love your son to come back from Hell to warn him.

And then she remembered that Miss Mary hadn't come back to warn Carter. She'd came back to warn her.

Her fever broke that same afternoon. One minute she felt drugged and sweaty, in a sleep so deep she couldn't crawl out. The next minute everything felt clear, and she blinked in the sunlight and sat up in bed, sweat drying on her skin, eyes sharp. She heard the toilet flush and Grace came out of the bathroom.

"Good, you're awake," Grace said. "Would you like a glass of water?"

"I'm hungry," Patricia said.

Before Grace could get her something, Carter burst into the room.

"She's awake," Grace told him.

"It's good to have you back," he said. "You've been running a fever. I was getting ready to take you to the hospital if it didn't break by tonight."

"I feel all right," Patricia said. "Just hungry. Where are Blue and Korey?"

"They're fine," he said. "Listen, we're going to lose—" Then he remembered Grace. "I appreciate you being here, but I'd like some privacy with my wife."

Patricia nodded to her, and Grace said, "I'll check back with you this evening," and left the room.

Carter sat in the chair Grace had been sitting in beside the bed.

"We're going to lose Gracious Cay," he said. "Leland can't hold on to it with James Harris gone. He had a lot of money in escrow, and some of it's just not there anymore. We're already getting nervous investors after that fire, and if they hear Jim's gone and Leland can't find a lot of the cash, we're going to lose what we put in. Do you have any idea where he's gone? His house is totally empty."

"Carter," Patricia said, pushing herself up in bed. "I don't want to talk about this right now. I want to talk about when we're bringing Korey home."

"A man is *missing*," Carter said. "Jim meant a lot to this family, he meant a lot to the kids, and he meant a lot to that project. If you know anything at all about where he might be, I need you to tell me."

"I don't know anything about James Harris," she said.

She must not have said it very convincingly because Carter took it as proof that she knew something.

"Is this about your obsession?" he asked, leaning forward, elbows on his knees. "Did you go off the deep end again and say something to him? Patty, I swear, if you've messed this up for everyone . . . you don't even know how many families you might have affected. There's Leland, us, Horse and Kitty . . ."

He got up and began to walk circles in the room, still talking on and on about James Harris, escrow accounts, missing money, and principal investments, and Patricia realized she didn't recognize this man anymore. The quiet boy from Kershaw she'd fallen in love with was dead. In his place stood this resentful stranger.

"Carter," she said. "I want a divorce."

Two days later, Patricia dragged herself out of bed and drove downtown to see Slick in the hospital. She was dozing when Patricia arrived, so Patricia sat and waited for her to wake up. Slick looked sallow, and her chest hitched occasionally as she breathed. They had her on a full oxygen mask now, trying to keep her levels up. Patricia remembered stumbling across James Harris asleep all those years ago and thinking he was dead. That was how Slick looked.

"Grace already . . . told me," Slick said, opening her eyes, pulling her mask away from her face to speak. "I made her . . . give me all the details."

"Me too," Patricia said. "I was out from what he did to me."

"How did . . . it feel?" Slick asked.

Patricia never would have said this to anyone but Slick. She leaned forward.

"It felt so good," she breathed, then immediately remembered what he'd done to Slick and felt selfish and insensitive.

"Most sin does," Slick said.

"I know why they hurt themselves," Patricia said. "It's this feeling of things being whole and stable and warm and safe, and you want it back so badly, but it's just slipping away over the horizon and you feel like you'll never get it back again and you don't want to live without it. But then you just keep living and it hurts all the time. Everything feels like knives on my skin and my joints ache."

"What . . . did he do to us?" Slick asked. "He made us . . . murderers . . . and we betrayed . . . everything . . . and now it's all falling apart . . ."

Patricia took Slick's hand that didn't have an IV needle in it.

"The children are safe," Patricia said. "That's what matters."

Slick's throat worked for a minute, and then she said, "Not the . . . ones in . . . Six Mile . . ."

Patricia's blood felt like lead in her veins.

"Not all of them," she said. "But your children, and Maryellen's children, and Kitty's. Mrs. Greene's boys. He's been doing this for a long time, Slick. No one's ever stopped him before. We did. We paid a price but we stopped him."

"What about . . . me?" Slick asked. "Am I . . . going to get better?"

For a moment, Patricia thought about lying but they'd been through too much together to do that now.

"No," she said. "I don't think you are. I'm so sorry."

Slick's hand gripped hers so hard Patricia's fingers felt like they were about to break.

"Why?" Slick asked behind her mask.

"Mrs. Greene told me he said something before he died," Patricia said. "I think this is how he makes other ones like him. I think that's what he did to you."

Slick stared at Patricia, and Patricia saw her eyes turn red and bloodshot and then Slick nodded.

"I feel . . . something growing . . . inside," Slick said. "It's waiting for me . . . to die . . . and then . . . it hatches."

She put a hand to the base of her throat.

"Here," she said. "Something . . . new . . . hard to swallow . . ."

They sat quietly for a while, holding hands.

"Patricia . . ." Slick said. "Bring . . . Buddy Barr tomorrow . . .

I want to . . . change my will . . . I want to . . . be cremated . . ."

"Of course," Patricia said.

"And make sure . . . I'm not alone . . ."

"You don't have to worry about that," Patricia said.

And she didn't. Someone from book club was with her all the way to the end. On Thanksgiving day, when Slick started having trouble breathing, and her oxygen count began to fall, and she lost consciousness for the last time, Kitty was there, reading to her from *In Cold Blood*. Even after the crash team burst into the room and surrounded Slick and crowded Kitty into a corner, she kept reading silently, just moving her lips, whispering the words from the book like a prayer.

A few days after Slick's funeral, Ragtag started walking in circles. Patricia noticed he'd follow rooms around their edges, always turning to the left, never to the right. He sometimes bumped into doors on his way through them. She took him to Dr. Grouse.

"I've got two pieces of bad news for you," he said. "The first is that Ragtag has a brain tumor. It won't kill him today or tomorrow, and he's not in any pain, but it's going to get worse. When it does, bring him here and we can put him to sleep."

The second piece of bad news was that the tests to find the tumor cost five hundred and twenty dollars. Patricia wrote him a check.

When she returned home, she told Blue. The first thing he said was, "We need to get Korey."

"You know we can't do that," she told him.

She didn't think they could do that? They'd paid for Korey to stay at Southern Pines for eight weeks, and she had a whole program of therapists and counselors and doctors, and they all kept telling Patricia she had trouble sleeping, and seemed restless, anxious, and unfocused, and it would be unwise to pull her out prematurely. But when she'd visited the day before, Korey had seemed clear-eyed and calm, even though she didn't say much.

"Mom," Blue said, talking like she was hard of hearing. "Ragtag is older than me. You got him for Korey's first Christmas. If he's sick, he's going to be scared. He needs her."

Patricia wanted to argue. She wanted to point out that they couldn't interrupt Korey's program, that the doctors knew best. She wanted to tell him that Ragtag wouldn't know whether Korey was there or not. She wanted to tell him that Korey mostly ignored Ragtag, anyway. Instead, she realized that she wanted Korey to come home very badly and so she said, "You're right."

They drove to Southern Pines together, and signed out her daughter against the advice of her doctors, and brought her home. When Ragtag saw her, he began to bang his tail against the floor where he'd been lying.

Patricia kept her distance while Blue and Korey hung all over Ragtag that weekend, soothing him when he barked at things that weren't there, driving to the store and getting him wet food when he wouldn't eat dry, sitting with him in the backyard or on the sofa in the sun. And on Sunday night, when things got bad, and Dr. Grouse's office was closed, the two of them sat up with Ragtag as he walked around the den in circles, barking and snapping at things they couldn't see, and they talked to him in low voices, and told him he was a good dog, and a brave dog, and they weren't going to leave him alone.

When Patricia went to bed around one, both kids were still sitting up with Ragtag, patting him when his wanderings brought him close, speaking to him, showing him patience that Patricia had never seen in them before. Around four in the morning she woke up with a start and crept downstairs. The three of them lay on the den sofa. Korey and Blue were on either end, asleep. Ragtag lay between them, dead.

They buried him together around the side of the house, and Patricia held both of them while they cried. When Carter came by the next evening and the two of them sat down to tell Korey and Blue they were getting a divorce, Carter laid out how it was going to go.

"This is the way things are going to be," he said. He'd told Patricia that kids liked certainty and he was the better qualified of the two of them to map this new reality for them. "I'll be keeping the house on Pierates Cruze and the beach house. I'll pay for your school and college, you don't have to worry about that. And you can stay here with me for as long as you want. Because this is your mother's decision, she'll be looking for a new place to live. And it may not be very big, and it may be in another part of Mt. Pleasant. She'll only have the one car, so you probably won't be able to borrow it to go see your friends. Your mother may even need to move to a new city. I'm not saying these things because I'm trying to punish anyone, but I want you to have a realistic idea of how things are going to change."

Then he asked them who they wanted to live with during the week. They both surprised Patricia by saying, "Mom."

IN COLD BLOOD

February 1997

CHAPTER 42

Patricia pulled into the cemetery and got out of her car, tote bag swinging. It was one of those sharp winter days when the sky looked like a great blue dome, white around the bottom, darkening to a saturated robin's-egg blue at the top. She walked along the winding road that ran between the grave markers and stepped onto the grass when she got to the right row. The dry grass crunched beneath her shoes as she walked to Slick's stone.

Her inner thigh throbbed like it always did when she walked over uneven ground. Korey felt the same kind of pain, too. It was something they shared. But Patricia refused to accept it was permanent for Korey. They'd already started going to see specialists, and one doctor thought a blood transfusion and a series of synthetic erythropoietin would help Korey produce more red blood cells and that might eliminate the pain. They planned to start as soon as school was out. They only had enough money for one of them to try this treatment. That was fine with Patricia.

Everyone was broke. Leland had declared bankruptcy just after the new year and was selling houses for Kevin Hauck on commission. Kitty and Horse had lost almost everything and were chopping Seewee Farms into parcels, selling it off piecemeal to keep the lights on. Patricia didn't know how much Carter had sunk into Gracious Cay, but judging by how many times her lawyer had to remind him to send the child support checks, it was a lot.

Everyone assumed James Harris had seen the crisis coming, packed up, and skipped town. No one asked too many questions.

After all, tracking him down would be a lot of work, and bringing him back would only lead to awkward questions and no one actually wanted to hear the answers. At the end of the day, some rich white people lost their money. Some poor black people lost their homes. That's just how it goes.

Patricia had driven out to Gracious Cay in January. The construction equipment had been taken away, and now the frames of the houses stood alone, stark and unfinished, like towering skeletons eroding in the weather. She drove the paved road through the center of the development all the way back to Six Mile. Mrs. Greene had moved to Irmo to be near her boys while they finished high school, but some people were moving back. A gaggle of little children bounced an old tennis ball off the wall of Mt. Zion A.M.E. She saw cars parked in a few driveways and smelled wood smoke coming from a handful of chimneys and settling in the streets.

Before she died, Slick had been working on gifts for everyone and Maryellen had driven around distributing them in December. Patricia had unfolded her pink sweatshirt and held it up to her front. It featured a picture of the baby Jesus asleep in the manger which was, for unknown reasons, beneath a sequined Christmas tree with a real bell on top. In cursive script it read, *Remember the Reason for the Season*.

"She made one of these for Grace?" Patricia asked.

"I got a picture of her wearing it," Maryellen said. "Do you want to see?"

"I don't think I could stand the shock," Patricia said.

She and the children had their Christmas dinner with Grace and Bennett. After they finished the dishes, while Korey and Blue went out to the car, Grace gave Patricia a bag of wrapped leftovers, then reached into the drawer of her front hall table, pulled out a thick envelope, and tucked it inside.

"Merry Christmas," she said. "I don't want to argue about this."

Patricia put the bag on the table and opened the envelope. It was stuffed with a thick sheaf of worn twenty-dollar bills.

"Grace—" she began.

"When I got married," Grace said, "my mother gave me this and told me that a wife should always have some of her own money set aside, just in case. I want you to have it now."

"Thank you," Patricia said. "I'll pay you back."

"No," Grace said. "You absolutely will not."

She used part of it to give Korey and Blue the Christmas they deserved. The rest she added to the $2,350 in cash she still had from James Harris and put a deposit down on a furnished condo with two bedrooms near the bridge. Where they were living now only had one and Blue slept on the sofa.

Patricia took a copy of *In Cold Blood* out of her tote bag and laid it in front of Slick's headstone. She took out a wineglass and a little screw-cap mini bottle of Kendall-Jackson and filled the glass and set it on top of the book. She made sure it wouldn't tip over and then did what she always did on these visits and walked over to the above-ground niches, where she found C-24 and C-25. They were blank, without even names on them. There never would be names on them.

Patricia wondered who James Harris had been. How long had he been traveling the country? How many dead children did he leave in his wake? How many little towns like Kershaw had he sucked dry? No one would ever know. He'd probably been alive for so long that he didn't even know anymore. By the time he came to the Old Village, she imagined, his past was probably one long blur and he existed in an eternal present.

He left no one behind, no children, no shared memories, no history, no one told stories about him. All he left to mark his passing was pain, and that would fade over time. The people he'd killed would be mourned but the people who loved them would move on. They would fall in love again, have more children, grow old, and be mourned by their children in turn.

Not James Harris.

If this were a book it would have been called *The Mysterious Disappearance of James Harris*, but it wouldn't be a good mystery because Patricia already knew its solution: the mystery of what happened to James Harris was Patricia Campbell.

But she hadn't solved it alone.

If Maryellen hadn't worked at Stuhr's, if Grace and Mrs. Greene hadn't been superior house cleaners, if Kitty hadn't had such a good swing, if Slick hadn't called them all and convinced them to come together again in her hospital room, if Patricia hadn't read so many true crime books, if Mrs. Greene hadn't put the pieces together, if Miss Mary hadn't found the photograph, if Kitty hadn't called to her in Marjorie Fretwell's driveway that day.

Sometimes, when she was doing laundry or washing dishes, Patricia would stop, her heart pounding double time, blood swelling in her veins, overwhelmed by the sheer horror of how close they'd come.

They weren't stronger than him, they weren't smarter, they weren't more prepared. But circumstances had brought them together and allowed them to succeed where so many others had failed. Patricia knew how they looked, a bunch of silly Southern women, yakking about books over white wine. A bunch of carpool drivers, skinned-knee kissers, errand runners, secret Santas and part-time tooth fairies, with their practical jeans and their festive sweaters.

Think of us what you will, she thought, *we made mistakes, and probably scarred our children for life, and we froze sandwiches, and forgot car pool, and got divorced. But when the time came, we went the distance.*

She leaned as close to the lid of the niche as she dared and listened. She heard cars passing on the distant highway, and closer by she heard birds in the trees, and the wind rustling branches, but behind all those she heard something quiet and relentless. She knew it was impossible, but behind the sounds of the outside world she thought she could hear the sound of something wrapped in plastic, writhing, crawling, blindly searching for a way out, squirming eternally in the darkness, relentlessly looking for the weakness that would set it free again.

Everything had changed. She was divorced. Her friend had died. Her daughter and son had a shadow on them and she didn't know how long it would last or how far it reached. Seewee Farms was being sold to developers. Six Mile had been scattered to the winds. Her mother-in-law had died. She had had some kind of communion with a man who wasn't her husband, and then killed him.

She didn't regret any of it. What had been destroyed made what remained that much more precious. That much more solid. That much more important.

She stepped back from the crypt, turned her back on the remains of James Harris, and walked to her car. She didn't stop by Slick's marker. She'd come back in the morning and pick up the wineglass and the book. But for now they could wait.

She needed to get to her book club.

Happy Holidays, Book Clubbers!

What a wonderful year for the Literary Guild of Mt. Pleasant, y'all!

As we get ready to head into the new millennium,
I think we can all look back and say that our 12th year was
truly the best one yet for our book club. Who knows what
the future will bring, but as you spend time with your loved
ones this holiday season I hope you enjoy reflecting on all
the great books we read in 1999. And if you don't mind, and
have the time, may this little poem help you rewind!

We learned a lot this past year
About horror, terror, murder, fear.
We learned about Theresa Knorr, a real bad mother,
And also we learned a lot about each other.

Jhanteigh Kupihea turned out to be a good talker
On Philip Carlo's book, *The Night Stalker*.

We had a wonderful discussion of *And Never Let Her Go*
Conducted by our own Nicole De Jackmo.

Using diagrams and pictures, artist Andie Reid
Made us wonder whose child was the real *Bad Seed*.

And after two years of asking by Kate McGuire
We're all glad we finally read *Interview with the Vampire*,

Although we will admit Moneka Hewlett caused us all angina
By insisting we read *Bastard out of Carolina*.

Rick Chillot summed up our October book best,
When he said, "Nobody's perfect, but at least
we aren't Fred or Rosemary West."

Then Julia, Kat, and Ann Hendrix, our sisters three,
Had a lot to say about *The Killer Inside Me*.

As the last century scurries away,
We really musn't forget to say
Thank you, also, to Amy J. Schneider, our favorite grammarian,
And let's not forget Becky Spratford, number one librarian.

Of course, behind every woman there's a man, usually somewhere parking the car or asking why there isn't any rice on the table, and several in particular went above and beyond this year, so big hugs to Joshua Bilmes, Adam Goldworm, Jason Rekulak, Brett Cohen, and Doogie Horner for all their support, and for staying out of the way when book club descended on their houses like a barbarian horde. We couldn't have finished all these books without you, fellas!

Let's also not forget some of the wonderful people who provided special snacks this year like David Borgenicht, John McGurk, Mary Ellen Wilson, Jane Morley, Mandy Dunn Sampson, Christina Schillaci, Megan DiPasquale, Kate Brown, and Molly Murphy.

And finally, a big thank you to the Literary Guild of Greater Charleston, who have been a part of my life for as long as I can remember: Suzy Barr, Helen Cooke, Eva Fitzgerald, Kitty Howell, Croft Lane, Lucille Keller, Cathy Holmes, Valerie Papadopoulos, Stephanie Hunt, Nancy Fox, Ellen Gower, and, of course, Shirley Hendrix. May you all keep on reading for many years to come!

See you on the other side of Y2K!

Marjorie Fretwell

We hope you enjoyed *The Southern Book Club's Guide to Slaying Vampires*. The following pages include bonus material to enhance your reading experience, including a reading group guide for book clubs, a hand-drawn map of Mt. Pleasant that shows where each of the main characters lived, Marjorie Fretwell's letter to the Mt. Pleasant Literary Guild with a calendar of reading selections for 1993, Grace Cavanaugh's letter to the no-name book club with a calendar of reading selections for 1993, a letter from Kitty to her daughter Honey that recaps the major events of 1993, and an annotated true-crime reading list by Grady Hendrix.

Happy Reading!

READING GROUP GUIDE

1. After an uncomfortable introduction to the neighborhood, James Harris quickly and almost seamlessly transitions into being a trusted resident. Why does he fit in so well despite his sudden and surprising appearance?

2. Discuss the dynamics of the neighborhood. What are the pros and cons of living in a suburban community like Mt. Pleasant in the 1990s? Do these vary depending on gender, race, or social status?

3. The book is female driven, and much of the horror happens to women and children. How do all the women in the book club respond to reports of strange or downright scary events, and how does their environment influence the different strengths and weaknesses the women display?

4. "Something strange is going on" is a phrase Patricia repeats throughout the book. Are there red flags about James Harris early on that the women miss, or ignore? Are the women's reservations different from those of their husbands?

5. Patricia is the one person who remains suspicious of her handsome new neighbor despite his friendly and charming exterior. Why do you think she, out of all James Harris's new friends in their quiet neighborhood, is more prone to considering the possibility of a menace in their midst?

6. The response to reports of missing children in Six Mile versus the Old Village differs greatly, among both residents and law enforcement. What are the social implications of these differing reactions, and how do they influence the way the story plays out?

7. Despite the small-town charm and close-knit ties in Mt. Pleasant, Patricia finds her confidence broken again and again by people she trusts. How is her trust betrayed, both inside her social circle and beyond her community?

8. Although there is one obvious monster at the center of the story, we learn that fear, dread, and terror come in many forms. Is there more than one kind of monster in the book? What are the scariest elements of this story, and why?

9. Discuss how the women come together to end the threat to their community. Do you think the women's actions are justified, or do they go too far?

10. Discuss the novel in terms of other vampire horror fiction. What elements of vampire lore has Grady Hendrix expanded upon, discarded, and added to the genre? Do you think he has successfully furthered readers' expectations for the vampire novel?

The Marsh

A MAP OF
—

A MAP OF
—

MT. PLEASANT
CHARLESTON, SOUTH CAROLINA

DRAWN AND ANNOTATED BY GRADY HENDRIX

The Harbor

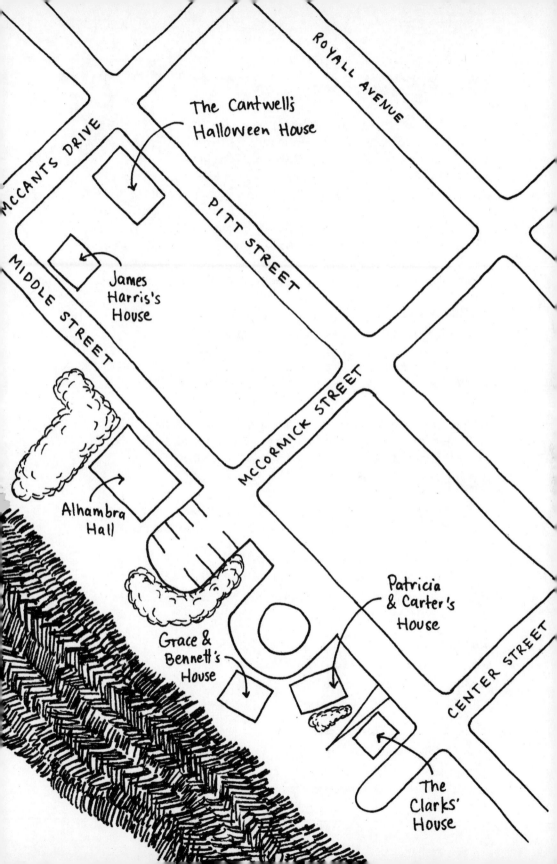

Happy November, y'all!

The turkeys are basting and we're all busy bees with
football, and schoolwork, and finding the perfect gift
for all those special someones—Christmas is right
around the corner! But I implore y'all, do not lose this book list for
1993. You're going to need it! You'll find the names of all the hostesses
and conversation leaders on the next page. You'll note that after some
certain members felt we were reading too many "old" books last year,
I've updated our list to only include two books that are more than five
years old. (Three if you include *A Child's Christmas in Wales*, but I
think I can be excused for not uprooting all of our traditions at once.)

JANUARY

Waiting to Exhale (Terry McMillan, 1992)

A very interesting look at friendship from the "other side."

FEBRUARY

One (Richard Bach, 1989)

Who didn't just love *Jonathan Livingston Seagull?* Mr. Bach is back
with more profound insights on love that I believe will make us all do
some thinking around the true meaning of Valentine's Day.

MARCH

The Agony and the Ecstasy (Irving Stone, 1961)

So divine! The life of Michelangelo is sure to uplift and inspire!

APRIL

The English Patient (Michael Ondaatje, 1992)

Thought-provoking and tragic. Make sure you have some tissues
handy!

MAY

Nectar in a Sieve (Kamala Markandaya, 1954)

It's the busy time of year, so I selected a shorter work by an
"international" author, which is no less profound for being short.

JUNE

Scarlett (Alexandra Ripley, 1991)

Everyone's brain is just going to be in a whirl from the heat, but don't
we all want to know what Scarlett and Rhett have been up to since
Gone with the Wind?

JULY

WLT: A Radio Romance (Garrison Keillor, 1991)

Everyone's favorite radio personality is also <u>quite</u> the writer.

AUGUST

The Bridges of Madison County (Robert James Waller, 1992)

Set in August, I couldn't think of a more profound meditation on "the one who got away" than this.

SEPTEMBER

Every Crooked Nanny (Mary Kay Andrews, 1992)

We're all going to be so overwhelmed getting the children ready for back to school, so here's our annual "fun" book. It's a real tidbit of a mystery by a fellow Southerner. Such a treat!

OCTOBER

Loves Music, Loves to Dance (Mary Higgins Clark, 1991)

Who inspires chills around Halloween like Mary Higgins Clark?

NOVEMBER

Smilla's Sense of Snow (Peter Hoeg, 1992)

Our second "international" book of the year, but one that has received plenty of praise. And I think we'll all want something challenging as we stay indoors by the crackling fire and sip a nice cup of Sleepytime tea.

DECEMBER

A Child's Christmas in Wales (Dylan Thomas, 1952)

The year draws to a close with our traditional Christmas read-aloud of Mr. Thomas's beautiful and moving book.

If anyone foresees any problems finishing the books, please let me know as soon as possible so arrangements can be made.

Gobble gobble,

Marjorie Fritwell

Greetings,

I hope this note finds you well. Below, you will find the 1993 reading selections, along with the name of the hostess and the discussant. You may have already read some of these books but I encourage you to reread them. Everyone should be refreshed on the details of each book, not merely the discussant. Kitty, this means you.

JAN - *On the Trail of the Assassins* (Jim Garrison, 1988)
Hostess: Slick Paley
Discussant: Grace Cavanaugh

FEB - *The Name of the Rose* (Umberto Eco, 1983)
Hostess: Kitty Scruggs
Discussant: Slick Paley

MARCH - *Raven: The Untold Story of the Rev. Jim Jones and His People* (Tim Reiterman, 1982)
Hostess: Patricia Campbell
Discussant: Kitty Scruggs

APRIL - *Rebecca* (Daphne du Maurier, 1938)
Hostess: Maryellen Papadopolous
Discussant: Patricia Campbell

MAY - *Helter Skelter* (Vincent Bugliosi, 1974)
Hostess: Grace Cavanaugh
Discussant: Slick Paley

JUNE - *The Bridges of Madison County* (Robert James Waller, 1992)
Hostess: Patricia Campbell
Discussant: Maryellen Papadopolous

JULY - *The Stranger Beside Me: The Shocking Inside Story of Serial Killer Ted Bundy* (Ann Rule, 1980)
<u>Hostess</u>: Slick Paley
<u>Discussant</u>: Maryellen Papadopolous

AUGUST - *Psycho* (Robert Bloch, 1959)
<u>Hostess</u>: Kitty Scruggs
<u>Discussant</u>: Grace Cavanaugh

SEPT - *Zodiac: The Shocking True Story of the Nation's Most Bizarre Mass Murderer* (Robert Graysmith, 1986)
<u>Hostess</u>: Slick Paley
<u>Discussant</u>: Patricia Campbell

OCT - *We Have Always Lived in the Castle* (Shirley Jackson, 1962)
<u>Hostess</u>: Maryellen Papadopoulos
<u>Discussant</u>: Slick Paley

NOV - *The Dead Girl* (Melanie Thernstrom, 1990)
<u>Hostess</u>: Grace Cavanaugh
<u>Discussant</u>: Kitty Scruggs

DEC - *And Then There Were None* (Agatha Christie, 1939)
<u>Hostess</u>: Kitty Scruggs
<u>Discussant</u>: Grace Cavanaugh

Looking forward to our conversations,

Grace Cavanaugh

My Honey,

Once again it's your old mom writing you her annual letter that you'll probably never read. I understand. Your grandmother used to do this and I never opened a single one of them. But when I turned thirty, I found them all in that beat-up secretary in the living room Daddy is always cursing because he can't find anything in it. I don't know what he's doing wrong because I found these 19 letters Mama had written, and when I read them (because I was putting off doing the dishes—when you're older you'll tally up every single second you spent washing dishes and want every single one of them back), I felt very lucky to have a record of what was going on around me when I was too caught up in myself to notice.

So let's see, 1993 . . .

It snowed in March and everybody just about lost their dang minds, even though it was barely more than a hard frost. It was a cold and rainy Christmas last year. Summer was hot, hot, hot, and we had a drought all the way past you all going back to school. I stayed inside, mostly keeping up with the trial of those Menéndez brothers. May I ask you, please, if you or any of your siblings ever decide that you just can't tolerate Daddy and me anymore, would you consider moving out instead of shotgun murdering us in our sleep?

Daddy spent most of the year upset because first Shannon Faulkner could go to the Citadel, but then they said she couldn't, but then another court changed their mind and said she could again, and you know Daddy, he doesn't care if they let a woman into his alma mater or not, but he can't say that to all his friends who act like it's the end of the world. He just had to gnaw his knuckles bloody, nod and smile, and drink a lot of brown liquor to keep quiet. Then Coach Ken quit the Tigers, which depressed Daddy even more—and to top it all, he shocked himself so bad with that Worm Gitter doodad he bought off late-night television that he went unconscious in the front yard and scared me half to death. I told him it was a waste of money and if he wanted bait he should just pay Lacy or Merit to dig up some worms, but nobody ever listens to me around here even though I'm right 99.9% of the time.

It was a tough year for animals. The mayor of North Charleston's little Vietnamese potbellied pig, Harley Dude, passed away. I don't know if you remember meeting that little pig, but he was just like a tiny dog, except more even-tempered. Then the Supreme Court said you could sacrifice animals as part of your religion, which is hard on the animals and unfair, I think, because it's not like you can sacrifice children—and I've met some dogs in my time who are worth twice some people's children (not mine, of course, you all are practically perfect in every way). But over the summer, a great white shark ate a groom on his wedding day in Australia and got away with it, so sometimes animals get to chalk one up in the win column.

A bunch of Canadians whose names I won't even dignify by writing down won the World Series this year, and our poor Twins could not seem to get their act together. They can't keep coasting on 1991 forever.

The Branch Davidians, who were cult people down in Waco, TX, got in a disagreement with the government and wound up having their compound burned down. It was a real mess, but you shouldn't tangle with the government, as they always win in the end. Daddy says that every year at tax time when I try to get him to take more exemptions and things, and it's words you should live by. Daddy doesn't say many wise things in the course of his life (especially after he electrocuted himself with that Worm Gitter), but when he does they're worth remembering. The attorney general who ordered the ATF and FBI to burn down that compound was a woman, by the way, so the Citadel may want to rethink their low opinion of the gentler sex, as they call it.

I don't know how much you remember about the goings-on last year when your mother (me!) got sick over the holidays, but I want you to know that I'm all right now. You don't ever need to know what happened, but the Campbells were having some real difficulties and you know how close I am with Mrs. Campbell. I tried to do the right thing for her, but things in her life just took a turn. She's a smart woman, and a good friend, and she's always game for anything I throw at her, which makes her fun, but sometimes life can get the better of you. I made myself sick with worry over her but your father got me through it. He is a rock and he did yeoman's duty looking after you all while I was indisposed.

I hope one day you find a man who makes you as happy as your daddy makes me. Life is not all sunshine and roses, as one day you'll unfortunately find out, so it helps if you find someone who'll stick by your side and take the rough with the smooth and never let it upset them too much. Your daddy puts his family first, even if he doesn't always listen to us and winds up shocking half his brains out with a contraption he never should have spent $28 on in the first place.

I won't think less of you if you don't read this letter until 2004.

Your loving mother,

Kitty

A TRUE CRIME READING LIST
BY GRADY HENDRIX

A lot of people believe that Truman Capote's 1966 book *In Cold Blood* established the true crime genre. This is what's known, in purely technical terms, as bunkus. Capote's account of the Clutter family killings made true crime writing respectable to cultural gatekeepers and high-minded prudes, but we've been gobbling up stories of human criminality for approximately as long as we've been able to speak.

PAMPHLETS AND SONGS (15TH TO 17TH CENTURY)

Gutenberg invented the printing press, and about five minutes later they started grinding out pamphlets recounting that week's most gruesome murders. They were given titles like "A true and most horrifying account of how a woman tyrannically murdered her four children and also killed herself, at Weidenhausen near Eschwege in Hesse," and the texts could be sung along to the tune of popular hymns such as "Come Unto Me, Says the Sons of God." Their writers adopted tones of headshaking bewilderment at the state of this fallen world ("My dearest reader, this is, unfortunately, may God have mercy, one piece of horrifying news after another") before launching into vivid verses such as the following.

> *She first went for the eldest son*
> *Attempting to cut off his head;*
> *He quickly to the window sped*
> *To try if he could creep outside;*
> *By the leg she pulled him back inside*
> *And threw him down onto the ground;*
>
> *. . .*
>
> *O please don't kill me! Spare me, do!*
> *But no plea helped, it was in vain;*
> *The Devil did her will maintain.*

She struck him with the self-same dread
As if it were a cabbage head.

AMERICAN EXECUTION SERMONS (17TH TO 18TH CENTURY)

In colonial America, some days were extra special. Those were the days when a sodomite, murderer, bad parent, or burglar was led in chains before the church and a celebrity minister preached an execution sermon before that wicked child of God got the rope. Crowds of up to five thousand people traveled dozens of miles (which was a long way back then) to hear the minister weave great clouds of biblical wrath over the head of some poor sap before they were led away with all convenient haste to meet their maker for stealing grapes, or picking pockets, or killing their baby. These flowery sermons were printed and distributed, so if the trip was too far, you could still wallow in every odious detail of your neighbor's sinful life that had finally led them straight to hell.

NEWGATE CALENDAR (18TH TO 19TH CENTURY)

Originally a simple calendar of executions kept by Newgate Prison in London, *The Newgate Calendar: Or, Malefactors' Bloody Register* became the most widely read book in England for one hundred years. (The American equivalent was *The Record of Crimes in the United States.* Nathaniel Hawthorne was a big fan.) The lives of noted ravishers of women, like the aptly named James Booty, were spun off into solo pamphlets, but the regular calendar still featured a cavalcade of criminals such as William Duell, who was hung for rape and murder. His corpse was taken to be dissected by medical students, at which point Duell to sprang back to life. Embarrassed, the court commuted his capital sentence to exile in North America. Another standout was Alexander Balfour, who, obsessed with his sister's tutor, informed her that if she ever got married, he'd murder her husband. Then she got married and he murdered her husband. Scheduled for a beheading, he escaped, disguised as his sister, and died of natural causes fifty years later.

MURDER BALLADS (18TH TO EARLY 20TH CENTURY)

Like the poems and songs in fifteenth-century pamphlets, only with better tunes, murder ballads were uniquely American, often relating the story of a young woman murdered for getting pregnant, or falling in love, or just plain old hanging around with the wrong people. Songs about the 1808 murder of Naomi Wise in North Carolina have outlasted anything we might know about the real Naomi, and the beheading of the pregnant Pearl Bryan in 1896 spawned three distinct ballads, none of which mention the fact that she probably died of a botched abortion performed by her dental student boyfriend who sawed off her head in a failed attempt to prevent her identification. By the 1930s and '40s they'd morphed into popular songs, like Patsy Montana's "I Didn't Know the Gun Was Loaded."

GANG BUSTERS (1936 TO 1957)

For twenty years, working-class Americans religiously tuned into *Gang Busters*, a radio show about real-life criminals based on interviews with their victims, witnesses, and the men who put them behind bars. Actor Phillips Lord had achieved national fame on the airwaves playing the folksy backwoods philosopher Seth Parker before producing this true crime show as a public service. Unfortunately, he reached out to the head of the FBI, J. Edgar Hoover, for assistance, and Hoover's suffocating sanctimony almost sunk the first season. Lord kicked the stuffed shirt G-Man off the show for the second and insisted on more: more gunshots, more sound effects, more blood, more action, more excitement, and more crime. Most of his audience earned less than $3,000 per year, rich people ignored the show when not writing editorials about how it encouraged crime, and kids gobbled it up. Capturing the populist anger at banks and the forces of law and order with its romantic audio portraits of the renegades who bucked the system, the show was also groundbreaking for its opening—so loud, lurid, and exciting that to this day when someone says something "comes on like gangbusters" they're referring to a radio program that went off the air perhaps before they were born.

TRUE DETECTIVE MAGAZINE (1924 TO 1995)

Printed on the grittiest pulp paper and laid out with all the aesthetic appeal of a body bag, *True Detective* rocketed to popularity in the 1930s and sold two million copies per month for its first twenty years. Founded by the intense, muscular vegetarian Bernarr MacFadden, the magazine was a carnival barker of American crime: "Weird Case of the Rapist Who Wanted Romance!" "Brooklyn's Vicious Thrill-Kill Kids!" "What Powerful Lure Drew Him from Ogling Nude Dancers to his Brutal Slaying?" "Corpse at the Picnic!" "House Full of Skulls!" Though it's about as reputable as a freak show, its defenders cling desperately to its handful of respectable accomplishments, such as the 1931 series, "I Am a Fugitive from a Chain Gang," which exposed the brutality of convict labor in Georgia. The magazine also published work by pulp stylists Jim Thompson and Dashiell Hammett. But its greatest accomplishment was spawning an avalanche of detective magazines, scare sheets, and supermarket tabloids for decades to come.

IN COLD BLOOD (1966) AND *THE EXECUTIONER'S SONG* (1979)

When people try to justify the appeal of true crime, these are the books they cite. Capote's account of the Klutter family killings launched a cottage industry of movies, books, more movies, and even more books, but it still stands as a great read. Norman Mailer's account of Gary Gilmore's decision not to oppose his own death sentence for the murder of two men in two separate robberies won a Pulitzer but is long-winded and exhausting, like Mailer himself. These books invented true crime for the literati because the "right" kind of writers—upper class white men who subscribed to the "right" magazines—were finally tackling it, which totally ignores the fact that the "wrong" kind of writers (female, nonwhite) had been doing the same thing for decades, including Celia Thaxter in 1875, Edna Ferber in 1935, and Zora Neale Hurston in 1956.

THE STRANGER BESIDE ME (1980)

Ann Rule was a harried single mom trying to support four kids on the money she made freelancing for *True Detective* under the name Andy Stack when she landed her first book deal. Hired to write a quickie about the so-called "Co-ed Murders" in the Pacific Northwest, Rule didn't have a clue these would become some of the most famous serial killings in modern history, nor that they were being committed by Ted Bundy, Rule's good friend who worked next to her at a suicide hotline. She went on to write numerous true crime paperbacks, but none rival the queasy intimacy of her first. *The Stranger Beside Me* established the template for the contemporary true crime genre, but Rule warped it into an uncomfortable blend of forensic analysis and autobiography. Forget the cold, clinical, God's-eye view of *In Cold Blood*. If you want to read the sweaty, disquieting, elegiac masterpiece of the genre, no book does it better than *Stranger*.